# SCHOOLLAND
## a novel

## Max Martínez

**Arte Publico Press**
Houston, Texas
1988

This volume is made possible by a grant from the National Endowment for the Arts, a federal agency.

Arte Publico Press
University of Houston
Houston, Texas 77004

Martínez, Max
  Schoolland.

  I. Title.
PS3563.A73344S36   1988      813'.54
ISBN 0-934770-87-5
LC 87-35127

For Elizabeth Jean

# ACKNOWLEDGEMENTS

The person most responsible for the completion of this book is my mother, Antonia V. Martínez. In addition to being my mother, she gave me rent money, cigarette money and sometimes even a little beer money. And meals, wonderful meals. My sister, Santos Gloria Martínez, and my brother, Ricardo Martínez, were always good for a few dollars. My cousin, Guadalupe de León and his wife Jimmie Lee also gave me room and board for many months when I wanted a feeling for Schoolland and when I needed to be in Schoolland. I am very grateful, indeed. My aunt Simona de León, my cousins, Pablo de León and Dorotea, Juan de León and Gloria, Eusebio de León, were also helpful and generous with their warmth and sense of family. Likewise, my friends, Tatcho Mindiola, Jr., John McNamara and Cynthia, Rolando Ríos and Anna, Nelson Allen, Cecilio García-Camarillo, Patricia Montoya, José Luis Montalvo and Carlos Guerra, helped as well as only friends can and I am deeply grateful. The Méndez sisters, Cat, Ali and Angie, operated *Los Padrinos* and made it one of the best bars in the history of San Antonio. One day I promise to pay my bar tab. And, Nicolás Kanellos never gave up nagging me about completing this book. I hope this book is worth the impositions I made on everyone. If not, I can only try again.

# Chapter 1

My Grandpa was in his usual place at the far end of the porch, sitting in his straight-back chair with his head tilted to one side, snoring gently. His snore was a long continuous buzz that trailed off into eternity just about the time you began to wonder if it was humanly possible to hold a snore that long.

The sound of it was mesmerizing.

Then, suddenly, Grandpa would grunt and the buzz would erupt again, beginning slowly and sounding as if it were far away and gradually it would become louder and louder, seeming to zoom past my brothers and me.

Paulie and Jose and I were outside along with Grandpa. We were on the porch without particular purpose, waiting for the stroke of midnight. It was New Year's Eve.

My father had joined us on the porch earlier in the evening to enjoy his after dinner Bull Durham. He said it had been too many years since he had much of a reason to celebrate the coming of the new year. Speaking to no one in particular, he said he saw little use in picking up the habit again.

That Grandpa was all excited about it was kind of strange to me. He had spent the entire day in anticipation, definitely looking forward to it. None of my brothers had seemed interested in celebrating.

My grandfather had started sucking on the jug of whiskey right after supper and was already drunk and asleep by the time it got to be eleven o'clock. All night long he had repeatedly said he wanted to be awake at the stroke of midnight. It was a New Year's Eve he did not want to miss.

Earlier in the evening, about nine o'clock and a quarter of the way into the bottle, Grandpa had kicked off his brogans despite a mild chill in the air. One enormous toe poked out of a hole in his socks.

During the day, when he found the whiskey that my brother Heriberto had given him for Christmas, when he had decided to drink it that evening, he had made me responsible for making sure he was awake at midnight. I asked how he expected me to do that since he was usually sound asleep shortly after sundown and it would probably take a goddamned big John Deere to drag him awake. He grunted, saying I was getting the same smart-mouth from my brother Paulie. I hadn't meant to hurt his feelings, but then you can't always tell about old people.

Paulie was the first to notice that Grandpa was asleep. He nudged me in the ribs to make sure I was watching. Whatever Paulie was up to, I knew two things for sure: it was going to make me laugh, and I was going to feel ashamed for doing so. Paulie wouldn't try anything if my mother or my father were there to see it, but they had already gone to bed. Paulie kept grinning as he went inside the house.

It was my mother's custom to leave on the kitchen light whenever any of us was out of the house at night. Out of the corner of my eye, I saw Paulie's shadow cross through the swath of dim yellow light. As he came back to the porch, he blocked it out altogether. When he was sure I was watching him, a twisted little smile crossed his lips and he waved a fistful of kitchen matches in my direction. I nudged my brother Jose, who was watching him as well.

Paulie began to creep stealthily toward Grandpa, kind of like a cat stalking a bird. The warped boards on the porch groaned as he took each step. When he got as close to Grandpa as he dared, Paulie struck a match on the seat of his pants. He had intended to toss the match underneath the arch of Grandpa's foot; however, as the match flared, sending a thick sulphurous stench into the air, Grandpa jumped instantly upright, landing on his feet. Paulie jumped back, out of reach, tossing the match over the side of the porch. Only the foul, acrid odor of the sulphur remained.

Grandpa, doing a little whiskey reel on his feet, took a step toward Paulie. My brother scampered away, saving himself from a cuff behind the ear. Grandpa weaved uneasily on his feet, his fists rubbing away sleep from his eyes. He tried to shake some of the drunk from his head, too. It seemed for a second that he wobbled out of control and it sure looked like he was going to pitch forward, but actually he was bending over to pick up the bottle of bourbon.

He had lost the cap to the bottle and in his confusion he looked around for it. Before too long, he gave up and took a long swig. Grandpa gesticulated toward Paulie with one hand in the air. In the other, the bottle in his hand slapped against his thigh.

"Son of a bitch!" my grandfather said. "Your father should have drowned you in the creek when there was a chance to do it!"

"You mean, Paulie came to us floating along the creek, like that little Moses story that Father Jack loves to tell?" my brother Jose asked.

"Naw, I don't mean any of that church shit. I mean, when the little turd was born, somebody oughta've taken him to the creek and sat on him," said my grandfather.

Sometimes I couldn't tell if he was serious or not.

"Well, I wasn't drowned, old man!" said my brother Paulie, defiantly. No matter who or what it was, Paulie insisted on having the last word.

My brother Paulie, it was generally agreed, was a gift to the family from the devil himself. Paulie had buck teeth that swept forward like the cattle-catcher on a train and he had pointy ears. When he was up to something, which was most of the time, he got the look of the imp on his face.

Paulie was usually blamed for every disaster, misfortune and calamity that befell our family. Once, when Paulie and I were out riding, my horse spooked and took off on a run. I slammed my head into a beehive and got half a dozen beestings out of it. It scared the hell out of everybody when I swelled up from the stings. It was Paulie who got the blame. He protested that he didn't have anything to do with it, but my father said he should have been looking out for me.

Still, he was so often guilty of so much that even when innocent he got the blame anyway. Many times, as I remember, Paulie took punishments which some one or other of us deserved.

My mother and my father agreed that my brother Paulie was both cursed and a curse.

My mother was convinced that doña Casimira, the oldest human being in Schoolland, had said something in jest while my mother carried Paulie. When it became evident that something was amiss, my mother required that doña Casimira come and touch her swollen belly. The old woman feared that she would become known as a *bruja,* a witch, and refused the small kindness asked of her. Her refusal left her innocent comments to fester into a full-fledged curse. And, to make matters worse, Paulie's birth was an easy one and my mother was on her feet in a matter of days. This was an ill omen of what Paulie would become.

My father had an altogether different version of the curse. He believed, quietly but quite forcefully, that out of nine children, one of them was bound to grow up and be like Paulie. No man could claim nine normal, decent children. My father's belief was just common sense, a rational way of explaining the world.

Most of the time, my father didn't bother to explain himself but when it came to Paulie, somehow we could figure out what he meant and it seemed to make sense. Our friends and relatives thought that my father's version made good sense. Still, my mother's version was preferable as there was something biblical about it; a sign from God. The way my father told it, as an aberration of nature, it was grounded too much in the every-day randomness of things. My mother provided something fearsome and awesome to teach the lesson of how puny human beings are.

Grandpa's feeling were indeed hurt. He stomped on the porch, full of the anger that eventually passes to frustration and then finally subsides into a bewildered resignation. The whiskey had made my grandfather maudlin and sentimental.

Paulie was well out of reach and there was little danger that Grandpa would actually hit him, no matter how much he might want to. Anyway, Paulie was too quick.

"He was just trying to be funny, Grandpa," I said. "He didn't mean anything by it."

My brother Jose shifted position on the porchstep where he sat. "You know by now how he is. Why do you pay attention to him."

"The little bastard should apologize," said my grandfather, grouchy and refusing for the moment to be placated. He took another swig from the bottle, glaring at Paulie, who shifted his weight on the balls of his feet and prepared to make a run for it should Grandpa move toward him.

"Tell him you're sorry, Paulie, goddamn it!" said my brother Jose.

"What the hell for? I didn't get to do anything," protested Paulie. "Besides, you can't make me! Not even all three of you put together!" So saying, he spread his feet wide apart and crouched low on the floor as he had seen the wrestlers do on television.

"Oh, the hell with him!" said Grandpa. It was hard to tell whether he was still angry or not.

"There you go, Grandpa," said my brother Jose. "Just don't pay any attention to him."

My grandfather sulked. "Somebody's going to shoot him between the eyes one of these days. It's too goddamned bad he's my daughter's boy, else I would do it myself," he said.

Maybe Grandpa really meant what he said. Or, maybe Paulie realized he had gone too far this time. In any case, the defiance went out altogether from my brother Paulie. Paulie relaxed his body, standing straight up on his feet, his shoulders pressed forward and his head bowed a little. He said, "The hell with it," just to have the last word.

My brother José began to laugh. He had a deep rich voice which made him the best singer in the family. When he laughed, though, out came a squeaky giggle, like Porky Pig in the movies. Moreover, when he got his laugh going full tilt, we were drawn into it, laughing more at his laughter than anything else.

I began to laugh as well because of my brother Jose's giggling, and then Grandpa joined in. We laughed because neither Grandpa nor Paulie had managed to get the best of the other. Grandpa was particularly proud of himself because a draw with Paulie was as good as anyone ever got.

Paulie, seeing Grandpa's laughter as an expression of victory, felt himself beaten. He jumped off the porch and disappeared into the darkness. He went to sulk where no one could see him.

Grandpa's laughter was more than he could manage in his condition and it slipped into a round of coughing. To settle his throat, he took another swig from the bottle of bourbon, which didn't help things much. My grandfather rarely drank and on this evening he had already put away nearly half of the bottle of whiskey. He didn't get loud or belligerent. He just couldn't figure out why none of his movements came out as he intended.

"You better turn in, Grandpa, it's late," said my brother José, referring to the liquor and not the hour.

"What time is it?" asked Grandpa.

"Damned if I know," said Jose.

"I want to be up for the New Year," said Grandpa.

Grandpa, dropped his chin to his chest, made poking motions at his shirt on the wide part of his belly where his vestpocket ought to be. Because of the whiskey, he was a younger self, decked out in his only suit with a vest. As he did so, he swept his left foot forward to regain his balance and when that didn't help, he swept it back around to where it had been. He was standing perfectly still, in balance, but I don't think he believed it. So he repeated the motion a couple more times. It looked to me like he was dancing to some inaudible tune. My brother Jose, who had gotten to his feet to stretch himself, was smiling, watching the old man.

Grandpa remembered that his watch was in his trouser pocket and in one abrupt movement, like a gunfighter going for the draw, he pulled it out by the chain. The sequence of events eluded him momentarily and he glared at his palm expecting the watch to be in it, not realizing that the watch dangled at the end of the chain.

Somewhere out in the darkness, my brother Paulie farted. The sound of it distracted Grandpa. He tilted his head, bird-like, listening for more. Jose and I held our laughter. In the dim light cast from the kitchen, we saw him concentrate all the more intently, wrinkling his brow, his body leaning dangerously to one side. He started to sway again in increasingly larger half circles until it seemed he would go down. I ran to him.

"Here, Grandpa, let me do it," I said.

"I don't need any goddamned help, goddamn it!" he said.

"Come on, Grandpa, let me help you," I persisted. Before he could say any more, I took the watch from him, opened the solid gold flap and told him the time. It was eleven-thirty.

Christmas is when we did a lot of celebrating at our house. Actually, it was not so much celebrating as it was that a lot of people came to visit: people we didn't see all year, who brought us tamales and cookies and things like that. And when no one was visiting, my mother would go visit people she had not seen all year to take them tamales, and so on.

There was the noise of the kids, so many of them it was impossible to tell whose they were. There was the rushing back and forth of my mother and my sisters, the last minute panic when one of my brothers was dispatched to town to bring something back from the store. There were cars and trucks coming in and going out bringing and ending the visits of our many friends and relatives.

My sister Celia—she was the oldest—came in from San Antonio to stay the entire week. Although San Antonio wasn't but fifty miles away, each time Celia brought her family for a visit, she made it seem like they had travelled thousands of miles.

After the first night, probably during the night, she and her husband Frank had a fight. He went home, saying he had some things to do. We figured something was wrong when Celia wouldn't go out to the car to see Frank off. She and the three children stayed as planned. Frank returned two days after Christmas, spent the night and, all of them went home the next day.

My father said there was a bad business there, and my mother told him to be quiet as it wasn't any of our affair. Whatever it was, they would have to settle it themselves. It wasn't right to meddle in other people's troubles. My father kept quiet, but he kept thinking.

Since early December, my brother Heriberto had taken to visiting more and more. He carried a washtub in the trunk of his car which he filled with bottles of beer and large chunks of ice. He'd get himself so drunk he would have to sleep over, which meant either me or Paulie ended up sleeping on the floor.

Heriberto had brought the bottle of Four Roses bourbon to Grandpa as a Christmas present. It was one of those exchanges where you give what you most want for yourself. Heriberto had expected to be invited to the drinking of it right then and there, but Grandpa decided to save it. Heriberto got himself all pissed about it. He wouldn't say anything to Grandpa, not even a joke that they crack it open and get it going. Instead, he let his anger chew on his liver for as long as he could before he wheeled out to West-hoff to bring back a case of Falstaff.

My brother Heriberto was the only one of us who ever drank in front of my father. There were fathers in Schoolland who never allowed their children to drink in front of them. My father was more modern, figuring that if a man had a family of his own, he had a right to do pretty much as he pleased. Heriberto defended himself, claiming he was free, white and twenty-one. Every time he said that, we couldn't help but laugh because my brother Heriberto was black as the ace of spades, black enough anyway to pass for a Negro.

We figured things were not going well between him and his wife Alva. My father had a lot to say about that, too, but my mother wouldn't let him. As the trouble between Heriberto and Alva got worse, my mother got to see less and less of her favorite grandchildren. My mother loved Heriberto's two kids. She tried not to play favorites when Celia brought her children over, but the kids themselves could tell, even if it wasn't so readily apparent to anyone else.

My father said Heriberto was drinking too much and my mother said it was none of our business. My father felt that Heriberto's drinking was separate from his family trouble. My mother didn't see it that way. As far as it went, it was one subject no one dared to bring up.

Right after Christmas, our house would get back to normal. After all those screaming kids racing all around, the constant bickering of my twin brothers, little Julian and little Albert, the house was again tolerable.

By New Year's, none of us was in the mood for much of anything. I especially didn't see much point to celebrating. I was desperately in love with Cristina Sifuentes, who lived in Smiley only half of the year. The other half, her family lived in West Texas where the crops were. There they remained until the last part of January, when they came back to Smiley and I got to be with Cristina once more. I was hopeful that this year her folks would see that she was old enough to go out with me.

My brother Elpidio and my sister Juana had gone to visit the Arreaga family who lived a few miles down the road from us. They were the closest thing we had to neighbors. My sister Juana, from the looks of it, was more or less engaged to Tony Arreaga. Thing is, every time my sister Juana went to visit the Arreagas, my brother Elpidio would tag along. Tony was his best friend, sure, but it didn't seem that Tony paid much attention to Elpidio when Juana was around. Fact is, so my father said, Elpidio was sweet on one of Tony's sisters. My grandfather recognized the signs of it himself. Asked how he knew, my grandfather said that a man in love has his nostrils flared.

There were four Arreaga girls and as Elpidio seldom spoke about anything, much less the women in his life. Because he was so niggardly with his words, it was impossible for any of us to know which one it was. Nevertheless, over the years, it was assumed that some from our family would marry some from their family. There was more than enough sons and daughters to go around.


"Come on with me, squirt," said my grandfather.

He started to walk forward as though his feet were glued to the planks of the porch and he had to jerk loose each time he took a step. Once he was at the edge of the porch, it took him quite a while to negotiate the four steps leading to the ground. I stayed close to him on one side while Jose poised himself on the other. We didn't touch him at all as he would have resented it. When Grandpa was standing on the ground, satisfied that his footing was right, he took another swig from the bottle. He had a little trouble remembering where he was supposed to go and when it finally came to him, he pointed himself in the direction of the bunkhouse. Only when he was sure that it was the right direction did he take the first step.

# Chapter 2

To the side of our house was an old line shack which served as a bunkhouse for Grandpa and my brother Elpidio. My brother Heriberto and my cousin Lupe had come upon the shack on Bernie Robertson's place. The bunkhouse was more than fifty years old and still in reasonably good shape. Bernie Robertson figured it was probably left over from the days when Schoolland was mostly cattle country. Last he heard, the line shack was used in the 1920s by a couple of bootleggers who came in from San Antonio to make whiskey.

My brother and my cousin wanted the building for a playhouse. They had been working days for Bernie Robertson from time to time. He gave it to them on the condition they cleaned up after themselves and didn't leave anything behind to mangle any of his cows. It took Heriberto and my cousin Lupe about a month, working on weekends and days when they didn't have jobs, to take it apart, board by board, and bring it to the house where they reassembled it. They replaced all of the rotted wood, water-proofed the roof, and nailed two bunks to the walls. Thereafter, it became their private territory, meaning that no one could go inside unless invited. My sisters could pick up dirty laundry and deliver clean clothes, but that was as much intrusion as was allowed.

My cousin Lupe came to live with us after my aunt Marcela died. She left four children, of whom Lupe was the oldest. My uncle Andrés was not able to take care of them, so he gave them away. My mother would have taken all four of the children except that we were his last stop and only my cousin Lupe was left by the time Uncle Andres came to the house to see if he could give him away.

After my uncle Andres got back on his feet, with a good job in Corpus Christi, he remarried and began to recover the children. My cousin Lupe had become attached to us and we to him and he refused to go. Lupe appealed to my father not to let his father take him away. My father knew better than to get himself in the middle of anything like that. In the end, they struck a deal where my cousin Lupe would live with my uncle Andres during the school year and he would spend Christmas and summers with us. That lasted about three years and by the time they got the line shack, my cousin Lupe was a permanent member of the family as he had quit school to go work and he wanted to work in Schoolland.

It was a well-worn footpath from the house to the bunkhouse. Grandpa could walk it out of habit, and while several times he took two steps back for each step forward, he stayed right on the tamped black dirt trail bordered by tufts of dried grass.

The bunkhouse had a forward tilt to it where the soil below had shifted over the years. Heriberto and Lupe had set it on mesquite stumps and over the years, the front part of it had sunk deeper into the soft soil. The lone step in front of it was lopsided now and pretty much even with the ground.

Grandpa threw the door wide and stepped inside. I remained outside shivering in the cool damp air, my arms wrapped around my chest. I could hear Grandpa inside shuffling his feet trying to find the light cord. When he found it and jerked it, the light came instantly on. I could see that Grandpa had swept his right arm to one side searching for the cord and his right leg had swivelled along with it. Grandpa dropped noisily into the nearest bunk, the one where Elpidio slept. He leaned his head against the wall, closing his eyes for a minute. The spine of his book was cutting into his buttock as he sat on the bunk. Once he got his bearings, he lifted it and removed the book. He tossed it on the pillow. All four corners of the book were fluffed up, brown and yellow from the years of its existence. The cover and the first few pages had long ago disappeared. The name of it and the name of its author were no where to be found on the book.

My cousin Lupe left our home for good after he fell in with a team of wildcatters in Westhoff. He won some beers from them shooting pool and the wildcatters decided they liked him and hired him for a week. After the week was over, they were impressed with his work, and so the wildcatters took him on permanently. When they finished the job, they took him away to Pasadena, Texas, where he eventually found work in a refinery. What it meant to us, simply, is that we lost a family member.

As might be expected, Heriberto was the most upset when our cousin Lupe went away. At first, he pretended that his best friend was coming back. Heriberto would never let anyone take over Lupe's bunk. But we needed the extra bunk. Our house was getting more and more crowded all the time. The twins were getting too old for the crib in my parents bedroom. And, the rest of us were simply getting bigger.

Well, suddenly, without the least bit of warning, without even the least hint that anything was up, Heriberto decided to marry his girlfriend. We knew, of course, more or less, that he had a girlfriend. My mother was upset because he had not bothered to properly introduce his intended to the family. I suppose she had a right to expect better, Heriberto being the eldest and the first to put her through this, and consequently she had a right to be upset. Not only that, but Heriberto would not hear of a proper wedding. My mother was furious, as could be expected. She was somewhat mollified by the priest in Nixon who agreed to perform a brief ceremony at the house, just for our family and hers.

As if that weren't enough, my brother Heriberto went to live with his in-laws until he could afford his own place. I guess he figured he couldn't very well bring his wife to live in the bunkhouse.

For several weeks after Heriberto left, the bunkhouse remained empty as if we half-expected that Heriberto and my cousin Lupe would come back.

My sister Juana had her own room in the house, acquiring that luxury upon the marriage and departure of my sister Celia. Little Albert and little Julian, the twins, had been sleeping in a crib in my parent's room. When they outgrew it, my mother decided they would sleep on the floor in Juana's room. She made a pallet for them every night. My sister Juana was not too thrilled about that. She agreed on the condition that they come in only for bed and nothing else. Juana's room had become a private world all to herself.

Naturally, the arrangement was not going to work. It was difficult to make the twins understand that they were guests in the room and as such they had to be respectful and not play or otherwise make themselves at home.

When it became impossible to ignore that Heriberto was gone for good, it was decided that Elpidio and my brother Jose would move into the bunkhouse. This freed their bed for the twins and my sister was left to herself in her private world.

My grandmother died soon after that. My mother worried about Grandpa and she insisted he stay with us for a while. This brought Jose out of the bunkhouse and into the house again. Jose figured it would be temporary, so he took to sleeping on the floor. My mother had something else altogether in mind. In her concern for Grandpa, she felt that he ought not to live alone. He was still strong and quite lucid, for all anyone could tell. It was just that losing my grandmother left him desolate, without much interest in anything.

In the year following my grandmother's death, I don't think Grandpa noticed much of anything. So, it was not difficult to convince him to stay with us. Actually, I don't think he so much agreed as he didn't offer resistance.

In time, of course, Grandpa came to accept and live comfortably with his grief. He was able to return to work with a renewed vigor and in general he became himself again. Not only that, but he got used to living in the line shack. Elpidio was quiet, easy going and respectful. Grandpa, once he was himself again, liked to talk a lot. Mostly, he told long stories during which he did not care for interruptions and it suited him that Elpidio preferred to listen more than to talk. Thus it was as good an arrangement as anyone could wish for.

The lightbulb dangled precariously from the ceiling, its yellow light dim and hazy, throwing moving shadows on the walls. Grandpa moved forward on the bunk to sit upright. It was an effort for him to breathe, his breath coming in short, labored pants.

It was the only sound in the still night.

He hugged the bottle of Four Roses to his belly.

"What the hell day is this, squirt?" he asked, his speech thick and slurred.

"It's Monday, Grandpa. What's left of it," I said. "In a few minutes it's going to be Tuesday, the first day of 1957."

"I'll be seventy-three this year." As he spoke, his gaze was on the floor between his knees. "You know how old that is, squirt?"

"No, Grandpa, I don't," I said.

"No, you don't know how old that is," he said, sadly. "Well, it ain't as old as the time when snakes had feet. Pretty damn close, though. I feel like it's pretty goddamned close!"

Grandpa started to laugh, but he was overcome by a fit of coughing and wheezing. Afterward, when he became calm again, his face settled into a faraway sadness.

I had seen the look before. I had mentioned it to my father and he said it was probably that Grandpa remembered something about my grandmother or happier times when he was younger and stronger. I guessed that he was thinking about what the world would be like when he was no longer in it.

"Are you thinking about Grandma?" I asked.

"No, I wasn't thinking about her at all," he said. "I wish I was, though. I hardly ever think about her anymore. She was a good woman. No, it's too late to be thinking about that anymore. What do you say?"

"About what, Grandpa? I don't know," I said, a little disturbed by the question.

"You really want to know what I was thinking about, don't you?" Grandpa lifted his face to look at me. In the bright light of the overhanging bulb I could still detect a little sadness, but there was something else in his face. A slight, wistful smile to cut the edge from the sadness.

"Dying. I was thinking of dying. As old as I am, it's best to know I can die anytime. I can be talking to you one minute and I could be dead the next. Just like that," he said and snapped his fingers. "That's what it means to be old. It happened to your grandmother. Only I never thought it would happen to her just when it did. Rest her soul."

Grandpa became quiet for a moment, before he lifted his head again. "I was right there when it happened. I saw it happen. It was like nothing I ever thought. She sat there, pretty as ever, and then she was gone."

"You'd figure, living as long as I have, I'd've seen a lot of people die. Well, I haven't. They say you only need to see one person die in front of you and that's enough. Your grandmother died right in front of me. You'd figure I'd be ready for my own dying by now. Thing is, I don't know if I'm ready. I do know that I think about it all the time. In fact, I can hardly think of anything else. And you know what?"

"What is it, Grandpa?" I said.

"Knowing about it, thinking about it, only makes me more afraid. That's all. If it's something that happens to all of us, then we shouldn't be afraid of it. I am afraid of dying, squirt," he said, and he turned his face away from me.

"You shouldn't really think so much about it, Grandpa," I said, lamely.

He had been speaking ever so softly, in a monotonous rumble, his voice thick and groggy. I could only just make out the words. From the way he began, it appeared to me that it was a preamble to a story he was about to tell. He had a way of saying something that confused me and then he would follow it with a story. The story was supposed to teach me something. Seldom did I make the connections he sought and he became impatient with me, but the stories were fine.

This time, Grandpa simply stopped talking. I wanted to say something that might be of comfort to him.

"You're not going to die, Grandpa. You're stronger than any of us, Daddy says so all the time." It was the best I could manage.

He was distracted for a moment and suddenly his face brightened up. "Your daddy's a good man. Couldn't have asked for any better for my daughter. You boys are going to turn out just fine. Even that idiot, Paulie!"

Grandpa became quiet again. He picked up the bottle of bourbon, bringing it half way up to his mouth before deciding against having another drink.

"Listen carefully, squirt," said my grandfather. "I'm going to die this year. I don't know exactly when, I just know that I won't see another year."

Then, as if the thought had just occurred to him, he added, "I wanted to stay up for the New Year because it's going to be my last. I want you to be the only one to know about it, understand?"

I figured it was the whiskey talking. I had heard how stupid my brother Heriberto got when he was drunk. The best thing to do was just listen to Grandpa.

"How come you don't want anybody else to know, Grandpa?" I said.

"If I told everyone else, they'd just worry about me. I'm not helpless. Not yet, anyway. It'll be our secret, just you and me."

I didn't believe him, exactly, of course. And yet, there was an undeniable finality to his words. Moreover, the brightness that crept into his eyes when he was pulling my leg was missing. Even more frightening to me was the way he sat on the bunk, elbows on his knees, his head hunched deep into his shoulders.

My grandfather seemed so sad and far away, almost as though he was becoming a memory while he sat in front of me. His voice was low and soft and it had a detached, beaten sound to it, as if he had confronted this business of death and had already been vanquished by it. A lump formed in my throat.

The tears began to flow down my cheeks as I remembered my grandmother's funeral. I remembered the way that my mother held my brothers little Albert and little Julian by the hand, one on each side of her. She sat in a folding chair in the front room of the house. The coffin was disproportionately large for the small room and the small body it contained. Its polished, lacquered surfaces were out of place inside our house. My mother had insisted that the wake be held in the house.

My grandfather had been in the kitchen warming up some tea for my grandmother. It was an herb tea, as she had been complaining about not feeling well. The tea was supposed to make her feel better.

When my grandfather returned to her side, she looked at him briefly and breathed her last. It was as if she had waited for him. My grandmother was dead for hours before my grandfather could bring himself to our house to tell us about it. Afterward, he went into a daze and could not bring himself to confront any details of the funeral.

The funeral parlor people were reluctant to bring the body all the way from Gonzales to Schoolland. It was the custom among our people, but one which the parlor people discouraged. However, in the face of my mother's insistence, they gave in to her wishes.

When the hearse came to a stop in front of our house, my brother Jose shook his head in disgust. "You get to work like a goddamn dog all your life and when you die all you get is one last ride in a goddamned Cadillac," he said, spitting over his shoulder.

The white man from the funeral parlor, who wore grey gloves, moved in light, gliding steps to the rear of the hearse. He withdrew and opened a folding stand with wheels on it. He positioned it to accept the casket and signalled wordlessly for my father and my brothers to help him. It was cumbersome moving the casket up the porchsteps but they managed to get it up on the porch without incident. After that, the funeral parlor man waved his hands for my father and brothers to move out of the way. The parlor man wheeled it inside the front room and clasped his hands together. If he thought anything about what he saw of our house, he kept it to himself. He flitted outside without seeming to lift his feet off the floor to bring in two stacks of metal folding chairs.

My mother had come to stand in the kitchen doorway, wearing a shiny black dress over which she wore a bright yellow apron that had a large red pocket in the center. She kept her arms folded, staring at the brightly polished box in her living room. The funeral parlor man had positioned the stand so that the length of the coffin was in front of the couch. It was obvious that those who would sit on the couch would have their knees touching the coffin. On the other side, he arranged the six folding chairs in a semi-circle. My father remained outside on the porch smoking a cigarette. The white man went over to whisper in my father's ear, as if my father was the one who made all the decisions. Receiving nothing but an impassive glare, the white man returned to the front room, careful to avoid looking at anyone directly in the eye. He fiddled with some things on the side of the casket and opened the front part of it. My mother stepped forward a little to peer at my grandmother in her final repose. My grandmother lay, white on a white satin pillow. They had dusted her face with powder which contrasted sharply with her dark brown features. There was a trace of color on her lips. She had never worn makeup of any kind in her life.

I recalled the moment when I gathered up my courage to look inside the coffin. As I pictured it in my memory, I saw my grandmother's face, stonelike and cold, her eyes closed in something more than sleep. The image of her face cushioned by the white satin gradually dissolved into the face of my grandfather. I shuddered a little more.

# Chapter 3

"Stop snivelling, will you," grouched my grandfather. "I'm not dead yet, I'm still here. And, I'll be here for a while yet, so don't start snivelling on my account. Not yet, anyway. Save it for when I'm gone."

"You can't mean what you're saying, Grandpa," I said. "You're just trying to scare me, and it's not funny."

"Scare you? The hell, you say. I'm the one that's going to die, son, why should I want to scare you?"

"I don't want you to die, Grandpa," I said, crying.

"Neither do I, son," said my grandfather. "Neither do I." He let a long minute pass before he spoke again. "Now, suppose you go over to that trunk there. On the bottom somewhere is my gun. Bring it to me." He said.

"What're you going to do, Grandpa?"

"Make me some noise. Shoot the hell out of the New Year. What do you say to that!" He said, gleefully.

In an instant, his countenance had changed completely. He became cheerful and playful again. Almost child-like. I was glad for it.

It was a cardboard steamer trunk with a humped lid. Its metal hinges had turned to a light chocolate color over the years. I opened the lid and dug into the contents, past clothes mostly, until I could feel the weapon. I lifted it up slowly, careful not to disturb the neatly folded clothes.

The pistol, a .45 Colt Peacemaker, was wrapped in an oiled blue bandanna. I handed it to Grandpa, who unwrapped it and held it firmly in the palm of his hand. He twirled the cylinder several times with his thumb to make sure it was empty. He hefted it in his hand, making a circling motion with his wrist.

"This is a gunfighter's weapon," said my grandfather. He held the blue bandanna in his other hand. It contained an old tobacco sack, its white cloth having turned brown with age. Inside the sack were four bullets.

"This gun used to belong to John Wesley Hardin," said Grandpa.

"Who's he?" I asked, although I knew already.

"John Wesley Hardin was an outlaw; a killer, some say. In fact, your great grandfather Cirildo rode with him for a time. They used to work cattle down around Pilgrim. Used to be a lot of dead men lying around in those days. That's what they tell me, anyway."

"Was great grandfather Cirildo an outlaw, too?" I asked.

"Hard to tell. Depends on whose side he was on. No, I guess not, he wasn't an outlaw. He rode on the Taylor Ranch. Seems the Taylors had a war going with the Suttons, from Cuero. When the white man came here, more than a hundred years ago, they fenced off all of the land; at least, what they could claim for themselves. Something about the white man that makes him want to know exactly what is his. It's not enough to know that something is there and that he can use it. Shit, no! The white man's got to know exactly what's his and exactly what ain't his, even if he can't use it at all."

"Wasn't much law in those days, either. And, what there was, was mostly crooked, favoring decent people and thieves all the same. The Taylors did a little thieving, but they had the law in Gonzales. The Suttons did a lot of thieving and they had the law in Cuero. It was a bad business."

"You mean, there were battles, like in a war?" I asked.

"I don't know anything like that. At least, nobody ever told me anything like that. It was probably a cowhand here and there got shot while they stole each other's cattle. They say John Wesley Hardin did most of the killing. My guess is your great grandfather Cirildo took down a few men on his own but he was not the kind of man to say so."

"So, how did he get the gun from John Wesley?"

"He didn't. I got it from a drunk gringo in Cuero one night. That was a long time ago, before the first world war. I won half of it in a dice game," said my grandfather with a certain brightness in his eye.

"How can you win a half a gun, Grandpa?" I said, my voice rising in disbelief.

"That's easy! You see, this goddamn gringo ran out of money just about the time he thought the dice were getting hot for him. All he had on him that had any value to speak of was this pistol. So, he goes and ups the stakes to five dollars on the roll. He hadn't lost but two dollars the whole night and I would say that was about all the money he had ever seen in one piece in the whole of his miserable life. I guess he figured he'd get rich on my money."

"Well, by the time the dice came around to him, he was down ten dollars on the pistol. Not only that, the son of a bitch was surely running saltwater through his veins. He couldn't have thrown lucky if you put chewing gum on the dice so they'd stick to the canvas. It took only two rolls and it happened so fast that by the time he stopped to breathe like a Christian, I owned half of the pistol. That gringo son of a bitch got Bubba the Nigger, who ran the place, to give him some more whiskey. It didn't take too long for him to get full of bottle courage. And sure enough, the whiskey got his courage going and he came back to bet his half against my half. It was my turn to throw the dice, but he insisted he was going to roll. I didn't want to argue with him. Anyhow, I won. The house rule said you had to strike the wall with the dice and they would fall back on a piece of canvas tacked smooth on the floor. The pistol was on the canvas.

"After I won, I let the pistol stay on the canvas. Nobody else did much of anything. That pistol meant the last thing of value that gringo owned and nobody likes to see a man lose everything he has. Besides, in those days, no decent man ever gambled away his weapon. So, the gringo got to thinking it was easy and he made a grab for the pistol. There was a Slick sitting across from me. He was from Victoria or San Antonio or some other place that ain't got too many Christians. When the gringo made his grab, the Slick stuck out his leg and kicked the gun toward me. He said to me, 'I believe this is your weapon.'

" 'What the hell did you do that for?' the gringo said.

" 'It ain't your gun, sport,' the Slick said.

"The gringo said, 'the hell it ain't,' and he looked at me half expecting that I was going to give him his gun back. The gun was under my knee where I crouched. I hadn't even touched it at all. He kept looking at me and I kept looking at him. Neither one of us said anything but he knew he wasn't going to have that gun, not without money. So, he gives the meanest look he's got and he leaves. I stuck the pistol, being that it was my property, in my belt. I went back inside the bar to have a beer for myself before going home for the night.

"I offered to buy the Slick a drink, being that I was friendly and he had a favor coming.

" 'You figure he'll be back,' the Slick asks me.

" 'With my money, he will.' "

"The Slick buttoned up his vest and suitcoat. I guess he smelled trouble coming and he said he had a long way to go and he had to move on. The gringo came back a short time later with twenty dollars. The gamble had gone all out of him. I guess the night air did him some good, too.

"He puts the twenty dollars on the bar and says he wants his pistol back. I told him the truth, that the pistol wasn't worth but twenty dollars. I reminded him that I had won forty dollars and that's exactly what it would take for him to get his pistol back. Unless he put another twenty dollars on the bar, he would have to wait until he could. He said twenty dollars was all I was going to get. He warned me about giving him his pistol back. I didn't see that there was any point in answering a threat he couldn't carry out by himself. He thought about it for a little bit. He changed his tone of voice and told me to go ahead and take the twenty. He had decided he would owe the other money.

"If he had been a Mexican or a Christian, I probably would take his word for it. Thing is, you can't trust a white man to owe you money. Money makes white people act funny.

"I told him I would be glad to take the twenty dollars but that I would not surrender the pistol until he had the rest of my money. Well, he was getting a little nervous about that time. He called on Bubba the Nigger to tell me his father had been the sheriff of DeWitt County and that the pistol had belonged to John Wesley Hardin himself. He even threw in that his cousin was the present sheriff of the county. Bubba the Nigger never moved from his place behind the bar. He didn't have one word to say, either.

"I guess he had heard the story often enough. The gringo said the pistol belonged to his family and he couldn't part with it under no circumstances. In fact, he said he really had no right to be gambling it away. I sort of felt sorry for the dumb son of a bitch. I told him it wasn't his to part or not part with anymore as I was now the owner of it. Again, I told him to go find another twenty dollars and I would be pleased to sell it back to him. Well, he was getting desperate on me. He said again how he had no right to gamble the pistol away like that and he said I had no right to win it, either.

"The other boys had given up on gambling and had drifted back into the bar for some serious liquid amusement. They were listening in on us and they got a good sized chuckle when the gringo said I had no right to win the pistol. He put on what was about his meanest face again. He didn't go so far as to threaten me, but he did say I had no right to keep the weapon."

"What happened, then, Grandpa? Did you have to kill the son of a bitch?" I asked, eagerly.

"Of course, I didn't kill the son of a bitch. And, don't let your mother hear you talk like that. You don't kill somebody just because he's a god-damned fool.

"Anyway. Bubba the Nigger, who was bigger than any Christian I ever saw, he made sure that things stayed friendly in the bar and out in the back where the dice games went on. Old Bubba got tired of hearing the same bullshit and told the gringo that he lost the gun fair and square and that there was no way out of it short of putting up another twenty dollars like I had been saying. He reminded the gringo that he would have to buy it back for what he bet on it. That was the rule, and his cousin, the sheriff, wanted a clean game where everybody obeyed the rules.

"The gringo said a white man's word ought to be good anywhere. Bubba the Nigger told him no man's word meant shit when it came to gambling. So, anyway, that gringo son of a bitch ran out of the bar saying he was going to go get his cousin. The sheriff would surely settle things.

"I asked Bubba, after the gringo went away, about the sheriff. Bubba told me he couldn't be sure what the sheriff would do. He said it wasn't the first time the gringo son of a bitch tried to welch on his losses. Most people were used to him, Bubba said. They just gave him his money back because they didn't care to find out what the sheriff might do.

"Bubba then gave me some unwanted but good advice. He said it would be better if I got over the county line before the sheriff came. He said the sheriff was paid to look the other way when it came to a little gambling and some whores who dropped in from time to time. Bubba said it seemed to him like this was family business and he wasn't sure how the sheriff would take it. There was no telling what might happen."

"You didn't run away, did you, Grandpa?"

"You're goddamned right I ran away.

"I had a purple mare in those days. She was mostly slow, but I convinced her we had to get the hell out of Cuero fast and the little four-footed thing was most obliging. I didn't slow down too much until I was two miles this side of Westhoff, inside Gonzales County. And even then I rode on looking over my shoulder. Afterward, when I safe on my own land, I figured if I stayed out of Cuero for a while, the whole thing would blow over. Turns out, as things do sometimes, I was wrong."

"Does the story get better, Grandpa?"

"No, it just goes on. Seems that a week or two later, I was working my land. I had a pair of mules that I got near Stockdale. One of them mules was just like your brother Paulie, mean and useless. Caused me a lot of trouble to get her to work with the other mule. Only reason I didn't ever shoot that mule is I needed her to get my cotton in the ground. It was only during planting time that I wanted to shoot her. Once the cotton was in, I didn't have any reason to shoot her. Went like that for years. I finally took to renting a tractor and I didn't have any more use for the mules. Couldn't sell her to anybody. Goddamn mule finally died of old age.

"Anyway, I was out there with the mules trying to scratch your grandma and me a living—none of the kids were here yet—when I be goddamned if that idiot gringo son of a bitch doesn't show up on my place, pretty as you please on horseback. He had the sheriff of DeWitt County, his cousin, with him. The sheriff wore the fanciest pair of chaps I've ever seen. They weren't chaps a working cowhand might wear. Cocky little banty rooster of a son of a bitch he was, sitting that horse of his.

"You know, squirt, things were mighty different in those days. White people didn't walk all over us like they do now. No, sir, they did not. We got respect from white people because we knew how to take care of our own and they knew it. It's not that they didn't try, mind you. It's just that they didn't know for sure whether they could get away with it. I don't expect that you understand that, but it was different then.

"I saw them coming up the road from Smiley and I saw them turn into my land, prancing their horses right toward me. They reined up beside my mules and that sheriff from DeWitt County comes right out and says I have stolen a gun that rightfully belongs in his family. I told him I had stolen no such goddamned thing. Furthermore, I told him I didn't appreciate being called a thief on my own land.

"He said he didn't care to hear what I thought about anything. He had come for that pistol and that's all there was to it.

"I told him to check with any of the boys that had been at Bubba's that night and he would discover the truth of things.

"That sheriff of DeWitt county stood up on his stirrups and gave my land a good looking over, like he had all the time in the world. He got through in his own time. Then, he told me to just give up the goddamned gun and be a good Mexican, stay out of trouble. The other gringo, his cousin, just sat in his saddle and didn't offer to say a goddamned word. They were pretty sure I wasn't going to make any trouble for them and anyway I didn't want to argue all goddamned day as I had plenty of work to do. So, I thought for a minute to myself and I decided the hell with it. I told that sheriff of DeWitt County if he was convinced that he knew what he was doing then he ought to just go on up to my house and tell your grandmother to hand over the pistol. She knew where it was and she would give it to them.

"It appears that's what the sheriff of DeWitt County wanted to hear and he began to turn his horse in the direction of the house. Before they could spur their horses I told them to hold up a minute. I wasn't quite finished. I guess he didn't like the sound of my voice because that sheriff of DeWitt County was mighty pissed when he reined in his horse.

"I told him—it was useless to talk to the other fellow—they could have the gun but that I would catch up to them before they reached Smiley and I intended to shoot both of them dead. I told them the gun was mine and it was not for sale. I wanted my money that night at Bubba's. Now, it was my pleasure to keep the gun. I intended to keep that gun or I intended to lie on the ground that very day. That was the only two ways to it.

"He looked at me like he'd been kicked in the back of the head. He reminded me that he was the sheriff and he wanted to know if I realized I was talking to a peace officer. I said as far as I was concerned, he was just another white man trespassing on my land. I told him we had our own sheriff in Gonzales county.

"Well, he didn't do much of anything for a while, except he stood up on his stirrups a couple of more times. I'd say he was thinking. His cousin tried to say something, but the sheriff told him to shut his damn mouth."

"Weren't you scared, Grandpa?" I asked again.

"Yeah, I guess I was scared. Your blood gets to flowing real fast and you can't hardly breathe. But, I wasn't thinking of that. There was not anyway I could know it at the time, but, yeah, damned right, I was scared. You don't remember too well the times when you're scared. The thing to remember, though, is this: you can't trust a white man with a gun. You especially cannot trust a white man with a badge and a gun."

"You're always saying that, Grandpa. All the white kids in school are pretty nice. They're okay, you know."

"You may be right, squirt. Maybe, there's something to the way they're growing them these days. But, even if white people can be nice, and even if you get to liking them, that does not mean you can trust them. Besides, you're too young to know too much shit, yet."

"Okay, Grandpa, have it your way. Just tell what happened."

"Well, the two of them had come in on the wagon road from Smiley. If they went to the house, they would have to turn left and go over the top of the hill. All you could see from where I stood was the roof of the house.

"When the sheriff of DeWitt county finished doing his thinking, he spurred his horse worse than he had a right to, and the animal jumped away at a gallop. His cousin followed. Those couple of seconds was the longest time I ever waited for something to happen. Sure enough, they turned back to the wagon road. I kept watching them until they were out of sight. After that, they didn't bother me again, except I knew to stay out of Cuero. It was too bad because there wasn't another place like Cuero to visit in those days.

"I ran into the sheriff of Gonzales county not long after that and he warned me to stay out of DeWitt county because the sheriff had pledged his vow to arrest me. I told him I hadn't done anything and he said it didn't matter. A sheriff can do just about anything he damn well pleases in his county."

"And, did you ever go back to DeWitt county?"

"Sure, I did. But, not until that sheriff son of a bitch was voted out of office. I even ran into him on the streets of Cuero one day. All he did was nod a greeting to me, like we were acquaintances from long ago, and that was that."

"I bet he was afraid of you, Grandpa," I said.

"No, he wasn't. He wasn't afraid when he came on my land. He came on my land knowing one thing, and he left knowing another. That's all."

"You just told me you scared him away, Grandpa," I said, exasperated.

"I didn't scare him away, son. What happened is this. I didn't threaten him. I told him what I was going to do. It was up to him to decide whether I meant to do what I said. When he couldn't be sure whether I meant what I said or not, he decided he didn't want to test it."

"Well, did you mean it?"

"That's hard to say because I didn't have to do anything. There was a chance I was bluffing, and he could just go and take the gun, and it would be the end of that. If it turned out I wasn't bluffing, then there was a chance there was going to be some killing. The point is, you never take a chance on getting yourself killed. You see, there was no trouble between me and that sheriff. It wasn't even a thing for the law to get involved in. He was just looking out for his family, same as anybody would. It was the other fool that got it started and he must've convinced the sheriff that there wouldn't be that much to getting the gun back from a Mexican. When the sheriff saw that it might go some other way, I guess he figured his cousin and the pistol were not worth the trouble.

"As for being afraid, remember this, you're never safe so long as somebody's afraid of you. So long as they remain afraid of you, they've got a hold on you, and they never let go. The only way they can ever stop being afraid is when you're dead. They'll likely wait until your guard is off and they'll take the advantage. It's a bad business having people be afraid of you."

"Nobody's afraid of me, Grandpa," I said. "There's lots of kids at school who are afraid of Paulie."

"Paulie ain't got the sense God gave to a pissant. Kids fear ain't the kind of fear I'm talking about. Kids forget, sooner than later."

Grandpa and I stayed quiet for a few moments. Although he was still a little groggy, his voice had cleared, and he did not seem to be as drunk as before.

Grandpa grunted and tossed the tobacco sack containing the bullets to me. The bullets were heavier than I had imagined.

"You want to load this pistol for me?" he asked.

"Sure, Grandpa. Can I shoot it once, too?" I asked, eagerly.

"No, you're not big enough to hold on to the pistol. Here," he said, handing it to me. "Put it on the bed when you load it. Otherwise, you might drop it and it'll go off."

I took the big .45 in both of my hands. I wanted to prove I could hold the pistol in one hand. Grandpa had insulted me. He didn't know whether I could hold it in one hand or not. Still, I didn't want to argue with him.

It took me a while, but I found the cylinder release. I held the cylinder up with one hand while I tried to pull the drawstring to loosen the pinched mouth of the tobacco sack. The brittle fabric cracked and crumbled in my hand. I was going to say something about it to Grandpa, but I realized that after I loaded the gun there wouldn't be any need for the sack.

Across the narrow strip of floor between us, Grandpa had reached into his trouser pocket to look at his watch again. He had sobered up enough to be able to read the watch without struggling to focus his eyes.

"Hurry, there's only a few minutes to midnight," he said.

I cautiously slipped the shells into each chamber and snapped the cylinder shut. Holding the grip with one hand and the barrel with the other, I stood up and brought the sixshooter over to Grandpa. I had the barrel pointing toward the back of the bunkhouse.

"Looks to me like you're really going to grow this year, squirt. You can shoot the gun for yourself next New Year," said my grandfather.

My heart gladdened and a big smile crossed my face.

"Is that a promise I can hold you to, Grandpa?" I said.

"No, it ain't a promise I can keep myself. I won't be here. I already told you that. But, I intend to leave you the gun after my death. I'll make sure and tell your daddy about it. After it's yours, you can do with it what you want."

I was too excited with having loaded the pistol and having received the promise that he would give the gun to me to pay much attention to all of what he said. He took the gun from me and stood up.

"Come on," he said, "let's go see what this New Year is going to be like."

"How can you tell things like that, Grandpa?" I asked. "To me, it's just the old year and then it's the new year. I mean, I can't tell any damn difference."

"You have to pay attention to things, squirt," he said. Grandpa snapped his fingers. "Nothing comes to you just like that." And, he snapped them again. "Pay attention to the ground. See how the dirt changes color. Read what's left when the topsoil drifts away. Look into the cracks in the earth you walk on. Watch the trees, especially. See how they bend one way and then another, how they resist against some winds and how they seem to flow with the breezes. Smell, too, the smells that the wind brings. Get to know the smell of the sea so that you can sniff it out of a hundred miles of other smells picked up along the way. Know the difference between the thick winds and the thin winds. Wildflowers, shrubs, weeds and brush. Look up at the sky, see and feel the colors up there; in your lifetime you will see a sky in every color you can imagine. Watch the clouds. Some will just hang there, large and fluffy, close enough to touch; some will lie scattered all over the horizon, and there will be days when the clouds stretch all the way to the ground and all of Schoolland will exist inside a cloud and instead of the rain falling on you it will be suspended in the air, without moving at all, and when you walk, you'll walk right into it and you can taste the rain right in the air itself and it will be sweet and sharp and cold and you will never taste anything like it ever again. The animals. Pay close attention to the animals. Animals are the ones that can teach you the most because they are flesh and blood, too. Animals don't talk Christian like you and me. If you know how to get it out of them, they can tell you things."

I didn't understand too much of what my grandfather said. I wanted to ask him to explain but he rose to his feet and was already walking through the door, out of the bunkhouse, following the footpath back to the house.

The kitchen light was on for Elpidio and my sister, Juana, who would not be back for another hour at least. I had expected that Jose and Paulie had already given up and gone inside to bed. In the faint yellow kitchen light that reached the porch, I could see the outline of my brother Jose, stretched out at the top of the porchsteps, asleep. Paulie had come back from his sulk and was sitting on the fender of Jose's truck. He was quiet, for a change. He roused himself when he saw us coming up.

"Is he got that old rusted piece of shit he calls a gun," said Paulie. Paulie was being mean, as the nickel-plated finish of the pistol was well oiled with nary a spot of rust on it.

"He's got it," I said. "I loaded it myself, Paulie. You had better watch yourself now that Grandpa is armed. He might just shoot you with it this time."

My brother Paulie loved a dare, especially of the kind I had just thrown to him. I wished I had kept my mouth shut.

"That old gun is going to blow up in your face, old man," said Paulie, warming up for his best shot. Then, he surprised me.

"I'll get you my shotgun if you want to make some noise," Paulie said. "I just got some shells for it the other day. A shotgun'll beat that popgun any day."

I couldn't see it very well in the dark, but Grandpa, slowly and deliberately, pulled the hammer of the .45 back. I heard the click.

"This'll do," said Grandpa.

"I'm telling you, it'll make a lot more noise, Grandpa," said Paulie. "All you want to do is wake up the dead, anyway. Ain't that what you're after?"

I tapped Paulie on his knee with my fist. "Leave him alone, will you?"

"That's all right, squirt," said Grandpa. "Let him flap his trap. I'm not going to shoot him, if that's what you're afraid of."

My grandfather then raised his arm way above his head and fired the .45 Colt. It was a thunderous blast, unlike the thin, spat-sounds of my .22 rifle. We heard the click again and there was another explosion. I could see a brief orange flame erupt from the barrel after each shot. My grandfather fired two more times and then the hammer struck an empty chamber. At the first shot, my brother Jose had awakened abruptly, groaned, but had continued to lie on the floor. As my grandfather dropped his arm to his side, my father came out on the porch, his feet bare, buckling his belt. My father figured Grandpa was still drunk.

"Has he got any more bullets left?" he asked of no one in particular.

"No, sir," I said.

"Well, then, that's it, isn't it?" said my father as he went back to bed.

# Chapter 4

The first day of the New Year was as clear and as bright as a summer's day. In the night a wave of cold air had rushed through, but by mid-morning the wind had died down, leaving a brisk, sunlit day. At noon there was not a cloud in a sky so rich and blue it seemed you could reach up and touch it.

It was shirt-sleeve warm and Paulie and I decided to go hunting in the Poindexter pasture across the road from our place. Huntley Poindexter had warned us repeatedly not to do it, but he lived in Gonzales and rarely came out to catch us. Anyway, we knew better than to shoot when cows were about. As we went out with our rifles, my father told us to stay out of Huntley Poindexter's pasture. We headed straight for it from the house and crossed the barbed wire fence behind our mailbox. I knew Daddy would be pissed off, but he'd be over it by the time we came back.

Inside the pasture the cowpaths were worn smooth and hard. Paulie and I followed them willy-nilly, staying within sight of each other. I froze in my tracks when Paulie fired into a pile of brush. Paulie was twitchy as a hunter, firing at almost anything that moved, even rabbits on the run, knowing he couldn't hit them. My cousin Lupe was the only one I ever saw who could hit a rabbit on the run. I stood still in case whatever it was he shot at ran in my direction. I saw Paulie beginning to move again and relaxed. He didn't volunteer to say what it was that made him shoot.

When we came to the mesquite treeline at the edge of the pasture, before us stretched a quarter mile of bottomland going right up to the banks of Espinoza Creek. My father had told us the story of how he and a cousin of his worked on this land for three months, trying to clear it into arable land. The cousin, whose name was Simon, was bitten by a rattle-snake and my grandmother on my daddy's side had to amputate his leg. We had asked my father to show us where it had all happened, but he said he couldn't remember and anyway there was no point to it.

It had taken us nearly an hour to make our way along the cowpaths to the end of the pasture. Once we were out of the pale shade of the mes-quite, out in the open and in the lee of the trees, it became warmer. Paulie wanted to go on across the ankle-high dry grass of the savannah toward a stand of huge oak trees. Just beyond, he swore, we could find swamp rabbits. I reminded him that no one at the house would eat swamp rabbit.

Just when I finished talking, Paulie began to plink at a buzzard flying low. The best he could do was hit one of its wings, tearing a few feathers away. All of a sudden, Paulie became disgusted.

"Fuck it," he said. "Let's go home."

We walked back along the curve of the pasture where I figured my father had worked clearing it. We saw a couple of stumps and I wondered if my father had been with the crew that left them there. We circled around on the soft grass in the direction of the road for the walk back home. It was much shorter this way than the zig-zag we had taken going out.

The next day would be the end of our Christmas vacation from school and I was worried that Paulie would be discovered. He had quit attending classes in the early part of December. He continued to go to school each morning, though, taking the yellow bus into Smiley. There would be a teacher in front of the large central building of the school to shepherd us inside. First, she would make us form two lines, no matter how cold it was, before we marched inside. Somehow, my brother Paulie would go right through the building without anyone noticing, go out a back door and disappear. In the afternoon, Paulie would be back, big as life, in time to line up and get on the bus for the return trip home, acting as if he had suffered along with the rest of us through the day-long drone of the teachers.

It was not uncommon for parents to keep the children at home when they needed extra labor and, I suppose, none of the teachers were particularly concerned about Paulie's absence. He was not one of the favorite pupils in school, anyway.

"What are you going to do about school tomorrow, Paulie?" I asked as we walked back to the house.

He had his rifle across the top of his shoulders, his arms hooked one over the barrel and the other over the stock. "I don't know. Nothing," he said. "Anyway, it ain't tomorrow yet."

That was a typical response from Paulie. Even years later, as an adult with children of his own, when he went through difficult times, he would not waste any time thinking. He preferred instead to react right at the precise moment when he had to.

"If you ask me, if Ma doesn't kill you, Daddy's going to knock the shit out of you."

"Nobody asked you, shithead. But, now that you say so, maybe they will and maybe they won't." He was more subdued than usual when he faced big trouble, so I figured he was worried more than he let on.

It didn't take us long to get back to the fence. We crossed over it to walk the rest of the way on the grassy road shoulder. We saw don Armando Gutierrez coming out of our driveway in his little green truck. He waved to us as he went by.

My mother, who governed such things, kept to a Sunday routine for New Year's, which meant nothing more than a large supper at three or four in the afternoon. All day long she fed whoever came to visit.

At the house, Paulie and I faced away from the porch to unload our rifles. I gave mine to Paulie so he could put it away and I went into the kitchen where everyone was gathered.

"You better clean those rifles," admonished my father, knowing it was useless to remind us.

He sat at the table with Grandpa and Elpidio. Each of them had a cup of coffee resting upon a saucer in front of him. My mother and my sister Juana were preparing food for the big meal.

"I didn't fire my rifle at all," I said, "so there's nothing to clean. I want some coffee."

"No, sir," said my mother, "you'll be up all night and tomorrow's a school day." Coffee never kept me up, but there was no explaining that to her.

"You anxious to get back to school, squirt?" asked Elpidio, who slid his coffee toward me.

"Yeah, I guess. The more I go the sooner it will be over," I said.

"Cristina Sifuentes will be coming back from West Texas any day now," said my sister Juana, smiling. "That's why he can't wait to go back."

"Who's Cristina Sifuentes?" asked my father. "That's not Cipriano Sifuentes' girl, is it?"

"Sure is," said Juana.

"It wouldn't hurt if he learned something," said my mother. She didn't turn around to see me drinking the rest of Elpidio's coffee.

"They don't teach nothing. Juana finished high school, and she doesn't know beans about nothing," I protested.

"Be quiet, elephant ears," said my sister Juana. "You shouldn't let him go out with Paulie, Momma, he's getting to be just like him."

"All you people ever do is talk about me behind my back," said Paulie as he came into the kitchen. He took a cup from the sink, rinsed it, and poured himself some coffee. My mother didn't say anything to him about coffee keeping him awake.

"You're not going to sit here and spoil this good company, are you, young man?" said my grandfather as Paulie approached the table.

My brother Paulie drew back a chair and said, "That sounds like an invitation to me." He reversed the chair and hooked a leg over to straddle it. "I do believe I will join you."

"Paulie," said my mother when she saw him, "it's not polite to sit that way."

"He saw Lash LaRue do it that way at the movies last Saturday," I volunteered.

"Elpidio, don't give him any coffee. I don't want him to drink coffee before school," said my mother, noticing the cup and saucer in front of me and knowing who gave it to me.

"I don't think anybody likes me in the family," Paulie said. "Why don't you just give me away to somebody. Give me away to a Negro family, one of them in Nixon. That way you won't have to see me again."

"Your father should have drowned you in the creek when he had the chance," said Grandpa.

"Daddy, don't say things like that, he'll think you're serious," said my mother.

"Who says I'm not serious," rejoined my grandfather.

"Yeah, old man, I bet you're serious," said my brother Paulie. "Well, what are you going to do when I run away to Africa?"

"What makes you want to go to Africa?" asked my sister Juana. "You don't even know where it is."

"It's on the other side of Gonzales, isn't it, Pa?" said Elpidio.

"Yeah, I know where it is. You just go east and you'll get to it eventually," said Paulie.

"I can understand Heriberto wanting to go to Africa," said my sister Juana. "He's black enough to be a Negro himself. And the squirt could fit right in with the elephants."

"Don't you start, too, Juana," said my mother. "And, don't talk about Heriberto like that." We are all pretty dark-skinned, but Heriberto was nearly black and my mother was touchy about it.

"How did Heriberto get to be so black?" I asked.

"We got Negroes in the family somewhere, I bet," said Paulie.

"Paulie!" said my mother, horrified. She turned to my father, who had a way of listening to everything without becoming involved in any of it. "Will you do something about him?" she insisted.

"Do what?" asked my father, giving up trying to stay out of it. "There are no Negroes on my side of the family."

"None on mine, either," said Grandpa.

"Not so fast, Grandpa," said my brother Elpidio. "I've heard there can be a Negro in the family a hundred years back and everybody will be white as anything and all of a sudden, there's a little pickaninny like Heriberto comes along."

My sister Juana began to laugh, as did the rest of us. "I don't believe you, Elpidio," she said.

My mother gave up. By the way she slammed the pots around on the stove, she was not too happy about the conversation. Worse than that, she couldn't stop it. My father decided to help a little and change the subject.

"Are those doña Marta's tamales?" asked my father.

"Daddy, you saw when don Armando brought them, you were outside talking to him when he gave them to me," said Juana.

"I guess I was," said my father, smiling.

"She always sends us a batch of tamales for New Year's Day," said my mother. "They've been doing it forever."

"The pigs are going to have a feast tomorrow," said Paulie.

"Did anybody feed the pigs today, by the way?" asked my father of no one in particular and no one answered right away.

"Paulie," said my mother, "don't be disrespectful toward doña Marta and don Armando."

"I saw Jose going in the direction of the pigpens this morning," said Elpidio. "I couldn't guarantee that he fed them, though."

"He was probably going to take a shit," said Paulie, and that got him a swat of the dishtowel from my sister Juana.

"You didn't see him actually feeding them, did you?" I said.

"He did. If Jose went that way, he fed them," said my father.

"I think it's your turn to feed them next week, Paulie," said my father, "you and the squirt, here."

"Are you really going to feed all those tamales to the pigs?" I asked.

"Don't be silly," said my sister Juana.

"Well, I'd like to know who's going to eat them," said Paulie. "We've been eating tamales since before Christmas. Whoever heard of anybody making tamales for New Year's?"

"There's some people who do," said Grandpa.

"Jews, probably, they ain't Christians," said my father.

"Doña Marta and don Armando are as good Christians as anybody," argued my mother. "And don't talk about Jews."

"Those tamales are so greasy," said my sister Juana.

"Anybody ever notice all those dogs doña Marta keeps around the place? And did you ever notice that right after New Year's there's not as many dogs around their place anymore?" said my father. Then he leaned back in his chair.

My mother looked at my father and shook her head. "You see why your children are the way they are," she said, exasperated.

"I don't think she uses lard on those tamales at all," said Paulie. "I think she wipes the sweat off her mustache and throws in into the masa."

"Paulie, get out of my kitchen," yelled my mother at last, having lost once and for all her long battle to keep her temper under control.

"Speaking of food," began my father, "are we ever going to get something to eat today?"

"Paulie, I meant it," said my mother, "get out of my kitchen."

Paulie sensed that my mother was serious now, irritated by all of us together, or maybe by something else. In any case, as was usual, she took it out on my brother Paulie.

"I think I will go check on the twins, see how the little shits are doing," said Paulie in a grand manner, rising and throwing his leg back high in the air. He wanted my mother to see his final act of defiance.

"And don't make the twins cry," she said, competing with him to have the last word.

"Why don't you do something?" she shot at my father.

"Don't start on me, he's your son," said my father.

"I always thought somebody found him in the creek and gave him to you," said Elpidio.

"That's right," said Grandpa, "and he should have been drowned right then and there."

"I can't have a cup of coffee in peace," said my father.

"My mother placed her hands on her hips and surveyed the room, stopping at each of our faces to give us a stern look. Juana, who had worked up a nice fat grin on her face, got rid of it as soon as my mother turned to her. My mother had had enough.

"I was going to start the tortillas," said my sister Juana.

Elpidio, my mother's favorite and the one who hardly ever got scolded, pushed back his chair and announced that he was going to feed his mare.

"Don't take too long, the food is almost ready," said my mother.

"Feed my black," said Paulie from somewhere in another part of the house.

"Feed him yourself," said my brother Elpidio.

"Feed all of them while you're out there," said my father, knowing that is what Elpidio would do anyway. Elpidio was also the one who always got after Paulie for neglecting his horse.

"Is this what this family has come to," asked my grandfather, "every man for himself?"

"I wouldn't call Paulie a man, Grandpa," said my brother Jose, who had come into the kitchen in the interim, dragging his jacket on the floor. "Anybody been outside lately? We're going to get a good norther tonight, that's all I can say."

"Come on, squirt," said my brother Elpidio, "help me feed the horses. You're going to get into trouble if you stay here."

Elpidio and I went through the kitchen door to the back porch. My dog Jeff rested his head on the floor, his paws neatly placed on each side of his jaws. When he saw us, he lumbered up on his three good feet, opened his mouth wide, giving his chops a wraparound lick and then he flopped his tongue so that it dangled from one side. His breathing speeded up as he took a step forward. Then, he whirled around, hopping on his one good rear leg and lay back down again in the same position from which he seldom stirred. He had decided we weren't going anywhere and he would stay put.

"That dog of yours is the most useless dog I have ever seen," said Elpidio. "He never does anything. He doesn't run, he doesn't bark. In fact, I've never even seen him get off the goddamned porch in five years. I don't think I've even seen him eat. How does he live?"

Jeff was given to us about the time I was born and that sort of made him my dog, which didn't mean a whole hell of a lot except that it allowed everyone to complain to me about him. I was expected to defend the son of a bitch.

"He eats, Elpidio," I said lamely. "He just wants to be by himself most of the time, that's all. What's wrong with that?"

"He doesn't act like a goddamn dog should act, that's all!"

"You just don't see him. I don't think he likes anybody to see him eat. Ma gives me scraps for him and I put them in front of him, but he won't touch them. When I leave and nobody else is around, he eats. At least, the scraps are gone when I come back."

"If I was as useless as he is, I would be ashamed to let anybody see me eat, too, I guess," said Elpidio.

"He used to be a good cow dog," I said.

"He was good before he was run over, I'll grant you that. You're too young to remember all of it, that's all," said my brother Elpidio.

I was only a few days old when Gypsum Davis brought the dog over to us. Seems that all of a sudden, old Jeff had gone crazy in the head and wasn't any good as a cow dog any more. Gypsum Davis hated to shoot the dog, which is what he would have to do unless my father took him in. It was more as a favor to the old man that my father took in the dog. And thereafter Jeff was known as my dog. Jeff didn't act like he was anybody's dog.

The story says that one of Gypsum Davis's longhorns, which he kept as curiosities, as there was little market for them, tried to gore Jeff. The longhorn didn't hurt Jeff at all, but he got to be afraid of cows. It was so great a fear that he took to barking at them every time he saw one. It is not good for a cow dog to be afraid of cows and to bark too much.

Everybody in Schoolland knew about old Jeff. My brother Heriberto took to breaking Jeff of his bad habits by taking him out with our few cows. There didn't seem to be anything wrong with him.

Heriberto hired himself out to work on Bernie Robertson's place and he brought the dog with him. Bernie said if that was old Gypsum Davis' old dog, he didn't want him on his place. Heriberto swore to Bernie Robertson that he had trained him out of his bad habits and old Jeff was as good as new. All it took was one afternoon and Bernie Robertson said he was going to shoot the son of a bitch. Old Bernie even thought about shooting Heriberto for lying to him.

Heriberto wouldn't give up on the dog, though. So he started to train him to chase cars. My brother Heriberto figured that by chasing cars, old Jeff would lose his fear of everything. When a car came by on the gravel road in front of the house, Heriberto would sic him on to the speeding car, whistling as if they were herding cattle. Maybe old Jeff began to confuse cars and cows, thinking of his best days. He would run up to the front of a car, nipping at the wheels, trying to turn the car around, as he had been trained to do with cattle, yelping as he did so.

It was during one of those times that he got too close to the car and slid himself under the body of the car enough so he lost his balance and the rear tire rolled over his hind leg. Heriberto and Elpidio saw Jeff tumbling on the road and ran to him. Before they could reach him, Jeff was already on his feet, coughing, tossing his head forward as if trying to dislodge something from his throat.

Elpidio tried to pick Jeff up to bring him back to the house, but as he approached him, the dog growled in a menacing way that no one had ever heard before. They stood there watching Jeff, circling to see if he had ruptured his stomach, looking for blood coming from his mouth. All they could see was the hind leg that dangled in the air. Once or twice, Jeff dropped the leg to the hard packed gravel and then leaped forward from the pain, emitting a high-pitched, mournful yelp.

Elpidio and Heriberto continued to watch old Jeff for a while. My brother Jose went to join them. He had played with Jeff more than the others, but the dog would not let Jose come near him either. The three of my brothers came back to the house where my father had been watching them from the edge of the porch. From the looks of it, they were convinced that Jeff would die.

For the next few hours, Jeff remained on the grassy easement, shying away from the occasional car that sped by, jumping away in a circular hopping as it was too painful for him to move. After the car had disappeared and its roar died away, they could hear Jeff whining.

As it began to get dark that day, Jeff moved across the road, eased himself under the fence into Huntley Poindexter's pasture and no one saw him again for three or four days. I was four years old at the time and no one bothered to tell me anything about it. I don't recall that I even noticed he was missing. Jeff returned several days later, gaunt to the point where his ribs made deep furrows along the ragged tufts of reddish tan fur on his skin. He came back quietly, embarrassed, something like a man who disappears from home for a few days. He went directly to the back porch.

My mother, to the surprise of everyone, fried some hamburger meat, tossing in some potatoes and pieces of corn tortilla. She tried to place the bowl of food in front of Jeff, but he growled at her. Jose was the next one to try, but Jeff growled at him, too. My brother Jose set the bowl on the porch floor where I picked it up and took it to Jeff, ignoring his growling. As I came near, he lifted up on his good forelegs and bared his teeth. I went no further, but slid the bowl of food close enough to where he could reach it. The entire family stood on the porch watching him, but he would not touch the food. Gradually, everyone lost interest and went inside. The next day, the food was gone. After that, we pretty much learned not to linger once we took Jeff his food. As the leg healed, Jeff got used to being a gimp. The leg set at almost a perfect right angle from his body, giving him the appearance of a dog always about to take a leak.

More than one visitor got a little jumpy as Jeff approached them to get a good sniff, fearing that he would piss on him. He was scolded so often that eventually he gave up greeting visitors. The best he did was come around the side of the house every once in a while, get a good look at who it was and then he'd go back to the porch.

Over the years, there were a couple of our neighbors who had done him some wrong or other, and these he would greet with a low growl. Unless someone came out, Jeff would not let them down from their vehicles. Other than that, old Jeff stayed on the back porch from where we seldom saw him move. We usually had anywhere from two to five other dogs around, and they too stayed away from Jeff.

On the southern side of our house was a narrow strip of mesquite land, a rectangle about one hundred yards wide and three hundred yards long. In the center of it stood an aluminum windmill that had an electric water pump as a back-up system in case of long windless periods. Adjacent to it was a round concrete water trough, some ten feet in diameter and rising up to mid-thigh, provided you weren't too tall. Over the years, the chaparral and brush had dried up and had been cleared away, leaving just the scrubby mesquite and here and there a few clumps of cactus. The mesquite grove was fenced in. It was as good a place as there could be to keep our four horses. We didn't need four horses, but we had four horses.

Immediately past the narrow man-gate, there was a tackroom, maybe six by eight feet, that formed the eastern wall of a horse shed. The horse shed was open to the south, with unevenly matched boards to form the northern and western walls. In a corner of the horse shed, we kept bags of horse chow, sacks of oats, and a good supply of hay bales that we brought from the barn at the old house. All of it was protected from the horses by a barrier of chicken wire. The tin roof was rusted in so many places, it was covered by an almost solid sheet of pitch tar.

As soon as the horses saw us, they came running. They stopped a few feet way from the wooden feeder trough, pawing politely at the ground, waiting to be served. Elpidio rolled back the chicken wire, while I parted a few squares of hay and spread them out on the ground at the horses' feet. The horses stood their ground, ignoring the hay. They wanted the good stuff.

Suddenly, Elpidio's mare kicked with both of her hind legs. None of the other horses were close enough to be bothering her. She was a wine-colored mare with a white mane and forelocks. Elpidio claimed that she had the blood of thoroughbreds in her, and sometimes he claimed she came from an Arabian sire. My father snorted that the mare was like the rest of us, a mix of so many bloods no one could tell exactly what we were. My mother, who overheard the comment, angrily scolded my father. She insisted there was nothing wrong with being Mexican and, further, she insisted that it was good enough for her.

"That mare is crazy, Elpidio," I said.

"Naw, she's just glad to see me, that's all," said Elpidio.

"Maybe she's starving. When was the last time you fed her?" I asked.

"I feed her every day, shithead," said Elpidio.

"Probably not very much," I retorted.

"That's true, I guess. They eat more than they're worth. I told Pa we don't need so many goddamned horses," Elpidio said.

"What did he say?" I asked.

"He said we might have to eat one, one day. Grandpa says there's people who like to eat horsemeat more than beef, can you figure that?" Elpidio said with a disgusted look on his face.

"You know, I should sell the mare. Bernie Robertson, when I went to help out with his cattle, offered to buy her," Elpidio added, trailing off into silence to think about it some more.

"What did you say?" I asked, impatiently.

"To what?" said Elpidio, as if he had completely forgotten what he had said.

"About what? About the mare, idiot!" I said.

"Oh, the mare? Naw, I don't want to sell her. I couldn't sell her. It cost me too much just to save up to buy her."

"I don't understand this. You just finished saying you want to sell her."

"I said no such thing, squirt. If I was to do the right thing, I would sell her. That's the thing to do. But, I don't want to. There's the big difference," said my brother Elpidio, satisfied with himself.

It was too confusing for me to follow. Elpidio moved to the opposite corner of the shed to take a leak. Meanwhile, I took a coffee can and began to fill the feeder trough with horse chow. The chunks of horsechow reminded me of horse turds. After the first coffee can of chow was in the feeder, the horses moved forward eagerly and began to butt each other out of the way. It was not until I filled the trough with a full ration for each that they settled down to eat properly.

Elpidio's mare did not join the other horses. She was special and she knew it. She stood to one side until Elpidio had finished his business. He took a burlap horse bag, which he had made himself, and filled it with the last of a sack of oats. The horse bag had straps made from an old belt sewn into it. Elpidio stuffed the mare's snout into it and buckled the bag over her head just behind the ears.

"Bitch eats like a queen, don't she," said Elpidio, proud of her and of himself.

I threw some more hay on the ground because the horse chow and the oats would not be enough. That finished, Elpidio relatched the chicken wire. We remained to one side of the horse shed to make sure the horses wouldn't bite or kick each other while they pushed and shoved for the last share in the trough. None of them seemed interested in the hay, but they were going to have their fill of it as soon as the horse chow was gone.

Elpidio's mare stood alone to one side, tossing her head occasionally to get at the last of the oats in the bag. When she was done, Elpidio slipped the bag off her head and we returned to the house where our supper was waiting.

# Chapter 5

In the morning, the norther predicted by my brother Jose failed to arrive. The explosive reaction to Paulie quitting school also failed to materialize. It was difficult to get such things by my father and he had known about it all along, as our neighbors had seen Paulie loitering in Smiley and had reported it to my father. My father had already made his decision as to what to do with Paulie. It was a warm winter morning. A little of the night chill clung to the air, dry and solemn, but otherwise it was going to be a warm day. The twins and I huddled deeper into our beds in an attempt to avoid the inevitable. My mother would stick her head into the bedroom, calling us half-heartedly, knowing we would not get up. She did this several times each morning with no results. My father would then take over from my mother. He would call us the first time and he didn't mind that we didn't get up. The second time when he poked his head into the room, we knew from the sound of his voice that we had better get up.

Once we had our blood flowing, we discovered it was much warmer than we had thought. Nevertheless, my mother made us wear warm clothing, much heavier than what we thought was necessary. She made the twins wear their fleece caps with the stupid-looking earflaps. I wanted to make fun of them, as I always did, but I decided it was too early in the day to make trouble for myself.

My mother would place our lunches on the kitchen table in the order we would likely be ready to grab them and run outside to wait for the bus. Mine was first, followed by the twins, and then Paulie's, as he was always the last. Except, this morning Paulie's lunch was missing.

"Where's Paulie?" I asked, fearful of the response.

"You know he hasn't been to school for weeks," said my mother in a sarcastic, exaggerated way.

I sat down to eat my breakfast consisting of an egg, refried beans and some cornpone. I ate quickly because there was something coming and I had nothing to say in my defense.

Whenever she was the last to know something, my mother naturally figured we conspired to keep it from her. It was going to take her a long time to get over this business with Paulie. To my surprise, once I finished eating, she said, "Go on, now, you'll be late for the bus."

The twins stayed behind, picking at their breakfast until she looked out of the small window over the sink and saw the school bus in the distance.

It was only then that she sent the twins out to where I waited.

Riding on the school bus, the only thing I could think of was Cristina Sifuentes. I knew it was too early for her to return, but just the thought of going into the classroom where she would sit in just a week or two, made me feel good. Nervous, too. How much would she change in the six months I had not seen her? She had kissed me the year before. To me, that was a pledge more binding than if she had actually told me she loved me, which she hadn't.

To keep from going crazy thinking of Cristina Sifuentes, I began to think about Paulie quitting school. The only thing I could figure was that my father had given Paulie a job. He was only a year and a half older than me, but leaving school and having a job brought him to the brink of adulthood. Paulie in fact had to be reminded of his age as he tended to act much older than he was. Moreover, he wanted to do things which children of his age didn't do.

With his new position in the family, he was bound to make life difficult for me, just as my brother Jose had made life difficult for Paulie a few short years before.

While we where outside playing in the schoolyard during the noon recess, the norther blew in. At first, the winds began to blow a bit harder, carrying with them a blanket of wet, thick cold. As the winds whistled through the sides of the buildings and through the trees, they picked up dry leaves and dust from the ground, making it difficult to see. This was followed by a faraway roar that sounded like a threshing machine. The roar became louder as it grew stronger and it seemed to rev up to a high-pitched whir.

The teachers were having their lunch while we played outside. As the storm intensified, it knocked loose an eight-foot-long branch. The teachers heard the crack of the branch and turned to see it come crashing down into the playground. We heard it coming and were well out of danger when it struck the ground.

The teachers gave up on their lunches and rushed outside, holding onto their skirts and hair, holding their forearms against the cold. In no time, we were ushered inside the school building. We had plenty of time left on our lunch-time play period and so we resented it when we were told to sit at our desks and place our heads down.

The roar of the storm continued gathering speed. Gusts of wind crashed against the stone walls of the school building and the sound of it made us imagine that the building itself was swaying with the wind. The glass panes rattled. The dust that swirled outside made a wall of dirt form against the windows. Through the roar and the intermittent swirls of dust we saw the trees bend with the wind. We heard the sudden, terrifying crack of thunder and the thunderbolt struck again. This time it split a tree in half down the middle of the trunk until one part of it came to rest on the ground. The other half, wounded and obscene with its insides exposed, stood erect.

After an hour's incessant pummeling, the winds subsided as abruptly as they had begun. The temperature began to drop steadily, making the classrooms cold and dreary. Not sure of what else was in store for the day, the principal decided to close the school early. The teachers were only too eager to get home as they feared for storm damage on their own property. They lined us up in the foyer long before the driver could be summoned to get the buses ready. No one said anything as we waited in line, but we could hear teeth chattering all along the line of little bodies, some shivering from the cold, others from fear.

My mother was surprised to see us come home so early, as the storm had not passed by our place at all. I was just as surprised to see Elpidio sitting in the kitchen drinking coffee.

"The teachers sent us home early on account of the storm," I said by way of explanation.

"Broke your little heart to have that happen, I bet," said Elpidio, casually.

"Leave me alone, it wasn't my fault," I whined.

"He didn't say it was your fault," interrupted my mother, who defended Elpidio all the time. "And don't whine like that," she added, "I hate it."

"I don't mind going to school," I protested, which was true as far as it went. If it weren't for seeing Cristina Sifuentes every day, I wouldn't like school as much.

Elpidio and my mother exchanged looks. They were about to stress the importance of school to me and how they hoped I could be something more than a farmer. I had been hearing the discussion for the last two years and they seemed to be the only ones convinced of it. My father, of course, went along with the idea, but I was never sure whether he believed in it or whether it was an easy way to keep the peace. It didn't seem to me that I had much choice in the matter.

"Where's Grandpa?" I said in an attempt to change the subject. "I think I'll go and drop in on him."

"He's gone. He went out for a ride," said Elpidio.

"His truck's parked out front," I said.

"He went out on horseback," said my mother.

"Grandpa hates horses," I said.

"He didn't go out on just any horse. He took my mare," said Elpidio.

"He hates your mare most of all. She tried to bite him, once. I saw it for myself. That mare is crazy," I said.

In another part of the house, one of the twins screamed. Little Julian liked to study everyday after school, whereas little Albert insisted that they play. Little Albert was barrel-chested, although the rest of his body was that of a scrawny child. My brother Heriberto had taken them to see the wrestling matches at his in-laws', who were the only people we knew with a television set. Heriberto's father-in-law made the comment that little Albert had the build of a wrestler. Thereafter little Albert wanted to be a wrestler. He needed little Julian to practice with and little Julian would have none of it, as he preferred coloring-in his school assignments or practicing his letters and numbers.

The scream that reverberated throughout the house and into the kitchen came from little Albert. Little Albert had been taunting little Julian until little Julian had enough of it and punched little Albert in the nose.

My mother ran to the double bedroom and Elpidio and I heard the door to the back porch slam shut. We saw the top of little Julian's head behind the glass in the door. My mother returned, leading little Albert by the hand. His nose was bleeding. She took him to the sink, where she wiped his nose and told him to stand still with his head tilted back.

"I'm going to spank that boy," said my mother.

"When little Julian doesn't want to play, little Albert should leave him alone," said Elpidio.

"I will not have fighting in this house," said my mother.

"Speaking of fighting," I said, "where is Paulie working?"

"Who knows. Pa took him along this morning, probably to help out a little and just get in the way of things," said Elpidio.

"He'll wish he was back in school, I bet. He thinks working is a lot easier," I said.

"He'll get used to it," said Elpidio. "He'll learn that work is not something you can run away from, like he does most things."

Elpidio became pensive and without him noticing I slid his cup of coffee away and drank from it. My mother decided that little Albert was well enough to send back to the bedroom, where she admonished him to take a nap and not bother little Julian anymore. In the meantime, little Julian had slipped back into the bedroom to continue his homework.

"I can't figure out Grandpa riding your mare, Elpidio. He told me you keep her just to piss him off," I said, sliding the coffee toward him.

"I don't know anything about that, squirt. He asked if he could take her out and I thought she needed the exercise. Didn't seem to me he was going out for the fun of it. You know how he gets. He's probably on to something," said Elpidio.

"It's going to freeze tonight," said my mother.

"I guess we'd better go move the pigs," Elpidio said, wearily. "Come on, squirt, let's go do it now before it gets too cold and too dark."

"Put on some warm clothes, both of you. We can't afford to have anybody get sick in this weather," my mother said.

My brother Elpidio and I did as my mother ordered. We began a brisk walk, hands in our pockets, to the old house. The old place was a little over half of a mile away. To our right as we walked, adjacent to the highway, was my mother's garden. Later in the spring, most of the garden would be planted with sweet corn, potatoes, beans and tomatoes. My mother liked to experiment with different seeds each year. She tried strawberries one year, but that didn't yield anything. Over the years, though, she'd plant a vegetable none of us would eat, like okra, carrots, cauliflower and such. She claimed they were good for us and we should eat them, except no one did. These would be planted in a small section, fenced off from the rest of the garden. For a while, she kept chile pitín and cilantro plants in a grassy area between the bunkhouse and the house, but the dogs pissed on them, or so my daddy said one day. After that, she developed a repugnance to the chile and especially to the cilantro. My sister Juana told us my mother was convinced of what my father had said and even after Juana had washed the cilantro, my mother insisted that she smelled dog piss. She tried to transplant them across the fence in the larger garden, away from the dogs, but they never took.

Elpidio and I stayed on the dirt tractor road. To our left were the fields that would turn a bright green immediately after the planting in early spring. We would know it was summer when the milo heads turned into rich golden and russet colors. Next to us in the enveloping cold of winter, the ground lay black and empty. The catchment terraces swirled along the downward slope like giant snakes.

"Come on, I'll race you," I yelled to Elpidio and took off running. I turned back to see if he was catching up to me, but he had kept up his brisk pace, in no mood to overexert himself.

Our pigpens were on the old place built by my grandfather, my father's father. It was the place on which he and my grandmother had lived and had had their children and on which my grandmother, following my grandfather's death, had raised their children alone.

The house itself had been abandoned for many years. It leaned sad and forlorn to one side, with gaping holes in the walls. In a corner room, which used to be the kitchen, there was a pile of rotting, moldy cottonseed. For many years, to save money, my father had brought home the seed for the next year's planting. Much of it was ruined because the house was not weatherproof and he figured finally that it was cheaper to deal with the ginners.

When we were growing up, we used it as a sort of clubhouse. We finally had to stop when one early evening, Jose, Paulie and I were lying about telling ghost stories. From time to time we watched the rats that peeked out of the holes in the baseboards. A young rattlesnake came slithering into the room. The rattler had come in through some rotted wood in the floor and had inched its way under a torn piece of linoleum. The snake was headed for Paulie's rear end. Luckily, my brother Jose saw it and yanked Paulie out of the way. Paulie grabbed for Jose, thinking they were going to horse around.

I began to laugh until I saw Jose's expression. Paulie noticed it, too, and turned to look at the little bitty shit of a snake. The rattler, not much more than a foot long, kept crawling toward where I lay on the floor. It was too young or too stupid to be frightened yet.

Paulie, who amazed all of us with his stunts, bent over and pinched the narrow part of the snake behind its diamond-shaped head, holding it between his thumb and forefinger. When Paulie picked it up, the snake struggled a little, but mostly it just hung limply from his hand. Jose and I came up to get a good look at it. As we approached, the snake opened its mouth wide. It seemed to be yawning, harmless. Jose told Paulie to take it outside and kill it. Paulie said he wanted to keep it for a pet. My vote said let it go. I hated the sight of snakes, even dead ones.

The three of us went outside, Paulie in front. He kept the snake as far away from him as he could. Once outside, Paulie tossed it into the middle of a red ant hill, where the snake landed on its back and in a slow, undulating movement, righted itself. That was when Jose tossed the rock which landed square on the snake's head, smashing part of it. The snake continued to move, trying desperately to reach the safety of the high grass nearby. By this time, Paulie had joined in and he took a large, flat rock, going forward to where he was right above the snake. He dropped the rock, which landed at an angle, almost cutting the snake in two, pinning the front half down. The two halves of the snake continued to move. We soon lost interest knowing it was dead already. We cut short our storytelling and we began to walk home.

When we told the story at supper, my father and mother warned us not to play in the old house anymore. The warning was not something we felt particularly compelled to obey. However, our fear of snakes kept us from playing at the old house after that.

There was no wind blowing as Elpidio and I got to the barbed wire fence separating the old homestead from the milo field. It was a curious dry cold that had settled in, made even more abrasive by a brittle, metallic light that seemed to hang in front of our eyes like smoke.

I pushed down the middle strand of barbed wire and crossed over. The barn was located a little ways to the left. To one side of the barn was a small corral, large enough for a dozen cows. At one end, facing the house, was a chute made of tin and wood, the upward slope filled with grass-growing dirt.

I looked forward to going inside the barn. It had always had a smell which combined stale, musty air with the sweet smells of decaying old hay.

Inside the barn it was as cold as the inside of an icebox. Though shielded from the wind, the lingering cold was even more unbearable. As I walked inside, it was pitch black; I could not smell the familiar odors. There was such an eery feeling inside the place. It was quiet, too quiet. When Elpidio spoke to me, I was startled.

"Goddamn, it's cold," said Elpidio, slapping his hands together.

"Yeah, let's get this shit over with, quick!" I said.

Behind the barn were the pigpens. Inside the barn we kept three 50-gallon oil drums in which we made corn mash for the pigs. My brother Elpidio filled one of the buckets and handed it to me. He filled another bucket and we walked out to the pigpens. By the time we got there the pigs were ready for us, jostling each other to be first at the trough, grunting as they did so. We poured the mash and the pigs squealed in their rush to get at it.

As we walked back to the barn to refill the buckets, Elpidio said, "They eat like pigs, don't you think?"

"Like some people I know," I said.

"You notice anything strange about Grandpa?" Elpidio asked me, becoming suddenly serious.

I was proud to have a grown-up question put to me. I was determined to make a good answer for it.

"Grandpa told me he was going to die and he asked me not to say anything about it, but I have to tell someone," I said.

Grandpa's only concern had been to keep the family from worrying about him. So, I didn't feel I was breaking a confidence given to me by my grandfather.

Elpidio missed it altogether. "I guess he's going to die. We all will, sooner or later."

"No, stupid, he said he's going to die soon. This year."

"What the hell are you talking about?"

"The other night, on New Year's. He told me it was going to be his last New Year's. What do you think about that?"

"Are you sure you know what you're talking about?" said Elpidio, now paying close attention to me.

"Sure, I'm sure. He told me. Big as life. I couldn't make something like that up!"

"No, I guess you couldn't. So, that's what's been bothering him," said Elpidio.

"Must be. He told me I could have his gun when he dies."

Elpidio laughed at that, then he said, "I guess it must be something serious, then. He don't look sick. He just has been acting different, that's all."

Elpidio seemed satisfied about Grandpa, but we continued talking nonetheless as we worked. Soon enough the pigs had their fill. I wanted to ask Elpidio which of the Arreola girls he went to see every night, but if I were to ask, I knew he would say he went to visit Tony and the family and no one of the girls in particular. We had asked Tony plenty of times, but Tony would not admit to shit, either. To save myself the trouble, I decided not to ask him anything.

There weren't that many chores to do during the winter. The silver butane tank fed the stove and heaters inside the house and so we didn't have to chop wood anymore. All there was, in fact, were the horses, the pigs and about a dozen laying hens. Occasionally, we would take a pick-up full of hay out to the cattle.

Since Elpidio took everything he did quietly and seriously, we finished feeding the pigs in no time. He noticed that Paulie and me had not been very careful about our work in previous days. He cursed at how sloppy we were. He and I began to stack hay bales and to clear out some of the rubbish which had accumulated since the last time someone had cleaned it. I sure wanted to go home. My fingers were turning purple and blue. "What the hell is this?" asked Elpidio.

Paulie had made a knot in the rope pulley which he used as a swing while I did the work, which is why I hated pairing up with Paulie to do the chores. Elpidio undid the knot, got the pulley to working again and sent me up to the loft. He wanted to move some of the hay up to the loft before the spring rains, I told him it was too much work to do by ourselves and, anyway, it was too damned cold to do it. Elpidio grunted and said we would just do a little bit to get started. We would have to finish it another day.

Elpidio sent each bale up to me with the pulley. While he hooked and pulled on the next one, I stacked the previous one. The first tier was too high for me and so I began another stack. There were still dozens to get up when Elpidio said we would quit. I lowered myself down on the pulley, holding on to both rope ends.

"Where did you learn that?" Elpidio said.

"I learned it from a Tarzan movie, him swinging from the vines. He's the king of the jungle," I said, not wanting to say that I had learned it from Paulie, who had probably picked it up from Tarzan at the movies.

We had worked up a pretty good sweat and we went to rinse our faces at a wooden catchment barrel. Dust and bits of hay stuck to our faces, arms and necks. The water was numbing cold. Although it could not have been five o'clock as yet, it was bleak and dark.

# Chapter 6

Some of our cows were grazing near a row of mesquite trees that bordered the contours of the dry creekbed. Something spooked them and they scampered away. We squinted our eyes in the gray twilight, both of us thinking it might be a coyote. Then we saw that it was Grandpa on his way home. I cupped my hands into a funnel over my mouth to call out to him, but Elpidio tugged at my shoulder.

"Leave him alone, he's tired," he said.

Elpidio's mare was also tired, her long sleek neck hanging level with her body. The reins were loose in Grandpa's hands, resting on top of the saddlehorn. Grandpa's body was limp. His broad shoulders were hunched forward. His head rolled back and forth, swaying with the graceful strut of the mare.

"Why don't you run and catch up with Grandpa. Help him put up the mare. Don't let her drink too much water, and give her some extra oats," he said.

"The oats are all gone, you used them all up yesterday," I said.

"Jose should have brought some from Nixon today," said Elpidio. "They should be there by now."

"Oh," I said, embarrassed.

"If you can stand it, walk her around for a little bit. I can't tell how hard Grandpa's ridden her, but she looks hot to me. Put a halter on her. I don't want her loose for a couple of hours."

I ran at a fast trot until I caught up to the mare. Despite her long legs, I could walk as fast as she. Grandpa did not acknowledge that I was walking alongside them. I patted the wine-colored mare on the neck and found it sopping wet. I thought of asking if he had been running her, but didn't.

When we arrived at the horse shed, Grandpa glided down from the saddle and was loosening the cinch in almost the same motion. I stood a little distance away until he finally saw me and he asked me if I wanted to take care of the mare for him. I told him I would and he trudged off on tired feet to the house. He didn't go into the house. Instead, he circled around the back and went directly to the bunkhouse.

The saddle was heavy but I managed to carry it to the tackshed. I couldn't lift the saddle to hang it on its hook, so I placed it on top of some burlap sacks on its side. I was short of breath and the whole world smelled of horsesweat when I finished. I grabbed a halter draped over one of the rafters and went outside.

Elpidio's mare, though very thirsty, stood her ground where the reins lay. It was not until she saw me going to the water trough that she moved to follow me. She began to drink as I unbuckled the bridle. I waited until she raised her head before sliding the bit out of her mouth. I didn't want to interrupt her drink. I dipped the bit into the cold water to rinse away the foam that had collected on parts of the metal and leather. When I figured the mare had had enough to drink, I slid the halter over her head and led her back to the shed. I tied her to a mesquite post where she could get at the oats Jose had brought and left for all of the horses. Later I would put her out and turn her loose. The other horses came close but kept their distance.

Supper was ready and the first sitting was busy midway through the meal. Grandpa, my father, Elpidio, Jose and Paulie ate during the first sitting. My grandfather was not at the table on this evening. The rest of us, including my mother and my sister Juana, ate during the second. Now that Paulie was officially an adult, he sat with the first sitting.

As I came in, Jose was making fun of Paulie.

"How do you feel, Paulie. It ain't the same as playing hookey, is it?" said Jose.

"I can work circles around you any day, idiot!" said Paulie.

Jose turned to Elpidio to inform him that, "Daddy had to send Paulie into town just to get him out of the way. He's a runt anyway, but working all day I figure made him shorter by a couple of inches."

Paulie was touchy about his height. "At least I don't have the body of a goddamned grayhound."

"Paulie!" snapped my mother, as expected.

"By the way, Daddy, I heard that Oscar Burns stopped Paulie in Nixon today. Casimiro Diaz told me about it when I went to pick up some oats for Elpidio," said my brother Jose.

"He stopped you on the road?" asked my father.

"No, I was coming out of Brown's and he stopped me on the sidewalk."

"What the hell were you doing in Brown's?"

"I went to look for some boots."

"So that's what took you so long to get back. What did Oscar Burns say?"

"He said to tell you I don't have a license and that he don't care so long as I just go run errands for you. He said there's a highway patrol that's been riding up and down between Cuero and Stockdale, on 87. He said to be careful because the highway patrol don't know shit about nothing."

"You should take a couple of pillows with you to sit on. Make you look like a man, a short one, but a man, anyway," said Jose to no one in particular.

"They'll mistake him for a wetback if he does that," said my brother Elpidio.

"What else did he say?" asked my father.

My mother stood, with her arms crossed, near the stove. She finally shook her head and said, "You just let him go on just like he's the sweetest angel on earth!"

My father and Paulie ignored her. "Oscar said you should hire a wetback," said Paulie.

"I don't think a wetback can get a license, can they?" said Elpidio.

"Oscar Burns can say anything he wants. He doesn't have to pay for a wetback," said my brother Jose.

"Oscar's a good man," said my father. "He's just trying to do what's right."

"He put Heriberto in jail," I said.

"Heriberto was drunk," said Elpidio. "Besides, it wasn't Heriberto that got himself in trouble. It was Efrain that started the trouble."

"Didn't cousin Lupe get thrown in jail, too, that time?" asked Jose.

"Yeah, there was five of them, altogether," said Elpidio.

"My compadre Carlos got his boys off. I had to pay for the other three," said my father.

"Efrain?" asked Elpidio.

"The same one," said my father.

"Efrain must have been raised by armadillos. He never did have any family," said Jose.

"No wonder he never learned to take a bath," said Paulie.

We all laughed at that and turned to look at my sister Juana, who stood near the sink. As we looked at her, she shifted her weight and became uncomfortable as she feared, with cause, what was coming next.

"Tell what happened next, Daddy," said Elpidio.

"No, I don't want to embarrass Juana," he said.

"You all leave Juana alone," my mother warned us.

"It wasn't her fault," said Jose.

"That's right," said Elpidio, who took up the story. "Efrain got out of jail with Beto and Lupe and we dropped him off in Smiley. He was living with some people in Smiley."

The first sitting had finished eating and began moving away from the table, one by one. My sister Juana wanted more than anything to interrupt Elpidio's story. She began to place clean plates on the table for the second sitting. She kept her eyes on her work, except that when she got close to Elpidio, she elbowed him in the ribs. It was a warning that didn't take. Elpidio began to tell his story in earnest.

"Yeah, it was a Friday night when they all got into that trouble and it wasn't until Saturday morning when Daddy got all of them out of jail. And that was the end of that.

"On Sunday morning, I was on the porch waiting to take Ma and the girls to church, when I see somebody on foot way off on the road. Well, little by little finally he gets to the house. It was Efrain, all right. His face was black and blue and there were these black things on his lips, like something fell on them and dried. I don't know what it was, but it sure looked ugly. It seems somebody had punched Efrain good."

"I asked him what happened and he said he got into it with the Velez boys on Saturday night. You remember them? They lived in Smiley for a while but they were really from Yorktown?"

"Oh, yeah, now I remember them," said Jose. "There's some very contrary people in Yorktown, that's for damned sure."

"Well, the Velez boys thought they were still in Yorktown because nobody from Smiley is much of a fighter. Not like in Yorktown or Gonzales, anyway.

"Anyhow, they beat the holy ghost out of Efrain. I asked him what had started it, but he wouldn't say anything about it. He said he was all right, though. What he really wanted was to talk to Daddy about something."

"I know what's coming, now," said Paulie.

Juana was near tears and as Paulie was the usual target, she snapped a dishtowel at him, half-heartedly, striking him on his side. Paulie was eager to hear the rest of the story and he let it pass.

"So, Daddy was away to the outhouse for his morning walk and I told Efrain to wait," Elpidio went on.

"You couldn't say he was busy. Oh, no, you have to say where he was," put in my mother, embarrassed.

"Ma, let me get on with the story, will you?" Elpidio was exasperated.

"Listen to your mother," my father said, absently.

"Yeah, Elpidio," said Paulie, "Pa doesn't want anybody to know certain things."

"Paulie," was all my father had to say as he used his rare voice, the one that told us he meant business. Paulie snapped shut.

"Let me go on, now," said Elpidio. "While we waited for Daddy, Efrain began to get more and more nervous. I asked him what it was all about, I told him maybe I could help him, but he said he would wait for Daddy. I told him as far as I knew, we didn't need any more hands, but if he needed some money, I told him he could have ten dollars, which was all the money I had in the world. He said, no, hell no, he didn't need any money, either."

"You'd'a never seen that ten dollars again," said Paulie.

"I never knew Efrain when he didn't need some money. It's amazing how some people can tell a lie like that," said Jose.

"Daddy finally stops being busy, or whatever it was that he was doing," continued Elpidio, shooting a glance at my mother. "He comes out on the porch. Daddy looks at Efraín's face and decides to look somewhere else, like at the cactus over by the side of the road there. Efrain begins to stutter at the same time, kind of like when you first crank up an engine and then all of a sudden he gets out what he wants."

"What was that?" I asked, with a mouthful of food.

"Not you, too, you little insect!" said my sister Juana, popping me with a dishtowel.

"I was just asking a question," I protested, not quite so innocently.

"You know very well what happened already," she said. "It's all anybody ever talks about here."

"I only heard the story once, from my cousin Lupe," I said.

"Oh, Lupe is no better than the rest of you," said Juana.

"Can I go on now? Are you two through?" asked Elpidio.

"Efrain rattled out what he wanted so fast, Daddy and I couldn't figure out what it was exactly. So Daddy told him to say it again. What he said is that he wanted to marry Juana. Once he got that out, it seemed to me that he felt a whole hell of a lot better. Daddy then asked him if he had spoken to Juana about this and Efrain said it wasn't necessary, that these things should be decided between men of honor, and he apologized for not having a father to make the arrangements for him, but he also said he couldn't let a thing like that stand in the way of the future he had planned out for himself and Juana."

"Too bad he didn't know Juana's already decided to be everybody's old maid aunt," said Paulie.

"I have not!" said Juana, shocked.

"What about Tony Arreola?" I asked.

"You could make Tony sit on top of the stove and it wouldn't get him to move any faster, or at all, if you ask me," said Jose.

"You leave Tony out of this," said Juana.

"Looks to me like Tony's blood runs very slow," said my father, laughing.

"Daddy, don't you start in with them," said Juana.

"Listen to me, now," said Elpidio, who had not finished. "Efrain stuck out his hand to shake with Pa, just like they had a deal. Daddy, I don't think, had even given himself a chance to think anything of it and so he shakes Efrain's hand and the idiot really thought he had a deal. Except that Daddy said, Juana is inside getting ready for church. If you can talk her into it, you can have her. One less mouth to feed around here, as far as I can see. But, you and I can't decide for her. You know that, don't you? She's got to decide for herself."

"Daddy, you're terrible," said Juana.

"I told him you would decide, honey," said my father.

"No, not that. What you said before," whined Juana.

"I don't recall that I said such a thing. That's Elpidio making up his own story. I probably would tell it different," said my father.

"Elpidio, you liar! You're just making up things," said my sister Juana.

"Daddy didn't say I'm telling it wrong. He just said he would tell it different. Besides, Daddy can't tell a good story. He just tells what happened and he leaves out all the good stuff. Anyway, let me go on. Efrain gets confused and says that he has a deal and Daddy says he can't make a deal unless Juana wants to go along with it. Women don't have to get married anymore unless they want to."

"Heriberto had to get married," said Paulie.

"You be quiet, do you hear me?" yelled my mother in Paulie's direction. "Don't bring up what you don't know anything about."

My mother had suffered for a lot of Sundays when Alva got pregnant and Heriberto had to marry her. Everybody knew what the true story was, but my mother liked to pretend it wasn't true. When my aunt Tencha said that brides in Alva's condition sometimes turned out to be good wives after all, my mother turned livid, hunted my father down and demanded that he take her home, saying she was not going to be humiliated anymore. It had started out as a very small wedding. But more and more people got on to it and came, even though they were not invited. Before long, it got to be a bigger wedding than anyone had intended.

My father was still a drinking man in those days and no matter what my mother said, he didn't want to leave just yet. So what my father did is he went to a few relatives to tell them my mother was crying and upset because her very first born was leaving her to begin a life of his own, to begin his own family. Of course, everybody knew the family Heriberto was beginning was already on the way.

My mother thought that my father was saying goodbye to everybody. That got my mother a lot of sympathy from people who came up to commiserate with her and she changed her mind about going home. My father was able to go on getting as drunk as he intended to.

Even so, after four years, and two additional children legitimately conceived, she became upset when somebody brought up the marriage. As a kind of self-imposed punishment, my mother lavished a goodly portion of her affection on Heriberto Junior, who was conceived out of wedlock.

Elpidio went on with his story, mildly annoyed at the interruptions. "When Juana came out of the house, she was wearing her high heels that made her look like she's trying to avoid stepping on cow patties. Daddy says, 'Here she is!' Efrain just stood there, not saying one blessed word. Juana made a face like she had stepped on a cowpie when she got a good look at Efrain's banged up face. He wasn't too good looking on a good day, anyway. She walked right past him to the car. Ma and Celia came out next and Efrain got way out of the way. He never said a word. We left, and then what happened, Pa?"

"You just told all there is to it," said my father. When we kept looking at him, expecting that he would add something, he leaned forward on the table. "He never even spoke one more word. Didn't even say goodbye. He just started walking back to Smiley. I offered to take him back, but he said he had some thinking to do and the walk was just the right thing for it. I do not believe we ever saw him again. Anybody know whatever became of him?"

"He was around here for a long time after that, wasn't he, Elpidio?" asked Jose.

"Yeah, I guess so. I only saw him at a dance in Gonzales once and I don't know if I remember right, but I think I ran into him in Westhoff, too."

"I guess that explains why Juana is an old maid today, losing out on such a fine man," said Paulie.

"I am not an old maid," said Juana. "I'm only nineteen."

"She probably dreams of Efrain to this day," said Jose.

Juana started for Paulie, ignoring the last comment by Jose. I don't think she much cared who got it. From the look of her hands, she intended to pull out all of Paulie's hair. I grabbed her around the waist and held her back. Had she gotten to him, she would not have let go until she was the owner of a good bunch of the hair and then my mother would have gotten in on it and then all hell would've broken loose.

"Let me go!" screamed Juana.

"Stop it, you two," said my mother. It looked as if she might blame me for starting it, but she didn't say anything more.

Elpidio had moved out of the way and was safely beside the refrigerator, poised to run out through the front room. Except there wasn't any more fight left in Juana.

My mother took her seat and Juana served her and herself. My sister Juana liked to eat as she and my mother cooked. As a final ritual of the day, they sat at the table, eating a little and talking to one another.

"I'm going to go see about Grandpa," Elpidio said. "It's not like him to miss out on supper."

"Tell him I'll fix him a plate and I'll send it out to him if he's too tired to come to the table," my mother said.

"What's the matter with the old man?" asked my father.

"I don't know," said Elpidio. "He was out on my mare all day long."

"Grandpa hates horses," said Paulie.

At that, Grandpa appeared in the kitchen doorway. There was still heaviness of sleep lining his face, but he appeared more rested now. "I wasn't out riding for my health," he said.

"Nobody rides for his health," said Paulie.

"What were you doing?" asked my father.

"Looking for water," said Grandpa.

"Water? What the hell do you want with water, Grandpa? There's plenty of water in the wells," said Jose.

"I've been through something like this before. Long time ago," said Grandpa, getting a good look at the food on my sister Juana's plate. "That looks pretty good, there."

"I'll fix you a plate," said Juana.

Grandpa sat down next to me. "You take good care of Elpidio's mare, squirt?"

"Yes, sir," I said, "all I have to do is turn her loose in a little while. I got her tied to a post."

"What's this about water?" said my father.

"You get to know these things right about the start of the new year," said my grandfather. "I've seen it all before. We're in for a drought this year. A bad one. The signs are worse than I've ever seen them."

The twins began to get up from the table quietly. The noisy spirit of the evening had subsided considerably with Grandpa's entrance. His words lay on the table and made us all pensive. My father kept his place. It was difficult to tell if he ever worried about anything, but his remaining at the table was enough of a sign that he wanted to hear more from Grandpa. The rest of us, except for my mother who customarily ate slowly and daintily, began to push our plates away. For once, we were behaved, almost solemn, as we helped Juana with the dishes, clearing away scraps and piling the dishes up for her to wash before she went to bed.

"We're going to need more water," said my grandfather.

"Grandpa, we got two wells already," said Elpidio. "The one by the house here is real good. There was a guy from Gonzales, a well digger out of work, he stopped here one day, looking to dig us another one. He got a taste of our water and he said we had good, strong water running through here. Said he could tell by the taste of it."

"The two wells here come up from the same spring. That's not good. All I know, it's going to get real bad," said Grandpa.

"Hell, Grandpa, there's nothing wrong with those wells," said Elpidio.

"That ain't what I said, son!" said Grandpa, pounding the table with his fist. "I said we're in for a drought. Apparently, you boys don't know what that means."

"The well by the old place's got sand in it already," said Paulie, surprising me by siding with Grandpa. "Not much, though. You have to let it settle before you can drink it. I noticed it when I was last out to the pigpens."

"We've had some rains in the last month," said my father.

"Drizzle, mist, spray rain. Don't matter much. Dries just as soon as it falls to the ground. It's not even good crop water. We ain't had nothing that'll sink into the ground," said Grandpa.

"Looks like you're telling me I shouldn't bother planting this year?" said my father.

"I ain't saying anything of the kind. I may be wrong. It don't seem like it, though. Thing is, I ain't seen nothing that would make me change my mind about this. What I want to do is dig another well as far from these two as I can, maybe tap into another spring. That way, we can have drinking water and maybe save the animals," said Grandpa.

"You're in no condition to be digging wells, Papa," said my mother.

"Don't be too sure about that," said Grandpa. "I wouldn't do it if I didn't think I could finish it."

"She's right, Grandpa," said Elpidio, "you're not as young as you used to be."

"You're not as young as you think you are, either," said my brother Paulie.

"I didn't expect that any of you would believe me. And that's just fine with me. As far as me digging a goddamned well, I can do it alone. Planned to do it that way all along."

"Maybe you ought to get don Atilano to help you," said Paulie. It was generally agreed in Schoolland that don Atilano was crazy, so he wasn't trying to be particularly helpful.

"That old man that's got the stick he says points to water?" asked Jose.

"That would be the one," said Paulie, smiling, satisfied with himself.

"There are some who say he's good at it," said my father, winking.

"Don't need him at all," said Grandpa. "I found four good places today. I'm going to go out tomorrow with a shovel and do a little digging. I want to make sure the one I pick is soft enough. No sense in making more work for myself than I have to."

"Grandpa, I really don't know if you're fit enough to go on with this," said my father. "Maybe you should take it easy. If you're serious, I can send one of the boys out with you. Paulie's been helping me, but I can send him. He can do the digging for you."

"Paulie and hard work don't go together too well, Pa," said Jose.

"Let me think on it. I can tell you in the morning," said Grandpa.

"I want to go, too," I said.

"The only place you're going to is school, young man," said my mother.

The wind began to howl outside. The strong powerful gusts made the house shudder and shake. Supper had taken longer than usual. The noise in the kitchen gradually dissipated until no one moved and no one said anything. It became quiet and sad in the kitchen.

Right afterward, Grandpa announced he was going back to bed. He wasn't upset that no one had taken his prediction of a drought very seriously. He acknowledged that he was rude to my mother and praised her for a good meal.

Meanwhile, my father told my brother Jose to light the gas heater in the front room. I had a lesson to read for school the next day and in the bedroom I tried to make the best of it over the arguments between little Albert and little Julian.

The temperature began to drop precipitously and it got colder and colder in the room because the space heater couldn't shoot its heat into our room fast enough. Before too long I was forced to go under the covers and that was enough to make me forsake the studying altogether. Very soon I fell asleep. As the entire family drifted off to sleep, before the freeze started outside, it was cozy and warm throughout the house.

# Chapter 7

Some weeks after my grandfather somberly predicted the coming of a drought, we got one of those lugubrious winter rains where thick black clouds hang low in the sky and everything is wet and cold, and finally after threatening for the entire miserable day, the pressure builds until the reluctant rains come.

The rain started in late afternoon, right after we got back from school. It was dark and cold and we expected the sun to go down earlier than usual. Despite the weather, we still had our chores to do. What with the wind, the cold and the mud on the road, we waited until one of the boys came home so he could drive me and little Albert to feed the pigs.

Now that Paulie was working, I alternated doing the chores with little Julian and little Albert. Today, it was little Albert's turn. My mother wanted us to wait until the rain let up but it didn't seem as though it would. I took my father's raincoat, which was mostly rubber-coated canvas that dragged on the ground because it was way too big for me. I wanted to get a headstart on things by feeding the horses. I went to the mesquite grove and threw down some hay on the dry ground under the horseshed. Elpidio's mare and Paulie's black were gone.

My brother Jose had come in and was warming himself over the space heater when I returned. He agreed to drive us to feed the pigs.

Jose drove out on the ocher gravel road, turning into the old place, coming to a stop at the barbed wire gate facing the road. He said he wasn't going to go any farther and he made us crawl through the fence. He stayed in the truck listening to the radio while we hurried to finish our work.

Little Albert wore a thin little schoolboy raincoat over the heavy layers of clothing that my mother made him wear. The rain continued to pour steadily. Little Albert wanted to quit after a couple of trips, but I told him the pigs would die from the cold if we didn't feed them. Little Albert said he didn't care if the goddamned pigs died, he said they would probably die anyway, it was so goddamned cold. We hurried so we could get back to the warmth inside the truck cab and go on home.

When we got back to the truck, we thanked Jose for his help. My voice at least was full of sarcasm. Jose laughed and said it was important that we learn about life. "Beto and Elpidio never helped me when I had to do it," he said. "What makes you two think you're any more special?"

We didn't have an answer for that, except maybe that it was so cold. The heater was on in the truck, blowing out hot air directly onto our feet until it felt as if they were burning. As we warmed up, we stopped feeling sorry for ourselves.

By the time we were back at the house and had washed up, the rain let up. Although it was not yet sundown, it was pitch black outside. From a break in the clouds, way off in the distance, we could see daylight falling on another part of the country.

My grandfather and my brother Paulie had been out on horseback digging all day. When the rain threatened, they had hurried home at a full gallop, Elpidio's mare leaving Paulie's black nearly a mile behind.

The rain, nevertheless, had caught up with them. My mother made Paulie take a hot bath to keep him from catching pneumonia. She tried to get my grandfather to take one as well, but he refused, which added fuel to Paulie's protests. It didn't work for him, though.

During the second sitting at the table, it began to rain again. Thick, heavy drops of rain thundered on the roof of our house and little Albert and little Julian were afraid. Each time there was a thunderclap, my mother crossed herself and said, "Maria purisima!"

My father and the boys went to the front room while the rest of us ate. I had just finished eating and was chewing on a kitchen match, which for once did not upset my mother. The boys' conversation drifted into the kitchen. They were wondering if the dance for the coming weekend in Gonzales would be canceled because of the weather.

Once we became accustomed to the rain pelting the roof, it was possible to talk without too much interference. It was the thunder that made whomever was talking stop in mid-sentence. It was right after one such loud explosion of thunder that I heard something that sounded like a voice outside.

"There's somebody outside," I said.

"Yeah, it's the bogeyman," said Jose, smiling.

The voice called out again, asking if anyone was home, and this time my father heard it, too.

"There is somebody outside. I didn't see any lights drive up," he said. "Anybody see anything?"

"Probably somebody with a stalled car up the road," said Elpidio.

"Who the hell's going to be out on a night like this," asked Paulie.

"Never mind that," said my father. "Go see who it is, Paulie."

Paulie didn't argue and went to the door. As he opened it, a gust of wind blew in, bringing with it a sheet of water and a wide swath of cold. Paulie flipped on the porch light.

"Can you help me," said the voice outside. "I'm looking for a relative of mine."

He spoke in Spanish as we did, but it was a different kind of Spanish. It had a sing-song rhythm with a lilt upwards at the end of each pause. Paulie would have a fine time mimicking him. We could recognize immediately that he came from Mexico.

"Tell him to come inside," said my father, annoyed both at the intrusion and at Paulie's bad manners.

The man heard my father and came forward as Paulie stepped to one side. He stopped in the doorframe but did not come any farther. He shuffled his feet a little to wipe them, although he had already cleaned his shoes on the porchstep. We could see he was soaking wet. A puddle of water began to form immediately around his shoes.

"I don't want to ruin your nice home," he said.

My father told me to bring a burlap sack for the man to stand on. With the front door open, and the man standing there, the draft of cold wet air was unbearable. I ran to the back porch for some rags and hurried back. I came back and dropped a burlap sack and some other rags in a flat pile just in front of the door. The man came in, bowing to everyone, moving the rags so the door would clear when he shut it.

Very carefully, he smoothed his wet hair back, letting the water drip inside the collar of his shirt. Beads of rainwater dripped from his leather jacket, worn in places to the point where it resembled rawhide.

"Who did you say you were looking for?" asked my father.

"A relative of mine. His name is Aristeo Dominguez," the man said.

"There's no one in these parts by that name," said my father.

The extremely formal encounter was between the man and my father, none of us moved or said anything. It would have embarrassed my father had we done so.

The twins were looking at the man, poking their heads around a far door. I had looked at him and remembered that it is impolite to stare and lowered my gaze. I did lift my head to look at my brother Paulie, and he too was looking at his boots.

"Anyone of you ever heard of anyone by that name?" my father asked of all of us.

Elpidio answered. "There was a man working for Herman Beatty, on the other side of Pilgrim. That's the only stranger I know hereabouts recently. I never found out his name, though. But, it could be him."

"Where is this Pilgrim," the man asked. "I'll just continue on that way."

"Pilgrim's about ten miles away, sir. You're not going to make it tonight," said my brother Jose.

"Why don't you drive him out there, Jose," said Elpidio.

"Not tonight. I wouldn't trust that truck of mine. Besides, Herman doesn't have anybody working for him regular. Rafael and Eluterio Garza were working days with Herman, helping him clear some pasture land, I think."

"When was that?" asked my father.

"I ran into them in Smiley last week. Herman wouldn't hire daywork if he had somebody regular working for him. My guess is, that other fellow moved on."

"Did your relative tell you where he was working?" my father asked.

"No, sir," the man said. "He wrote to my mother saying he was in a place called Smiley. I stopped at the store to ask, but no one had heard of him. A gentleman there told me to take this road and that I might find him."

"Well, it don't look to me like you're going to go too far tonight," said my father. "Do you have some dry clothes with you?"

"In my suitcase," the man responded. "I crawled under some bushes when the rains came. I hid it next to a tree where it will stay dry, up the road a little, where the road to here breaks off. I left it there because I didn't want it to get wet. But, I didn't want to spend the night there, either."

"You'll get sick in those wet clothes," said my father. "Elpidio, you can sleep in the house tonight. He can sleep in the bunkhouse with Grandpa. And, why don't you loan him some of your clothes, you two look about the same size."

"Okay, Daddy," said Elpidio. He walked forward to where the man stood and told him to follow.

The man picked up the burlap sack and rags upon which he had been standing and which were now as soaking wet as he was. He carried the bundle outside with him, leaving it on the porch next to the door. My mother yelled for Elpidio to wait for a raincoat, but Elpidio was already running around the side of the porch to the bunkhouse in the rain.

"Fix him something to eat, he's bound to be hungry," said my father.

"Poor man," said my mother.

"I'll do it," said my sister Juana.

Paulie was about to say something, but my mother's stern look stopped him.

"There's only the ham I brought in from the smokehouse for tomorrow's breakfast," said Juana.

"Fry some of that for him, and there's some beans leftover from dinner," said my mother.

"You're acting like he's some kind of royalty," said Paulie, "he's just a *mojado.*"

"You should always help those less fortunate than yourself," said my mother. "You never know when you'll need help yourself."

Elpidio and the man in the night were gone for a long time. Juana had fixed some dinner for him and it was getting cold on the plate. Finally, when the rain had subsided to a gentle drizzle, Elpidio and the man came back. The man, now wearing Elpidio's jeans and a flannel shirt, came in after Elpidio opened the door for him. My father told him to go in the kitchen to eat a little something. The man protested that he was not hungry and that he already was ashamed enough at having put us to so much trouble. My mother told him to treat this as his home and that she would have none of his embarrassment.

"I'm very grateful," he said. "My name is Marcos de la Fuente."

My father then introduced himself and presented each one of us by name, except for the youngest, who were already bundled up in bed and occasionally screamed loud enough to be heard in the front room.

Marcos de la Fuente went into the kitchen, where Juana placed a plate of refried beans and fried ham before him. She reheated tortillas, one by one, for him, sliding a freshly hot one on the side of the plate each time he finished the previous one.

"I hope you like wheat flour tortillas," she said.

Marcos smiled and tasted one. "They're very good, you should be very proud of how you make them."

"Oh, I didn't make them," said my sister Juana. "My mother did. I understand in Mexico you don't have wheat flour tortillas."

"That's right," said Marcos de la Fuente. "But, I have tasted some like these before. In Los Angeles. I lived in Los Angeles for two years with my mother and father. That was many years ago, a long time ago. Have you ever been to Los Angeles?"

"No, I have never been anywhere," said my sister.

My mother could not help but notice the easy way in which Juana and the Mexican were talking. She was not pleased with the way Juana spoke so freely with the guest. None of us knew him at all and it appeared very forward of Juana to be speaking so casually with him.

"Juana, go see about your brothers," said my mother, sternly.

Marcos de la Fuente could not help but notice the rebuke of my sister and he lowered his head and began to concentrate on his meal. My sister had completely disarmed him and I think he realized that he had breached our hospitality.

Although it was still early, the bitter cold, the howling wind and the heavy rainfall made us all want to turn in earlier than usual. My grandfather was already snoring gently on the sofa, leaning over to one side. My mother brought a blanket for him and after Elpidio wrapped it around him, my grandfather stood up and Elpidio helped him walk out to the bunkhouse. Marcos de la Fuente followed them.

In the morning, the drizzle which had come down all night turned into another final shower. The only difference from the day before was the cold. It was so much colder. We begged, whined and wheedled in a vain attempt to stay home from school. My mother, of course, would hear none of it. She made sure we were warmly dressed and hurried us along as she had already seen the bus go by to the far end of its run. She was determined that we would be there when the bus came by.

Because I was the eldest still in school, she made me carry the large, ugly, black umbrella which had belonged to my grandmother and which had probably been handed down to her when she was my age. Since it had belonged to my grandmother, that made the umbrella a woman's thing and at my age then, when those things matter most, I was embarrassed to carry it. There was a mended tear in the material between the spokes and this gave it a strange distortion. She cautioned me to walk slowly so that little Albert and little Julian could stay dry under it. I hated the damned thing.

The rain stopped by late morning, leaving only the coldest day I can remember. The cold outside was just about the right temperature for what I felt. Worse than that, Cristina Sifuentes had finally arrived at school. I tried to catch her alone between classes, but I didn't have any luck. I spent the entire day at school trying to catch Cristina's attention. I was beginning to feel that she was avoiding me on purpose.

On the way home, we passed Marcos de la Fuente. When the bus dropped us off, Marcos de la Fuente, wearing one of Elpidio's coats, caught up to us. He carried a cardboard suitcase which he told us had stayed fairly dry where he had hidden it. I asked him if he had found his relative and he said Jose had driven him to Smiley and then to Nixon, but they could not find the relative and they had not found anyone who knew anything about him. I began to suspect that there was no such relative. My suspicions were further strengthened when he volunteered to help me slop the pigs; in fact, he told little Julian and me to go ahead and play for a while, that he could feed the pigs by himself in no time at all.

When we returned to the house, he stayed outside in the cold. I told him he could wait in the bunkhouse. All he did was sit on the porch with his suitcase by his side. Neither my mother nor Juana would invite him inside without my father present. For his part, Marcos de la Fuente could not go into the bunkhouse because he felt he no longer had permission to be in there. After my father came home, with Paulie driving the truck, he scolded Marcos, saying he should have gone inside; but, of course, both of them knew he wasn't supposed to.

While we were at supper with the first sitting, Marcos de la Fuente allowed as he was in limited circumstances. He explained that it had taken all the money he had just to get this far. He asked if we knew of anyone who would hire him and provide him with living quarters. My father suggested that Elpidio might take him later in the evening to visit a few places, see if anybody was taking on hands. Elpidio said he was supposed to go help Tony Arreola work on his car.

"You take him, then," my father said to my brother Jose.

Jose was annoyed, as he had had a tiring day, but he agreed for my father's sake.

Elpidio asked me if I wanted to go help him and Tony. Paulie said he wanted to go, but Elpidio reminded him that don Antonio was still angry at him for kicking the family dog. Paulie said the old man should have forgotten about it by now. It had been more than a year since it had happened. My father looked at Paulie and just shook his head.

# Chapter 8

Don Antonio Arreaga's dog was a weird little runt of a creature with a squeaky yelp. For some reason or other, Paulie and the dog never got along. In fact, each time Paulie visited, which was not often, the dog would bark constantly at Paulie and there was nothing anyone could do to make the dog stop.

One of the Arreaga girls would have to come and get the dog and put a leash on him before Paulie could get down from the truck or car. Even so, the squeaky bark of the tiny son of a bitch continued unabated.

If left to run loose, the dog's favorite attack would begin a short distance away and would come at Paulie at a run. The dog would leap into the air and bite a hand or arm, and once, part of a thigh. All Paulie ever did was brush the dog aside. The dog was such a runt that none of what he did hurt Paulie. The worst Paulie ever got was a little scratch.

It was Paulie's claim that he never kicked the goddamned dog. And, for once, Paulie seemed to be telling the truth and everyone believed him. What happened, so said Paulie, is he put up his boot and the dog came crashing, snout first, into it. The little bastard got a copiously bleeding split lip for his trouble.

Don Antonio heard the dog yelping in pain and came outside to see it bleeding from the mouth. Don Antonio, of course, knew better than to raise a hand to Paulie. That was to invite serious trouble between our families. Instead, don Antonio came to our house the following day with the dog in his lap. He showed my father where the dog's lip was split.

When my father was not particularly impressed with the dog's wounds, don Antonio insisted that he get a good look at it. My father did as don Antonio insisted and then he sent for Paulie. When Paulie came around the house, the dog leaped out of don Antonio's arms and went for Paulie. Tony, who was driving the Arreola truck, ran after the dog. Tony was not quick enough. The dog was tearing Paulie's trouser cuff before Tony could jerk him away. This new incident caused the dog's split lip to begin bleeding again.

"That dog just doesn't like Paulie at all, does he?" said my father.

"I want to know what you plan to do about punishing your son for the attack on my dog," said don Antonio.

"I've never known Paulie to strike an animal. He'll hit another human being, maybe, but not a dumb animal. He's been taught not to hit animals," said my father, with some concern. I could tell he didn't particularly care for don Antonio's accusation.

"I didn't hit him, Pa. I just raised my foot to keep him away from me and the little son of a bitch jumped right into it." Paulie was not as defiant as he usually was when accused of something.

"I say he hit my dog," said don Antonio. "You just heard for yourself how he cursed my dog. I expect that you will punish him for it."

"Very well, don Antonio. If you say so. On your word, I will punish him," said my father, sadly.

"I didn't do anything, Pa," said Paulie.

"That's enough, Paulie," said my father, gravely. "Go inside the house while I finish talking with my good friend and neighbor, don Antonio."

My father was usually patient and tolerant of almost anyone that might abuse his hospitality. Even when he was most offended he kept his silence and maintained a certain graciousness.

Don Antonio, in what amounted to a serious insult, said there was nothing more to talk about and returned to his truck. I guess he expected that my father would punish Paulie in front of him. The old man wanted his satisfaction, mean and on the spot. Even before Tony cranked up the engine, my father had turned his back to don Antonio and hurried back to the house. It was unusual for my father to be rude like that. He had not spoken a further word to don Antonio, not even his farewell greeting, commending them to a safe trip home. The way he gave his back to don Antonio made it clear to us that he was as angry as he was ever apt to be.

Don Antonio and Tony Junior could not but notice the rebuke.

Supper was not particularly pleasant that evening. At the table, my father asked Paulie what kind of punishment he wanted.

"None," Paulie protested. "I said I didn't do anything. I mean it. I'm not lying. You can't punish me for nothing."

"No, I'm not going to punish you for the dog. I'm going to punish you for don Antonio, for getting me involved in something I shouldn't be involved in."

"But, it's not my fault, Daddy," said Paulie, exasperated.

"Maybe it's not all your fault. I'll leave you to decide that, but it's the way it's going to be. I gave my word to don Antonio. Now, you pick something or I will. And, you may not like what I pick."

"Okay, I know," said Paulie. "Juana asked me if I wanted to go visit Celia in San Antonio with her this weekend. I can stay home."

"Liar! You said you had something else you wanted to do, Paulie. It wouldn't be giving up anything," said my sister Juana.

"I can change my mind, can't I? Anyway, you just want to stick up for don Antonio on account of Tony, that's all," Paulie accused our sister

Juana.

"Very well," said my father, "you'll give up your paycheck for this week."

"Oh, come on, don't make me do that, Pa. I was going to get a new pair of workboots. I'll be needing them now."

"We'll go to Brown's on Saturday. I'll buy them for you," said my father, tired of the whole thing.

"I got my own damned money! I want to buy them with my own money," whined Paulie.

"You've embarrassed me enough already. I don't want to hear you whine and this will be the end of it. Understand?" My father sounded exceptionally harsh and Paulie was on the verge of getting even more punishment.

Since that time, Paulie had not been welcomed at the Arreola place. In fact, none of us went there hardly at all, anymore. Don Antonio's bitterness toward Paulie and my father had been extended to the whole family.

When we saw Tony, and especially the girls, it was always in town. We would run into them either at the Mexican movies in Nixon on Wednesdays, or at the dances in towns close by.

Our families had been frequent visitors to each other and it was even expected that some of our boys would marry some of their girls. After Paulie's incident with the dog, it was still expected that some of us would marry some of them, except that don Antonio was not too keen on being friendly with any of us, especially not with my father and Paulie. I don't think he minded the relations so much as he just didn't want to be a part of them.

Elpidio asked me again if I would go with him over to help Tony. I wasn't paying much attention to anybody.

All of a sudden, Cristina Sifuentes had appeared in my thoughts. I was dejected because Cristina Sifuentes had not jumped into my arms as soon as she saw me when she walked into the classroom. Worse, she had made no effort at all to even talk to me in all of two goddamned days.

Elpidio's voice dragged me out of the low I felt. I agreed to go because more than likely we would be outside the whole time and with the damned cold I might get lucky and freeze to death.

"I'll go," I said, my voice just above a whisper.

"What the hell is aching him?" asked my father. Luckily, no one bothered to respond.

"Don't keep him out too late, Elpidio," my mother said, "he's got to go to school tomorrow. And, make sure he stays warm."

"Ma, I know how to keep warm. I'm not a kid anymore," I said, irritated. The way I felt, I didn't want anybody to be nice to me.

"I'll take good care of him, bring him back safe and alive," Elpidio said.

We drove north to the Arreola place. It was already dark by the time we arrived. In the garage to one side of the house, Tony had the hood up on his car. He was working beneath a naked lightbulb. To one side, he had an electric heater going, but you had to stand close to it to get warm.

They worked for several hours to change the starter on Tony's car. I didn't do much of anything except stand by and get cold. Once or twice, they had me hold a flashlight while the two of them struggled with some rusted bolts. Mostly, I kept out of the way and I kept my mouth shut.

When we returned home, it turned out that Marcos de la Fuente was again sleeping in Elpidio's bunk. Elpidio had to sleep in the same bed with little Albert and little Julian, and they were complaining about it the next morning at breakfast.

I went immediately to bed. There was no possibility that I would fall asleep. I had a lot to think about. There had to be some explanation or some reason for Cristina Sifuentes to act the way she did. I tried not to think about it. Sooner or later, I would find out.

Grandpa seemed more alive and friendlier than he had been for several days. It turned out that he had taken a liking to Marcos de la Fuente and had hired him to help dig the well.

Our breakfast, for the twins and me, consisted of chocolate milk and oatmeal. The twins hated oatmeal. I didn't care for it all that much, but it was easier to eat than to argue about it.

My father told us then that he had given Marcos permission to use either the old house, if he could patch it up, or the haybarn to sleep in for the time being. Just for the time being, he repeated.

"He'll freeze to death out there. In either place," said Juana.

"Well, we can't take him in," said my father.

"What about that relative of his? Has he said anymore about him?" asked my mother.

"He ain't said nothing to me about it," said Elpidio.

"That boy will do all right for himself," said Grandpa.

"He was just too late for a job with Herman Beatty. You know Alfonso Ruiz?" asked Jose.

"Skinny little guy, drives that green '45 Ford pickup?" said my father.

"That's him. He and his brother-in-law worked out a deal with Herman."

"Herman don't make deals unless he's going to make some money," said Elpidio. "That's one white man I wouldn't want to work for."

"Herman still believes slavery is good for ranching," said my father. "In fact, I think his first workers were slaves."

"Slavery was almost a hundred years ago," I said, "he's not that old!"

"What are you talking about, squirt," said Elpidio. "You don't even know the man." That was more or less a signal for everyone to ignore me.

"Well, Herman's got a patch of watermelon land near Leesville and Alfonso's going to go shares on it," said Jose.

"Halves or quarters?" asked my father.

"Halves, most probably. His brother-in-law is going to work days for him in the meantime and help Alfonso out now and then."

"I never heard of anybody going shares on watermelons, have any of you?" asked my father.

"Come to think of it, you're right, Daddy," said Elpidio. "Didn't Bronson Joyce have a ranch out near there? The land played out so much old Bronson couldn't get a nickel an acre. Had to leave for Houston or someplace to find work. What they say is, Herman Beatty bought out Bronson Joyce."

"If the land is dead, what do you think the deal is, then?" asked my father.

Elpidio thought for a moment before responding. "Well, I don't think Herman has got the money to pay Alfonso's brother-in-law. He'll get him to work as long as he can, promising that he'll get part of his share of the watermelon crop."

"And he'll get the both of them to do whatever other work he needs done as a favor," added Jose.

"I wonder how long it'll take Alfonso to figure out the land's not worth planting?" asked Elpidio.

"If he was any kind of a farmer, which he ain't, he could figure it out right now. But, I figure he'll find out in late spring," said Jose.

"Soon as he gets a good look at somebody else's crop and compares it to his own, he'll figure it out," said Paulie.

"Paulie actually said something intelligent," said Jose.

"Leave him alone," said my mother. "The way you pick on him, it's no wonder he is like he is."

"You pick on him most of all, Ma," said Elpidio.

"There's not a goddamned thing wrong with me!" yelled Paulie and he left the table to go outside.

"Paulie, put some clothes on if you're going outside," said my mother, but Paulie was already gone.

"He took his coat, Ma," said Juana.

"So, how long are we going to have Marcos de la Fuente with us?" asked Elpidio.

"He promised not to be a bother to us at all," began my father. "He said he would feed the pigs, fix up the pens and help out as we need. In exchange, he wanted to use the old house. I told him it wasn't livable, too many rats and probably snakes. He said, if it was all right with me, he could sleep in the hayloft for the time being. He says he can fix up the old house in no time at all. The place is just sitting there, rotting. What could I say? No?"

"Probably, not," said Elpidio. "God damn *mojados* have a knack for doing things. I just don't know what to think of them."

"He won't hurt anything by living in the barn. I'm only afraid he'll freeze to death. Is he going to sleep out there tonight?" asked my mother.

"I guess so, tonight, hunh, Daddy," said Elpidio.

"Yeah, sure," said my father.

"By tomorrow, he'll be through fixing up the house. Can't be too soon for me," said Elpidio. "I don't want to have to sleep another night with little mouses in my bed."

The twins were too pissed off at having to eat oatmeal to respond.

"Well, boys, it's time to get going if we're going to earn our beans for this week," said my father.

"Pa, I need some money for Friday," said my sister Juana.

"I could use some money myself, but I don't have anybody that I can ask to give it to me," said my father.

"I'm serious, Papa. I'm going to take Ma to visit Celia and the kids on Friday. We can't just leave and not give them something," said Juana. "The last time they were here, it sounded like Frank is not working and things are not going too well for them. Celia didn't say anything about it, but you know how Celia is."

"I'm going to be using my car this weekend, so you can't have it," said Elpidio.

"I didn't ask, crazy. We're taking the truck anyway," said Juana.

"I suppose you mean you're going to take my truck. You could ask me to borrow my truck, you know," said my father.

"If that truck belongs to anybody, it's me," said my mother.

"I'm the one paying for it," said my father.

"That's right, but it's still mine," she said.

"Give up, Pa, you can't win against these women," laughed Elpidio, sipping the dregs of his coffee as he stood up.

"No, I guess not," said my father. "All right, Juana, I'll stop at the bank on the way home tomorrow. Is there anything else you and your mother need while I'm at it? Like, maybe I can repaint the truck in a color that will suit you, or something?"

"Well, seriously, I don't know why you didn't put a radio in the truck when you bought it. It's boring driving all the way to San Antonio without a radio," said Juana.

"You could talk to one another, or just enjoy the scenery," said my father. "That's what people used to do, before radios, you know."

"They'll want a television set in there next," said Jose.

"That's all these two ever do in the house all day, talk and gossip. If not here, they go over to someone else's house to do it. Nothing and no one is safe from them," said Elpidio.

"That'll be enough from you, Elpidio," said my mother.

"I thought you were leaving, all of you," said Juana.

"You should come along with us to visit Celia, Daddy. You could play with the kids," said Juana.

"I just played with them when they were here last. That's enough," said my father.

"But, you haven't been to San Antonio lately, Daddy," said Elpidio.

"There's very little there that I want to see," he said.

"You haven't been out there since before they paved the highway," said my mother.

"It's still not paved all the way through. Wiley Barnett was telling me the state's going to do the last of it any time now," said Elpidio.

"They should pave the road out front," said my father.

"Well, Wiley, when I saw him over at Candy's Grocery, said he was close to convincing somebody in Austin to pave it," said Elpidio.

"Listen to him," said my sister Juana, "full of news, aren't you."

"Well, I don't spend all day reading movie magazines," he retorted.

"Go on now, all of you," said my mother. "Get out of my kitchen. Juana, help me clean the kitchen."

# Chapter 9

The first girlfriend I ever had was probably Cristina Sifuentes. I was at that stage where, physically, puberty had set in. I had no idea what this gift of nature was for, exactly. The problem was one of experience. And so I clung to my playmates and our games while slowly and reluctantly I was wrenched from the innocence of childhood.

Cristina Sifuentes was a year younger than me, with plenty of flesh around her middle and hips, and the beginnings of breasts under the furry sweaters she wore. Hers were the first meaningful breasts I ever noticed.

She wasn't very pretty, precisely speaking. Her face was nicely proportioned, except that her nose flared just a little too much at the nostrils. However, her full, wonderful lips made up for it. Her skin was the color of pecans, with a little copper thrown in. But the most striking thing about Cristina Sifuentes was her hair. It was straight and black and long and it reached all the way down to her thighs. Cristina's hair fell in a straight line on either side of her face, which, despite her pudgy cheeks and full lips, appeared thinner than it was.

It was everything put together that made Cristina so attractive.

Within five minutes of having seen her for the first time in my life, Cristina Sifuentes had sort of kissed me and I was hopelessly in love.

Cristina Sifuentes walked one morning into the classroom shared by the third and fourth grades of the Smiley school. Our teacher, Mrs. Pinckney, was doing her best to make Pedro Mendoza spell "Minnesota." She gave him two clues, one that it was settled by many Swedes and the other that it had many lakes. Pedro Mendoza had no idea what the hell she was talking about. All he wanted to do was act dumb, not much of an act, really, so she would call on someone else.

Cristina Sifuentes' entrance saved us all from enduring the same embarrassment as Pedro Mendoza. Mrs. Pinckney would surely have called on each one of us until she had her correct answer. I don't suppose it ever occurred to her to just spell it out for us.

Cristina Sifuentes came in holding a slip of paper in her hand, which she gave to Mrs. Pinckney. I thought it might be a message from the principal, or something. But, then, I had never seen her before.

Mrs. Pinckney was annoyed at the interruption. Mrs. Pinckney was one of those kinds of people who figure out the world at an early age and it never changes thereafter for them. Cristina Sifuentes' intrusion disrupted what she had determined would happen that day and all other days during that term.

Cristina Sifuentes felt the cold of Mrs. Pinckney's disapproval. The third graders were giggling openly, while we in the fourth grade simply stared at her. Cristina kept her head bent, looking at the floor.

She raised her head just enough to see where Mrs. Pinckney assigned her to sit. I sat in the front row where she would have to turn to get to her seat. As she was nervous, confused and probably pissed at the teacher, Cristina Sifuentes was unable to control her feet and thus she stumbled right in front of my desk. She went flying. She threw her books forward and brought her elbows down forcefully on top of my desk. Her knees buckled under her, but she held on.

Her long, straight, black hair flew into my face. It was still damp from her morning bath. Cristina's hair cascaded over me and I could smell the fresh, scented soap she used. A few strands of it got caught in my eyelashes, as I gazed upon the top of her head. She shifted her weight to her feet and lifted her face into mine. Her lips brushed a corner of my mouth. Her lips were pressed together, but as she relaxed somewhat, they blossomed full and soft before my eyes. She pulled back a little and I could see that she was mortified.

It was not a good introduction to her new school. I had other things on my mind, though. It was as close as I had ever been to a girl before.

"Hi! Do you know how to spell 'Minnesota?' " I whispered to her. She kept looking at me and I at her. I fell in love.

All of the third graders and most of the fourth graders roared with laughter as only smirking little shits can do. I slid out of my chair, taking her by the arms to get her to her feet. She shrugged her shoulders, maybe it was a shudder, to get free of my hands. She didn't need my help. I was going to pick up her books, but Marilyn Suzman had already done that. Cristina Sifuentes took her books, brushed by me and went to her desk. What she needed most was a place to hide.

Mrs. Pinckney's tired voice quickly restored order. Pedro Mendoza thought the Lord had spared him for the day. Not so. She called on him to finish spelling the word for the day. Bobby Adames had written it out for Pedro and had slipped it to him during the confusion. It didn't help because Pedro needed several hours to memorize so many letters.

At noon, we marched to the cafeteria for lunch. I usually bought either orangeade or chocolate milk to go with the lunch I brought from home. I searched the cafeteria several times looking for Cristina Sifuentes, but she was nowhere to be found. After lunch, during the play period, I saw her standing by the water fountain. I walked up to where she stood clutching her books and introduced myself.

"Didn't you eat lunch?" I asked her.

"I go home to eat," said she. It didn't appear that she was all too thrilled to be talking to me.

"I'm sorry about what happened to you," I said, apologizing in the name of Smiley, Texas, for her misfortune.

"It wasn't your fault," said Cristina Sifuentes.

"I know," I said.

There were lots of things I wanted to ask her, but mostly I just wanted to be with her. From the look of it, she wanted to be by herself or maybe she just didn't know how to talk to boys yet. I took the hint and left her alone.

Cristina was a year younger than me, which ordinarily would mean that we were worlds apart. We were in the same classroom and that meant I could see her every day. And see her I did, taking every opportunity to turn around to the back of the room. It quickly became evident to everybody that I was desperately in love.

None of the other boys in the fourth grade saw anything special about Cristina Sifuentes. In fact, they decided she was ugly. Not only that, they were sure she must be part Negro because of her complexion and the fullness of her lips. Of course, none of them said shit to me.

My best friend that year was Bobby Adames. He told me what everyone was saying. Bobby had seen how I tried to talk to her during recess and how she never responded and most of the time simply walked away. It seemed to him that she didn't care for me at all.

So long as she was not spending her time with anyone else, I had hope. There were days when my love for her was unbearable. I would be overcome with an anxiousness and a frustration that would leave me sad and forlorn. I was the saddest, loneliest person in the world. What I wanted to do most of all was cry for Cristina Sifuentes. As much as I tried to get my tears flowing, they didn't. The best I could do was a sort of lump in my throat. On other days I quite forgot about her for hours. I would go to my chores and be surprised that I had spent an hour or two without a single thought of Cristina Sifuentes. At home, I would be my old self.

No doubt my brother Paulie had explained to everyone the source of the change that had come over me. The folks were respectful of what I was going through and mercifully I was spared the usual bantering.

It took nearly a month of chasing after her like a puppy hungry for affection until Cristina Sifuentes finally acknowledged me sitting close by and asked me to come sit next to her. I had rehearsed everything I had to say to her so many times that I couldn't get the first word out. It was my chance to win her over and I had planned every last little detail.

The thing of it is that I sat there with my legs crossed, she looking at the kids playing on the merry-go-round, and me with my heart racing and my mind a dull useless thing. Cristina turned her head slightly to look at me out of corner of her eye.

"Everywhere I go, I see you," she said.

"We can be friends," I said.

"I have lots of friends in Tahoka, where we live," said Cristina Sifuentes.

"What about here in Smiley? Don't you live here now?" I asked. "Don't you want friends here?"

"I can wait. We're going back in September," she said.

"But, I thought your folks were going to live here in Smiley!" I said, excited, confused.

"We are, but just half of the year. The other half we will spend in Tahoka where my father can get work."

I was dejected. "You mean, you're going away when school is over?"

"No, we'll be here in the summer. To work. My father says there is lots of work in the summer. After, is when we go."

We didn't say too much more that first time.

The end of summer was four months away but I felt as though it was coming the following morning. I was anxious for her to be my girlfriend and there just didn't seem to be enough time for me to win her over.

When the warning bell rang, I sprang to my feet and offered my hand to Cristina Sifuentes. She took it and pulled herself up. On the way back to our classroom, I asked if I could walk with her after school, not home, mind you, but to don Pedro's for a soda. She said, no, that her mother was coming for her in the car.

Having sat with her and having actually talked to her was enough for me. From then until school ended for the year, we were inseparable. We sat together under the trees as the days became hotter and the breezes were pleasant and caressing. I would help her with her lessons, which was the same stuff I had learned the year before.

Cristina became friendly and comfortable with me. She seemed shy and there were days when we did not exchange a single word while we were together. My school friends, of course, obnoxious little bastards that they were, made fun of me. I had stopped being a part of the group, spending all of my free time with Cristina Sifuentes. After school, I might stay in Smiley for a ballgame or something. The boys would have to come for me.

With Cristina Sifuentes in my life, now, I would get on the bus and go home. It was proof that I was being faithful to her. My friends had as yet to discover what it is to be in love and to have a girlfriend.

As near as I could tell, Cristina Sifuentes was not the kind of girl to have a gaggle of girlfriends to giggle with. When she was not with me, she was by herself, reading her books, or drawing something in her notebook. I had asked her lots of times to tell me about her friends in Tahoka. She was reluctant to talk about them too much. The best I could do was to get four or five names out of her. They were just names, though. She didn't mention anything about them.

The high point of my fifth grade year was the time I came up to her from behind and caught her writing my name in her notebook. If I had not received any indication before that Cristina Sifuentes loved me back, that was it. She closed her notebook suddenly and smiled at me. I leaned over and took her hand in mine. For once, she didn't flinch or move it away.

With school out, I was not going to be with Cristina every day.

I tried to talk her into making some plans so we could see each other during the summer. She wasn't particularly interested in my elaborate schemes; in fact, she told me she looked forward to being out of school.

I told her to look for me at don Pedro's every day. I would have to work with the family, as we had already begun the harvest. It was going to be damn near impossible to come into Smiley every day. I wasn't worried about that, though. If she consented to meet me, I would find a way.

She said she might be able to go every now and then, but that I should not expect her to be there. Anyway, she said, if she were to be there, more than likely either her father or her mother would be with her. They were going to be picking cotton and wouldn't be in town until after dark.

The usual way of things in Schoolland was for pickers to ask for work. My father hated contractors because they seldom had good pickers with them. The old way of hiring people we knew was the best.

I was at the age where I should have been a good cotton picker, but I wasn't. And so, my father would assign me to the tally.

My father was working on something else, when he and my brother Paulie came in during the late afternoon to check on the picking. He got a dipper of water from the wooden barrel attached to the tractor. He rinsed his mouth and spit before he drank. I tried to sound like a grown-up.

"We could use some more pickers, Daddy," I said.

My father drank another dipper of water.

"There is a new family in Smiley, Daddy. Cipriano Sifuentes. We could hire them," I said, my voice trembling.

My father handed the dipper to my brother Paulie. Paulie hooked it back on the rim of the barrel and closed the lid.

"We don't need any more pickers," said my father.

I pestered my brothers Elpidio and Jose enough to where we went for drives in Smiley. They knew pretty much what I was up to, but it was still a pain in the ass for them.

The Sifuentes house faced a narrow dirt street that led to the main highway, but I could see it when we passed by on the highway. I was always too early and I never got a look at Cristina Sifuentes.

I figured her family had to go into Gonzales on Saturday afternoons. For that reason, I made sure I got to go along whenever anybody in the family went to Gonzales. As we rode into town, I would look in every direction trying to catch a glimpse of her father's car. Sometimes it would be parked in front of Schmidt's meat market and other times it was parked in the center of town.

The first time, Paulie and I had been walking in the direction of the bank, going up the street to the Western Auto. Paulie was going to get some .22's for himself and a box of .410's for my grandfather. As we got to the corner, Paulie elbowed me in the ribs. I turned to see Cristina and her mother coming out of the Rexall drugstore. Cristina's mother paused just outside the door to inventory her purchases. Paulie nudged me in the ribs again. I was smiling at Cristina but she did not return my smile.

Instead, she took her mother by the arm and led her away.

They walked in the opposite direction. I asked Paulie to walk after them with me. Paulie said, shit no, he had to finish his errand. I decided to follow Cristina and her mother. With luck, they might stop to look in a window and I could catch up to them without being so obvious. They didn't stop until they came to the Courthouse Cafe and they lingered there for a few minutes while her father and the rest of the children came out. I stopped a short distance away, leaning against a building, as if I were out to enjoy an afternoon in town. Another time, I was with my father and mother and my sister Juana when we parked a few cars away from them in the lot. Cipriano Sifuentes and his wife were eating fruit from a brown paper bag. Cipriano Sifuentes and my father exchanged casual greetings. Afterward, I asked my father if he knew them and he said it had been a long time ago.

The third time I saw her in town, I was with my brother Elpidio. Concepcion Arreaga's birthday was coming up and he was getting her a present. I suspected he was sweet on her, but he wouldn't admit to anything. Besides, he bought birthday presents for all the Arreaga girls.

Elpidio and I were standing in front of the Courthouse Cafe after having had some hamburgers. From where we stood, I saw her whole family across the square. They went up to the ticket box of the Lynn Theater. Her father paid the admissions and then he and Cristina's mother watched their children go inside.

My heart jumped into my throat when I saw Cristina go inside the theater. I asked Elpidio if he cared to go to the movies. He said we would be leaving shortly. Besides, you only went to the movies when there was a girl inside waiting for you. I, of course, was desperate. I begged him to give me just a little time. Elpidio had never seen Cristina Sifuentes and I was not about to tell him outright, but I did convince him to wait for me while I went in for a few minutes. He threatened to leave me stranded if I took too long. At that point, I didn't care.

Cristina sat downstairs, with her brothers and sister on either side of her. I waited a long time before my eyes got accustomed to the flickering darkness. It was difficult for me to find her. Eventually, I made out the back of her head. The worst part of it was that somebody was sitting behind her. I had intended to whisper in her ear that she should join me up in the balcony. It was impossible for me to get close enough to say anything without drawing the attention of her brothers. Fortunately, the movie was nearly over and I spent my time staring lovingly at the shadow of her head. When the movie ended, she came to the lobby for a soda and it was there that she saw me and smiled.

I asked her if she wanted to watch the beginning of the movie with me in the balcony and she said she couldn't because she had to take care of her brothers and sister. I did, however, make a date with her for the following Saturday. She promised to sit with me in the balcony.

When I came out of the theater, Elpidio was waiting for me in the truck. I was so happy, I didn't mind at all that he scolded me all the way home.

I never realized how long it took for six days to pass. I worked harder than I had ever worked before, thinking that by speeding up my work, time would pass by more quickly. It didn't, of course. After moving at a lightning pace, only a couple of minutes would have gone by. Not only that, I wasn't paying close attention to the tally. After I screwed up one wagon load by sending in a short bale, my father sent me to pick cotton as punishment.

The humiliation of it and the ribbing from my brothers was as nothing to me.

With unbearable slowness Saturday came. Only my mother and father were going to Gonzales. That didn't help me at all, since they usually went, bought whatever it was they went for, and came right back.

Elpidio and Jose were going to see a ballgame in Nixon. My sister Juana said she would take me if she only had a car, which was a hint to my father more than an offer to help me.

In desperation, I told my father I would go with them and they could leave me there and that I could get a ride back with somebody or other. When they asked, I told them I was to meet someone at the movies. They didn't embarrass me by asking any more than that.

My mother, though, wouldn't hear of me staying behind. She said I was crazy and if I went with them, I would return with them. Fortunately, Elpidio came to my defense, saying it was about time I learned to do things on my own. My father allowed as I ought to be able to find a ride back, being that half of Smiley would be in town anyway. My mother still refused, saying she would not allow one of her children to be a bother to anyone else.

I rode into Gonzales with my folks. On the way, I kept assuring them that it was fine to leave me in town. I could watch the movie and then catch a ride with somebody. But my mother had made up her mind and finished our discussion by telling me to not get too involved with the movie, that my father would be going in to drag me out when they finished their shopping. My father obviously had a plan in mind as he nodded reassuringly to me and gave me an extra two dollars to take care of myself.

I didn't see the Sifuentes car as I walked over to the Lynn. I was going to wait outside until Cristina came before going in, but I saw that my mother and father were watching to see that I went in. Reluctantly, I went in, found a spot near the stairs going to the balcony where I could see outside and waited.

The Sifuentes finally arrived, taking their own sweet time about getting out of the car. Instead of coming to the theater, Cristina walked with her family into the five and dime. It was nearly half an hour before Cristina bought her ticket and was standing in front of me, her head bowed, nervous.

"Let's go sit upstairs," I said, touching her elbow as we walked.

First, I tried to hold her hand. Each time my eager little fingers found her hand, she moved it away. I placed my arm on the padded backrest of the chair, easing my forearm forward to touch the back of her head. She moved her head forward, shaking it, as if a bug had landed on it. I then dropped my hand to her shoulder, and she brushed it away with her hand. I leaned over several times to whisper things to her, but each time she ignored me. The only time she spoke was to tell me I should let her enjoy the movie.

I leaned back in my own chair, eagerly and anxiously planning my next move. It had to be something bold, something I had not dared before; and yet, it could not be anything that would anger or frighten her.

The best I could come up with was cupping my hand at the base of her smooth, fragrant neck. Cristina sighed, expelling a long rush of annoyed breath. She didn't remove my hand, though.

When the ecstasy of touching her neck began to wear a bit thin, I inched my fingers around until I found her earlobe, which I pressed between my forefinger and thumb. This time, she shook her head. Cristina turned in her chair, took my hand and made me a present of it in my lap.

The next thing I knew, the lights came up and there were people getting up from their seats all around us. I caught glimpses of the lucky bastards who were surprised in their clenches when the lights came on.

The afternoon and my first date had been a complete bust.

Two months earlier, the thrill of sitting next to Cristina Sifuentes would have been enough. As I had spent so much time with her in school, and as I had received so many of her smiles and as I had even gotten to hold her hand, I naturally wanted more. I couldn't say what, exactly. I had not expected things to go the way they went. It had been the first time that we had agreed to meet. Near as I could figure out, it had been a date, the movies being the most romantic spot in all of Gonzales.

In the lobby, while Cristina Sifuentes waited for her folks to come and collect her, I became bold. I stood next to her with my hands in my pockets.

"Don't you love me, Cristina?" I asked her.

"Don't be silly," said she.

"Will you come to the movies with me next Saturday?"

"Of course, I always come to the movies on Saturday," she said.

Cipriano Sifuentes parked by the curb and Cristina sprinted out the door before I could say another word. Right behind Cristina's father was Tony Arreaga. He motioned for me to come get in the truck.

"Your daddy asked me to look out for you," Tony said, as he released the clutch and the truck lurched forward.

"Thanks," I said.

"Is that your girlfriend?" said Tony, smiling.

"I don't know," I said. "I think so."

"You think so? Goddamn!" said Tony Arreaga.

The part of the year I most dreaded came upon us all too quickly. The beginning of school was but three weeks away and I expected that Cristina would just disappear into thin air for six months.

I had seen Cristina just about every Saturday that summer. She never mentioned going away and neither did I. I thought that if I didn't mention it, maybe her father would forget and stay, after all.

Elpidio and I were delayed by a flat tire, which made me late for my last date that year. To my surprise, Cristina was waiting for me in the lobby. Her face brightened when she saw me and she had an arm outstretched, ready to take my hand when I came up to her. I slipped my arm around her waist and she didn't seem to mind that either. I mentioned how it was a special time for us and asked if she might kiss me goodbye. Slowly and gracefully, Cristina leaned over to me. Once again I could smell her freshly washed, perfumed hair. Gently, as a wisp of breeze, she brushed my cheek with her lips. I put my arms around her and tried to draw her to me for another kiss on the lips.

"No, I can't," she said, placing both of her hands squarely on my heaving chest.

"But, I won't see you until January," I said, lamely.

"We can wait," she said. "You'll see, it won't be that long."

There was a lump in my throat throughout the entire movie. It was one of the Technicolor Westerns that I liked, but I had too much else on my mind.

All too soon, we were filing out of the theater, jostling past the waiting crowd for the next show. My mouth was open and my eyes were a little watery as I saw Cristina Sifuentes get in her family's car.

On the way home, my brother Elpidio noticed how sad I was. I had told him she would be gone for six months. He tried to cheer me up by saying she'd be back in no time at all. I just wanted to be alone with my misery.

When we got home, I stayed outside on the porch for hours. I didn't go in for supper and no one came out to ask me to come in. I watched the moon rise. Just a few miles away, the same moon shone on Cristina Sifuentes. Her folks would begin their journey at two in the morning. I must've dozed for a couple of hours. I awoke with a blanket around my shoulders. The moon was directly over me, brighter than it had been earlier in the evening and the sky surrounding it had brightened up with thousands of stars.

# Chapter 10

Labor Day weekend was noisy and crowded at our house. My sister Celia visited for a few days as did several relatives with lots of kids. Without being asked to, I fed the animals and kept pretty much to myself. There was too damned much cheerfulness in the house to suit me.

As if I needed more reminders, I heard from the men who gathered to talk at the gas stations and at the grocery store benches, that the Sifuentes family had gone. It was curious to them that someone would divide the year between Smiley and West Texas. The Sifuentes had proven that they were good and reliable workers. They had worked in Schoolland all summer. Now that all of our crops were in, the harvest was just beginning in West Texas.

The first day of school brought the ghost of Cristina Sifuentes to me everywhere I turned. I thought that by sitting quietly and alone where she and I had shared our precious moments, I could bear her absence. Instead, I was overcome with loneliness and doubt. Would she forget about me? Would she fall in love with someone else? Would her family really come back in six months?

The first few weeks of school were unmasked torture for me. It was not possible for me to escape reminders of her. Not that I wanted to forget. Almost everything had a secret and special meaning with Cristina at the center of it. Every inch of the school ground was a place where I had stood with her and some were more special than others, bringing back meaningful glances exchanged, or a smile, or maybe a conversation.

When my sad, lonesome, forlorn, tragic figure on the school grounds became too visible, I threw myself into all manner of games and activities with the boys. It didn't look as though I was going to die from grief. And, all the kids were having too much fun at my expense. I could pretend to be my old self, while inside my heart was truly lacerated.

Joining up again with the boys provided me with the cloak of normalcy rediscovered. We flirted with the girls from the safety of the group, which made of it a seemingly innocent ritual. Later on, as we went on to high school, it wouldn't be so innocent and we would discover how serious we had been all along.

I laughed once again. From all indications, I had a good time. But there were instances when I would suffer a relapse into misery and I would pine away for Cristina Sifuentes.

Samantha Coleman fell in love with me along about October of that autumn.

Samantha Coleman had blond hair, green eyes, and wore glasses that had rhinestones in the frames. She was a bit taller than the other girls and her ghostly white skin had a reddish tint to it in places.

It was more or less understood by all the kids in school that whites fell in love with whites and Mexicans with Mexicans. There had been one or two adventures between the races, but they ended before junior high; certainly none of them lasted past the sophomore or junior year of high school. In the senior year, boys and girls paired up for life.

There is no doubt that each of us, even as children, had a responsibility to our respective races. The differences became more evident as we got older. Mixing us up as children served only to humanize us. Just as we were to face fierce opponents on the football field, the races were similarly opposed.

The divisions were there all along as the teachers, who were white, tended to favor the whites. By the time we began to date seriously, we knew where we belonged and what our place in the world would be. We might bend over shoulder to shoulder in the line during the scrimmage. After we played the last football game, however, the fathers of our teammates hired our fathers, and our teammates in turn would hire us.

Another thing we understood quite clearly: the wealthiest Mexican was always somehow a lesser human being than the worst of white trash.

What made it permissible for Samantha Coleman to fall in love with me was the fact that she imagined herself to be Lana Turner. That fact alone made Samantha Coleman different from every one, white or Mexican. All the kids and many of the parents were convinced that something was not quite right with Samantha Coleman.

She was pretty and had larger breasts than any other girl and most adults. However, the imperfection of the eyeglasses seemed to override every other facet of her pulchritude.

In keeping with her conviction that she was Lana Turner, Samantha Coleman wore white dresses into which she fit quite nicely. Once, she had worn a white turban to school and the teachers made her put it away. Another time, she wore tightfitting white shorts cut so high up that her panties showed as she walked. The teachers sent her home that time.

I was sitting on the grass with Cristina Sifuentes. Samantha Coleman came up to us. She wore a tan sweater, a cream-colored skirt and red patent leather shoes. She had tied a red scarf loosely around her neck and she carried an outsized red patent leather purse.

"Are you a Latin American?" she had asked me.

"My father says we all came from Mexico," I responded.

"Have you seen the movie, *Latin Lovers?*" she asked.

"No, I haven't," I said, smiling at Cristina Sifuentes.

"Too bad. Ricardo Montalban is a Latin American," said Samantha Coleman before going away.

"What did she mean by all that?" Cristina Sifuentes asked me.

"I don't know. She's strange," I said.

I was in the first few days of learning to live in Cristina Sifuentes' absence. Pedro Mendoza, Rolando Ríos and I were leaning against the wall of the cafeteria building after lunch one day when Samantha Coleman comes up to us and just stands there, grinning and looking at me.

Pedro Mendoza said hi for all of us, but she didn't pay him any attention. Suddenly, she thrust out her hand, which held a picture of Lana Turner and offered it to me. I didn't know what the hell to do at that point but to take the picture. Samantha Coleman turned and went to rejoin her friends, who had been watching from a distance. They were looking at me and laughing as she joined them. Samantha Coleman turned to look at me over her shoulder and gave me a smile that resembled Lana Turner's in the picture she gave me. Other than that, there wasn't too much of a resemblance. The picture was a 5 x 7 glossy printed on one corner with, *Affectionately yours,* and Lana Turner's signature. On another corner, Samantha Coleman had written, *To John Garfield. Love always, Samantha.* I stuck the picture in one of my books.

At the water fountain a few days later, I asked her why she had given me a picture of a movie star dedicated to someone else.

"Don't be silly," said Samantha Coleman. "You're John Garfield!"

"Who is John Garfield?" I asked.

"Don't you know? He helped Lana murder her husband in *The Postman Always Rings Twice.*"

"What's that got to do with me?"

"You look like John Garfield, a little bit. Too young, but you look a little like him."

Thereafter, for the remainder of the school term, I noticed that Samantha Coleman always seemed to be with her friends close by wherever I was with my friends.

A few weeks later, my brothers Elpidio and Jose came with me to the football game, an important one against our archrivals, Nixon. I was sitting with them at the far end of the bleachers. Suddenly, I looked to one side, past my right shoulder, and saw Samantha Coleman standing there, alone. She was staring at me with an odd, serious look on her face. She gave me a thin smile, opening her eyes wide in a question.

I jumped down from the bleachers just as Elpidio and Jose exchanged grins with one another. Samantha and I walked away from the glaring lights of the football field over to where the cars were parked. It was a cool, windy night and we went to stand in the lee of the cars. We were next to my brother Jose's truck, shielded from any one who would care to look at us from the bleachers.

Samantha Coleman threw her arms around my neck and kissed me. I had been kissed before, but never in my life like that. It was wet, warm and wonderful. Her lipstick had a sweet aftertaste to it. Little did I know that a lot of it had been smeared on my face. When she let go of me, she touched my cheek with her fingertips.

"You're so dark. I like a dark man. Just like Richard Burton in *The Rains of Ranchipur*," she said.

A flush went through me as I felt the perfidy and unfaithfulness to my faraway Cristina Sifuentes. I dropped my head, resting my eyes on her ample bosom. I didn't quite know what to say. Samantha Coleman caught me looking at her breasts. She took my hand, raising it to rest in the middle of them.

"Is this better?" she asked. "Is this what you want from me?"

My massive, all-encompassing erection strained against my jeans.

She placed her hands on my shoulders, tilting her head to one side, expecting me to kiss her again. As I hesitated for just a second, she pulled on my shoulders. Her lips were parted and her eyes were closed. Being careful not to snag my nostrils in the rim of her glasses, I tilted my head and leaned over to kiss her.

Abruptly, she pushed me away and ran.

A couple of weeks later, she caught my arm in the hallway and dragged me into a broom closet. It was dank in there and smelled of disinfectant. Samantha Coleman shut the door and leaned against it. She wore a turquoise colored sweater and a blue skirt that reached down to her ankles.

I was nervous and afraid we would get caught by the janitor or one of the teachers. Samantha, though, wet her lips with the tip of her tongue.

"Look," she said, and she lifted her sweater, bunching it under her chin. My gaze was first concentrated on her bare midriff until I saw the brassiere. She had sewn hundreds of glass beads, in pearl, green, blue and red colors, to the cups. The beads were sewn in concentric circles, narrowing to a bright ruby red bead the size of a small grape.

"Do you like it?" Samantha Coleman breathed her question, huskily, just as Lana Turner would have.

"What is it?"

"I saw *The Prodigal* last weekend. Lana wears an outfit just like this," said Samantha, proud of herself.

She reached inside her black patent leather purse and took out a handful of glass beads. It took me a little while to recognize that tangled up in the strings of beads was a pair of white panties.

"See," she said, holding them up for me to get a good look. "She had these strings of beads on her underpants, too. Only thing, the beads were too heavy when I put them on." She pointed to a long rip on the side of them.

I didn't know what to say.

"Here," said Samantha Coleman, holding out the panties. "You want them?"

"No, I better not," I said. "We better get out of here."

Samantha Coleman slipped the sweater over her breasts, smoothed out her clothes before we came out of the broom closet.

For the rest of the afternoon, all I could think of was the two pointy lumps of the glass beads at the center of each brassiere cup.

Until Christmas vacation, I found Samantha Coleman at all the football games and at the movies in Nixon and in Gonzales. If we stopped for a couple of dollars' worth of gas, she would ride up behind us in the car with her mother or her sister. It got to the point where I was disappointed if she didn't show up.

We never actually planned anything, as I still considered myself the boyfriend of Cristina Sifuentes. I did think quite a bit more about Samantha Coleman than I should have. I wasn't in love with her, or anything. It was just impossible for me to ignore her, that's all.

Cristina Sifuentes had never pledged herself to me in so many words. Nevertheless, I felt it was my duty to love her and no one else. However, so long as I wasn't in love with Samantha Coleman, it was okay for her to console me in Cristina's absence. To be truthful, I liked it that Samantha was chasing me and gave all appearances of being in love with me. She had kissed me and shown me her underwear. I showed her the same restraint that Cristina Sifuentes showed me. In sum, what I felt for Samantha Coleman was never quite strong enough to make me turn away from Cristina Sifuentes.

Samantha and I were in the same grade and we took to sitting next to one another in class. We ate lunch together. Because I wasn't in love with Samantha, I felt no compulsion to be perfect in her eyes. I was never embarrassed that I brought a sack lunch, whereas she paid for hers everyday. She would share her desserts with me; in fact, it is possible that she would have given me all of her lunch had I indicated I wanted it.

During recess, we spent most of our time together. She helped with my schoolwork, volunteering to do all of my homework for me. I ended up doing it myself, because it was a pain in the ass to copy it before the teacher called for it.

When we had our school pictures taken, her folks ordered every pose sent to them by the photographer and without even taking them home, Samantha displayed them all to me and asked me to take all of the ones I wanted. I think she meant I could have all of them. Just to be nice, I took a small one which she insisted I put in my wallet. I did so, vowing silently to remove it before Cristina Sifuentes came back to me.

Since it was so obvious to everyone that Samantha Coleman and I were more than just friends, I panicked one day when I realized that someone would surely rat on me to Cristina Sifuentes. I knew that Cristina didn't have very many best friends among the girls, but Samantha and I made such an odd couple that someone was bound to tell her, just for curiosity's sake.

I wasn't worried in the least because I had never encouraged Samantha Coleman. Though the temptation was strong and unavoidable, my heart was pure. In fact, I made it very clear to Samantha that I would be going with Cristina in the Spring.

Samantha had tossed her shoulders forward. Pursing her lips, she spoke in a little girl voice, saying that Lana Turner had lost John Garfield, Richard Burton and Edmund Purdom. She would have to learn how to lose a man.

At the last football game of the season, Samantha and I were seated together on the bleachers. Smiley, as had happened at every home game, was losing. She had her arm hooked in mine and we each had our heads sunk into our coats against a very cold evening. When it became evident that not even a miracle could help Smiley, more and more people began to leave. Samantha Coleman whispered in my ear to follow her. We walked from the football field back to the schoolyard and there in a dark corner in between some buildings, Samantha Coleman unbuttoned her thick coat and pulled the zipper on her sweater.

I slipped my hands inside her sweater, pressing them flat against her bare flesh. Samantha moaned as she kissed my ear. Then she whispered, saying I could unsnap her brassiere if I wanted to. Try as I might, I could not undo the hooks of the brassiere. Samantha became impatient, reached between us and pulled it over her breasts.

"There!" she said, and gave me a long, lingering wet kiss.

Her bare breasts were not doing me any good as she pressed against me so tightly, I couldn't get my hands on them. She asked urgently if I loved her breasts, if I loved kissing them. I said, yes. What else could I say? Each time I tried to slip my hands between us, she pressed closer to me.

Again, she urged me to kiss her breasts, pressing her lower body against mine. I did manage to shove her hand between us so she might grab hold of my pecker. Once her hand was in the general vicinity, she turned her hand the other way. I ended up grinding my pelvis against the back of her hand.

At long last, Samantha Coleman relaxed a little. In the slack, I managed to take hold of her breasts. They were large and soft and felt as though they might flow through my fingers. Remembering the grape-sized glass beads, I bent my head and began to suck on her nipples which were hard and rough. Once I got that far, I held on to those nipples for the remainder of the time we were clenched in that dark corner.

The walk back to the bleachers was uncomfortable for me as my crotch was in pain. There was a gooey wetness on my shorts. Samantha Coleman asked me if I had enjoyed myself. It seemed important to her. I reminded her that there could never be anything between us because I had given my heart and soul to Cristina Sifuentes, who would be coming back in a couple of months.

Samantha Coleman said she knew all about Cristina, that she would be coming back soon and that there was a chance she was going to lose me. I asked her why she wasted her time. She said she wasn't wasting her time. She always got what she wanted.

The school vacation started and I saw a lot less of Samantha Coleman. The respite from her made my yearning for Cristina Sifuentes all the more unbearable. I began to appreciate the good that Samantha had done for me.

A couple of days before Christmas, my brothers and I were all sitting on the porch when a strange car came up the driveway. My brother Paulie said it was goddamned gringos. And sure enough, Samantha Coleman got out of the car, opened the door to the back seat and took out three gift-wrapped boxes. She had brought me Christmas presents!

I was embarrassed because of how bold she was, getting her mother or whoever it was that drove the car to bring her to our house. I was also embarrassed because it had never occurred to me to buy her any presents. But, mostly I was embarrassed because my brothers were not going to let me live it down for months.

The second term began and without actually counting the days I could sense the return of Cristina Sifuentes. She had not written to me even though I had asked her to do so. I had written our mailing address in her notebook. She had not given me an address where I could write to her, even though I had asked for one. She said her father did not allow her to receive mail from boys. And therefore, every school day in January, I left home with my heart thumping in expectation that Cristina would come into class, maybe an hour or two late, as she had done the year before.

On weekends, I would make damned sure that we would cruise by her house to see if there were signs of life. On the roads, I was impatient until I could make out an approaching vehicle, hoping that it might be them and that I might catch a glimpse of her.

I tried to keep my distance from Samantha Coleman. Cristina's return was imminent and I didn't want to cut it too closely. Besides, I thought that being all to myself until her return would purify me, absolve me of my involvement with Samantha.

Samantha, though, wasn't ready to give up. When I couldn't get away from her, we would sit and talk. I avoided secluded places to prevent any smooching, for fear that Cristina might find out.

I was afraid that the imprint of my unfaithfulness would be there for anyone to see.

"I missed you over Christmas," Samantha told me one day. "Did you think about me at all?"

"Yeah, I guess. A little," I said.

"I bet you thought a lot more about Christina Sifuentes, didn't you?" she said.

"That's right," I said.

"Maybe they aren't coming back anymore, did you ever think about that?" Samantha Coleman said to me another time in the hall. She caught me in the afternoon just as I was going out for the bus.

"They'll be back," I said, with youthful certainty.

"My mother says you can come over to the house to study, if you want to," said Samantha Coleman. "She said it would be all right, even if . . ."

". . . I'm a Mexican," I finished for her.

"My mother is not like that. Well, maybe a little," said Samantha Coleman. "Anyway, she knows that after I saw *Latin Lovers* with Ricardo Montalban, there is going to be a Latin man in my future. I just love South Americans."

"I can't study with you, Samantha. I don't have a way to get around," I told her.

I could probably get one of my brothers to drive me over. Except I wasn't interested in her. I was sort of ashamed that she even asked, being as Cristina was so close to being back.

"I have to get on the bus," I said, "or it'll leave without me. Then, I'll catch hell from my folks."

"Send word back with the twins that you're going to study with me," she persisted. "My mom'll drive you back. You can have supper with us."

"I can't," I said.

I couldn't bring myself to believe that her father would allow me to eat at the same table with them. Before she could say anymore, I ran to the bus.

The day I had been waiting for for six months finally arrived.

Cristina Sifuentes returned to Smiley and came back to school later the same week. Only it was a far, far different Cristina Sifuentes than the one I had kissed goodbye the previous summer. For one thing, she had lost all of her baby fat and she had grown a couple of inches taller. She was now lean and shapely. Her movements were slower and more graceful, and she was no longer shy and self-conscious. Her clothes were different, too. She wore tight skirts, scarves tied to her neck, all of which made her appear a lot older.

When she made her entrance into our class, the attention she got was much different from the year before. It was as if she was doing more than standing by the teacher's desk. She made subtle shifts in her posture as if she enjoyed the attention she was getting.

Pedro Mendoza punched me in the shoulder. When I turned to look over at him, he pursed his lips in a silent whistle. I seriously considered fighting him at lunch because of the lewd smile on his face.

I could hardly wait for the bell to end the period so I could talk to Cristina in the hallway. I fully expected that she would be anxious and eager to be alone with me. When the bell did ring, Cristina bolted out of the classroom and as much as I looked for her, I didn't see her until I came in for our next class. The same thing happened at lunch. I concluded that there were lots of things she had to do on her first day back in school. Nevertheless, it did seem odd to me that she had not made a special effort to be with me.

In desperation, I sent her a note, relayed along the row of desks. When she got it, she looked in my direction, smiled and slid it between the pages of her notebook. At least, she now knew I was in school, too. In the note, I had asked her to meet me after school. I figured I could skip the bus and have the twins send someone to get me at the store later in the evening.

She never even opened the note, that I could see. Undaunted, I knew she would read it and come to me. When the last bell of the day rang, I didn't get on the bus, figuring it would take her a little time to find her way to me. I lingered on the school grounds with some of the guys, stretching my neck to get a look at every exit of the school building, expecting at any moment to see Cristina Sifuentes.

Almost every one of the kids who lived in town went by don Pedro

Longoria's for cokes and moonpies after school. When it was evident she was nowhere on the school grounds, I went there. She failed to show up at all.

My brother Elpidio came for me about six o'clock. I expected that my mother would be upset, but Elpidio said he had gone to feed the pigs for me and once that was covered, no one paid any notice to my being in town.

Within a couple of days of Cristina Sifuentes' return, she was the most popular girl in school. The year before she had been reclusive and had hardly spoken to anyone except me. Now she was always with a coterie of a half dozen girls or more. And, when not surrounded by girlfriends, I stared as she walked and sat and talked and laughed and smiled with almost every boy in school—except me, that is. Cristina Sifuentes was not only avoiding me, it was like I didn't exist anymore.

Cristina Sifuentes was especially attracted to the boys older than she, those sons-of-bitches who already had their own cars. My friends, those who lived in town, would tell me that so-and-so had taken her to the dance and to the out-of-town baseball games, and so on. I personally had seen her riding around in Nixon with some fellow in a red car.

Samantha Coleman tried to console me on several occasions. I would not have any of it, as I still held a vanishing hope in my breast for Cristina Sifuentes.

"She doesn't want you anymore," Samantha protested.

"She will," I said, stubbornly.

Samantha Coleman laughed and touched my arm. "You can come study with me whenever you want," she said, leaving me to myself.

It was nearly a month before I finally got the chance to talk to Cristina Sifuentes alone. It was going to be awkward and painful for me and for that reason I had not really pressed her until we were as alone as we could be.

I tried to get the words out quickly, just to get it over with. Instead, all I could manage was a whimper, which brought an expression of contempt from Cristina Sifuentes.

"What is it," said she, curtly. "What do you want?"

I stammered some more. Cristina swivelled her head from side to side.

I just couldn't find the right words to demand the explanation I wanted from her. I think she sensed what I wanted to know and she told me that she was no longer a child and that she had to start thinking like an adult.

I never could figure out what that meant, exactly. One thing was clear, though. If she had been in love with me, something I was beginning to doubt, it was no longer true. Of course, it was sadly over between us. It had been obvious from the first day she had returned. I simply had struggled against it within me.

Her last words to me are baffling to this day. "Who knows," she said, touching my cheek, "maybe one day I'll discover you were the one I always wanted."

I eventually got to go to Samantha Coleman's house to study. Her folks were pleasant about it and her father didn't seem to mind when I ate supper at the table with them. In her home, Samantha was altogether different. There, she stopped being Lana Turner.

# Chapter 11

The last rain we had that year came during the last week in January. For what remained of January and through February, the fog rolled in. Every damned day, everywhere you looked, there was the fog.

Each morning, as I looked out of the windows, it seemed as if we were living inside a cloud. I could see the limbs of the trees black and grim as balls of fog the size of a house rolled by. All you had to do was stand outside for just a few minutes to become drenched in a sticky, clammy wet. Above the fog, as if there was a layer of sun in between, clouds hovered low and thick.

For most of the month, we did not see the sun on the ground. The thick morning fogs were not burned away as was usual. Instead, they were replaced by low, rolling fogs that enveloped your legs as you walked and it seemed you were stepping upon clouds. It kept the land moist and damp, but my grandfather told us not to pay too much attention to it. We still didn't know what to make of Grandpa's prediction. Toward the end of February, even the damp brought in by the fog stopped.

March, Crazy March, as we called it, came in with a decided change in the weather. February had been wet and cold. March came in dry and cold, colder than anyone could remember for March. For a couple of days, the temperatures remained at the freezing level until mid-morning but the warm would barely get going and then the temperatures would begin to drop again long before sundown.

Periodically, a bit of sunlight would get through the clouds, but for most of March it was murky and gray all day long, and you had to strain your eyes to look into the distance. It was frustrating to have familiar landmarks obscured at such short distances, you knowing exactly where they were but you just couldn't see them. It was as if the world we knew had been taken away from us.

From gray and miserable, the daylight slowly became extinguished and it seemed that you just noted how the haze would go on forever and then it was dark already. Indeed, we could feel the days getting longer, but we never saw the sunlight.

As was bound to happen, we had more than our usual share of illnesses in the family. Light, nagging, miserable illnesses, nothing to worry about; just enough bellyaching to keep us all pissed at one another. Little Albert and little Julian stayed sick most of the time. Their teacher came out to visit us one day, saying she was worried about them.

Although no one paid any attention to truancy laws, every once in a while, the school officials decided to make trouble for someone. I guess it was our turn, because we never believed for a minute that the Anglo school teacher gave a shit about my brothers' condition. It was just an excuse to file a complaint against us.

The boys had taken a turn for the worse the night before and my mother had stayed up, checking on them for most of the night. My mother was in no mood for a truancy visit.

At breakfast, the boys were finally resting easy and my mother went to get some sleep, entrusting the breakfast chores to my sister Juana.

We didn't like Juana to be completely in charge of the cooking because she had taken some home economics courses in high school and she cooked stuff like biscuits with sausage gravy that nobody liked.

She had cooked omelettes that morning and only my father had the nerve to finish his. He said it only looked funny, but it didn't taste too bad. I didn't like onions at all, and she knew it, and I think she put extra onions on mine. In any event, it was not the best breakfast we ever had.

My mother had just gotten up. She was grumpy as she waited for her coffee to boil. In their delirium, almost in unison, the twins had asked for *buñuelos,* which Juana, taking directions from my mother who was still very tired, was trying to make for them.

Juana was at the stage where she rolled out the dough before frying it when the teacher drove up, tooting her horn. She stayed in the kitchen to finish making the twins some hot chocolate.

My mother could not speak a word of English, in spite of the fact that she was born just a few miles away from our house. At the time it was never important for Mexicans to attend school, especially girl Mexicans, and she never had. The other thing is we never had much to do with gringos, except in school, at work and when we bought things in town. Thing of it is, my mother understood quite a bit more than she let on she did.

My sister Juana did all of the talking with the teacher. At one point during the conversation, Juana became dark with anger. My sister Juana was very dark complected, anyway. When she became angry, her eyes would narrow and her hairline seemed to flow over her forehead. In the process, her complexion became darker and more menacing.

My mother who well knew of Juana's moods became apprehensive. She asked Juana to explain to her what it was that the gringa wanted. Juana explained that the teacher did not believe the boys were sick and that she was going to file a complaint with the constable's office. The teacher, who had been Juana's teacher not many years before, scolded Juana for speaking Spanish in front of her, insisting that it was not polite to exclude another person from a conversation.

My sister Juana turned angrily to the teacher and demanded a suggestion from her as to how she might communicate with my mother, who spoke only Spanish. She had been left out of the prior conversation altogether.

The teacher remained calm and averred that this was America and people ought to learn to speak English. This was not, she said defiantly, Mexico, after all.

Juana held her peace for fear of the teacher's retaliation against the twins, not to mention me. My mother then told Juana to take the teacher in to see the boys if she doubted they were sick. And, this is what Juana did.

The teacher wrinkled her nose as she went into our bedroom with its two double beds on either side of the room and clothes hanging from nails on the walls, an old dresser with a pock-marked mirror, and shoes and boots all over the place. Try as she might, my mother never could make us tidy up the room. The best we did was to pile our dirty clothes in one corner of the room.

My mother told my sister Juana to tell the teacher she could file all the complaints she wanted but that the boys would stay home until they were well enough to go back to school. The teacher then sternly warned Juana that she was not entirely convinced that the boys were too sick to go to school, but that she was going to take her word for it this time. She also said we ought not to expect generosity from her every time. She knew very well, she said, how Mexicans, or, "you people," were. "You people," as she called us, made a mockery of the educational system.

She had filed a complaint about Paulie before but no one seemed to care and one of the school officials informed her that at thirteen a boy was more valuable working than in school.

The teacher left in her brand new car. My sister Juana then repeated the entire exchange to my mother. After she finished, Juana, who was proud beyond anything about our family, was near tears. She told my mother that she had wanted to slap the bitch. My mother told her that that would not have solved anything. My sister said it wasn't meant to solve anything so much as it was meant to make her feel a whole hell of a lot better.

My grandfather was beginning to act stranger than ever. During the days of the fog, he went for days without coming out of the bunkhouse. He had an old dog-eared copy of a novel by Sir Walter Scott which was translated into Spanish and which he would read at random.

One day he was reading near the beginning and later in the afternoon, he would be reading near the end. Grandpa said he had read the story before and knew every bit of it. He said he enjoyed reading a little here and a little bit there, because it kept his reading in practice. He liked the sound of the words.

But, most of the time, he lay in his bunk, staring at the ceiling, the opened book lying on his chest. We asked Elpidio about him, thinking that as they readied for bed, Grandpa might say something he kept from the rest of us. More than that, Grandpa always confided in Elpidio the most. Elpidio would say that Grandpa hardly spoke two words to him each day.

Marcos de la Fuente had helped Grandpa with some digging until they struck a layer of solid rock. Marcos had volunteered to go at it with a sledgehammer and break through it, but Grandpa almost absent-mindedly had told him he had been mistaken in choosing the spot for the well. He had another place in mind for the well and promptly fired Marcos. Marcos was a very good worker but I think Grandpa wanted to dig that well all by himself.

For two or three days, not respecting weekends, Grandpa would ask my mother to fix him some lunch, because he would not be back at noon. He would ride out early on Elpidio's mare, a shovel, a pickaxe and his lunch tied to the saddlehorn.

Some days he would come back before noon and sit at the table to eat his cold lunch. Other days he would not come back at all until after both sittings at supper were over. He would tell my mother he was too tired to eat and he would go directly to bed.

Then, the fog rolled in. For days and days he would not come out of the bunkhouse at all.

Despite the cold and miserable weather, my father and the boys got all of the crops in the ground: milo, corn and cotton. My father put forty acres in the soil bank and seeded it with Johnston grass for hay. We lost four calves, one of which was strangled to death by its umbilical cord. But, we managed to get a couple of dozen calves to market. My father decided we didn't need to be pig farmers and he sold most of the pigs, saving four of them for slaughter and keeping two sows and a boar for breeding. It seemed to me we were still in the pig business but I wasn't going to argue about it.

March had been damned good weather for slaughter. We killed the four pigs one Saturday. It was decided that little Albert and little Julian would shoot the pigs. My father loaded up a little .22 rifle that had belonged to his father and which I used most of the time. He gave the twins lengthy instructions on how to cock the rifle and to point it directly at the pig's forehead and then squeeze the trigger.

We had separated the breed sows and the boar into another part of the pen. The pulley had been strung over the barn doors to raise the carcasses for dressing. Nearby, Grandpa was tending a large cauldron full of boiling water. Little Julian took to the task with relish, shooting the first pig square in the forehead. The animal squealed and rolled over, dead.

With little Albert, it was another matter altogether. Seeing the pig roll over, kicking a little before he was stone dead, was too much for him. He began to cry, saying he couldn't do it. Little Julian, the quiet, studious one, shot his twin brother a look of disgust. He grabbed the rifle away from him and went and shot another pig. That made little Albert cry all the more. Little Julian was chasing down another of the pigs when my father told him it was enough. Little Julian said he was not afraid to kill all four of them. My father took the rifle from him and shot the other two himself.

It took most of the day to dress the pigs. My brothers Paulie and Jose made several wooden boxes which were packed with curing salts and large slabs of bacon. My grandfather did most of the cutting all day until he was covered with drying blood all the way up to his armpits. My father saw that Grandpa was too tired to go on and took over the cutting. Elpidio and I came back to the house where we started the fire in the smokehouse.

The meat was loaded up haphazardly in the truck. Jose drove slowly as if fearing to damage it. Everybody else walked alongside the truck. It was nearly sundown.

My mother came out to make sure each piece of meat was washed well. She complained that we should have bought a freezer the year before when we had the chance. My father had bought a new truck which, according to my mother, we didn't need.

Marcos de la Fuente was a good worker and he quickly earned the respect of anyone who hired hands and of everyone he worked with. It didn't matter much that he was from Mexico. We were Mexicans, too, of course. But, Marcos de la Fuente was from Mexico. That difference was always present, even though it seldom came to the surface.

As he promised, he completely rebuilt the pigpens in his spare time, made them larger and then he asked my father if he might throw in an animal or two of his own with ours. My father gave him permission to do so. Marcos also built a chicken coop for the laying hens that he bought somewhere. Every other day or so, he would bring my mother a pile of eggs in a basket. We had our own laying hens but there were never enough eggs from them. We discovered that he kept the Red and White in Smiley supplied with eggs.

He went into the haybarn one Sunday and when he came out, it was neat and orderly. He completely rebuilt the corral which had become rundown after my father lost a lot of money in cattle. We kept a few dozen head of cows which mostly took care of themselves, no more than could graze on what pasture land we had.

Elpidio mentioned that now that the corral was in good working order, Marcos would probably ask if he might keep a few cows, which is exactly what Marcos did and, again, my father gave him permission. Marcos bought two cows and was very scrupulous about keeping and feeding them separately from ours.

Marcos de la Fuente had used lumber from the old house to rebuild the pigpens and patch up the corral. With the remainder, he cleaned out the kitchen of the old house, the best surviving room, and made it usable again. The screened porch still had a good portion of the roof over it and the floor was still good. He sealed that up and turned it into a bedroom. The old house had been low and elongated. After Marcos was done with it, there remained only the floor in what had been a front room and back bedroom. The two other bedrooms at the far end were gone completely, the only thing left being some wooden posts sticking up out of the ground.

The old house, the shape of it fixed so firmly in our memory of it, seemed abused and mutilated.

# Chapter 12

The old house was built for my grandfather by his two brothers. My grandfather Jose Maria, who was always known as Chema, died while still a young man.

As my father always told it, my grandmother had consented to marry my grandfather only if he would build her a house first. It wasn't a dowry or even a challenge to his stamina. She did not want to live with anybody and simply wanted her own house. The fact is, my great-grandparents had no use for my grandmother. It wasn't anything she did, except, maybe, breathing the same air they did.

There was something altogether different about her. To hear anyone tell it, my grandmother had her own mind, did things in her own way and wasn't too particular about what people thought when she did. It seems that my grandmother thought she was marrying down and my great-grandparents thought she was marrying up. I don't think my grandfather thought much about it either way. To compound matters, she was older than my grandfather by a good five years. The difference in their ages may account for the fact that she did not intend to be a meek little housewife.

It was agreed by most people who knew her only slightly, and this included my grandparents, that my grandfather Chema was her last chance for matrimony. I think she probably waited all of her life for a man good enough to come along and finally settled on my grandfather. Whether he was good enough or not, he died far too young to have proven anything.

My grandfather Chema was eighteen at the time he met and fell in love with my grandmother. My great-grandmother thought it was a scandal for someone so young to marry someone so old, someone with so much "experience." My great-grandfather probably didn't think too much of it. Not too many years into his marriage he had surrendered to my great-grandmother. For better or worse, she managed the household.

My grandfather, as was pretty much the custom, planned to marry my grandmother and then live with his folks. Young people lived with either one or the other of the relatives.

My grandmother's people, her father, mother and one sister, were killed in a fire that destroyed their house. Her remaining brothers had taken control of all of the property and had promptly lost it, including her share, because they had no idea of how to hold on to it. Therein lay my grandmother's pretension that she was a woman of property, even though she was landless and penniless. She lived her life as a virtual housekeeper, going from one brother's family to the other.

My great-grandmother was not one to let something like that pass. She expected some sort of deference, a recognition of the natural order of things, from my grandmother. When my grandmother held her head up a little too high, when her manner was anything but demure, my great-grandmother beheld someone who needed desperately to be corrected.

They say she once accused my grandmother of living on charity in a house with a dirt floor. She added, just to be mean, that my grandmother had gone barefooted until my grandfather bought her shoes.

It wasn't so much that my grandmother wanted to be a woman of property again as it was that she was tired of living in other people's homes. Considering my great-grandmother's feelings toward her, feelings that ran pretty high and close to the surface, it was impossible for the newlyweds to have begun their lives together by moving in with my great-grandparents.

In anticipation of a wedding, my grandfather had hired out to a German farmer on the other side of Gonzales, near Shiner. The German had promised him a house in which to live. My grandfather figured that that's what my grandmother had in mind when she insisted on having her own house. And, being kind of young and not too experienced, it rankled my grandfather when he thought of the manner in which his intended was being treated by his own family. So far as he wanted, he needed to be as far away from the family as possible.

Now, my grandmother had something else in mind altogether. When she told my grandfather she wanted her own home before she married him, she meant exactly that.

My grandfather had two brothers and my great-grandfather's land was eventually to be divided among them in three ways. My grandmother figured that if she allowed my grandfather to go through with his plans, that is, turn his back on the family, he might be excluded from the eventual division of the property. The only way to prevent that was to have my grandfather build her a house on my great-grandfather's land.

As things were going, my grandfather and my great-grandmother were not talking to one another. My great-uncles, who were older, considered the whole thing as a source of amusement, but in general they stayed out of it. The only one to talk to about building a place was my great-grandfather. It was going to be difficult to get my great-grandmother to stay out of it.

That's when my grandmother played her best card. She agreed that my grandfather should take the job with the German farmer in Shiner. Then, she moved in and lived as wife to him. She would not marry him until the house was built, but she would live with him, denying him nothing. She told him, frankly, that until he built that house for her, all of his children would be born bastards.

My grandfather's brothers knew of the arrangement as soon as he moved to Shiner. In a compact with my great-grandfather, they conspired to keep it from my great-grandmother.

My grandmother was not one to avoid controversy of any kind. When her brothers, especially their wives, demanded to know where she was going, she told them in no uncertain terms. With the way news travels in Schoolland, my great-grandmother found out quickly enough.

The distance to Shiner in those days was considerable. It was several months before my grandfather came for a visit. He was hardly in the door when my great-grandmother walked up to him and slapped him as hard as she could. She glowered at him, her face contorted in anger and shame. When she had given him a good look at the anger in her face, she slapped him again, making my grandfather lose his balance and fall back against a wall. As he planted his feet firmly on the floor again, she slapped him once more, this time with her left hand. My grandfather just stood there with his mouth agape. Without a word, she turned and walked swiftly to her kitchen. She prepared a plate of food for my grandfather and dropped it noisily on the table.

"Eat," she said, "and get out!"

My great-grandfather and my grandfather's brothers had watched everything, powerless to intervene. My grandfather went to the table and began to eat, the tears which streaked down his cheeks mingling with the food he chewed in angry, impotent bites. When he finished the food, she threw the plate against the wall. It did not break, bouncing off the wall and rolling to a rest beside a sack of potatoes.

Before he left, he told my great-grandfather that he wanted to build a house on the property. In the months he had lived with my grandmother, he was desperate to marry her.

My great-grandfather was ashamed of what my great-grandmother did to his son. The request was not at all unreasonable and he would have granted it out of hand. However, there was the question of my great-grandmother.

My father says that my great-uncles came to the rescue. They saw that my great-grandmother was carrying things too far. They knew it was useless to talk to her about it and they prevailed upon my great-grandfather to give my grandfather a small piece of land that wasn't much good for anything. The best part about it was the distance from the main ranch house. In their spare time, they would build the house for my grandfather since it was too far for him to come from Shiner to do it.

My great-uncles had some money coming to them from my great-grandfather. They told him they would take the piece of land in payment and then they urged him to advance them some money for materials. They promised to pay back the money between them. It took some doing, but my great-grandmother went along with it mainly because she had no good argument against it, at least, not where my great-uncles were concerned. It was a cash deal.

It took nearly a year for them to finish the house. My grandfather and my grandmother did not know anything about it at all. More important to them was the baby they were expecting. My grandfather worried about his first child being born a bastard. My grandmother didn't give a shit, either way. It wasn't any of her doing. Anyway, whether married or not, she would still love her child.

My great-uncles made the journey to Shiner to tell my grandfather he could come home now. They had papers to the land and they had finished the house for him. He could get married. My grandfather was relieved and overjoyed. Instead of proposing to her again, all my grandfather did was present the deed to her. My grandmother didn't display one bit of emotion.

My grandfather stayed on with the German to finish out the harvest year before moving back to Schoolland. He and my grandmother were married before a judge in Gonzales with only my great-uncles present. My great-grandparents didn't care to attend the ceremony and her brothers didn't bother.

My grandmother's baby was stillborn. My grandfather was heartbroken. My grandmother was up and about in no time at all and whatever she felt, she kept inside.

My great-grandmother died in her sleep. She had been her usual self the evening before when she went to bed and in the morning she didn't get up. She was just gone.

My great-uncles, when they came for my grandfather and grandmother, couldn't understand it. My great-grandfather sat at the kitchen table, drinking his coffee as usual, half-expecting my great-grandmother to periodically refill his cup for him.

When my grandmother came in, she went directly to the bedroom where my great-grandmother lay. One arm rested across her breast while the other lay extended at her side. My grandmother closed the door behind her and began to prepare her mother-in-law for burial. She chose the one black dress for my great-grandmother to be buried in. My grandfather and one of my great-uncles went to town to get some fresh lumber to build a box for her. My great-grandfather remained in the kitchen, sipping his coffee, oblivious to everything.

Most of the family is buried in Wrightsboro, for no particular reason other than it is convenient for everyone in the family to get to. It was there that they went to dig the grave.

My grandfather and his brothers carried the coffin out to a mule-drawn wagon where they placed it with one end on the ground and the other on the wagonbed. They removed the lid. A photographer had been hired to take pictures. My grandfather and great-grandfather stood on one side and my great-uncles stood on the other. After the pictures were taken, they began the long ride to Wrightsboro.

Shortly thereafter, my great-grandfather had a stroke which left him bedridden for many months. My grandmother went out to care for my great-grandfather. My grandfather did a little farming on his little patch; mostly, though, he hired out for day work.

One afternoon, my great-grandfather began to toss and turn in his bed, making noises like he was choking. By the time my grandmother got to him, the second stroke had killed him.

There was quite a bit of insurance money coming. My grandmother took to handling the business for my great-uncles. With my grandfather's share, they bought more land, which she kept separate.

After the passing of my grandparents, my great-uncles lost interest in ranching and farming. They borrowed on their share of the ranch and they took a trip to New Orleans where they stayed for several months until their money gave out. When they returned, they spent a lot of time lying around the house they had built for my grandmother. There was the matter of my great-grandfather's place, which my grandmother wanted badly. She didn't have the money to buy it and my great-uncles didn't say they wanted to sell it. Instead, the three brothers made a handshake agreement whereby my grandfather would work the land and turn over to them their share of the increase in money. Other than borrowing against their share, this was the only interest they took in the place.

By the time the Great War came, my father had a sister and a brother. My great-uncles had settled into a life where they went off for days, sometimes weeks, to drink and gamble. They would return, spend a few days until they got restless enough to ask my grandfather for an advance on the money they had coming and then they would disappear.

One of my great-uncles had strayed away as far as Victoria, where he took a room behind a saloon. He awoke one morning, sick from the drink he'd had and sick of the way he was living. He decided to go back to farming, but didn't have the money to come back right away and so he enlisted in the Army. He was sent to France where he was killed.

My other great-uncle was mortally wounded in Gonzales in a saloon gunfight just a year later. It wasn't even his fight, but he got caught in the crossfire. A doctor had patched him up as best as could be done and my great-uncle was brought home by some friends. In all the commotion to bring my great-uncle into the house without killing him, no one particularly noticed the young girl and the baby. She remained outside the whole time and it wasn't until she came in to ask for some milk that anybody noticed her. She was sixteen years old and the baby was my great-uncle's son. Her name was Teresa, and the baby was named Simon, after my great-uncle who died in France.

My grandmother, uncharacteristically for her, became very excited about the girl and the baby. She made a big deal out of it and made the little girl welcome and comfortable. It took my great-uncle about two weeks to finally die. Teresa had enough to do with her baby and so my grandmother took care of him and her children, too.

Teresa spent almost every minute of every day with my great-uncle, sitting in a rocking chair in the room with him. When the baby got too heavy for her arms, she placed him beside his dying father. My great-uncle never even knew they were there.

After my great-uncle died and was buried, Teresa and little Simon became members of the family. It was as though my grandmother now had two more children to care for. Teresa stayed with the family for several years fleshing out into a full-grown woman, devoting herself entirely to her little boy. She was known as my great-uncle's widow, even though they had never married.

My grandfather argued that she was in fact his brother's widow, if for no other reason, because of the child. When my great-uncle died in the war, my great-grandfather's place would have been divided in half, and one half of it now belonged to the baby, Simon, if not to his mother. My grandmother wasn't keen on it, but she wasn't going to take what didn't belong to her. And so my grandmother who took care of the finances, began to set aside one half of the ranch earnings for little Simon and his mother.

During the yearly round-up, where all the neighbors came to help, my grandfather rode back and forth, keeping an eye on things. He sat atop his horse, watching some cows go into the corral, waiting to drag the gate shut, when he fell to the ground. He was dead at the age of twenty eight.

Not long after, Teresa brought home her new man to ask my grandmother permission to marry. My grandfather had treated her as a sister-in-law while my grandmother treated her as one of her children. My grandmother knew she had to respect my grandfather's wishes and it came as a surprise to Teresa that she and little Simon were the owners of half of my great-grandfather's place. She told Teresa that she wanted the land and would buy her out just as soon as she got the lawyer in Nixon to draw up the papers. The money lasted them for a few good years, after which, Simon's stepfather settled into being a good father to him and the other children he had with Teresa.

My grandmother turned out to be a pretty good businesswoman. She managed to keep the place against the odds and despite all kinds of offers to buy it and threats to take it away from her. She took pity on an Anglo sharecropper and hired him for a while. From the very first day, the Anglo son-of-a-bitch decided to cheat my grandmother. But there was not a human being alive who could cheat my grandmother and get away with it. When my grandmother confronted the Anglo about his cheating, he figured he could get rough with her, being that she was a woman and a Mexican. He grabbed her by the hair and threw her to the ground. He told her from now on it was his place, one hundred percent, and for her not to come around no more.

She went home and got her thirty-thirty and rode back on the same horse from which my grandfather had fallen to his death. My grandmother rode right up to the shack where the Anglo lived and fired one shot into the porch. The Anglo came out, mad as hell. He was trying to load an old Civil War revolver when my grandmother calmly aimed the rifle and shot him through the fleshy part of his arm. That took the fight out of the gringo altogether. She ordered him off her place.

The gringo filed a complaint with the sheriff, who came out, saw the proof that my grandmother had showed the gringo was a thief and that was the end of that.

Once the bullshit with the gringo was settled, my grandmother sort of got the reputation that she was indeed someone to respect. She paid damned good wages and most of the cow hands liked working for her because she was not above getting into the work with them and putting in as good a day as they did. Better than most other bosses, she would get into her Model T and go to Gonzales on Sunday mornings to get her cow hands out of jail. So long as they were at work on Monday mornings, she wasn't too particular about what they did the rest of the time. In fact, she probably expected that they would get drunk and in trouble and she expected that it was up to her to help them out.

In 1933, when my father and mother were married, my grandmother took in the surviving widow of one her brothers. Her brothers and their wives had not been particularly kind to her, but she felt a responsibility toward them anyway. She did make it clear, however, that the widow would earn her keep and a little money besides, by taking care of the house for her.

My father, without my grandmother seeming to notice very much, grew to his manhood. When my father decided to get married, rather than parcel out what she had worked so hard to put together, she prevailed upon the owner of the adjacent piece of land to sell it to her as a homestead for my father. It was about ten acres altogether. In a bold move for the time, she moved my great-grandfather's house, all in one piece, to my father's homestead.

My grandmother had lived with her tuberculosis for years, keeping the fact of it secret from the family. She went to see a doctor in San Antonio who tried for years to get her to spend some time in the sanatorium. But she refused because she could not bear to be away from her work. Instead, she lived on her medicines, being very scrupulous in the things she touched, to make sure she didn't pass it on to anyone else in the house.

She kept her contact with the children to a minimum. She also set aside her own tableware and utensils, cleaning them herself, to avoid the contagion. As she kept her illness to herself, she was perceived as a cold and distant woman and that, too, was fine with her. For most of her life, my grandmother was a tall and sturdy woman. As she got on in years, little by little, day by day, she simply began to shrivel as the disease began to claim more and more of her strength. She withered away until on some days she did not have the strength to ride her truck. And, then, later, she would spend long days in bed without either the strength or the will to be up and about.

My father who worked for her as a ranch hand, took over as foreman, the job which she had always reserved for herself. She knew she was dying and she tried to teach as much as she knew to my father.

In 1939, she passed away at the age of fifty-eight.

When my grandmother died, my father found that running the ranch by himself was not as easy as he thought. The ranch hands both feared and respected my grandmother, as she thought nothing of whacking one of them across the face with her ever-present quirt. They were not, however, afraid of my father and he had yet to earn their respect.

My father made a couple of wrong decisions, which caused him to lose a couple of hands he could ill afford to lose. If being the ramrod over cowhands was all there was to it, then my father would have made a go of it. It was the making of deals with cattle buyers, keeping track of the sharecroppers, paying the hands and borrowing money from the bank that did him in. Once he was reduced to the homestead place and a small herd of cattle, he was much better off.

At home, our family was growing; my brothers and sisters kept arriving every eighteen months to two years. My grandmother's sister-in-law had gone from a servant to a companion and, following my grandmother's death, she expected that my mother would wait on her as she had waited on my grandmother. She stayed in my grandfather's house, refusing a bed in my father's house. My mother had to cook and deliver three meals a day to her and she had to do everything else the woman demanded. My mother took it until she decided not to take it anymore.

My father then found the woman's children, who were by now grown and living near Hebbronville, and told them that, as he had his own family to care for, he could not afford to take care of their mother. They weren't too happy about it, figuring that after so many years the woman had rights on the place. Besides, my father owned land and they didn't and he ought to be able to afford it. They ignored my father's request that they come for her. My father finally packed her up in the truck and took her down to Hebbronville himself. Her children weren't too happy about it, but they took her in.

Several weeks later, they brought her back. My father had rented out the house and there were people living in it already. My mother told them there was no room in her house for the woman. Her children then told my father that it was going to cost them extra to take care of her and wanted my father to send them money. My father promised he would, but he didn't.

My grandmother left the ranch to my father outright, making a provision that he always take care of his brother and sister. My aunt and uncle hardly ever came to visit, which meant my father didn't have to make any provision for them.

My grandfather's house was lived in on and off for about ten years. There wasn't as much money in farming or ranching as there had once been. And my father was not as astute in the business of it as my grandmother had been. He borrowed a lot of money at the wrong time and then was not able to pay it back. He had to sell a small ten acre piece to keep from going to court. Right after the Second World War ended, my father had lost most of my grandmother's herd and all but a hundred acres or so of the land.

My father tried as best he could to make a go of things. It was a matter of bad luck and hard times. No one could fault my father, though, because he had worked very hard all of his life.

The sharecroppers went with the land. One by one, he let go of the hands who had been with us since my grandmother ran the place. My brothers were growing up and he relied on them to keep things going.

Except for renting out my grandfather's house from time to time and mostly loaning it to friends, relatives and neighbors in dire straits, the house was rarely used and it fell into disrepair; then we began to use it as a storage shed for cottonseed and as a playhouse.

No one was pleased with what Marcos de la Fuente did to the house. There was too much of the lives of our ancestors in it.

# Chapter 13

As we drove by my grandfather's house, we marveled at how grotesque it looked after its butchering at the hands of Marcos de la Fuente. I sat in the middle, between Elpidio who was driving and my father, who smoked another of his Bull Durham cigarettes.

"God damn," was all my father could say as he looked at how much Marcos de la Fuente had done to the house.

"Did you give him permission to do that?" asked Elpidio.

"Hell, I don't know what I gave him permission to do. What do you think?" said my father.

"I think you didn't know what the shit he was asking for," said Elpidio, who understood what my father said in the first place.

My father chuckled. "You could tell me a lie, you know."

"Wouldn't change things," said Elpidio.

"I guess not." He tousled my hair. "Let this be a lesson to you, squirt."

"Me? I didn't let the son of a bitch do anything."

"Listen to the little shit, Pa," Elpidio sneered.

"I didn't teach him any of that," said my father.

"Well, you can guess where we got it, then," said Elpidio.

"Anyway, all I'm worried about is what else Marcos is going to want," my father said in a resigned voice.

"I can tell you that already," said Elpidio.

"Don't tell me. I don't want to know. Not just yet, leastwise," said my father.

"What is it? I want to know," I said.

"Actually, I think there is something you should know, Pa," said Elpidio. "I ran into Tony Arreola over in Nixon a couple of days ago. He said he had seen Juana and she didn't want to talk to him."

"I thought she and Tony already had some kind of an understanding. With things the way they are between don Antonio and us, I figure it's hard on them, too," he said, hunching his shoulders to think a little.

"Tony says the wetback has been sniffing around her," said Elpidio.

"That's not a nice way for him to be talking, is it?" said my father.

"Probably not. The point is, Marcos has been paying a lot of attention to Juana. Too much. And, Juana seems to spend all of her time either with him or talking about him," said Elpidio.

"Juana is going to marry Marcos," I said.

"Don't be starting any rumors, squirt," said Elpidio.

"It's bad enough that that damned old fool still holds a grudge over Paulie and that goddamned dog of his," said my father. "I don't want Tony or the girls getting in on it."

"Well, shit, I promised not to tell anyone, but I guess I better. And you had just better forget you heard any of this, squirt. Hear me?"

"I can keep a secret," I said.

"Elvira Arreola ran off with the Watkins drummer. She was gone for about a week before he brought her back."

"Is she the one you were after?" asked my father.

"Naw, she's too fat and ugly," said Elpidio. "Turns out the drummer promised to marry her and she went off with him. They got as far as Schulenburg because he was still on his route. I don't know all that much about it, but it was around Moulton or something that the drummer confessed to her that he already has a wife and children in Austin."

"Is she back home? How do you know this?"

"Well, he brought her back. Tony says the drummer just dropped her off at the entrance to their place and he took off, just like that."

"What the hell would you expect him to do? Go and ask forgiveness?" snapped my father, sarcastically. I couldn't tell what he was so angry about.

"I don't know, Pa. It's hard for me to think about something like that. I haven't told you the worst part. It wasn't the first time she was out with the drummer. She's going to have a baby."

"Jesus Christ! That poor girl. I'm not even going to guess about Antonio."

"Tony says the old man wanted to shoot her. Doña Matilde and the girls think he didn't mean it, but Tony thinks he does. He's been making her sleep outside ever since she came back. Won't let her in the house. Makes the girls take food out to her and everything."

"How's Elvira taking all this?" asked my father.

"Tony's afraid she's going crazy, or has gone crazy. Says she sits in the car and cries. Whines like a puppy dog and these big tears make her cheeks wet."

"He makes her sleep outside," said my father. "That's hard to believe."

"I only know what Tony told me. They're going to take her to San Antonio, see if doña Matilde's sister will take her in until the baby comes. There's also a good chance don Antonio will never allow her back home."

"And, who's gonna want to marry her, with the baby and all," I said.

"Well, we, and I mean all of you, had better stay out of it, Elpidio. I mean that. Don't get involved in it in any way. Don't even talk about it."

"That's why I didn't want to say anything about it."

"These things have a way of getting you mixed up in them and, before you know it, you're answering up for somebody else who doesn't owe you a damned thing. Bad business," said my father, "bad business."

"The reason I'm telling any of this, is that if Juana is getting sweet on the wetback, then Tony has reason to act squirrely as shit. That scares me. If Juana throws Tony over for a stranger she's only known a couple of months, then he's going to want to blame somebody."

"And you think he'll blame you, is that it?" asked my father.

"Nope, he knows me better than that. But, he sure as hell might go after Marcos. Wetbacks don't have it all that easy among our people, as it is."

"How do you feel about that?" My father was concerned.

"I just don't know. We've never had much to do with *mojados*, Pa. When you've hired them, you've always treated them same as anybody else. Besides, there just ain't been too many of them around these parts."

"Wiley Barnett says there's going to be a lot more of them around here," said my father.

"Don't get me wrong, I think Marcos is nice enough and everything. It's just that I think Tony has been expecting Juana to marry him ever since they were in school together. The damned thing of it, Tony is my friend and, hell, I've been expecting him to be my brother-in-law. In fact, he's already asked me to be his best man when the time comes."

"I don't suppose Juana knows anything about this?" said my father.

"Naw, not at all. It's always been something we all have known from a long time ago. You knew it, too, Pa. Even don Antonio has mentioned it to me. It don't seem right that all of a sudden, things are so different and none of us knows what's gonna happen next."

"What the hell's been the matter with Tony? He's been working steady now for three or four years, hasn't he?"

"Yeah, I guess, about that long," Elpidio sounded defensive.

"Is it because of that whore he was seeing in Yorktown, or Karnes City or wherever it was?"

"How'd you find out about that?" Elpidio was nervous, surprised.

"You know there aren't too many secrets in Schoolland," said my father, tired.

"I guess not. To answer your question, I think he gave her up or she gave him up a long time ago." Elpidio thought of something else. "Now that you mention it, there was a gringo that was going out with the woman at the same time. One of the girls who worked with her in the saloon told Tony where she lived and Tony went out there."

"You didn't go with him?"

"No! Shit no! I wasn't even there. He goes out to her house and he finds the gringo there with her. So he calls the gringo outside. Apparently, from what Tony says anyway, he was a big son of a bitch. And, Tony, short shit that he is, throws a punch at the guy. Tony says the guy stepped out of the way and threw a big bear hug on him and told him he didn't want to fight. Not over her, anyway. The gringo tells Tony that if he wants her that bad, he'd just as soon be on his way, being as he hadn't paid her anyway."

My father broke out laughing. "God damn!" was all he said.

"Old Tony never figured she was a whore. He said he was even thinking of marrying her. Then he said . . . , no, that wasn't it at all. Then he said he couldn't figure out what the shit was going on."

"Seems like I recall times like that when I was the same age," said my father, and a small, wistful smile crossed his face. "And now, you think Tony is liable to cause some trouble for us, is that it?"

"I couldn't tell you that for sure, Pa. Tony's expecting me to tell him everything I know about Juana and the wetback. Trouble is, I don't know anything. If there is something going on with those two, they sure keep it to themselves. Maybe it just looks like something is going on, that's all."

"If there is something going on, your sister is getting to be a sensible woman. It's not our place to interfere. In any case, whatever happens, we have to think of your sister first."

"Yeah, you're right there. Thing is, Daddy, Tony's going to find out sooner or later if there is something going on. I think he's going to want to fight Marcos over her."

"That's likely, I expect. And if we're lucky, that's all there will be. A nice fistfight. Sometimes it's a good thing to have a nice fistfight. Thing to do is not worry about doing anything and just wait and see what we can see."

"I guess you're right. I think I'm getting to be like Grandpa. I feel something is going to happen."

"Speaking of Grandpa, how's he doing?" asked my father, who took to calling him "Grandpa" after the rest of us.

"He's still digging. I went out to feed my mare and he's been using my good rope, probably to haul dirt. It was muddy as hell."

"Well, it keeps him busy working at something. And, how're you doing with your school work, squirt?" he asked.

"Okay, I guess."

"Okay? What the hell kind of an answer is that?" said Elpidio.

"Okay means okay, shithead! I don't want to go to school anymore."

"I'm afraid there's no help for you on that count, squirt. Your mother has got herself convinced that you're going to be the first of her sons to finish school. She's even talked of sending you off to college," he said.

"You'll probably become a priest, squirt," said Elpidio, laughing.

"Bullshit," I said.

"If Paulie had quit after the first day, your mother wouldn't have cared either way. In your case, she's got her heart set on it. I've known your mother a long time and I don't see that she's going to change her mind. It'll probably make your life a whole lot easier if you just go along with it, seeing that there ain't no way out of it. Come to think of it, it would make my own life a whole lot easier."

"Looks like you better start doing better than okay, squirt. You're in for it," said Elpidio.

"Listen, boy, I got something for you to do. Tomorrow I want you to do a favor for me. Stay home from school and go with your grandfather. Take the black, he's gentle enough."

"I can ride any of those scrawny nags we got," I said.

"You're not going to get out of graduating from school by breaking your neck," said Elpidio.

"Don't let on to your grandfather that I put you up to this, you understand? Just say you want to go with him, or something. Start in on him tonight. Tell him you want to see what he's doing, maybe you can help him. Something like that."

"Can I tell him I believe him when he says we are in for a long drought?" I said.

"You don't have to lie to him, son. I mean, it's one thing to spare his feelings, but lying to him is something else again." My father was uncomfortable when it came to lying.

"What if I really believe him?"

"You'd be the only one, then," said Elpidio.

"Well, I do," I said.

"Don't make something out of it that it isn't, that's all. I want you to find out where he's digging and from now on, I want you to go out there when you get home from school. You can get in a couple of hours helping him before he quits for the day," said my father.

"Isn't that going a little too far with it, Daddy?" said Elpidio.

"Maybe so. My father used to go out riding all the time. He had no use for motor cars. He bought an old truck once, but he could never get the hang of it right. I was seven or eight then and I could drive it better than he could. If he had to go to Candy's Grocery, he would go on horseback. One of the hands told me one time he thought my father wasn't quite right in the head. He meant that my father would round up the cattle when there was little need for it. When they were ready to sell calves or something, they could've ridden out to the herd and cut them out. Not my father, though. He wanted the entire goddamn herd brought in. I remember my mother getting so damned mad at him for that. It was a waste of time and money, she would say to him, but he liked working cattle and riding around on his horses. He dreamt of having thousands of cows just so he could be out with them every day.

"He had a palomino with the bushiest mane and tail I ever saw, and he had a bay pony that he used for cattle work. I was nine years old when one day one of the hands came to me and said, 'looks like your Pa's having such a good time he's fallen asleep in the saddle.' Well, they decided to play a joke on my daddy, but as they were coming up to the bay pony, the animal spooked and my father just fell over. He just leaned to one side and dropped down. All I can remember after that is when we ran over to him, one of the hands was feeling around his head to see if he crashed into something. All he said was, 'he's cold already!' Only thing anyone could figure was my daddy had been dead for a while, still sitting on his horse."

My father became silent for a while. Suddenly, he said, "Imagine that! He died on his horse. Goddamn!"

"And you don't want that to happen to Grandpa," said Elpidio.

My father took his time in responding. "More than seeing my father slumped over the saddle was a thought I had that he could have been out riding alone and he would have died out on the range. Maybe his horse wouldn't make it back to the barn. It might take us a long time to find him because there weren't that many fences in those days and he didn't always stay on our land. He just wandered wherever his horse had a mind to go, sometimes. The coyotes or the buzzards could have gotten to him and that's what scares me the most."

"That was in the old days, Pa," said Elpidio. "Everything's fenced up now. We ain't got hardly any land at all here. Wouldn't take us any time at all to find Grandpa if something were to happen to him. Besides, there's not much place for the horses to roam, and they'd head right back home. Shit, it's all anyone can do just to get the lazy bastards out of the horseshed."

"You're right, I know you're right. Still, I can't get the thought out of my head. Seeing Father eaten by coyotes and buzzards."

"There's something strange about that, Daddy," said Elpidio.

At that point, I had an image of the dogs jerking around rabbit skins and entrails and I imagined it was grandfather. A chill went through me.

Elpidio turned the truck into the wide driveway to the house. Jose's truck was there, as was Elpidio's car. And, there was another car we had not seen before.

"Who's that?" asked my father.

"Beats me," said Elpidio.

"Celia wrote to Juana last week, said they got a new car. That must be it," I volunteered.

"They never come visit during the week. Maybe something's wrong," said my father.

"Yeah, that goddamned Frank of hers gets into more shit than any two human beings combined. Maybe he lost his job, again," said Elpidio, angrily.

"Shit, that's all we need now, two more mouths to feed," said my father.

"Five, Daddy, there's the kids," I said.

# Chapter 14

My sister Celia wore a red dress which was not very becoming to her. She also wore too much makeup. When somebody pointed it out to her, Celia said it was the way women were in San Antonio. What with the makeup and the matronly heft that her hips were taking, my sister Celia appeared much older than her twenty-two years.

She cradled her newest baby, a dark-skinned little thing with Indian features, in her right arm. In the other, she held a cup of coffee. My father went into the kitchen first. Celia stood up to greet him, turning to one side so as not to crush the baby between them when she hugged my father.

My father took an obligatory look at the wrinkled face of the baby, making a face.

"Ugly little thing, isn't he?" he said. "Where's the rest of those creatures of the wild that you call children?"

"Papa, stop it! We just got here and you're trying to make us feel like you're not happy to see us," said Celia.

My father turned to my mother. "What's she so nervous about?"

"You better behave yourself, old man," said my mother.

"I'm not old, woman," said my father, "but I will be if you keep talking to me that way. You treat me like an old fool, sometimes."

"It's the way you act that calls for it," said my mother.

Celia came around to greet Elpidio and me, and to show off her baby. Elpidio and I made cooing noises at the baby, wiggling a finger over his face, and said nice things about his looks. Celia's other two kids, we discovered, were in the boys' bedroom where little Albert and little Julian were using them as toys. A screech from the bedroom brought a look of concern from Celia.

"Are they all right in there?" she asked.

"Juana, go see what they're doing," said my mother.

While Juana ran out of the kitchen, my father settled down at the table with a cup of coffee.

"Is Frank working? Why didn't he come?"

Celia turned her head away and then inclined her face to see about the baby. My father looked up toward my mother who gave him a signal with a nod of her head to go easy on her. There was a long pause during which no one said anything and no one wanted to say anything.

It was obvious that my mother and my sisters had already had a long talk about whatever had brought Celia home. It seemed to me that they had decided as well how much to tell my father in front of the boys. My mother would tell the rest of it to my father in one of their pre-dawn talks. It was during these talks that they decided all of the family business and other important things. Once or twice I had interrupted them. From the way they hushed when I came in on them, it was always something just between them.

"You might as well tell him, Celia," said my mother.

"Frank left me," said my sister Celia.

I had expected her to begin crying or something, but she spoke evenly and calmly as if she had gotten all the rest of it out of her system long before.

I remember when she first got married and Frank took her to live in San Antonio. For many months, each time they came to visit, Celia would break out crying for no apparent reason. My mother explained that Celia was homesick, as she had never been away from home. Heriberto, when he married, lived nearby and so it was like he still lived with us. He and his wife came to visit every other day, it seemed. My sister Celia was the first to get married and, except for me, the only one who had left School-land for good.

No one said anything in response to Celia's revelation about Frank leaving her. She would tell us about it, sooner or later. All we had to do was wait for her to take her own time.

My sister Celia handed the baby over to my brother Jose, who stood closest to her. Jose took the baby, fearing that Celia would drop him if he didn't. Once the baby was safe in his arms, Jose looked helpless. He looked beseechingly at my sister and realized that she had no intention of taking him back for the moment. Jose appealed to my mother for help.

"Just hold the baby, Jose," said my mother, "and be careful."

Jose had no idea what that meant and so he held the baby as if it would break any minute. Celia left the kitchen to look after her other children.

"He sure is ugly," said Paulie, trying to lighten up the moment.

"Takes after his mother," I said.

My mother turned to me angrily. "You!" she said, "one more remark and off you go, you'll sleep with the pigs, tonight."

"What's this about Frank leaving Celia?" asked my father.

My mother had been crying all along. I never saw her shed tears, exactly, not even when someone died. The tip of her nose would become red from her constant daubing at it with a handkerchief. That's how we could tell she was crying.

"He left her. What more do you want?" said my mother.

"Man doesn't just walk out on a wife and three kids," said my father.

"There has to be a reason."

"Why don't you go find him and ask him, then?" said my mother, turning her back to everyone.

The rest of us shifted uncomfortably wherever we stood or sat. My father was very aware of it.

"Well, now," he said, clasping his hands together. "Where's Grandpa? Is he back, yet?"

Elpidio moved to the back kitchen door and pulled the curtain aside. "My mare is in the corral, so he must be back already."

"He hasn't come in at all?" asked my father.

My mother answered without turning to face us. "He's been going directly to bed after work everyday. Sometimes he doesn't eat supper. I'm worried about him."

"He's stronger than all of us put together," said Jose, bouncing the baby. After his initial fear of dropping him, he now enjoyed holding him. It wasn't until the baby pissed on him that he panicked again.

Celia and Juana came back to the kitchen, visibly worn out from separating the twins from the kids, or vice versa.

"Why did Frank leave?" asked Elpidio.

It was what we all wanted to know and he thought it would be better to ask directly.

"I don't know," said my sister Celia. "Frank has had about four different jobs in the last year. It's mostly because of his drinking and he fights all the time with the people he works with. So, he gets fired."

"I never thought Frank was like that," said Jose.

"He wasn't. It's just in the last year," said Celia. She couldn't hold back anymore and she burst into tears.

My sister Juana, trying to be helpful, handed her a dishtowel. My sister Celia covered her face with it.

"Leave her alone, now," ordered my mother.

My father thought for a moment. "What do you boys think about all this, anyway?" he said.

Before anyone could answer, Grandpa come in. It was Grandpa who answered my father's question.

"I think we ought to sit down and eat. Never saw a family that talked so damned much," said my grandfather. "What's for supper, anyway."

"That's right," said Paulie, "let's eat! All this bullshit makes me hungry."

My mother went into a panic. "Juana, what are we going to do about supper?" she yelled.

"I don't know," said my sister Juana. "There's beans, that's all. We can fry some bacon and corncakes to go with them."

"No, that's not a meal," said my mother.

"I'll go to Smiley and get something," said Juana.

"Good," said my mother. "Bologna, cheese and a loaf of bread. No, get two loaves."

"Celia can go with me."

My father hated bologna, as did most of us. We were forced to eat it when we worked too far away from home and we had to take something to eat in the fields. But, we never liked it. Any other time, my father would not allow it in the house. He took five dollars out of his pocket and handed them to Juana.

"Here, stop at don Pedro's and see if he's got some meat. If not, go to the Red and White, see what they have. I don't see that we have to eat bologna. Tell your mother to give you some more money so you'll have enough."

"What the hell are we going to do in the meantime, anybody?" said my grandfather.

The great feast to celebrate my sister Celia's arrival consisted of bologna and cheese sandwiches for the little children and there was fried steaks in a red chile gravy for the rest of us. It was late when we ate and after supper my mother and my sisters went into the my parent's bedroom to gossip some more. Probably stuff they would be embarrassed to say in front of anybody but themselves. The kids went to the big bedroom to play and fight. Elpidio said he was going to visit the Arreola's. He told no one in particular that he had some things he wanted to talk about with Tony.

Being that it was a warm enough night, the rest of us went to sit on the porch. I lay at one side of the porch, where a steady wind flowed in layers over me. Once in a while, a stray chill raised goosebumps on my forearms. But, it was mostly warm and pleasant.

My father tried to limit himself to three cigarettes a day and he was smoking the last of them. My father smoked his cigarettes regular as clockwork. In the morning, he went to the outhouse where he rolled his first cigarette. We had an indoor toilet but only my mother and sisters used it. My father stayed in the outhouse until he had smoked the cigarette down to the point where it burned his fingertips. The second one he smoked after lunch. Wherever he was, he would take out his tobacco pouch and fiddle with it, twirling it in his fingers, bouncing it up and down; anything to delay rolling the cigarette. He knew he was going to do it but he delayed it, savoring the thought of it until the very last moment. When he finally made one, we knew that we had to return to work once he put it out. The last one was at night, as soon as supper was over.

Grandpa sat in his straight-back chair. My brother Jose sat on the porchsteps, strumming his guitar. Paulie was feeling playful and he kept punching Jose on the shoulder trying to pick a fight. Were Jose to put aside the guitar, Paulie would as likely take off running to keep from being wrestled to the ground, or worse, having his ears boxed. Jose had discovered that tapping Paulie on one of his ears made Paulie's eyes water. Once that happened, Paulie would give up. My brother Jose had fists which were disproportionately large to his muscular arms and with just a light tap, Paulie stopped being a pain in the ass. Knowing there was a risk to it, in fact, enjoying the danger of it, Paulie kept taunting Jose. He made sure, however, that he could spring out of the way in the event that Jose got tired of it.

Jose began to play *Camino de Guanajuato,* making the guitar whine, mournful and sweet, the way Antonio Bibriesca did in the movies. Paulie started to sing, straining to stay on key. He had a raspy voice that drifted into a pig-like squeal from time to time, but undaunted, Paulie held on to the tune even though it seemed like another song altogether.

"Makes you wonder," began my grandfather, speaking to my father, "what it was that makes the Lord give one man more decent children than you can count on the fingers of one hand and then He gives him another child like Paulie."

Jose kept playing his guitar and smiled when he heard Grandpa. Paulie was too busy concentrating on keeping up with the guitar to have heard him. My father took his time in answering, as if he were considering the gravity of Grandpa's comment.

"It's the law of averages, Grandpa," said my father. "The way I figure it, no man's luck can hold out for the long run. You gotta come up snake eyes, sometime."

"If you're gambling, that's true enough," said Grandpa. "In the matter of children, I don't know. I just can't say."

"No one can, Grandpa. That's the shit of it."

"Maybe so," said Grandpa. "I think I'll get in some reading tonight before I turn in." Grandpa said goodnight to us and walked off the porch.

# Chapter 15

It was a clear night with the stars high up in the sky. To the south we could see the haze from the lights of Smiley. Without the breeze, it was a warm enough night but when the wind did pick up I could feel the sting of cold that it carried. Grandpa stopped at the bottom of the porchstairs to stretch his arms and then continued on to the bunkhouse. I walked with him, staying a step or two behind.

"Where do you think you're going, boy," said my grandfather.

"Just making sure you don't get lost, Grandpa," I said, trying to be funny.

Grandpa snorted, and I felt good that it was as adult a response as I ever got from him.

"You want something, do you, squirt?" said my grandfather, going into the bunkhouse. "I never rush a man on his talk. If's he's got something to say, he'll get to it when he's ready."

Inside the bunkhouse, he went for his bunk and sat down; the flat boards that supported the mattress seemed to sag under his weight. He placed his large, rough hands on his knees. He kept his silence, waiting for me to come out with what I had to say.

"Grandpa, can I go with you to see that well you're digging," I asked.

"What for?" he said. It was not a question, it was more of an irritation.

"Maybe I want to learn about these things, sometimes, Grandpa," I said. "And, how am I going to learn if nobody teaches me anything and I don't get to see nothing."

"What about your brothers? Don't they teach you nothing besides how to make a fool of yourself?"

"Yeah, I guess so. They're not digging any wells, though. You could teach me that, I want to learn how to dig a well," I said.

"What the hell for? They got digging rigs now, with machines and motors. You won't have to dig a well, ever. You can hire somebody to do it," he said.

"Maybe. But, you're digging one. How come you didn't get one of those digging rigs?"

"I ain't got the damned money to pay anybody to do it for me, squirt, and that's the damned truth!" I knew he was telling me a part of the truth, but not all of it.

"You're always saying you never know when something you learned a long time ago can come in handy," I said.

"You just watch your father, see how he does things, that's more teaching than anybody could give you. Your father knows what he can do and he does it well. You couldn't ask for better than that."

"I just thought you might let me come out with you tomorrow, that's all," I said, dejectedly. My grandfather had not heard me.

"You can learn more things by just watching people. Watch how they do things. If you sit on your ass and let them jaw at you all day, well, you might learn a thing or two. But, unless you actually see how it's done and then do it for yourself, it ain't worth a rat's ass."

"Well, that's just about all I do in school, Grandpa. All those teachers ever do is tell us things. Sometimes, they show us a picture."

"That ain't what school is for, son. You've got to learn how to read and do your numbers. Besides, it seems your mother has plans for you that don't allow you to be a goddamned farm hand all of your life."

"What's wrong with being a farm hand, Grandpa? That's all you ever were and that's all my daddy's going to be, and my brothers, and every goddamned body I know. Why should I have to be different?"

"You won't be any different than any of us, squirt. Get that shit out of your head. You'll still be just like everybody else, except you won't be doing what we do for a living. That's all."

"We're not doing too bad, are we, Grandpa?"

"That's just it, son, you can't tell. You can't ever tell. No, we're not doing too bad right now. Unless I miss my guess, we'll be doing pretty bad before the year is out when the crops don't come in and your father has to start selling off some of the cattle. And, then, there's next year."

"You've seen it worse than this, haven't you, Grandpa. Things got better, didn't they?"

"Yeah, things get better. But, they don't go back to what they were. They never do. There used to be all kinds of people in Schoolland. It was good, rich land all around. Every time something like what's coming happens, we lose more of the people. And, it ain't just old fuckers like me who get tired of living and just die. The young ones, like you, go away. Without as many people to work the land, it don't produce nothing. The land goes back to being wild, except people leave scars on the land, scars that don't never heal."

"There's still a lot of people in Schoolland, Grandpa."

"Not like there used to be, son. Remember Schoolland like it is right this minute, with your family all around you. By the time you grow up, it will be changed. Schoolland will be like a widow woman whose children have left her for good. It'll be a gray, sad place. If you remember it the way it is right now, you'll always have that."

"You sound like I'm going away somewhere, Grandpa."

"You might, son, you just might."

"Is that why Ma says I should stay in school? So I can go away some day?"

"I don't think that's why she wants you in school, boy. I do know this much, if that's what she wants you to do, then I wouldn't fight it, boy. She's just like your grandmother. Maybe worse."

"You could talk her into letting me stay home from school tomorrow, Grandpa, then you could take me with you."

My grandfather thought for a minute and then became his gruff self, annoyed with me.

"I already told you, I don't need anyone to be watching me. And, I don't need any help. I know you all think I'm crazy with all this talk of a drought. Well, maybe I am crazy. But, it'll be good to have an extra well if there is no drought at all than to not have a well if there is one. You understand that much?"

"Yes, sir."

"Good. The other thing is more tricky. Now, don't get mad at me. It's all I can do to take care of my own self out there. I don't want to take you and have to look out for you, too."

"I won't be any trouble, Grandpa. I know it. Besides, you always like to talk and I could be somebody you could talk to. That way, you won't have to talk to yourself. I could learn to dig a well by watching you and I could learn other things by listening to you."

"That could be. I'm tempted to take you up on your offer, son, but don't get your hopes up. Your mother is damned difficult on a good day and impossible the rest of the time. I expect she'll be worried about your sister Celia for right now. And with Paulie leaving school, she might be afraid I'm leading you through to the path of perdition."

"The path of what?"

"Never mind. I'll talk to her in the morning. If you have your heart set on it, I'll see what I can do. You better be up and ready to go in case she's still half asleep when I talk to her and she gives her permission. We better be gone before she wakes up fully and changes her mind."

My father would as likely get permission for me to go before Grandpa asked. The only thing to do was get Grandpa to agree to take me along. Once I got Grandpa to agree, I had done what my father set me out to do.

"Goodnight, Grandpa, I'll be ready in the morning. I know you can do anything," I said, going out the door.

In the morning, everything had been arranged. My father and mother settled these things in their pre-dawn talks.

When I was awake earlier than usual, my mother asked, "what are you doing up?"

My father was already back from the outhouse, sitting over his cup of coffee. I walked behind him without saying a word, going to the back porch to wash.

"Friendly little cuss, isn't he," said my father into his coffee cup.

When I returned, my grandfather was also in the kitchen, drinking his coffee. He didn't look in my direction at all. I poured myself a glass of milk.

"I want to take this boy out today," said Grandpa.

"If you need some help, old man, I can send a couple of the boys tomorrow. I need them today, though," said my father.

"No, that's all right. I don't need any help," said my grandfather. "I just thought it might be good if the boy went out with me."

"So, that's what you two were talking about in the bunkhouse last night," said my mother, suspicious as ever.

"This may be the last time anyone ever hand digs a well in Schoolland. There's too much of the old way of doing things that's being lost, you know," said Grandpa, sadly.

"Maybe that's because the old ways just aren't good enough, Daddy," said my mother.

"Maybe so," said my grandfather. "When you do something with a machine, it just ain't the same."

"I think we've had this argument before, Grandpa," said my father.

"And we'll keep having it as long as I'm alive," said Grandpa.

"I wouldn't be surprised if they dug your grave with a machine. What about that?" said my father, chuckling in a low voice as he lifted up his cup of coffee.

"Won't make much difference to me when that happens," said my grandfather, testily. "As I said, I just thought maybe you wanted the boy here to learn something of the way things used to be."

"He needs to learn the new way of doing things, Daddy," said my mother. "When he's educated, he'll know how to do things quicker and better. You're still living like it was thirty years ago."

"It was good enough. It was always good enough," said my grandfather.

"You bought yourself a truck and you won't even use it. You have to go out on horseback everyday. If we hadn't taken over your place, you'd still be using mules to do the planting," said my mother.

My mother worried that since my grandmother's death, my grandfather had retreated far too much into the past. He talked more and more of the old days as if he had been plucked out of them and had been dropped into a time he didn't understand and didn't care for very much.

"That's not fair, my daughter. I was one of the first men in this county to learn how to use a tractor. You were probably too busy learning to paint your face to notice."

My father grinned at that one. He often told us how he had courted the prettiest woman in the county. He never knew, until after they were married, that what made her so pretty was the paint she put on her face. My father would say that he got the surprise of his life when he finally got to see her without the makeup. It was the woman he had married all right, only now she looked like somebody else. My mother would always slap him across the shoulders when he exaggerated like that.

"Go on," said my mother, in a threatening voice, to my father.

It was also a warning to my grandfather, except that she couldn't address him directly in that tone of voice.

"What for? That's all there is to tell," said my father, "anybody can figure out the rest of it."

"What about the boy?" said my grandfather.

I became impatient to know whether I was going to school or not. The three of them could go on talking forever, it seemed to me.

"Yeah, what about me, I want to go with Grandpa today," I said.

"It's all right with me," said my father, as if he didn't care one way or another.

My mother went into a fit. She was angered by my father's complacency. She accused him of being in favor of whatever it was that the children wanted and she accused him of letting her be the one with a firm hand. If it weren't for her, she said, we would all be mangy, ill-mannered brutes.

"They're your children, you do with them what you want," was all that my father said.

"I think the three of you planned this out." She pointed at me. "And, you, you didn't just wander out of bed at this hour. You were the one who started it all, am I right?"

"It was my idea," said my father speaking up, his face serious and his voice firm. "I think it would be a good idea if the boy went out with his grandfather for one day. It shouldn't hurt his school work. Right, squirt?"

"I don't think I'm the smartest son of a gun in class, but I get by," I said.

"Go ahead, go on and waste the day," she said, speaking to the wall behind the stove.

Turning to my grandfather, she added, "And, you, you watch that he doesn't fall into that hole you're digging and hurt himself. How deep have you gone, anyway?"

"I just started digging," said Grandpa.

"You've been out there every day for weeks," said my father.

"Took me a while to find the right place. I started one that went deeper than this one, but it's wasn't right. I'm ankle deep on this one right now."

"What are you going to use for shoring?" asked my father.

"I ain't gone that deep, yet," said my grandfather. "I'll think of that when I come to it. Looks like it'll be limestone and I won't need any. But, I don't know for certain right now. The ground is holding up pretty good. I get callouses on my brain if I think about it too much."

"Take a coat with you," said my mother to me.

"It's not cold outside, Ma," I said, resentful that she talked to me as she did to little Albert and little Julian. She said nothing further and I knew I was going to take a coat with me. Besides, although she had given permission for me to go without having said so exactly, we were still in the house and so long as we were there, she was in charge and she could change her mind, just like Grandpa said.

My mother had been frying eggs, one after the other, tossing them into a deep bowl. Ever since Marcos, the *mojado,* thought to win her over by bringing eggs to the house, we had eggs for breakfast every morning. Marcos de la Fuente would bring a handful of them every morning on his way to work. As he had a long way to go on foot, he was usually at the house long before anyone was up and he would place them on the back porch. With what he brought and our chickens laid, we ate more eggs than ever. On this morning, before the boys woke up, I was eating with the grown-ups and that was something special to me. As soon as we finished our breakfast, my grandfather arched an eyebrow and I knew right away that it was time for us to be off. My brothers Elpidio and Jose were just coming into the kitchen when Grandpa and I walked out into the increasing light of the morning. I was in front of Grandpa as we walked out to the horsesheds. The metal latch to the gate felt frozen and unyielding and I had to jerk it back and forth before it finally let loose and I could swing it open. Grandpa just stood behind me, snorting, with big mustaches of steam snaking out from his nostrils. I wore the jacket that my mother had warned me about and it wasn't quite as cold for me.

"Shouldn't we wait until there's more light, Grandpa?" I asked.

"You see why I don't want to bring anybody out with me," said Grandpa.

The horses must've thought it was feeding time and gathered quickly at the horseshed.

"Get me Elpidio's mare," said Grandpa.

None of our horses were so wild that they balked at being roped. In fact, all I had to do was walk up to the mare and slip the rope around her. That done, I simply led her over to where my grandfather waited. I brought her to Grandpa, slipping the rope off and going to stand at one side. The little mare just stood there, knowing that the bridle came next and then the saddle. The only thing she did was lower her head to the ground, shake her neck briskly and snort. My grandfather worked slowly and methodically, without much wasted motion, slipping the bridle over her forehead and behind her ears. My brothers would kid him about the slowness of his movements and how it took him forever to saddle up a horse. He invariably finished doing his part of things long before anyone else. Once he fastened the buckles the mare shook her neck again to make it comfortable.

"Grandpa, this is Elpidio's mare, right?" I asked, kicking a toeful of dirt in the mare's direction.

"We'll have shit to pay if it ain't," said Grandpa.

"We have four horses and none of them has a name. Why is that?" I asked.

"They're Mexican horses, that's why," said Grandpa.

"How come they don't have names? All the kids at school who ride horses have names for them. All I know is this is Elpidio's mare and that's Paulie's black. Not one of our animals has a name. Why is that?" I asked.

"I told you. They're Mexican horses who don't understand English and the ways of white people. These animals belong to Christian people, that's why."

"You mean, only white people name their animals?"

"That's right. Horses, cattle, sheep, dogs, cats. White people name every one of God's creatures. I wouldn't doubt it if there's white people who give names to snakes, mosquitoes or buzzards."

"Why is that, Grandpa?"

"I've always thought that a white man can't make life miserable for a living thing unless he can call it by a name of some kind. It ain't enough that there's horses and cows and sheep and dogs and cats. And trees and flowers and cactus. No, sir. The way I figured it out, if a white man can give an animal a name, it's almost like the poor creature is human. You see, this is all you have to know about white people. No matter how dirt poor they might be, they have to be better than somebody else, even if it's a goddamned animal. That's mostly why they give names to as many creatures of the woods as they can get their hands on.

"I thought about it, once. The way the Good Lord intended, names are for humans on account of all humans is different. Just so you know it's the Christian thing to do, we name every living child after a saint, on account of saints was the very best human beings who ever lived.

"Your name lets you know you're different from everybody else. It's a way, too, of letting you know that you're going to live long after you die. Mention your name and people will remember who you were. While we're still alive, we need names because we have to talk about people when they're not around. Otherwise, we could just point to everybody.

"Now, suppose you were some kind of idiot, like the one that comes out in the movies, Roy Rogers, if that's his name. Now, suppose you had a fine palomino and you named it Trigger. Now, there ain't no such thing as a Saint Trigger. But, then, there ain't a damned saint that's a gringo, either.

"Now, suppose you was in the desert and you didn't have water or food and you had to kill your horse to stay alive. Drink horseblood and eat horsemeat. You wouldn't want to do that to something you knew by name, would you?"

"I don't know, Grandpa. Don't seem like I would kill my horse just to stay alive."

"Yeah, you would. You just wouldn't want to, that's all. Difference of staying alive, that's all. Where you going?" he said.

"For the black. Pa says I can ride him."

"Boy, you don't even have a saddle and I ain't got the time to stand here while you stitch yourself a stirrup length to fit your legs. Besides, I ain't too sure you have permission from your brother Paulie to use his saddle like that."

"Well, how am I going to get out to the well?"

"We can ride double. You're not that heavy where this mare will mind your weight too much, and besides, we're not going that far."

"I don't want to ride double, Grandpa. That's for little kids."

"Little boys go to school whining, just like you're doing right now. You can ride double behind me or you can go on to school. Take your pick."

"I'll go with you."

"That's what I like to hear, no arguments," said Grandpa.

"You sure don't make things easy, Grandpa," I said.

"Wasn't my intention," he said, morosely.

My grandfather slipped the toe of his workshoe into the stirrup, hopped once or twice to get going, and easily swung himself into the saddle. He slipped his toe out of the stirrup for me and he leaned over so I could grab his arm. It wasn't graceful, but I got on the mare behind my grandfather.

We rode along the stand of mesquite and chaparral. There was a mixture of shadows and bright streaks of light all over the mesquite. My grandfather didn't need to guide Elpidio's mare. He simply let loose of the reins and she followed the meandering trails made by the horses and cows.

Elpidio's mare settled on a winding trail that cleaved to the barbed wire fence. The spindly chaparral brushed against our legs. Elpidio's mare liked to pace as she had been taught before Elpidio bought her. The mare knew that when Elpidio got on her, he liked for her to pace at an angle, almost as if she trotted sideways. Grandpa didn't have the patience for that kind of fancy riding. Not on a working morning. His idea of a good horse was one with four legs and a head that didn't think too much, better yet, a head that didn't think at all, so it wouldn't spook. More than anything Grandpa demanded a horse that could be ridden all day without working up too much of a sweat. A light eater was even better, but sometimes that was too much to hope for.

Elpidio's mare that morning swayed from side to side, not minding the extra weight so much as the division of it on her back.

The way my grandfather rode, he remained erect in the saddle, neither his head nor shoulders wavering more than an inch either way. I had decided not to make more of a pest of myself than necessary and had not bothered to grab on to Grandpa's belt at the back as he told me to do. However, the swaying of the mare wobbled me to and fro so much that I thought I had better grab the cantle to keep from sliding off. Elpidio's mare wasn't that tall, but it was high enough from where I sat. What scared me the most were the thorns on the cactus where I would surely land if I fell.

We came to the barbed wire gate at the far end of the mesquite stand and I slipped down from the mare to open it. The gate wasn't exactly in disrepair, but the barbed wire was not as taut as it could be, which was fine because horses were not curious or anxious enough to knock it down to go graze on the bright green milo sprouts. I was able to open it with ease and pulled it aside only enough to allow Grandpa and the mare to get through.

# Chapter 16

We followed the old wagonroad that bordered the milo field. As we rode along, in the lows between the terraces I could see the milo sprouts which seemed to be a river of green to the eye, which then as it sloped upwards and downwards became thin, sparse ribbons.

During the time of Franklin Delano Roosevelt, some gringos had come by to tell the family that we had been farming all wrong and that they could make things better for us. With bulldozers and drivers from the government, and other men in white shirts and string ties looking through telescopes, they came to terrace the land. They left several long, snaking bumps in the land that circled around the slope of the land. It was meant to prevent water run off and soil erosion thus yielding better crops in the long run. Except, the government fuckers weren't the ones who would plow the land. The plowing became more dangerous as the tractors were thrown into a steep angle when following the rows of crops that curled and wound their way along the contours made by the terraces. My grandfather hated the terraces, claiming they gave the land an unnatural appearance.

Elpidio's mare was feeling frisky. Whenever Grandpa slackened the reins, she would speed up her pace into a slow trot. My grandfather tightened up in the saddle. It was too early in the morning to have a man's body shake and jerk. My feet dangled loosely and I was bounced up and down until he reined her pace in. When Elpidio's mare slowed to her long graceful strides, I swayed to and fro and then it wasn't so bad.

It was a gray, bleak morning with enough of a chill in the air to break through the haziness of sleep. Looking back, our house in the distance seemed stark and solitary just behind the crest of the hill. We were descending the slope of the land and I kept looking back until the house was swallowed up entirely.

I looked around my grandfather's shoulder to the westerly direction in which we were headed. A bright morning light shone all around us now. I could see the treeline off in the distance ahead of us. It seemed we were headed into a black pit.

My grandfather jerked his hat off his head and readjusted it.

The act was nothing more than a preliminary to something he was going to say.

"Look what those goddamned government dickheads did to this land! Land ain't supposed to look like that. It's bad enough that people have been clearing away every damned tree and every rock to plant God knows what shit that man was never intended to grow. Look at that!" said my grandfather.

"Daddy says those terraces are good for the crops," I said.

"Your daddy also uses store-bought fertilizers on the land and they say that's also good for the crops. That kind of farming might make you some money right away, but a real farmer has got to think about things that'll happen another day when it ain't right now anymore."

"Are you saying my daddy is doing something wrong, Grandpa?" I asked.

"Naw, I ain't saying that. Farmers these days ain't got much choice in what they have to do. Goddamned government agents come in and they think they can run things for you. And when they ruin everything, they leave and you're left to pick things up," said my grandfather.

"How come you're feeling this way, then?"

"Sometimes I think I've had too much of living. The land is a living thing, son. Same as animals and plants. And, people. You can use land just like you can use this mare we're riding on. But you can't do more with it than it can stand.

"If we was to ride this mare all day, what she'll do when she'd had enough is she'll drop her forelegs and then she'll drop her hindlegs and then she'll roll over, hoping we're too stupid to get out of the way and if she's lucky she'll squash the shit out of both of us. So, we ride her a little and let her rest a little. Give her a chance to catch her breath, get up her strength again. Take care of your animal and chances are your animal ain't going to like carrying you around any better, but the animal ain't got much choice in the matter and it'll last you longer.

"Always take care of your animals. If they were wild, they could take care of themselves. When we make them work for us, we take the wild out of them and we have to take care of them. The land's the same way. By itself, wild, land'll grow lots of things. When you uproot it, carve it up, put fences around it, and then you decide what it will grow, you've taken the wild out of it. That's when it's important for you to take care of it. You don't treat the land right and it'll choke on you. It'll take every damned seed you put in it and just chew it like you would a bag of peanuts.

"Thing is, an animal will let you know when you ain't doing right by it. Land has a different way of saying things, a way that I don't believe we have yet to puzzle out."

"What do you think my daddy should do, Grandpa?"

"I don't know, boy. He's as good a farming man as any around here. He ain't never been very good at handling money. That's because he don't care about money. He cares about you, his family, that's all. I know he owes the bank a lot of money and them bankers, vultures, they don't give one rat's ass about the land. None of them have ever had to make a living off it. It ain't nothing to them if the land goes dead and you can't get nothing out of it. As far as they care, they'll sell your equipment, your animals, and the land itself if they have to. It wasn't like that, a long time ago, when I was starting out. You could owe the bank for years and they never sold you out from under. This part of the world hasn't been right once Hoover and them that followed got into office."

"Who was Hoover, Grandpa?"

"A son of a bitch!"

We followed the road that went straight into a clump of mesquite. Beyond, the road stretched across a dry creekbed. The milo field went right up to the treeline and the final part of the wagon road disappeared into some dry Johnston grass. The creek banks were no more than a foot high. The ruts in the road were washed away periodically when there was runoff from the spring rains.

We had another patch of milo on the other side of the creek. My grandfather turned Elpidio's mare away from it, to the south, in the direction of a dirt road that angled its way from Candy's Store westward and then southward back into Smiley.

The sun was a little higher now and the milo patch seemed to be thin strips of green paint on the black soil. The land here was flat and was not terraced.

"That's what land should look like, boy," said my grandfather, satisfied with the sight of it.

Although the sun was rising into full daylight, it was a shadowy dark as we rode along the bend of the creek, past the milo patch into a pasture loaded with mesquite trees. My grandfather cautioned me against the overhanging branches full of thorns. It grew darker as we went along the faint outlines of the wagonroad. The few cows we had left were black lumps in the morning quiet. In this part of our place, the smells were deep and rich and ripe from the dew which glistened on the waist high grass highlighted by shoots of sunlight penetrating the sparse leaves of the mesquite. As we rode on, droplets of water thudded on my hat brim from the lime colored leaves sprouting on the moss covered branches. It was peaceful and quiet, with only the sound of Elpidio's mare swishing through the brush.

My brothers had hunted and played over just about every inch of our land, but even they would not be familiar with this part of it. We seldom came this far to the west and south of the house. I was still trying to get my bearings when Grandpa reined in the mare and told me to open the gate. He also told me to be careful of snakes as this was the time of year when the young ones grew to be dangerous and he said baby rattlers were especially fond of biting baby Mexicans.

It was an in-between kind of light that made it difficult for me to make out objects. I broke out into a sweat as I couldn't be sure of where I stepped and all I could think of was stepping on a pissed-off rattler. I was not going to let my grandfather know I was as afraid as I was. I opened the barbed wire gate just enough for my grandfather to get through and then I ran forward to the safety of the graded road.

"How did you know there was a gate here, Grandpa? It's hardly light enough to see anything," I said.

"No secret to it, son, it's been there for years."

We rode on a ways on the graded road that had been packed with sand, which was a sharp contrast to the black soil knifed out of the way by the grader. I was curious about the road; I had never seen it before.

"Is this the road that goes to Candy's, Grandpa?" I asked.

"That's right. Back that way, you can ride right up to Candy's front porch. And going the way we're going, if you go far enough, you end up in Smiley, by the road where the grain storage is. I thought you knew this country as good as anybody, squirt."

"I only know the places where I've been, Grandpa," I said. "I've never been out this far. Didn't somebody say Heriberto lived out here somewhere when he first got married?"

"That's right," said Grandpa.

"Now I know where we are. I was only out here once at night."

We stayed on the road for about a mile until we came to another barbed wire gate. This time, all he had to do was stop the mare and I jumped down to open it.

"Is this where you're digging the well, Grandpa?"

"This is it. It's up a ways, over by those oaks. You can see them over there."

"How can you do that, Grandpa?" I asked "I mean, dig a well on somebody else's property? That's against the law, isn't it?"

"If a man just went into another man's property and started to dig a well, and if he didn't get shot first, I expect it would be against the law, son. It's getting so every goddamn thing a man has a mind to do will get him up against a government agent or some kind of law. Except, if some fool took to digging a well on my property, I don't believe I would complain. I'd probably bring him ice water and warm tacos and be grateful, too."

"What if the owner of this place finds out what you're doing? What happens then?" I became worried.

"The owner already knows, son."

"I still don't understand why you want to dig a well on somebody else's place, Grandpa. Couldn't you dig one on our place?"

"Goddamn it, boy, I own this place," said my grandfather.

"I never knew it, Grandpa," I said.

"It's fifty acres of pastureland. I've been leasing it out for about fifteen years, now. If I'm not disturbing my renter's cows any by digging a well, I figure I get a headstart on reclaiming my land. Besides, I agree with you about the law. I don't see where a man can't dig a well on his own property even if it is rented out to somebody else. More than that, I decided not to renew the lease because by the end of summer, we're going to need all this grass, not that there's that much here for a full grown cow to starve to death with in dignity."

"You kept this as a secret all this time?"

"Hell, no, it ain't no damned secret, boy. I don't give all of you an inventory of everything I own every day. I leased it out and I ain't hardly thought about it being mine for many years. It's to be mine again, soon enough. Shit, look around you, boy. Who would want this piece of land? It ain't good for nothing except maybe running a few scrawny cows on it."

"How come you bought it, then?" I said.

"There's water under it. I can tell. Good, clean, sweet, water. Got to go deep for it, though. It may not help us get through the drought that's coming in one piece, but we'll have plenty of water for the livestock, what we can keep of them. I chose this spot because we'll have to go deep. The deeper the well, the longer it'll give you water, clean water. Shallow wells is good for lazy men and they'll do in the good times, but you can't depend on them. I wouldn't trust one."

"I don't understand that, Grandpa."

"Simple. What the hell they teach you in school, anyway? The earth's surface has got layers to it, there's layers and layers of it. The top of it is mostly dirt, and some places it's mostly rock. Around here, we have black dirt. North of Candy's Store, it starts to turn into red clay and sand.

"The deeper you go into the earth, there's different layers. Right where we're going to dig, I'm two, three feet into it, it's still black dirt. I expect I'll hit a vein of clay pretty soon. What I want to avoid is rocks, there's layers of rock in the guts of this land. I've had two false wells already and that's when I have to rethink everything."

"How do you dig through rock, Grandpa?"

"Depends. If it's a thin enough layer, a foot, maybe, two, then we're fine. That much rock never hurt anybody. If it's more than that but it's soft rock, we can handle that, too. In any case, it's something to think about. Comes a point, when you're down too deep, where you can't afford but to go on ahead with it."

My grandfather nudged Elpidio's mare and she broke into a smooth gallop.

"It's over there," he said, pointing with an outstretched arm.

My grandfather's well was on a grassy knoll, some twenty paces from an hundred-year-old oak tree that leaned over to one side. The oak stood at the top of the horizon, its gnarled branches spread over a wide piece of ground. It stood alone and majestic inside a clearing where the cattle came for shade.

We were descending a low and gradual declension in the land before beginning a steep climb to the well. Here and there were traces where a road had been.

The Johnston grass came up to the mare's belly. When I turned to see how far from the gate we had ridden, the road had disappeared. I leaned over to look around his shoulder. Up ahead was the mound of black dirt he had gouged out of the ground. From the short distance, it seemed we were approaching a freshly dug grave.

"That's my well, boy." Grandpa's voice was weary in anticipation of the day of digging ahead of us.

Instead of going straight to the well, Grandpa kept going for a short ways before he stopped beneath the branches of another oak further away. Dangling from one of the branches was a short piece of rope. He slid his foot out of the stirrup and held out his hand to me. Holding on to the saddleseat, I slid down from the mare.

Grandpa loosened the cinch of the saddle and then he walked Elpidio's mare to where the rope dangled. He slid the saddle off the mare and held it in one hand while he slipped the end of the rope through the pommel. He tied both ends of the rope, leaving the saddle swaying in the air.

Elpidio's mare had been trained to stand where the reins touched the ground. Grandpa returned to her and removed the bridle from her mouth, hooking it on the saddle horn. He slapped her hindquarters and she took off running, disappearing among the trees and grass.

"How're you going to catch her when it's time to go, Grandpa?" I asked.

"Whistle. She'll come if you whistle. Horses have their own kind of smarts if you learn how to get it out of them. She's used to that worthless piece of mesquite patch where she's penned. She'd rather go back to that misery than stay here in this paradise of grass. Don't ask me to explain why. Like I said, horses have their own smarts."

"Is that like when we went to visit aunt Luisa and we had to spend the night and I wanted to be home in my own bed even if Jose kicks me all night long?"

"Yeah, except a horse don't whine and cry about it."

"I didn't whine and cry, Grandpa," I protested.

"Come on, let's see what we're going to do today."

To the side of the mound, there was a bucket upside down on the ground. He had a three foot square piece of tarpaulin inside of which he wrapped his tools. The tools consisted of a narrow spade, a long metal shaft with a spear-like point and a pickaxe.

The well hole was about four feet in diameter and as I squatted to get a good look into it, it was perfectly round and the inside walls of dirt were smooth and even. The bottom of it was jagged and uneven, like the muddy bottom of a watering hole.

"This looks like good work, Grandpa," I said, wanting to praise his efforts. "What are you going to want me to do today?"

"That one is going to be a little tricky, son. The two of us can work down in the hole. Only thing is, if I give you the pickaxe, I don't believe I'm going to have any toes by lunchtime. If I give you the shovel, you're going to be in my way. Like I said, it's going to be a little tricky."

"We can take turns in the hole, Grandpa," I volunteered.

"Naw, this kind of work calls for a strong back, which you ain't got yet. Why don't you stay up here and I'll go down. When I fill up the bucket, you pull it up and you walk it over there by the tree and begin a new pile of dirt. This one is too close to the well and it'll be trouble for us before we're through."

"Is that all I have to do?"

"Is that all? That's enough. It'll be a big help to me not having to jump in and out of the hole to get this goddamned dirt out."

"Don't seem like much to me, Grandpa."

"You tell me that about four o'clock, when the sun is good and hot."

Although a gentle morning breeze seemed to flutter in little eddies of cold because of the evaporating dew, Grandpa removed his shirt and jumped into the hole. He asked me to hand him the pickaxe and the spade.

I walked over to the mound of fresh dirt to sit down and the slope of it was so inviting that I leaned back. My grandfather would call me when he needed me.

The excitement of working with my grandfather had turned into a job of waiting. I was anxious to do something, but it would be a while before he had loosened enough dirt to begin passing up the bucketsful of it to me.

My grandfather's deceptively slow movements soon jarred me out of my daydreams when he yelled for me to give him the bucket. After that, he kept me busy for the remainder of the morning. I no sooner took the bucket he handed up to me, walked a ways to a place I had selected to pile the dirt, than I would hand it down to him and he had it full and was passing it up to me again. And so it went all morning. I was learning not to decide for myself how things were going to be. It became obvious I didn't have any useful experience in it.

Twice during the morning, my grandfather stood up to his full height down in the hole and rolled himself a Bull Durham. His upper body was glistening with sweat within the hour and as the time passed, it became caked with black dirt.

"Grandpa, you look like you could use a bath," I said, trying to be friendly.

"This is no work for a Christian, I can tell you that."

Each time, he dropped the cigarette butt into the hole without bothering to stamp it out. On the next bucketful, the butt would be in between the clumps of doughy dirt, still smoldering.

Along about eleven o'clock, the sun was out in full strength and I had lost my strength altogether. My feet became heavier than the bucketsful of dirt that I carried. It was taking me longer and longer to make the short trips to the steadily growing mound I had started. In no time at all, it seemed, I couldn't lift the bucket all the way and I had to drag it behind me, pulling on the wire handle. If my grandfather was annoyed at my slowness, he didn't complain in the least. My feet got so heavy I no longer had any control over them, or the rest of my body for that matter. My arms felt swollen and seemed to move on their own.

At first, I had felt sorry for my grandfather down in the hole as I bent over into the well to accept the buckets of dirt, placing my hands under the bucket to shift the weight from him to me as quickly as possible. Later, as the morning wore on, and the buckets kept coming, it was all I could do to just lean over and slip my fingers under the wire handle to jerk it over the edge of the hole.

My strength held up for five or six more buckets. I wanted to make an impression on my grandfather that I could keep up with him. But an overpowering fatigue made me lose control of my movements. Only when my strength gave out altogether did my grandfather begin to pile the dirt inside the hole. He started to lift the bucket out of the hole completely and place it on the flat ground outside for me to pick up. In that way, I could catch me a deep breath and summon strength I didn't know I had to pick up the bucket and carry on with my part of it.

The goddamned sun began to get on my nerves. It was a pleasant spring sun that wasn't hot so much as it was annoying, precisely because of its pleasantness.

About the time I was ready to give it up because I couldn't go on anymore, and hating myself all the while for it, my grandfather crawled out of the hole. I had been staring at the bucket for a long time, contemplating how I was going to find the strength to move the next load. My grandfather saw the bucket still sitting where he had placed it and he picked it up like it was nothing and took it to the pile I started under the branches of the oak tree. For all I could see, it might have been a bucketful of straw.

He first looked up at the sky and then, as if to confirm it, he took out his pocket watch. He grunted, hefted the watch in his palm a couple of times before he snapped the lid shut.

"I think we had better eat now if we're going to be any good for the rest of the day," my grandfather said.

He came back to the well and tossed the bucket into the hole. It clanged when it hit bottom. He was in midstride when he threw in the bucket and without looking back, he said, "Come on, I know a place where we can go eat."

The saddle blanket was on the ground, folded in half. My grandfather bent over it and took a brown paper sack from inside the fold. The sack contained our lunch and a mason jar full of caramel-colored coffee, the kind I didn't like.

My grandfather kept on walking for a quarter of a mile from where we had been working. I followed with my feet but the rest of me was numb and felt nothing. I was so goddamned tired all I wanted to do was drop down somewhere. My grandfather had a spring to his step and it seemed to me that he was purposely walking faster than normal.

"Come on," he said, "we don't want to take too much time."

I wanted to protest that it was our land, our work, and there was no reason to go about this as if gringoes were keeping our time. I knew somehow it wouldn't do any good to say it. As it was, I was beginning to fear that he was going to tell my brothers about me and knowing my brothers it would be a source of their fun for the rest of the summer. I was tired and miserable. The thought of the food, cold food, didn't help, either.

We walked along a worn cow path. It curved sharply around some trees and I was so far behind that my grandfather disappeared on the other side of it. When I began to circle the path, I saw a tall chimney spire made of limestone. Stretching to one side of the chimney was a wooden floor. It seemed to me that here had been a house at one time. What was left of it reminded me of a country dance floor, except that this was higher up from the ground. At the far end of the floor, on the right, a charred semicircle flared out from the edge.

My grandfather sat on the part of the floor where porchsteps had once been. He waited until I came to stand in front of him before saying anything. "Ain't as much fun as going to the movies, is it? Or making a fool of yourself in front of those little girls at the drug-store."

I felt resentful. It was bad enough that he had me doing the most back-breaking work a human being ever did, but to have fun at my expense made me tremble with rage.

My anger wasn't really directed at my grandfather. I was angry, though.

"Come here, sit down," he said, amiably. "We got here, tacos and more tacos. One egg, two bean, no, three bean tacos, a couple of loose pieces of meat from last night and some cold tortillas."

"I don't want anything," I said, my voice weak and whispery.

"Beans is good enough for me. Beans is the only thing a man ought to get used to that's good for him. You can have the rest. Unless, of course, you want some beans. In which case, since I'm going to eat two of them, I can be generous and let you have one."

I sat on the ground a few feet away from my grandfather. Toward the rear of what had been the house, a rusting cistern, most of it torn away, leaned to one side on stilts taller than most men. I took a few bites of my food and life reluctantly began to flow through me again.

"That's a cistern up there, isn't it, Grandpa?" I asked.

"What's left of it," he said.

"Well, don't that mean there's a well already dug around here?"

"Do you see a windmill around here, or what used to be one? Or, any damned thing that would draw water from down in the ground?"

"No, sir, but that don't mean nothing. There could be one, if you looked for it. I bet you didn't even hunt around to see if there was already a well around here."

"Didn't have to, son. I've known this place for more than twenty-five years. I've owned it for more than half of that. I remember when there was people living here, I used to come visit. Before I met your grandma, I fully intended to marry one of the girls who lived in this very house."

"Looks like it burned down a hundred years ago," I said.

"That's probably how long ago it was that everything happened." My grandfather ate some more of his food, taking his time to chew. "To answer your question directly," he said, "that's a catchment cistern. You hang metal troughs to the eaves all around the house. The rainwater runs down off the roof into those troughs. See, over there, that thing that looks like a cone lying on its side? That's what's left of one of them. The runoff flowed along a pipe into the cistern. It's as good a way as there is for rainwater. There's nothing like a drink of cool rainwater."

"The Arreola's have something like that, only it drips from the house and the barn into some barrels at a corner of the barn. Tony asked me if I wanted a drink of it once and I thought he was crazy."

"You should have taken him up on it. Won't be too long before catching water like that will be gone for now and forever. Then you'll never be able to tell your grandchildren what rainwater tastes like."

"I've tasted rainwater before, Grandpa," I said, defiantly.

"Well, I'll tell you. It ain't until you leave it set for a few days that you get the pure taste of rainwater. It tastes like nothing you've ever tasted before in your whole life."

"What kind of shit is that, Grandpa? That don't tell me nothing! I could just say the same thing and nobody would ever know the difference."

"There is a difference, boy."

"What's that?"

"The difference is, I know what I'm talking about and you wouldn't. That's what's important."

"Important? Why? Who's to know? It's all the same, isn't it?"

"No, it ain't and that's the point, son. You will know. That's what's important about it. It's one thing when a man calls you a liar and it's another thing when you know it for yourself. You tell one lie and just about when somebody's going to catch you in it, you have to tell another, just to save yourself. Pretty soon, it gets so you won't know the difference between what's true and what's not."

"Well, what about when you tell stories? I've heard you tell a story one way and then you tell it to someone else, and it comes out a different way. Which one is the truth? You change them all the time. I don't know if I can believe half of the stories you tell, Grandpa. They're supposed to be things that happened, but they always happen in a different way."

"Don't get squirrely on me, now, son. Maybe the stories I tell happened and maybe they didn't happen. And, maybe they didn't happen exactly the way I tell them. People learn better when you make a story for them to enjoy. That way they won't notice so much what you're trying to teach and they learn better."

"Well, then, why is it so goddamned important for you to teach people things, Grandpa?"

"It's one of the privileges that comes with being as old as I am, son. If I can spare people from making the same mistakes as I made and save them from some of the misery I suffered, then, maybe, just maybe, I will have done some good in this world."

"Grandpa," I said, exasperated, "you're always saying that it's good to make mistakes on account of you can learn from them."

"That's true, too, boy. But, if somebody's already made the same mistake, you can learn from it just as if you made it for yourself," he said.

"It's too confusing for me, Grandpa," I said.

The cold tacos didn't taste so bad once I got more of my blood flowing a little faster.

# Chapter 17

Grandpa and I didn't spend more than a few minutes wolfing down our lunch. I thought he was going to get us back to the well right away, but he didn't. Instead, he leaned back where he sat and instantly began to snore. My bones stiffened and became thick and heavy. I could feel my flesh become an unyielding mass, resisting any movement. It was a slow and laborious act to get on my feet. I didn't want to sleep for fear of not waking up when Grandpa was sure to call. Nevertheless, I leaned over to one side and was asleep before my shoulder touched the ground. The next thing I knew, Grandpa was shaking me.

"Let's do some more work. What do you say?" he said, gently.

Although the spring days were pleasant and warm, there were times during the day, especially in the afternoon, when it became cold and windy. As we walked back to the hole, the cold and wind came in.

At the well, Grandpa dropped into the hole and immediately was swinging the pickaxe. He was down a little below waist level. He continued to talk as he worked, occasionally allowing a loud grunt, when he swung the pickaxe, to interrupt the flow of his words. It was not any easier for me to keep up with him; in fact it was more difficult than it had been in the morning. I thought the nap at lunch would produce a resurgence of my strength. It did, but not enough. Within the hour I had nothing left. Grandpa told me to go on and dump the dirt beside the hole. I wasn't about to give in. Somehow, I found the strength to haul it to the dump I had started.

Grandpa adjusted the pace of his work to mine and we worked well for the remainder of the afternoon. About all I could do was suggest that we get a wheelbarrow. Grandpa liked the idea and he said he would get one of the boys to bring him one in the truck. Seeing that I was not going to last much longer, my grandfather decided to call it quits along about four o'clock. There was still plenty of daylight left, even though it was overcast.

"Work like this ain't fit for a damned dog," said Grandpa.

"How come you do it, then?" I asked.

"Keep busy. When school lets out, you can come help me every day. We'll put some muscle on you."

"Grandpa," I asked, "how come you never told anybody you had this place?"

"I never told hardly anybody I had it because frankly I never had much use for it. I don't think even your mother knows about it. Since I've been digging I guess they think I'm still on your daddy's place somewhere. That's good, because I don't feel like answering any questions.

"I had it for a long time before old Mr. John Crook came out and said he heard I owned this piece of land that bordered on his and he needed it for something and he leased it from me for five years and I just kept renewing it. Must be fifteen, twenty years that he's had it. The old fart probably thinks it's his. John Crook is not going to like it, but once we strike water in this little patch, we're going to need it for your daddy's cows and whatever else."

"What if he's gotten so used to having it that he won't want to give it back?" I said.

"Oh, he'll give it back, all right. You can't forget a thing like that," said my grandfather.

The overcast had swept in from the northwest. When I saw it through the trees it looked like the rolling fog that came in above the highway when we rode the bus to school. I pointed it out to my grandfather and told him maybe it was going to rain after all.

"It's not going to rain," he said, confidently. "Not for a long damned time."

We headed back to the house in time to catch part of a fight between little Albert and little Julian. I was worn out to the point where I could just wash up before coming to the table. My mother placed a cup, half coffee and half milk, in front of me. My arms grew heavy and my eyelids would not stay open. I did manage the strength to slide an arm in front of me for my forehead to rest on. And, then I dropped down on it and fell fast asleep. I awoke briefly to the silence of the night, with only the sound, low and peaceful, of my family asleep. I fell asleep again and it seemed that instantly it was morning. All of my joints and muscles were sore and I had to hurry and dress for school.

I could not recall being carried to bed, undressed and tucked in. Even as I slipped into my trousers I recalled the horror of my face asleep on the kitchen table. I realized I was not going to live it down for several months. I knew my brothers would take full advantage of it. I would have to wait maybe months before something happened to replace me as the object of their ridicule. The only defense I could think up was a downcast face and a sullen manner. That would indicate at least that I would find any reference to my falling asleep at the table inconvenient and not funny. It wasn't going to stop them, of course, but it might make them feel sorry for me. Fortunately, my father and my brothers Elpidio, Jose and Paulie were hurrying up the cultivation of the planting and had already gone to work.

There still remained my sisters and my little brothers. From them, it would not be quite so bad, after all.

On the way to school, the little boys told me our older brother Elpidio was in trouble. I took that to mean that my father was angry with him for some reason or other.

When school was over, I was anxious to find out what kind of trouble Elpidio had gotten himself into. He usually was the cause of the least trouble. My father always relied on him to do the right thing, whether in his work or in anything else, for that matter. I could not imagine what he could have done that would upset my father, or anybody. It wasn't like Elpidio.

My mother and my sister Juana were usually in league as Elpidio's protectors, defending him against even the slightest ribbing or criticism. They could not stand for anyone to say things about Elpidio. Elpidio didn't gloat about it, either. In fact, he was mostly embarrassed by it.

With my sister Celia, who was living with us, my mother and Juana allied themselves as a group and the three of them considered themselves a majority against the remaining seven of us. With Celia once again living with us, the flow of information was freer, as my mother and sister had to share more of what they knew and Celia was never one to keep her mouth shut. It wasn't long after we got back from school that I discovered Elpidio's trouble. It had to do with the Arreaga family.

Don Antonio Arreaga was the father of five daughters and two sons. The Arreaga farm was down the road from us, about six miles away, just north of where the Schoolland road angles south toward Smiley. The farm was not very big, not big enough anyway for them to make a go of it without having to do day work to get along.

Don Antonio was a small man, thin and wiry, who smoked one cigarette after another and whose hands almost always trembled. If that were not enough, don Antonio had a way about him that caused almost everyone who knew him to make jokes about him. His son, Tony, had heard most of what people said about don Antonio. Try as anyone might, it wasn't always possible to shield Tony from our comments. In fact, Tony himself poked a little fun at his father, just to show he was a good sport about it. In general, though, out of respect for Tony and because of an underlying respect for the old man as an elder, we kept our references to the old man down to a minimum. But only if either of them was nearby.

My brother Heriberto, who had no such respect for anyone, would say that if don Antonio had the guts to act like the little shit he was, no one would make fun of him. Heriberto claimed that assholes should take pride in being assholes. Most of us don't have much choice in what we are. It was when assholes pretended to be someone else that problems arose.

All of the Arreagas, the girls and the old man included, were good workers. When my father needed help with the crops or anything else, he would send one of the boys over to hire two or three of them. He didn't mind if Tony was not with the girls who came to work. In fact, my father claimed the girls were as good or better workers than Tony, who had a tendency to daydream, probably about my sister Juana.

Don Antonio was the first to introduce the idea of migrant labor to Schoolland. There were people in Smiley and Nixon who went north at the end of summer to harvest crops, returning late in the fall or early winter with enough money to last them until the Schoolland harvest season began in late spring. A few of them would go south a bit earlier to begin the harvest season there. The Arreagas began to follow the crops because it was the only way for them to get through the year. One year, my brother Elpidio went with them to pick cotton. My father convinced all of us that Elpidio would come back married. That scared my mother; Elpidio was only about fourteen at the time.

My grandfather always said a man ought to have his own piece of land, not that anyone ever really owns land. What you own, said Grandpa, is the right to keep every other son of a bitch off of it. He meant that when a man drops over dead he at least ought to fall on something that belongs to him. I didn't see where it mattered too much to a dead man where he might fall, but my grandfather repeated it often enough to where I understood its importance if not its relevance.

The Arreagas came to be as close to us as two families who are not related can be. Even after the incident with don Antonio's dog and my brother Paulie, our families still exchanged intermittent visits.

It wasn't the same as before, given that the old man, don Antonio, refused to visit or have anything to do with us. The old man remained reserved and polite when we took my mother and sisters to visit. For the year or so since Paulie had kicked the dog, don Antonio had not visited our house. My father had accompanied the family on one or two visits to sort of give don Antonio a chance to patch things up.

Each time, though, don Antonio had refused to say anything except grudgingly answer a few of my father's questions. The last time my father visited, when don Antonio was in a very bad mood, he had just walked out on everybody. No one could help but notice how rude he was.

My father didn't care about the incident in particular. He figured that don Antonio bore him and Paulie a big grudge, one that might take years to get over, if ever. My father had done all he could to smooth over the dispute. It would have to be up to don Antonio to decide when it should end. My father encouraged the rest of the family, except for Paulie, to continue the friendship. My father didn't have much to say about don Antonio. There are people who care for animals in the same way others might care for human beings. They tend to be, according to my father, people who are not quite right to begin with. An animal is a goddamned animal, that's all there is to it. My father speculated that whatever it was that bothered don Antonio had more going into it than just that damned dog which my brother Paulie kicked.

The unspoken certitude existing between our family and the Arreagas that one of our boys would marry one of their girls was becoming more remote. Heriberto had been just about the right age for the oldest girl; however, Heriberto never expressed even the slightest interest in her or in any of the others, for that matter. So, it wasn't so bad that he ended up marrying somebody else. However, hope of our families uniting rose considerably when Elpidio fell in love with Concepcion, the middle Arreaga sister. And, in no time at all, Tony and Juana were no longer children and it was evident that they had a crush on one another. Even don Antonio, in better days, had jocularly mentioned the prospect of a double wedding.

Our mounting problems with the Arreagas were made worse by Juana.

In the time since Marcos de la Fuente, the *mojado,* had been living and expanding his empire at our old house, he and my sister had become less secretive about the fact that they had something going. Marcos had asked for my father's permission to visit with Juana at the house. Against my mother's wishes, my father gave in, figuring that whether he gave it or not, Juana would do what she set her mind to do.

Things came to a head at a dance across the road from La Tacuachera, the bar that was just past the county line south of Nixon. Juana went with Heriberto and his wife. Marcos de la Fuente got a ride from somebody, and he was there, too. Not only did they dance every dance, but in between dances they sat together. At one point they even disappeared and were gone for a long time.

Paulie and I were busy with a contest to see who could eat the most hamburgers. Elpidio couldn't take his eyes off Tony Arreaga's sister, Concepcion. My sister-in-law, Alva, was worried that Heriberto was drinking too much. More than just drinking the beer being sold out of iced-down washtubs, Heriberto had a pint of whiskey in his hip pocket.

Whatever Tony Arreaga expected from my sister Juana came to an end when he asked her to dance and she refused.

"You'd rather have a wetback!" said Tony Arreaga, viciously.

Juana knew better than to respond. She moved a step or two closer to Marcos de la Fuente. Tony Arreaga became even more upset when she did that. He demanded Marcos de la Fuente go with him into a nearby field to settle it. From across the dancefloor, Elpidio saw that something was wrong. Paulie and I were finishing our third hamburger when we saw Elpidio rush over to Juana.

"Fight!" said Paulie, dropping the last bite of his hamburger. He ran after Elpidio.

My brother Elpidio took Tony Arreaga by the arm and led him a short distance away. There was a crowd gathering around by the time I walked over. Elpidio held Tony by the arm as he tried to talk to him. Finally, Tony jerked his arm away and went off in the direction of where the cars were parked. The crowd kept looking at him as he disappeared into the shadows. More than one person there that night, myself included, feared that Tony would return with a pistol and start shooting. The crowd took their time about dispersing. The owner of the dance platform got the musicians to cut their break short and begin to play again. For the rest of the night, from time to time, we would look in the exact same spot where Tony had been swallowed up by the dark to see if he would return.

The incident at the dance was altogether unnecessary. For too many damned years, Tony and my sister Juana just thought that it was inevitable for them to marry. I doubt if they ever spoke about it at all, at least to where each of them understood that it was what they were supposed to do. When Juana fell in love with Marcos de la Fuente, there was nothing Tony Arreaga could use as a claim on her. The bond between them was one from childhood and it had dissolved as they became adults.

Tony became distant and at times downright unfriendly. That was the only time I can remember that Tony had acted as anything but close to us. We were closer to the Arreagas than even some of our cousins that we didn't get to see too often. Now, Tony Arreaga was becoming an asshole when there wasn't any need for it.

Juana took to spending so much time with Marcos de la Fuente that my mother began to think up things for her to do just to keep her in the house. There's no doubt my mother wanted her to stay away from him. As soon as her chores were done in the morning, she would rush to the old house to put in a full day's work there. Marcos would be off somewhere working for wages while my sister Juana continued with the work he left for her to do.

He had already mentioned to my father that he was building up some money and would very soon offer to buy that piece of land from him. My father flatly told him he would not sell it. Marcos de la Fuente became impatient, betraying his frustration and anger. He protested that he had put a lot of work into the place and that it wasn't fair. My father told him no one had asked him to do a goddamned thing. My father was kind of touchy about his land.

Paulie, as the rest of us had already noticed, remarked that Marcos, if he couldn't buy the land fair and square, would probably marry Juana in the hope of getting it for nothing. That had earned Paulie a wet towel across the face from Juana who was standing by the sink when he said it. That dishtowel was her favorite weapon.

Up to the end of April, Elpidio had been visiting the Arreaga place on the pretext of seeing his friend Tony. Tony knew, as did everyone else except for don Antonio, that Elpidio actually came to visit Concepcion. Up to that point, Tony had figured Juana would get over her infatuation with Marcos de la Fuente and things would return to the comfortable way they had been before. He was determined to be very understanding about the whole thing. Tony was also determined to do his part in helping my brother Elpidio and his sister Concepcion. He would disappear wordlessly to allow them some time together alone.

At the dance, Elpidio had intervened to prevent a fight between Tony and Marcos de la Fuente. If forced to it, there is no doubt he would have sided with his friend Tony. At that precise moment, however, he had simply wanted to stop the fight. However, Tony interpreted my brother's interference as taking sides against him. For this reason, Tony decided not to help Elpidio with Concepcion anymore. Out of consideration for his sister, he wasn't going to do anything to stop him, though. There was no point any longer in pretending that he went to visit Tony. Tony wasn't being exactly an asshole about it, but it was clear that things were tense between him and Elpidio. Elpidio felt bad about losing his good friend; that's the truth, but he was not about to stop seeing the girl he loved.

Brave as you please, Elpidio took to going there full front to visit Concepcion. Luckily, he did not confide his foolhardiness to anyone in the family, else my father wouldn't have allowed him to do it. Things were bad enough without Elpidio making them worse.

The first time he appeared at the Arreaga place, Tony saw him coming up the driveway and he told Concepcion to go outside to wait for him. Tony stayed inside the house. Tony didn't think anything of it; he wasn't the kind who would make everyone miserable just because he was miserable. Concepcion was his sister and if she wanted Elpidio, there wasn't much he could do about it.

That first time, don Antonio was in Smiley playing dominoes, which he did every day. Concepción and Elpidio spent a couple of hours out in the front yard, leaning against the hood of Elpidio's truck, keeping a respectful distance apart just in case anyone in the house was watching, which, of course, they all were. Don Antonio did not return home until after Elpidio left.

Elpidio's visits went without incident and Elpidio became more confident, staying with Concepcion until after dark. Don Antonio returned from Smiley at the same time every day. It didn't occur to Elpidio that the days were getting longer. But, then, love can do that. Don Antonio Arreaga caught my brother and his daughter Concepcion at twilight, just as they were inching closer together, and were holding hands. They noticed but paid no attention to the headlights of his truck coming up the driveway.

When Concepcion recognized her father's truck, she simply moved away from Elpidio. As far as she knew, Don Antonio had never objected to Elpidio's visits.

Don Antonio was in a rage when he stepped down from the truck. "I don't like that," said don Antonio. "Coming to my home when I'm not here, sneaking behind my back!" His face was full of anger, his thin lips twitched.

It appeared to Elpidio as if the old man had been building up his steam for quite some time in order to let go with the full force of it. As Elpidio remembers it, the old man was primed for a fistfight. Elpidio was probably twice his size, but it didn't seem to matter to the old man.

"Papa," said Concepcion, "Elpidio always comes to visit!" Her tone was half pleading and half scolding.

"Get inside the house," the old man raged.

Concepcion started running toward the house, shouting for Tony to come outside. Tony came to the front door.

"Do something about our father," Concepcion said to him.

"Go on inside," said Tony.

The entire Arreaga family was bunched at the door and at the lone window facing the yard. As Tony came walking up to them, Elpidio apologized because he felt bad that the old man was so angry. He told the both of them that he had always felt he could visit them any time, just as they could visit our place any time. For that reason, he said sincerely, he had not thought it necessary to ask proper permission to visit Concepcion.

Tony could have done something to calm his father and help out Elpidio. However, the shoe was now on the other foot and he was going to enjoy himself and see if Elpidio could stay out of trouble.

Elpidio got the idea of making everybody feel better about the whole thing. "Don Antonio, I would like your permission to bring my father to ask your permission for a proper courtship between Concepcion and me," said Elpidio.

"Never!" exclaimed don Antonio. "I don't want you on my place, I don't want you near my daughter, I don't want any of your family to have anything more to do with any of my family. You go back and you tell your father what I have said. Now, get out!"

"Tony?" said Elpidio, turning to his friend for help.

Tony couldn't bring himself to turn on Elpidio, but he had to side with his father.

"Maybe you shouldn't come here anymore, Elpidio," said Tony. "My father is right."

Elpidio was embarrassed and angry, but mostly he was confused. He became so frightened of losing Concepcion that he cried all the way back to our house.

Grandpa was sandbagging my father in a game of gin rummy. Elpidio rushed into the kitchen and immediately everyone saw how upset he was. I was nearly asleep in a corner of the kitchen, leaning my head against the long white counter that stretched from one wall to the other. My mother and sisters were in Juana's room sewing. Jose and Paulie had been outside singing. They followed Elpidio into the kitchen.

"Don Antonio ran me off his place," said Elpidio.

When my father said, "Goddamn it!" I was startled awake. Grandpa also said, "Goddamn it!" because it didn't look as if he was going to win his game.

"What happened?" asked my father.

Elpidio took his time before beginning. He was disturbed because of so many things going to shit at the same time. For one, it meant the end of a friendship with Tony that had lasted almost twenty years, which was all the years they had lived. Elpidio felt that he could have done something to stop all of the stupidity that seemed to be controlling things. Because he had not stopped it, he felt himself to be the cause of it. Elpidio could live with his own mistakes so long as no one else was involved. He didn't mind paying for his mistakes, either. In this case, though, there were too many people involved, people he loved.

The worst part of it, of course, was Concepcion. For about two years or so, Elpidio had been in love with her and she with him. Both of them were too shy to flaunt themselves in front of either family. They pretended their

meetings were chance encounters. If they ever said or did anything inti-
mate, no one had ever seen them. All our family had to go on was a strong
suspicion that Elpidio went over to the Arreagas to see one of the girls.

Elpidio had already discussed it with my father. He thought it was his
duty to do so because of the problems it might cause. My father's only
concern was about don Antonio. Elpidio couldn't be of too much help
because he wasn't sure whether don Antonio knew about him and Concepcion. Elpidio was pretty sure the old man knew, but thus far he had not
been confronted by it. What he would do when it happened was the problem. Now we knew don Antonio's reaction.

My mother and sisters heard the commotion and came into the kitchen.
My sister Celia put on a pot of coffee, figuring that it might be a long
night for everybody. Grandpa was the only who could drink coffee at night
and fall instantly asleep.

Elpidio wasn't one to draw too much attention to himself. He wasn't
exactly bashful, but he wasn't exactly as outgoing as the rest of us. Elpidio
stood beside the refrigerator, leaning against it, his eyes red and glassy. I
moved closer to the table, beside my grandfather who still held his gin
rummy hand. I ran a finger along the corners of the cards. My grandfather
shook his head in disgust.

The coffee finished percolating. Celia and Juana served everyone, except me. I tried to sneak a sip from my grandfather's cup, but I saw my
mother looking at me. My brother Elpidio answered the question on everybody's mind by saying, "I'm going to marry Concepcion as soon as I
can."

It wasn't much of a surprise. For once, the devil was asleep and my
brother Paulie kept quiet. My father seemed to relish the moment when all
of his children were silent, their eyes fixed upon him, waiting for him to
speak his mind.

"First of all," he said, "we are not going to do anything. We're not
going to let this thing get out of hand. The trouble here didn't begin with
Paulie and don Antonio's dog." My father had not intended anything
funny, but nevertheless there was a generous round of laughter, the loudest
of which came from Paulie.

"I ran into Jim Boetticher from the bank when I was in town the other
day," my father continued. "He asked me if I was interested in buying the
Arreaga place. He said one of you boys is likely to get married one of
these days and you'll need a place to live."

"Don Antonio is selling out?" said Jose.

"Mr. Boetticher didn't say the place was for sale, but he was sure it
would be, very soon. Unless don Antonio comes up with a good deal of

money right quick, the bank is going to sell his place."

My father lifted his cup for my mother to refill with coffee. It was disturbing to all of us. Anything that happened to a neighbor might happen to us, too.

"That old fool should be nicer to people if he's in that kind of trouble. How's he expect to get help from anybody? And it looks like he's going to need it," said my grandfather. He spoke kindly, but there was a hard edge to his voice, a response to the way Elpidio had been treated.

"Well, when Mr. Boetticher told me that, I asked him to go back to the bank with me and see how we were doing. My idea was to see whether I had enough to maybe make don Antonio a loan, or at least offer one, not that the proud son of a bitch would take it.

"Mr. Boetticher advised me to begin thinking of my own problems before I threw away good money. It seems we can buy don Antonio's place, but we don't have enough to make him a loan. I have to borrow on this place some more if I want to help don Antonio out. I can't do that, of course.

"Mr. Boetticher says I should take it as a warning, though. Unless we get some good crops this year, we might end up like don Antonio. Don Antonio stands to lose everything they have. We'll stand to lose more, but it won't be everything. I'd hate to lose even one square inch of our land. It would be worth it to buy the place if don Antonio's land was worth anything, but it's not. Besides, I would hate to profit from another man's misfortune."

"I don't understand this," said my brother Paulie. "It always seemed like we were poorer than they were because we owed so much money."

"Some people spend a lot of money when they want to look good to impress other people. People look up to you if you have nice clothes and you have pretty things in your house," said Celia. "Everybody in San Antonio is like that."

"That's not our way in Schoolland," said my mother. "Don Antonio and doña Gertrudis have never pretended to have more than they do."

"Paulie's making things up again," I said.

Paulie threw a piece of wadded paper at me for that.

"These things just happen, that's all," said my father. "For the time being, I want everybody in this family to be polite and courteous to the Arreagas. Treat them as you always have. Let's hope that all of this will be over soon."

"What about Juana," asked Celia.

"Celia, don't say anything!" screeched Juana.

"That's why Tony's pissed off, isn't it?" said Celia.

"Celia, you have children of your own, which is all the more reason to watch your tongue," said my mother, the constant guardian of the language.

"Sorry, Ma," said Celia, who, under the glare of my mother's gaze, was reduced to a naughty little girl.

There was something my father was not telling us. Usually, once he told us what to do, that was the end of the discussion. This time, he kept on. "Just remember, it's no shame to be in the kind of trouble they're in. It could happen to us. They'll get on their feet again. There's no reason things can't go back to the way they were with us. After what Jim Boetticher told me, we have to do everything we can to get a good crop this year. Else, we'll be in the same trouble ourselves," said my father.

# Chapter 18

Grandpa had been sitting at the table, listening passively. He suddenly got to his feet and went to the sink for a drink of water. He drank an entire glassful. He wiped his mouth on his shirt sleeve.

"There ain't going to be a crop this year," he said with finality.

"Here he goes again," said Paulie sarcastically.

"Paulie," said my father, almost in a whisper, but it was enough to silence him.

My grandfather had no intention of beginning an argument with Paulie. Instead, my grandfather leaned against the counter to look at all of us.

"Children," he said, "you're not going to get a good crop this year. You'll be lucky if all the planting you've done will produce stalks with enough juice to turn the cows loose on them. It's not a year for good or bad crops, there'll be no crops this year. For anybody. We might as well get used to that."

My father bristled at my grandfather. The crops my father and brothers had planted came up nice and brightly green. However, in the last couple of weeks, the sprouts had paled. A few, particularly along the crests of the terraces, had begun to wilt, the tips of the leaves turning brown here and there. We couldn't help but feel there was a little truth to Grandpa's constant harping about a drought. Nevertheless, my father wanted to bolster our feelings. It was his view of life that hard work was enough to overcome any hardship. Even if there was a drought, my father felt we would get by with the sheer power of our work.

In all the time that my grandfather had been insisting on the drought, not one of us had taken him seriously. I believed my grandfather at the same time that I believed my father and brothers. It was too early in the spring to prove anything, so it was easy for me to believe both sides. My father, though, on this particular night, was more worried than usual that the family would begin to lose our spirit.

The thing about a drought is the way that the life of things simply evaporates. There isn't anything to see or to feel right off. It isn't like a hard freeze where it leaves a grotesque reminder of life suspended in a matter of hours or a tornado where in an instant the life of things is uprooted and strewn all about. A drought begins slowly, cautiously almost, not any different from any other dry spell. It begins to draw every drop of moisture from the earth, going deeper and deeper each day as the sun beats relentlessly on the cracked, parched soil. When it is too late, when the plants and the trees become ashen and then brown, water is deadly. A drought is living in the presence of brittle death.

My father was not going to let my grandfather have his way. "I checked with the county agent and the rainfall so far is running just a shade below normal for this time of year," he said. "I told him what you've been predicting, Grandpa, and he told me you're not the only one making those kinds of predictions. The county agent has all kinds of instruments and charts and there's a machine that sends in information from the Air Force and his opinion is that it will be a little dry this year, but that's all."

"You'd take the word of some slick wearing a necktie over the voice of experience," said my grandfather, in mock reproach.

My father went on. "Maybe we ought to expect ten percent less on the yield from last year. Other than that, he says there will be no drought. I'm going to see if we can't cultivate the crops a little more than last year, and I've even put in a little extra fertilizer to make up that ten percent loss."

My grandfather was not convinced. "That poison you use for fertilizer will probably kill the plants in another month," he said, contemptuous of the belief people placed in machines and gadgets and chemicals. "A man who depends on the weather for his livelihood had best spend a lot of time paying attention to it. There is not a machine invented by man that can substitute for a man's own observation. You have to pay attention to the changes in the color of the ground, that tells you how much water there is below. You have to feel the wind when it blows, see the direction it comes from. Why, you even have to notice what kind of sweat your body makes."

We laughed at the thought.

"Laugh if you want to," said my grandfather. "Those are the signs that tell you what kind of a year it's going to be. There might be a surprise every once in a while. Especially if something gets by that you ought to have seen. I can tell you this much, though, no squint-eyed bastard coming to this county from Dallas is going to solve anything."

"Jeez, Grandpa, are you finished?" said my brother Paulie.

My father was patient to an extreme and while he was disturbed by my grandfather's persistence, he remained calm. My brothers were clearly annoyed with my grandfather's stubborn predictions, particularly with the way in which Grandpa used the force of his experience. My father nevertheless felt compelled to say something. He could not bring himself to openly question my grandfather's opinion. Yet, it was important to keep his authority over the family.

"I'm not going to say I trust that county agent completely," said my father. "If what you say is true, Grandpa, then there is nothing to be done about it. If we're in for it, we're in for it. So far, it could go either way, I'll grant you that. In the meantime, what the county agent says is what everybody has to rely on, and I have to go along with it, too. What would you have me do to prepare for this drought of yours?"

"It ain't my drought," said my grandfather. "If it was mine to give, I'd just as soon send it to New York, or wherever there ain't too many Christians. That ain't the point, though. The point is, times is going to get tough before they get better. The only thing I would have done different is plant hay on every spare inch of land. That way we could save the animals, at least. What's in the ground right now will burn up by the end of the month. By the end of next month, it'll be so damned dry and so goddamned hot your sweat's going to boil on your skin."

"It won't get that hot, Grandpa," I said, incredulous.

"Maybe not, son, but you'll think it is," he said gravely.

After the attention of the family shifted to my father and grandfather, my brother Elpidio moved away from the refrigerator to stand somewhat apart from the rest of the family. Elpidio still felt responsible for the rift between our families. But of more importance to him was a way to keep seeing Concepcion.

There was more that we had to say, and yet, there was nothing more to say. We felt very keenly about the plight of the Arreagas and we wished there was something we could do for them. There was nothing more that needed to be said that night.

Elpidio borrowed my father's tobacco sack and went outside. My mother told us all to get to bed. No one argued with her.

In the morning, my father, my mother and my brother Elpidio were sitting at the kitchen table. Elpidio's eyes were red and his face looked worn out. He wore the same clothes as the night before and so I figured he had been on the porch all night.

Outside, the sun was bright and intense, seeming to be an explosion of light above the trees in the pasture in front of our house. The trees cast shadows so long they came almost up to our front porch. There was a frail, almost delicate stillness in the air. It was a far different kind of morning. It was not cool and neither was it warm. There was not a cloud in the sky.

My father and the boys were in no hurry this morning to go off to work, which made the kitchen unusually crowded. Even Grandpa straggled in, cheerful and surprised to see so many people. My sister Juana, trying to draw as little attention to herself as possible, took a curved wicker basket from the counter top and started for the door.

"I bet I know where she's going," said Jose, smiling into his coffee.

"You want breakfast, don't you?" snapped Juana.

"Be careful, Juana," said my mother, "I think there's a king snake out there somewhere."

"I thought the wetback was supplying us with eggs these days," said Grandpa.

"Grandpa, he's not a wetback!" expostulated Juana in horror.

"What the hell is he, then?" said Grandpa.

"The King of Spain, I think," said my brother Jose.

"King snakes don't bite," said Paulie, responding to my mother's warning.

"If he swam his way over here, he's a wetback, child," said Grandpa to my sister Juana.

"He's not a wetback in the way you say it," whined Juana.

"King snakes sure as hell do bite, if you stick your face in front of one," said Jose.

"They don't bite like a rattlesnake," I said.

"Bite your damned nose off if they get a hold of it," said Paulie.

"Ah, what the hell do you know," said Jose.

"Is anybody in this family going to work today?" I said.

"I am," said Grandpa, "soon as your sister finishes telling me what a wetback is."

"I always thought Marcos was wetback. Looks like one, anyway," said Paulie.

"Well, something out there's been getting my eggs lately," said my mother.

"And you can't expect Marcos to feed the whole family," said my sister Juana.

"Maybe it's Marcos. That wetback is going to sell little Albert and little Julian if you don't keep an eye on him," said my father.

"Yeah, that's right," said Paulie. "Marcos is making us a present of our own eggs."

Juana had given up trying to argue and was just out the door when my father's comment got to her and she came rushing back in, her face almost in tears. "That's not true, Daddy!" she squealed. "Marcos is only trying to make a little something for himself. Which is more than I can say for some people. I don't see any hope for any of you!"

With that, giving each one of us a stern look, she spun on her heels and went out the door again.

"What's wrong with her?" asked my father. "Touchy, all of a sudden."

My brother Elpidio spoke for the first time. "You should leave her alone," he said.

"Yes, all of you. You should leave her alone," said my mother.

"I think I've seen something like that before," said Celia.

"When you met Frank," said Elpidio, smiling and briefly forgetting his troubles.

My mother screamed all of a sudden. We turned to see what was the matter and all we could see was that she had the heels of her palms pressing against her temples.

"Jesus Christ, Ma!" said Paulie. "You're going to scare us to death!"

My mother didn't even notice the blasphemy. "Elpidio, Jose, somebody, this afternoon I want you to go to Nixon," she said.

"I'll be glad to, Ma, I haven't been to town all week," said Jose.

"I'll go with him," said Elpidio.

"Doesn't take much to get them into town, does it?" observed my grandfather.

"Not you, Elpidio," said my mother. "You haven't been to bed all night. You're going to sleep today."

"Not today, I need him to work," said my father.

"Get Grandpa to work for him," said my sister Celia.

"I got my own work to do," said Grandpa.

"Daddy, this is important," said my mother.

"Grandpa has his own work. It is important to him," said my father.

"I'm not tired at all," said Elpidio. "I can work."

"What about Nixon?" said my brother Jose.

"I'll go, I need to think," said Elpidio.

"Go to the outhouse. Daddy says that's where he does his best thinking," said Paulie.

"It's the best place to think," said Grandpa.

"That's enough!" said my mother.

"You boys don't leave without me, I want to go to town, too," said Paulie.

"Ma, if Paulie goes, I want to go too," I said.

"When you get back from school, you're going to go look for the king snake. Take the .22," said my father.

"I'll never find it, Daddy," I protested.

"You will if you look for it hard enough," said Paulie.

"If you're so damned smart, why don't you go out and kill it," I said.

"Can't," said Paulie, "I'll be in town looking at the girls."

"Be quiet, both of you. I have to remember what I need from town," said my mother. "Listen carefully, I want you to buy a cake of some kind, any kind, and some candles. No, no candles. I have candles. Oh, my, there are so many people in this house. And, bring a lot of sodas and candy."

"Ma, it's all right. Never mind," said my sister Celia. "I'll go. Juana can go with me. I know what to get."

"Good, good, you go. I forgot all about you being here, no, I didn't," said my mother. "I don't know what's come over me."

"Forgot about what?" asked my father.

"Oh, I forgot to tell you, too. Heriberto came by on the way home for lunch yesterday. It's Heriberto Junior's birthday today and they're having the party here, now that Celia's children are with us."

"We're going to have a houseful of kids?" asked my grandfather. "I believe I will stay out at my well until dark. If my luck holds up, they'll be gone by the time I get home."

"Grandpa, we're having the party this afternoon. It should be over by four o'clock," said my sister Celia.

"Nothing for the grown-ups?" asked my brother Jose.

"We'll save you some cake," said my mother.

"I've never had a birthday party," said Paulie.

"Me neither," I said.

"There goes the bus," said Celia.

"Get going, all of you," said my mother.

"Are you coming to work with me tomorrow, squirt?"

When Grandpa asked me that, everybody laughed, reminding me of the last time I went with him.

"I have to go to school," I said, pouting because I was not going to get to go to town.

"Tomorrow is Saturday, son," said Grandpa.

Everyone, including my mother, laughed once more.

"If you don't want to go, just say so," said my grandfather.

He didn't sound angry or hurt by my response, just irritated. He preferred direct answers to direct questions.

"I'm sorry, Grandpa, of course, I'll go," I said. "You might have to wake me up if you go real early, but I'll go. I wasn't thinking before when I answered you."

My sister Celia began to hurry little Albert, little Julian and me out the door in the same mother-hen fashion she used with her small children. She probably found it so useful that she tried it out on us to see how far she could get by with it.

On the bus to school, I thought about my sister Celia. In no time at all, it seemed, she reclaimed some of her girlishness and became again as young as she really was and was acting as she had before she went away to be a married woman. We had noted that marriage, the children, and her shithead of a husband had brought on a high seriousness about her, making her look older. The way she moved and spoke made her seem as old as my mother. But now she laughed and told jokes and remembered silly games and things from the time she was a young girl.

Celia went with me one afternoon to slop the pigs. She wanted her kids to see it. As we walked along the road, cutting through the wilting milo field, she remembered that it was once planted in cotton. She remembered trying to pick cotton while holding her doll under her arm. My brother Elpidio she said was just beginning to walk. My brother Jose was a baby and everything my mother did for him, she did for her doll. She had a cotton sack which was five feet long, the shortest my father could find at the store. He had tied a knot in the sack toward the end, shortening it to three feet or so. That way she would not have too much trouble filling it up, and more importantly, dragging it back to the bale wagon. It would be as much as she could fill the entire day. She spent as much time picking cotton as she did playing with her doll, trying to teach the doll to help her pick the cotton.

My mother would make her wear a large, bulky sunbonnet which Celia hated to wear because it didn't fit properly. The bonnet was heavy and by mid morning she would leave it hanging on a cottonstalk and my mother would have to go look for it. Sometimes, one of the picker's children would find it and return it to my mother at the bale wagon. My mother was at her wit's end. My father had work to do elsewhere and my mother had to keep tabs on the bale. In addition, she had to keep track of Elpidio, who, having discovered that his legs could carry him from place to place, took to walking off by himself. She was afraid that snakes or sunstroke would get him. That Elpidio had a fascination for the needles on cactus pads didn't help any. If that weren't enough, my brother Jose rested in a bassinet under the shade of the bale wagon. She had to mind that he was fed, that his diapers got changed and that ants, spiders, beetles and curious lizards didn't crawl into his blanket. My mother expected that my sister Celia would take care of herself.

One day, my mother saw that Celia was so tired it took her a long time to come in for lunch. After lunch, my mother told Celia to stay under the shade of the wagon, but that struck at the heart of Celia's pride. Her cotton sack was still stranded somewhere along the quarter mile rows of cotton. She had been left behind by the other pickers and the cut was already more than a dozen rows over. My mother prevailed upon one of the pickers to take up Celia's row, leaving a five yard stretch for her to pick. The remaining string of her row looked like a white chalk mark in the dark brown expanse of stripped plants.

Little Celia insisted that she be allowed to finish the row, at least. My mother relented, as she was busy with the tally. She was suspicious of a certain family who cheated on their weight by tossing in green leaves, pebbles and cotton bolls. It didn't add that much to the total weight, except that there were five of them together. My mother, working alone, couldn't empty the sacks after they were weighed. This made the culprits a bit bolder, as they emptied their own sacks and then tried to blend their tainted contents with the rest of the bale. She had seen enough to banish them from the fields, only my mother would not do that without consulting with my father. It was a busy season for everybody and hands were hard to come by. Between the five of them, little by little they were stealing five or ten dollars a day. It irked my mother to the point of distraction. She believed in scrupulous honesty and she meant to enforce it upon others.

Meanwhile, little Celia wandered off to continue picking her row of cotton. Her morning exhaustion was compounded by the blistering sun, but she was determined to finish the row. She was too exhausted to carry the doll under her arm anymore. Very shortly she was dragging it by an arm and picking cotton with the other. It was slow going. The cut was now farther away, which meant it would be a long way to drag her sack once she finished.

To relieve her burden a bit and to speed things up, she stuck the doll into the sack along with the cotton. Little Celia began to pick in earnest until the sack was full. She was not strong enough, even if not exhausted, to toss the shortened sack over her shoulder as did the other pickers. Instead, she dragged its dead weight behind her to the wagon which had been moved up twice already to keep up with the cut of pickers. It took her nearly as long to reach the wagon as it did to fill the cottonsack. Once she got to the wagon, she had a sip of ice water and decided her pride had been salvaged. She slipped under the wagonbed, next to my brother Jose's bassinet, and promptly fell asleep.

My mother didn't bother to weigh the cotton. Because it was light and loosely packed, she merely tossed it over the side of the wagon, shaking out its contents until it was empty. My mother never noticed the little pink arm of the doll pointing upward, as if drowning, from the mound of cotton.

My father finished his other work and came to the cottonfield at just about the time he calculated that the wagon would be full to its two bale capacity. He had been unable to find another wagon, so he scouted up the sideroad a ways until he found a tall mesquite from which he could hang the scale. He took the pickaxe from the truck and cleared away a patch of cactus. Until he came back from Candy's, they would have to dump the weighed cotton on the ground. He hated to do it like that, but he had no other choice.

He drove the truck back to the loaded wagon. Before hitching it, he helped my mother gather up the children. They decided it would be best if they went with him, since he could buy Celia and Elpidio some sodas at Candy's. Celia especially needed a reward for her work. My father smiled as he placed her in the truck. She was still asleep as he did so.

It turned out to be another busy day at Candy's cotton gin. There were about a dozen wagons and trailers full of cotton waiting to be ginned. The foreman told my father they intended to work through the night to clear up the backlog. He suggested that my father unhitch the wagon and they would take it from there. He could come for it in the morning.

My father, after he bought some cookies and sodas for the kids, went to the house for a tarpaulin to toss over the cotton on the ground to keep the dew off it. If the wet got down too deep in the night, he would have to spread it out further on the ground to dry it. The tarpaulin would help. He returned to the cottonfield where he helped my mother with the children and the tally.

The next morning, after the dew dried and he gave a nod to the pickers to begin, he went to Candy's for the wagon. He got his receipts for the bales and my father thought it odd that the workers came forward with smiles on their faces. The foreman handed him a badly mangled arm from the doll. He said the ginners had been scared shitless when they caught sight of the doll's pink body rolling around in the drum. One of them had wanted to stop the gin until they could make sure of what it was. The foreman had recognized the doll's head and decided there was nothing to be done about it. The workman was superstitious, though, and he went to the back of the gin where the chopped husks flowed into a mountainous pile and there he found the arm. My father laughed along with the men, but on the way back to the fields that morning, he worried about what to tell little Celia.

When he arrived at the cotton patch, he saw her, her head and shoulders just visible above the level of the plants. The first thing he did when he reached my mother was to show her the doll's arm. My mother became sad. Neither of them said anything while my father began to shovel the cotton on the ground into the wagon. During a lull in the weighing, my mother came over to ask what they ought to do about the doll. Thus far, little Celia had not missed it. My mother's solution called for my father to run into town and buy another one just like it. He said they had bought it two Christmases before and it was unlikely there would be another one just like it to be found. Besides, he said, she would know it wasn't the same one. My father suggested that they tell little Celia the truth. My mother agreed, reluctantly, but she didn't have the heart to break the news to Celia herself. My father felt he would be too brusque with her at a time when she would need some compassion, which was my father's way of trying to get out of it altogether. In the end, they decided it would be best if both of them told her.

My father wanted to wait until lunch to tell her, but my mother wanted to do it once and for all. To the surprise and disgust of several of the pickers who had come in to be weighed and were left waiting, both of my parents went to get Celia where she slowly and patiently picked cotton. As gently as they could they explained what had happened to the doll. My mother and father expected grief of tragic proportions. They were prepared to promise anything to make up for it. Instead, Celia calmly informed them that she was tired of the doll anyway. She felt she was now old enough to have her own pony. All my father could say, was, "Shit!"

I laughed when my sister Celia finished telling me about her doll. I asked her if she ever got the pony.

"Shit!" she said.

# Chapter 19

My sister Celia returned from Nixon loaded down with a bunch of stuff and it didn't occur to anyone that my mother had not given her any money. She had taken all of the money that Elpidio and Jose had between them to pay the bill. Celia told them to get it back from my mother. Elpidio and Jose scoffed at the idea, lamenting their loss. It was a favorite trick of my mother when she was short on money to send them to the store, conveniently forgetting to give them any money. They would pay for the groceries, and if they asked her to pay them back, she would pretend she couldn't hear or understand them. Complaints to my father, which amounted to demands that he settle up her account, came to nothing. My father insisted that they should know better than to expect her to pay them.

When we came back from school, Heriberto's blue Buick was parked in the yard. It was such a warm afternoon that the kids were allowed to play outside. Little Albert and little Julian threw their school books on the porch and went to play with the kids. Inside, my mother, Celia, Juana and my sister-in-law Alva were sitting at the table, appearing exhausted from having so many children to contend with. My brother Jose remarked that the place was overrun with kids. My sister Celia said it was bad enough to try and keep up with her own. She said one kid alone was just one kid, but two of them caused enough trouble that it seemed like four and three kids had the force of nine and it went on multiplying like that.

"Don't forget, your father wants you to go hunt for that king snake at the old place," my mother told me.

"Marcos told me to tell you that he found the snake," said my sister Juana.

"Did he kill it?" I asked.

"No, he chased it away. He said it won't come back anymore."

"How's he know it won't come back?" I asked, not believing the message.

"He just told me to tell you that the snake is not going to be bothering anything anymore." She became irritated with me.

I went to sit with Heriberto on the porch. He was sitting on Grandpa's straight back chair, trying out a few melodies on his accordion. Whenever he brought his accordion, it meant he intended to stay and drink for a while.

My brother Elpidio came in from work, driving up slowly to keep from hitting one of the kids. As soon as he stopped and stepped off, the kids ran to the truck, lining up at the door, going in one door and coming out the other.

"They look like one of those cars in the circus where more clowns come out of it than can fit into it," he said, laughing as he finished with the rhythm buttons on the accordion.

"I don't suppose you want to go out to Westhoff to bring some beer," he asked Elpidio.

Elpidio went inside the house without bothering to answer. For some time now, it seemed that all Heriberto had on his mind was getting drunk.

"You're too damned young to drive, yet, aren't you," he said to me.

"Even if I could drive, I couldn't buy any beer," I said.

"I guess not," he said absentmindedly, slipping into a spirited version of *La piedrera,* which was the polka he could play best.

The music had a good effect on my brother Heriberto. By the time he finished the polka, he was in a good mood. As he played, he lifted his left knee high up in the air and stomped it loudly on the wooden floor of the porch. When he caught someone watching, Heriberto would stretch the bellows of the accordion in a wide arc and squeeze violently in, making the instrument screech and peal at the margins of the tune.

My father and my brother Paulie were the last to come in from work. They must've been arguing about something. My father spoke in mock anger to Paulie and Paulie pretended to not understand, which served to provoke my father even more.

We sprawled out on the porch listlessly, waiting for supper. Paulie had gotten a piece of cake from which he licked all of the frosting. He wadded up the remainder and tossed it to the dogs, who refused to eat it.

Seeing that we were not in a particularly festive mood, Heriberto's playing trailed off into silence. Thereafter, we heard him playing the rhythm buttons, accompanying a tune he played in his mind.

"Come on, guys," he said, "it's my son's birthday. Jose, let's get some beer, get the guitar, let's play something, have a goddamned party!"

"Tomorrow's a work day," my father warned from inside the house.

"Tomorrow is Saturday," said Heriberto.

My mother came outside to tell us supper was ready. Heriberto said he couldn't afford to eat more than once a day. Paulie said no one was inviting him, anyway.

"Don't have to be invited," said Heriberto. "Home is where they have to feed you."

"Don't press your luck," said my father, irritated.

"You shouldn't have children unless you intend to take care of them," he retorted. My father had already gone to the kitchen, not bothering to answer.

"Make us a loan of your truck," Heriberto said to Elpidio.

"Your car's right there! What's wrong with your car?" asked Elpidio, more annoyed than any of us had ever seen him.

"It's almost out of gas, that's what wrong with it. Beats me how you have to keep putting money into your car. Just like the kids, gotta keep feeding them. Anyway, all the gas I got is enough to get home, that's all."

Elpidio knew why he wanted it. "The Sinclair is still open," said Elpidio.

"Yeah, but they're not giving it away, which is what he wants," said Paulie. "You loan him your truck, and he's gonna want somebody else to give him the money for beer."

"I do believe brother Paulie has got me figured out," said Heriberto.

Still, Elpidio made no move to give him the keys. It was unlike him. We didn't know if Heriberto had been told about the Arreagas.

"Here, take mine," said Jose, holding out the keys to him.

"Yours might get me to the creek, but I don't think it'll bring me back," said Heriberto.

"Have it your way," said Jose, "but that's the only truck you'll be getting around here tonight."

Elpidio raised himself up to his feet and went inside the house without saying anything to Heriberto. Before Jose could slip his keys back in his pocket, Heriberto grabbed them out of his hand.

"Not so fast, son," he said, jingling the keys in his hand.

"Come on, squirt, are you going to go with me?" said my brother Heriberto.

"I'm hungry," I said, getting up to go inside. "I'll go if you wait for me to eat."

"Some things a man can't wait on," said Heriberto.

A few minutes later we heard the roar of Jose's truck. Heriberto raced the engine several times. Paulie giggled at the sound of it.

"It's not funny, Paulie," said my brother Jose.

"I wouldn't have loaned him my truck," said Paulie.

"You don't have a truck," I said.

"Why did he borrow your truck?" asked my sister-in-law Alva, afraid of the forthcoming answer.

"He's going to Westhoff for beer, probably," said my father.

"But, why does he have to take Jose's truck?" said Alva.

"He said he didn't have any gas in the car," said Elpidio.

"The car is full of gas," protested Alva. "He filled it up in Smiley on the way over."

"Heriberto was never one to spend his own money when he could spend someone else's," said my father. "Who loaned him the money for the beer?"

"I don't think he asked for any, Daddy," I said.

"Looks like he pulled one over on you, Jose," said Paulie.

"Shut up, Paulie, I don't feel like putting up with you," said Jose.

"A fine birthday party for my grandson," said my father. "What's gotten into everybody?"

At that, Elpidio pushed his plate of food away and excused himself from the table. Grandpa was just coming in when he did so.

"Here, Grandpa, take my plate. I didn't touch anything," he said. With that, he disappeared out the front door. A few moments later, we heard his truck start up, the brief buzz of gears grinding, and he was gone.

"What's wrong with him?" asked Grandpa.

"Nothing, leave him alone," said my father.

"Where's he going?" asked Celia.

Juana was busy helping Alva with the tortillas. "He just wants to be alone, that's all," said Juana.

"That boy has not had any sleep since yesterday," said my mother.

We finished supper more subdued than usual, almost everybody thinking in some way or another about Elpidio and the sorrow he must have felt at having his visits to Concepcion stopped. Even though no one had mentioned it, that's what concerned us most.

Out on the porch, Grandpa took his chair, bending over to loosen the laces of his workshoes.

"Grandpa," said Paulie, "you're the only man I know whose feet swell up from eating."

"They're not swollen, idiot! I'm going to relax them," retorted my grandfather. "A man ought to take care of his feet."

"You always do the same goddamned thing after supper every day," said Paulie, spitting in the direction of a red ant hill, which was too far away for him to hit.

My brother Jose took his place at the corner of the steps. "I wonder if Heriberto is on his way back, yet," he asked of no one.

"He probably went right past Westhoff into Cuero. Today's Friday, right? They used to have those dime-a-dance girls on the dancing platform behind Jimmy Cross-Eye's saloon," said Grandpa, leaning back in his chair.

"Jimmy Cross-Eye died ten years ago, at least," said my father, as he spit over the side of the porch. My father rolled himself a cigarette and passed the sack of tobacco over to Grandpa.

"Is that a fact," said my Grandpa, closing his eyes, letting the last word drag out of him with a drawn out exhalation.

"Don't you remember he got something wrong with his leg? Used to sit at the entrance of his place with that swollen leg of his on a chair. Had a cushion to rest it on. You told him once he ought to cut that leg off and hang it in the smokehouse."

"Did my bad manners show that bad?"

"Yeah, and Jimmy Cross-Eye had just bought us each a beer on top of it. He got so mad, he tried to spit but it landed on his chest."

"News to me," said my grandfather, "I always believed you ought not to make fun of a sick man."

"Poor bastard didn't live too long after that," said my father.

"Now that I remember, I think that's right," said Grandpa. "Didn't his brother-in-law, or somebody, keep the place open after that, though?"

"I don't know about those things, anymore. The boys tell me there's always somebody trying to run that place. I guess old Jimmy Cross-Eye was the only one who knew how to make it pay," said my father.

"Yes, sir, you sure can't put those kinds of smarts away to leave to somebody when you're gone. Me, I never had a knack for business. Closest I ever come to it was this sweet little girl in Gonzales. Sara Ibanez. Her father owned a grocery store. Thinking I was going to marry her was the closest I ever came to going into the mercantile business. And I'd only have it in the family at that."

"The Ibanez? They still run that store, Grandpa. When was the last time you were in Gonzales?" asked Jose.

"The last time I was in Gonzales was the time Franklin Delano Roosevelt himself was supposed to make a stop on his train. They had a whole group of fools going all over the countryside tacking up billboards asking folks to come and see the President of the United States himself. I can't say exactly what he ever did for me, it wasn't like he was a Christian."

"Baptists are Christians, too, Grandpa," I said.

"Baptists speak English and I ain't never met a Christian born speaking English. Anyway, knowing how gullible people are and how high an opinion everyone had about Franklin Delano Roosevelt, like the fools we deserve to be, we all went to Gonzales just to see him."

"I hope this isn't another of your long stories, Grandpa," said Paulie, "it's too damned early to be falling asleep."

"If you slept less and paid more attention, you wouldn't be like you are, Paulie. There might still be some hope for you."

"Finish telling us about Franklin Delano Roosevelt, Grandpa," I said.

"There was a big crowd at the station when the train pulled in, but there was no Franklin Delano Roosevelt. No, sir. Some fat old fool said the President couldn't get away from important business in Washington having to do with the war. But, he said, old Franklin himself had sent him to tell the people of Gonzales how much he had wanted to be there. Before folks started to drift away, the fat fool asked everybody to wait and hear something from Governor Coke R. Stevenson. Seems that the governor wanted to stay on being governor."

"You actually saw the governor, Grandpa," said Paulie, doubtful.

"Surely did, son. It wasn't the first time, either. I got to see Ma Ferguson when she was governor."

"They would never have a woman as governor of Texas, Grandpa. There you go, again, making up your damned stories," said Paulie.

"They did have a woman governor, Paulie. That lady Grandpa just mentioned, she was the governor," I said, proud of myself for having listened in class.

"I don't believe either of you," said Paulie.

"Heriberto better get here with my truck pretty damned soon, that's all I know," said my brother Jose.

"Why'd you loan it to him?" said my father.

"Beats me," said Jose. "Hell, I'd like to know that myself."

"No doubt he ran into somebody he knows in Westhoff," said Grandpa.

"That's right," said my father. "Heriberto has never been one to leave good company behind."

"Sociable, ain't he?" said Paulie.

"I don't think he'll be back till after midnight, when they close all those stinkholes up there," said Jose, miserably.

He didn't need his truck for anything in particular. He loaned it so Heriberto could pick up some beer and come right back. Heriberto was always very good at taking advantage, stretching good will into more than people were willing to give.

"What about Junior's birthday?" I said.

"The kids had their party this afternoon," said my father.

My sister-in-law Alva came outside. She carried the youngest child in her arms. Alva had never felt completely at home with us. With the birth of her grandchildren, my mother had pretty much forgotten her first reaction to Heriberto's marriage. Alva had not forgotten.

She took her time, standing on the porch, before speaking. "Heriberto didn't say he was going to stop anywhere, did he?" she asked, bouncing the baby on her hip.

My father became gentle toward her. "No, he didn't say anything. But, you know how he is. He'll be here soon," he said, almost too matter-of-factly. Alva was embarrassed.

"He's only been like this in the last couple of months," said Alva, defending him.

"I'd say he's been like this his whole damned life," said Paulie, spitting over the side of the porch.

My sister Celia came to stand in the doorway. "Well, there's not much to do about it. You all come inside and get some cake and Kool-Aid before the kids eat it all," she said. She then disappeared inside the house without waiting for a reply from any of us. Alva followed her inside.

"Go and get me something, dog," said Paulie, kicking my leg.

"I ain't going no where," I said.

"I don't want any," said Jose.

"Can't ask a favor of anybody around here," said Paulie, rising and hitching up his pants, in a sulk.

He asked Grandpa and my father if they wanted a plate; both of them answered with a shake of their heads. Paulie did not come back to the porch, the kids probably having gotten him into one of their games.

Outside, on the porch, the early evening breeze was chill but not uncomfortably so. The lights in every room in the house were on. The stillness of the night would be shattered from time to time by the shrill noises of the children inside. At the turn-off from Smiley, the headlights of a car came into view. Jose noticed it right away, as if he had been expecting it all along.

My father allowed as it was probably someone passing through. We could count on knowing the occupant of every car that went by. I waited to see who it was. As the car approached our place, it started to slow down.

"That's not my truck," said Jose, and went back to drawing circles with his forefinger on the porchstep.

It was Ramiro Martinez, a distant cousin and godfather to Heriberto's birthday son. As he drove into the yardway, my father and my grandfather stood up to go greet him and his family. Jose stayed where he was. I didn't move either.

Ramiro Martinez made his greetings from the ground, looking up at my father. His children formed a semicircle behind him. He asked, as he always did, if everybody knew or remembered his wife, who stood next to him, and then he introduced each of his four children, the eldest of whom was ten. His wife excused herself and went inside, where my mother waited for her to join the festivities with her godchild and *comadre*.

My father asked Ramiro to come up to the porch. Jose and I stood up to shake his hand. Juana brought a chair for him to sit on. She motioned for the children to go inside with her. They remained standing near their father. He had to tell them to go on inside before they moved.

Ramiro Martinez asked about his *compadre* Heriberto. My father told him that Heriberto had gone to buy some beer. Ramiro smiled and said that that would be the last we saw of him until the saloons closed for the night. We forced a bit of laughter, out of politeness. When *we* said something like that, it was funny. When somebody else said it, it didn't sound right. Jose wouldn't have thought it was funny, no matter who said it. He kept quiet, glancing out to the road every once in a while.

Fortunately, within the next few minutes, Heriberto came home. It was obvious he had had a few in Westhoff and had been helping himself to the case he brought on the fifteen mile ride back. Heriberto told me to bring the case out of the truck. I did as bidden and when I set it on the edge of the porch, Heriberto asked Ramiro Martinez if he cared for one and Ramiro said he didn't want to but could not refuse a drink with his *compadre* Heriberto in honor of his godchild.

Neither my father nor my grandfather wanted one. Jose was so glad to have his truck back in one piece that he leaned over on his side and took a beer out of the case. He motioned to me to toss him the churchkey.

"Who told you you could have one," said Heriberto, who was about half drunk and belligerent.

"It's a holiday," said my brother Jose.

"I guess it must be," said my father, giving his tacit permission. He did not have to add that Jose was to keep out of sight of my mother who fought valiantly but in vain against any of her children touching alcohol. Heriberto began to drink when he was thirteen or fourteen.

Neither Elpidio nor Jose followed his example, except on occasion. We more or less knew that Paulie would begin to drink just as soon as he began to earn his own money.

Along about ten o'clock, the children in diapers were taken into a pallet on the floor of the front room. Not long after, the older children began to drift off to sleep, including little Albert and little Julian. From time to time we could see inside and either Juana or Celia or Alva would pass by the door carrying another sleeping child.

"I can see we're not going to have a bed tonight," said Jose, who was on his third beer. Paulie was still enjoying himself inside with the remaining kids and the women.

It was after eleven o'clock before it grew quiet and still inside the house. The wind coming through the kitchen toward the front porch carried the hushed female voices and their dainty laughter to us.

Paulie came out patting his stomach to indicate he had eaten a lot of cake and candy and whatever else there had been for the kids. My father said goodnight and went to bed. Grandpa decided to go read his book, but he reminded me that I was to go help him in the morning.

The case still contained seven or eight warm beers. Ramiro Martinez' wife came out to tell him it was late. A little later, Alva called out Heriberto's name. Just his name. Heriberto and his *compadre* Ramiro laughed together. They were not going anywhere until they finished all of the beer. My brother Jose finished his last beer, stretched out on the porch and went to sleep. We knew our beds were full of kids. We were not going to have them until Heriberto and his *compadre* went home.

My sisters, Alva and the wife of Ramiro Martinez were the only ones awake inside the house. Paulie snored loudly and I dozed a little. It was after midnight. Alva came out and told Heriberto it was time to go. She was not angry so much as there was desperation in her voice. Heriberto was quite drunk by this time. Heriberto exaggerated his politeness to mask his anger. He told her that they would leave after one more.

Instead of asking again, Alva and her *comadre* began to take the sleeping children to the cars. They woke up the older boys, who whined all the way, until they found a place to lie down on the carseat.

Once all the children were loaded up, Alva got into the car and sat. Her *comadre* got into her car and sat as well. There they sat for another hour until the men finished the case.

My sister Juana shook Paulie, Jose and me, telling us to go inside to bed. I wanted to stay on the porch, just to keep from getting up, but it was too cold.

# Chapter 20

Grandpa grabbed Paulie's foot and shook him awake. "Come on, it's morning," he said. "It's late."

Paulie, still deeply asleep, kicked at Grandpa, which is when Grandpa knew I was the other sleeping body huddled in the blankets. He leaned over to pull on my leg and as soon as he did so, I was instantly awake.

"I want to sleep," whined Paulie. Just to be mean, I shook him by the shoulders until he was fully awake.

"What the hell do you want," he growled, angrily.

"Let's go with Grandpa," I said.

My grandfather was standing by the doorway to make sure I did not fall asleep again.

"I don't want him with me," he said, in a low voice.

"I guess you can't go, then, Paulie," I said, knowing that was all the invitation he needed.

Paulie pulled the covers over his head and tried to go back to sleep. I got up and scrambled around looking for my trousers. I tripped over Heriberto's snoring body. I couldn't find my pants. Somebody had moved them for me so that Heriberto could have a place to sleep on the floor. After a frantic search, shivering in the morning cold, I found them behind a box in the corner of the room. I remembered that I had kicked my boots off on the porch. I found them stiff and damp.

Paulie's voice, deep from his grogginess, groaned from under the covers. "Is he really digging a fucking well?" he said.

"You were out with him once," I said.

"I thought he was just fucking around," said Paulie.

"Well, I was there on Thursday helping him with it. He's down about five feet already," I said, slipping into my shirt.

"Yeah, well, maybe I'll go with you," said Paulie, lifting his head partially from under the covers.

"Come on, hurry it up," I said. "Grandpa leaves as soon as he has breakfast. He probably is finishing up right now."

In fact, my mother and father were still asleep and there was no one to fix breakfast. On his own, my grandfather was making some coffee, by which he waited as it percolated on the stove.

"No breakfast today, squirt," he said, as I came in, rubbing sleep from my eyes.

"Where's Alva and the kids?" I asked.

"She probably went home by herself, leaving Heriberto here," he said.

I stared at him, making a considerable effort to keep my eyes wide. If I relaxed them, they might clamp shut for another hour or two. I went outside to wash my face and brush my teeth.

"Paulie's coming with us," I said.

"No, he ain't," said my grandfather, calmly.

"We could use the help," I said.

"Not his kind of help," he said, flatly.

"Maybe I'll just watch, then," said Paulie, yawning and scratching his head. Grandpa did not respond.

"We'll take this coffee. Later on, we can go on up to Candy's, see what they have ready-made to eat. Maybe some bologna and cheese. How's that grab you?" he said and smiled. I hated bologna.

When the coffee was done, he filled two mason jars, pouring liberal amounts of milk and sugar in each. He wrapped each jar in a dishtowel to keep it warm.

As we went to the mesquite clump to saddle up Elpidio's mare, I told him I wanted to take my own horse. He understood that I did not wish to be seen as a child who had to ride behind him to Candy's. I especially did not want to ride double with Paulie along. My grandfather respected that. Riding a horse of my own would surely earn even more respect for me from our neighbors who would be spending something of a Saturday morning lazing around the store as was the custom in Schoolland for so many years. I wanted to be recognized for my own self and not simply as one of my father's children.

The horses in the mesquite clump were noticeably nervous as we approached them. Normally, when they saw one of us, they came running, certain that we were about to feed them. This time, they threw their heads in the air, snorted and whinnied and bucked.

"There must have been a coyote around here last night," I said, "or maybe there's a rattler coiled up in the cactus somewhere."

"I would say there's a lion somewhere close," said my grandfather.

"A lion? I thought this was the wrong kind of country for cats," I said.

"It is, but they don't always know that. Every once in a while, one of them gets off his feed a little and ends up around here."

Grandpa thought for a minute. "If they have to come this far south for food and water, that can only mean it is parched up where they belong."

We got a pair of ropes from the tackshed and went along the trails between the cactus and chaparral to bring in the horses. I wasn't entirely convinced that one of the horses hadn't been scared by a snake, so I kept a close eye to the ground. I was going to ride my father's paint mare. Twice I paid so much attention to the ground near my feet, looking for a rattler, that the black reared up on its hind legs and scampered away bucking and kicking.

Grandpa roped Elpidio's mare on the first try and stood by her, rubbing her neck for a while to calm her down. On my next try, I got the rope over the paint's head. Ordinarily, she was supposed to stand still once a rope was on her.

This is what she did, but when I approached her, she bolted, jerking the rope out of my hands. She stopped a short distance away and let me get close enough to pick up the rope. Again, as I came near, she ran. This time, she ran toward the feeder shed. Paulie ran over and picked up the loose rope, twisting it behind his back as he dug his heels into the dirt. The paint didn't run, but she tried to back away, dragging Paulie along. I came around, avoiding her nervous hind legs, holding out my hand to calm her down. The paint reared high up on her hind legs, pawing at the air with her hooves. I got the hell out of the way.

"That damned mare is going to kill you both!" shouted my grandfather.

I started for the mare again. She backed away, despite Paulie's pulling on the rope. The paint kept her feet on the ground, but her head was high in the air, her eyes wide with terror, her ears pointed sharp and crisp. I got close enough to where I patted her on the neck, rubbing my hand along the coarse hair. She calmed down a little, but when I moved suddenly, she was afraid all over again. It took several minutes before she was settled enough to where I could turn my back and pull on the rope, leading her along to the feeder shed. After some resistance, she followed meekly. Whatever had spooked her, she was over it and she became as gentle as ever, once she was in front of the feed shed. Not that it did any good, but I gave her some of Elpidio's oats.

It had been a while since anyone had ridden my father's paint mare and she kept ducking and twisting her head out of the way as I tried to hang the bridle behind her ears. Grandpa, who had just tossed the saddle on Elpidio's mare, came over and hugged the paint by the neck, holding her head still. As quickly as I could I put the bridle on, forcing her jaws apart to slip in the bit and then, hooking the strap behind her cheeks, I loosely wound the reins around a post, fearful that if she spooked again, she might snap them apart. Once she got the bridle, she became quiet and settled.

"I think I better ride the paint," said Paulie. "You can ride my black."

"I can ride as well as you can," I snapped.

"Have it your way," said Paulie. He stuck two fingers in his mouth and whistled for his horse. The horse came running.

"It helps to have a trained animal," Paulie gloated.

I was going to have to use José's saddle, which was larger and heavier than the one my father had bought for me and Paulie to use. Since Paulie would be going with us, he had first claim on it. My brother Jose didn't mind me using his saddle, provided I left the stirrups adjusted to his legs. This meant I would have to adjust them for my legs and return them to their proper length in the evening. The lacing was a pain in the ass, but it was preferable to bouncing in the saddle, with my feet dangling and riding up to Candy's where everyone would surely laugh at me.

It took me several tries, but I finally got the saddle over the paint's back. I cinched it up tight, jerking on the saddlehorn to make sure it didn't slip. Grandpa had finished saddling Elpidio's mare and he came over to check my work. He loosened it a little, saying it was too tight.

Paulie saddled his horse in no time. While he waited for us, he opened one of the mason jars full of coffee that Grandpa had placed on the oat bin. Grandpa joined him in drinking the coffee while I relaced the stirrups for my short legs.

"There's a lion around," said Grandpa.

"Bullshit!" said Paulie, spitting out some of the coffee after he rinsed his mouth with it.

"I wouldn't expect an idiot to believe something like that," my grandfather said.

Paulie shrugged his head in complete indifference. Instead of handing the mason jar to Grandpa, Paulie walked over to his horse. He poured a little of the coffee into the palm of his hand and let the horse lap it up. He did this several times before he handed the jar to Grandpa. My grandfather didn't say anything as Paulie mounted the horse.

Grandpa tied a piece of twine to the tops of the mason jars and draped them over the neck of Elpidio's mare. Paulie got tired of waiting for me and Grandpa. He jerked the reins of his horse, kicked the horse briskly and took off at a gallop.

"That boy is crazy," said my grandfather. "I don't think we'll get much done today with him around."

"Paulie only does the things he does when there's people around, Grandpa," I said.

"Maybe so," said my grandfather.

By the time we were mounted and on our way, Paulie had reached the gate, opened it, and remounted. He was off again at an easy lope, following the curve of the road. My grandfather whistled to him to stop, but instead, Paulie turned his horse around and came back.

"You were going the wrong way," I said, to keep the two of them from arguing. "We're going to Grandpa's piece of land," I said, by way of explanation.

"I know where it is, idiot!" yelled Paulie. "If there's a goddamned lion around here, we should be checking on the cows, just in case."

I felt my jaws go slack. For the first time, I realized that my brother Paulie was more responsible about things than he let on.

"Not a bad idea, Paulie," said my grandfather.

Curiously, Paulie was neither pleased nor his usual insolent self about the comment. He simply rode away to hunt up the cattle and check to see if anything was amiss. In parting, he shouted over his shoulder that he would catch up with us. By the time we got to the gate going out of our place, Paulie caught up to us. We rode past the gate and abreast of one another on sandy gravel road. Paulie was looking at the milo to the left as we rode south. There was a frown on his face.

"That milo's in trouble," said Paulie. "I wonder if Pa has seen it."

"He's seen it," said Grandpa. "You check on those cows?"

"Naw," said Paulie. "They're not at the north end. I figure we can check on them across the fence up ahead. They're by those trees up there." Paulie nudged his horse into a gallop and rode on ahead of us.

There was a shady area where the oaks had not been cleared away. It was left there for the cattle. The only pasture land we had began at the edge of the milo. It was sparsely dotted with a few oaks and lots of mesquite trees. The cattle tended to gather under the oaks, venturing out to graze and to water at the tank nearby.

Many of the cows were lying down; a few others, those with calves, were up for the morning feeding of their calves.

"You remember how many there's supposed to be?" asked Grandpa.

"Yeah, there's forty-seven cows and there should be fourteen calves from this spring," said Paulie.

"Let's see if we can make a count from this side of the fence," said Grandpa.

"There's bound to be one or two son-of-a-bitches off where we won't see them," said Paulie. "I better go on through. You two can wait here if you want to."

He walked the horse until he found the gate. He leaned over on the saddle, not bothering to dismount, to open the barbed wire gate. When he got it loose and began to pull it toward the horse, the animal spooked and shied away from it, causing Paulie to lose his grip on the gatepost.

"Son-of-a-bitch!" said Paulie.

He nudged the horse forward, but he could not make him go near the barbed wire. Cursing under his breath, Paulie had to dismount to open the gate wide enough for the horse to go through.

Paulie went in and remained just inside the pasture, standing up on the stirrups, straining to count each cow. Without looking our way or saying a word, he raised his elbows perpendicular to his torso and whistled, which sent his horse flying in the direction of the stock tank.

"I count three missing," said Grandpa.

"A lion wouldn't take down a whole cow, would he, Grandpa?" I asked.

"No, not at all," said Grandpa, spitting over his shoulder. "But, those new calves are just about right."

I found it difficult to believe that Paulie and Grandpa knew so much about the cattle. The only time I ever noticed them was when they grazed near the house, and even then I just made sure they didn't chase me when I went to feed the pigs.

Paulie came riding back at an easy, graceful gallop, which seemed unusual, as his horse was large and ungainly. He slowed to pass through the gate and jumped off the horse. He told us he had a good count and closed the gate.

"I found the missing cows over by the stock tank," said Paulie. "There's not more than a foot of water in there. We're going to have to start watering them at the trough by the house." Neither Grandpa nor I said anything.

We took our time getting to the well dig. The first thing I looked for was the size of the mound I had started. It seemed to have increased in height but not by much.

"I guess we can make some good progress today, with three of us along," said Grandpa.

"You mean the two of you, don't you, old man," said my brother Paulie. "I just came along for the ride. I'm not going to do any goddamned digging. Cowhands don't dig."

"Where the hell did you get the idea you're a cowhand," said my grandfather.

Paulie ignored him.

"Goddamn it! I should've brought a rifle, do some squirrel hunting when nobody's looking. Nobody ever comes here so there must be lots of animals to shoot at."

Grandpa glanced over at Paulie, shook his head, and began his preparations. Grandpa got his tools together and lowered himself into the hole. He was down to where the lip of the hole came up to his chest. Grandpa labored methodically for nearly an hour. He was on a layer of soft earth, which he pried with the shovel, quickly filling up the bucket. Within the hour, he advanced a couple of feet down to where I could see only his head bobbing in and out of the hole.

I kept pace with Grandpa, taking the buckets and running them over to the mound beside the oak nearby. I was rested and only had a vague reminder of the soreness from the last time I helped with the well. This time, too, I was not going to allow Paulie to poke fun at me. Paulie was having a hard time entertaining himself. He went down to the remains of the house, picking over things, trying to find something he could use. He wasn't there for too long before he got bored and came back. He saw me struggling with the bucket of dirt. I was already sweating and I could feel the signs of my body playing out. I dropped the bucket and while I wiped the sweat from my brow, I asked if he intended to help.

Paulie's answer was, "Shit, no!" He crawled to the top of the mound of dirt begun by Grandpa beside the hole. He saw me continue to struggle with the buckets of dirt, saw how it was becoming more and more difficult for Grandpa to hold them over his head for me to take them. After what seemed to be a very long time, Paulie finally slid down the mound of dirt, placing his hands on his hips, and saying as he slid down, "You two are doing it all wrong."

"Suppose you show us a better way, smart-ass," said Grandpa, out of breath, the pace of his work having gotten to him.

"Tie a rope to the bucket," said Paulie, as he paced around the hole. "There's some mesquite posts back at that house we could use. We need three of them and a pulley. In fact, I could probably ride out to the barn right quick and get the one we have there. I don't mean to tell you your business, Grandpa, but it might save you some work."

"You wouldn't want to get off your ass and put it all together, would you?" asked Grandpa, breathing heavily, having to toss his head way back in order to see out of the hole.

"Not right now. I figure everybody's at Candy's by this time. I'm going to go get a soda. How about you, squirt? Want me to bring you one back?" said Paulie.

"Why don't you wait and we'll go together," I said.

"What the hell," said Grandpa, "let's go now. We shouldn't have to work so damned hard on a Saturday."

"If you buy the sodas, Grandpa, I'll help with the well all day today. I ain't done anything stupid for a while," said Paulie.

"I'll buy because you're my grandson, that's all. If you want to help later, that's up to you. You don't have to. I won't pay for your labor."

"Have it your way, all I want is a coke."

Paulie was the first on his horse and was back on the road before we mounted. Paulie kicked his horse into a swift run, leaving a dust funnel behind as he rode. When he had gone a quarter of a mile, he stopped to wait for us. I wanted to get the paint mare some decent exercise, too, but I couldn't leave Grandpa behind. We had seen a movie with Tony Aguilar during the Mexican night at the Nixon Theater where Tony made his horse lift his paw to shake hands. Paulie had gotten off his horse and was trying to teach him the same trick, but the horse would have none of it. We asked him what he thought he was doing when we came up.

"You go on, I'll catch up later," he said, continuing to try and teach the horse.

I twisted back in the saddle and saw Paulie grab the saddlehorn with both hands and swing into the air trying to land in the saddle as we had seen the gringo cowboys do in the movies. His ankle landed on the hard surface of the saddle, but it was enough for him to pull the rest of his body up until he was astraddle.

Paulie's stunt made the horse nervous. Paulie nudged him in the ribs, but the horse would not gallop. Then Paulie's feet went out at right angles to his body and he kicked several times, but the best he could get his horse to do was work up to a fast trot, which forced Paulie to stand up in the stirrups, else his tailbone would have been pummeled to a month of soreness. He next tried odd noises and whistles to scare the horse, but that didn't help, either. Paulie was not one to doggedly pursue the impossible. He gave up trying to get the horse to move, allowing him to stay several yards behind Grandpa and me all the way to Candy's.

The crowd at Candy's was fuller than it should have been for the time of year. Normally, there was plenty of work to do seven days out of seven. Although Saturdays were full working days, it was forgivable to take an hour or so to visit at Candy's.

The men at Candy's on this Saturday had the look of men with little to do. Without work, they sought the company of others. There were only a few of the old people at the store and Grandpa looked forward to joining them in a conversation, which probably began when the store first opened twenty years before and had probably gone on ever since.

The talk here was of drought and how many of the gringo bosses were already starting to ship cattle to market trying to beat the forthcoming onslaught which would surely drive prices down.

I didn't understand too much of it. I had yet to detect any effects of the drought, except for the stunted milo field and Paulie saying that the stock tank was almost dry.

Old man Candy had spent so much of his life in a wheelchair that no one much remembered what put him in it in the first place. His wheelchair was on a riser in a corner of the store. The store's office was just to one side of him. Candy's daughter, Miss Gretchen, took care of things, pointing him in the direction of the shelving and the doubledoor entrance, so he would have something pleasant to see.

In recent years, old man Candy had had a stroke, which left him paralyzed to where Miss Gretchen, who was getting on in years herself, had to feed him and do everything else for him. Nothing in him that one could detect moved, except for his eyes. His eyes seemed fixed on some spot which gave his peripheral vision a view of the entire store. If you looked straight into his eyes, it seemed he looked right past you. Old man Candy could never trust Mexicans and so he spent all of his life now watching that no one stole anything. Since his stroke, old man Candy was imprisoned by the straps of his wheelchair. He could see everything but he couldn't do anything about it.

Paulie and I were in the store once when Candy's daughter went outside to burn some trash. Paulie got himself a Payday peanut bar, walking right up to the old man, waving it in his face, and then stuffed it in his mouth, chomping on it until he finished swallowing it. He did it in front of the old man's face. Except for his eyes twitching, nothing about him moved.

"We're going to get in trouble," I remember saying to Paulie.

"There's nothing the old fart can do about it," said Paulie. "He can't talk. If you see something and can't tell about it, as far as anyone knows, it didn't happen. This old fool can't do a goddamn thing about it. Fuck him."

When Miss Gretchen came back, I expected trouble. Paulie wasn't too sure he was going to get away with it, either, so he went to sit out on the porch, leaving me to face Miss Gretchen. All she did was ask about my father and how we were all doing. Although Miss Gretchen smiled and was friendly to us, as she was with everybody, she too feared we, any Mexican, were robbing her blind. And so it was that the presence of old man Candy was enough to scare some people. Paulie and I took to calling him a human scarecrow.

Grandpa dismounted in front of the store and handed me the reins. I rode off to the side of the building to tether the horses. Paulie was just coming in as I rounded the corner of the building on my way inside. The RC Cola's were in the back cooler, right under the gaze of old man Candy. I tried to avoid looking at him, but the more I convinced myself I should avoid his gaze, the more drawn I was to look at him. There was something intractable and menacing about the old man which made looking directly into his eyes even more irresistible. His eyes were large and glassy, like marbles made pale by the sun, full of hatred as if he held me and anyone who looked at him responsible for the loss of his human movement. Every time I saw the old man, I was sure he remembered the candy bar which my brother Paulie had stolen and I knew he would surely hold me responsible for it. Maybe the old man just hated anyone who walked and talked.

I got me an RC and a Moon-Pie and told Candy's daughter that my grandfather would pay for it. Paulie had come in behind me and had gotten himself a can of sardines and a stack of Saltines, paying for it himself. One of the old people sitting with my grandfather, when he saw Paulie peel back the lid and pour the oil into the grass on the side of the porch, remarked that sardines had the distinct odor of some whores he could remember that used to work the saloons in Gonzales. Paulie ignored the remark; any retort from him would have embarrassed my grandfather.

Paulie and I were too young to join the men who made up the remainder of the crowd at Candy's porch. There was no one else present of our age and so we contented ourselves with drinking our sodas and listening. I didn't mind that too much, but Paulie, who was in such a great goddamned hurry to become an adult, found it unbearable.

Just about the time we were ready to leave, going on toward noon, my father drove up with my brother Jose. We were mounted already and Paulie, who had not seen them, had crossed the road and was waiting for us. My grandfather reined in so as to greet my father. My father came over to Elpidio's mare and began to tighten the cinch. It was a pretext on my father's part. He spoke low enough so no one sitting on the porch could hear.

"Did you happen to notice when Elpidio came in last night?" My father was serious, a stern look fixed firmly on his face.

"No, I didn't," said my grandfather. "I was sound asleep, which means it was pretty late, since it takes me several hours to fall asleep at night."

My father nodded and slapped the mare's bottom as Grandpa gave her her rein. I had not heard the question, but could figure out it had to do with Elpidio.

Back at the well, Paulie got to work with a vengeance. Paulie would struggle against everything to keep from doing something. He just didn't like to be told to do anything. Once there was no getting out of it, he threw himself into a task with an unnatural ferocity.

"I'll dig in the hole, Grandpa," said Paulie. "Why don't you go find some wood and shit and build a rig to draw out the water. We can use it in the meantime to draw up the dirt."

I thought it was a good idea. Not only that, but it was nice of Paulie to offer it. Grandpa became grouchy.

"I'll just find me something good enough to bring out the dirt," said my grandfather. "No sense in building something for nothing if it turns out to be a dry hole after all."

Paulie's lips curled into a sneer. He didn't like his ideas rejected like that. He took his anger out with the spade, shovelling dirt at a rapid pace.

Grandpa found some old fenceposts and a long strand of barbed wire. With his pocketknife, he notched each post. He had Paulie come out of the hole and each of us held one of the posts, while he carefully laid the third one so the tips met. He bent the barbed wire back and forth until he cut a short piece of it which he wrapped around the top of the fenceposts, guiding the wire into the grooves he had cut. It was a little wobbly but it held.

With the spade, he dug a hole under each post to further buttress it. Grandpa used the remaining piece of barbed wire to secure the posts about a foot or so from the top.

"What are we going to use for a pulley?" said Paulie.

"We won't need one today," said Grandpa.

Paulie dropped back down in the hole, while Grandpa went to get a short rope which he had stuffed into his canvas toolbag. He tied the rope to the handle of the bucket. Paulie was nearly a foot shorter than Grandpa and he had trouble handing the bucket up to me. The rope made it easier.

For the rest of the afternoon, Grandpa and I hauled away the dirt, while Paulie dug furiously below.

"I'm going to have to bring a ladder to get in and out of the hole," said Grandpa, during a rest period.

"You're going to have to shore up that thing, too," said Paulie, "else, that thing is going to cave in and you're liable to save the family the expense of a funeral."

"Paulie," I said, "don't even think something like that."

"You'd like that just fine, wouldn't you, you little shit," was the calm response from my grandfather.

"Have it your way," said Paulie. "I was only making a suggestion."

Grandpa began to put his tools away. "Let's get on home, I think I've had enough for one day," he said.

"What's the matter, old man? Can't take it?" Paulie said, baiting Grandpa.

Grandpa grumbled that he was going to take a few days to scrounge up some more tools and some lumber. With Paulie helping, we were able to get everything put away and we went home. Paulie tried to interest me into going hunting with him, as there was still plenty of daylight left, but I was too tired from hauling dirt and didn't feel like it.

My father and my brother Jose were still out working when we got back. Grandpa left Elpidio's mare for me to unsaddle and feed. Paulie walked his horse around the mesquite clump to cool him down, although he had not thoroughly exercised him. After making the widest circle he could, following the cowpaths, he brought the horse to water making sure that the horse didn't drink too much before being turned loose.

"Goddamn horses are too goddamn fat," said Paulie. "We need to ride them more often."

"We probably are going to have to sell them if what Grandpa says is true," I said.

"That drought shit he keeps talking about? Bullshit!" spat Paulie. "They're going to have to sell me first before they sell my horse." He spoke the last with a solemnity that could be taken seriously or not.

"Well, don't give anybody any ideas, idiot!" I cautioned him.

Celia, Juana and my mother were preparing supper in the kitchen. The kids were chasing each other through the rooms of the house, making such noises as only a mother can endure. Grandpa said he was going to the bunkhouse to listen to the black widows spin their webs, maybe read and take a nap before supper. My mother told him supper was almost ready, but he wasn't listening to her.

Paulie got some cards and talked me into playing a quick game of gin rummy. We ignored my mother's warnings to get out of the kitchen while they prepared the food. We figured they were gossiping and didn't want us to hear any of it.

My father and Jose came home earlier than usual. They didn't appear to have been at work. Paulie said something to them about it, but they ignored him. My father asked about my brother Elpidio.

"I don't know," said my mother. "He said he was going somewhere and he left as soon as he drank some coffee this morning. He wouldn't even eat breakfast. He hasn't been back at all today."

"Maybe I should talk to that boy," said my father.

"Leave him alone, Daddy," said my sister Celia. "He just lost his girlfriend. Don't you know what it is to be young and in love?"

"Not hardly," said my father, irritably.

"He's all sick inside about it," said Celia.

"Can't a man get a cup of coffee in this house?"

"Go on to Smiley. The Blue Goose is bound to have plenty of coffee," said my mother, testily.

"If I wanted coffee in Smiley, I would be there already drinking it," said my father.

"Don't start," said my mother.

"Oh, stop it, you two!" said sister Juana.

"You can't win around here, Pa," said Paulie.

"I guess not," said my father.

"Make your father some coffee, Juana," said my mother and that was the end of it.

# Chapter 21

The ground was parched and dry. The drought had gone deep into the earth, past the soft loam into the hardpack. As we walked along the fields, there were crevices in the ground that went down a foot and more. I wondered how far into the earth the cracks could go. My grandfather made the observation that if it stayed dry long enough, a crack would open up straight into hell itself. My brother Paulie countered that we would all have starved to death by then and it wouldn't matter much.

The crops, stunted and spindly, shrivelled sharp and black. As we walked across the furrows, the stalks would crumble into a black powdery mist around our ankles. The residue resembling black ashes stained our boots. The incessant breezes blowing for nearly a month had swept away most of the top soil. It had been swept away a grain at a time over and around the terraces built by the government to prevent such a thing from happening. My grandfather made no attempt to display the scorn he felt toward the government agents who had terraced our land.

The temperatures were not as hot as they ought to have been for the month of June. The nights were unusually cool. The dawn lasted only for an instant and then there was the sun, white and relentless. Without a cloud in the sky, its unrelenting rays burned everything. What made the heat bearable, pleasant almost, were the breezes. Soft, gentle, apologetic breezes that swirled and Standing on the porch of the house, we would see way off clouds of dust like a brown fog, low to the road, rolling toward us. We could measure how fast they came by the steady wind that pressed against our faces. The breeze wasn't strong enough to make our hair flutter, but we could still feel it on our faces, on our necks, on our arms. We felt the breeze brush against us first thing in the morning to the last thing at night. If we awoke in the night, we could hear it against the window panes, pressing against them, making soft tapping noises with the loose ones.

The talk at the gas stations and at the grocery stores and wherever men gathered to pass the time of day concerned the length of the drought. The old people remembered the hot spells and the dry spells of yesteryear. They recounted vividly stories of farms and ranches lost, carried away by the winds. They told of cattle and horses dying and decaying completely from one day to the next, of whole herds weak from thirst, unable to find safety in a ravine or a gulch, choked and strangled by the wind and dust.

They talked too of good men gone bad, not weak men or foolish men, but men who were unlucky, who had salt mixed in with their blood. The old people called up memories of having survived the droughts of the past, but they could not say whether they would survive this one. From the droughts of the past they went on to tell of floods and tornadoes and northers that froze cattle on the hoof. The calamities of nature were God-sent and therefore mysterious and none of them could bring himself to curse them.

They also raised the specter of truly evil men, men in white shirts and black ties, who drove cars that a decent working man could never afford, who carried clipboards and briefcases and who spoke in tongues that even other white men could not understand. Men who came to claim the lifestuff of those who worked the land, men who left in their wake the No Trespassing signs that resembled gravemarkers posted where a brother, or an uncle, or a cousin, or a neighbor, used to live.

The younger men listened to the old people, impatient for their turn to talk, for their brief opportunity to turn aside in words hurried and brash the ineluctable persistence of the past as it lived and breathed in the old men. And the young men, not having had as yet a past to relive, had but one thing to look toward and that was tomorrow. They flaunted, though still respectful, the countless days and months and years left to them. If they could hold on for a month, for two months, for four months, there was winter wheat to plant, and oats, and if the weather held up, they might just make it with hay bales alone. If they could hold on, there was the cattle market, too. If they could hold on to their beef, there was bound to be a shortage and prices would have to go up. If they could just hold on, the young men thought, they might just get rich out of the drought. If the banks could hold off and if they had money to lend, there were those who planned on putting up chicken ranches, even though the money wasn't as good, but it was steady and that meant a man could pay his bills and maybe salt a little of it away for tomorrow.

That's all the young men had. Tomorrow.

The one thing everyone in Schoolland wanted to know was how long the drought would last. It had not rained since March and it was already well into July, and no one, not even the County Agent knew anything. The severity of the drought itself was sinking in in little ways that, by themselves, didn't need notice. With the crops gone, no one seemed to care much about it, either. With the crops gone, a whole year's worth of borrowing, planning, sweating and hoping was destroyed. When they speculated as to how long the drought would last, it was useless. They had no need to know how long it would last.

For most everybody in Schoolland, the year ended toward the close of June. For everyone in Schoolland, there was nothing to do but wait and hope and look forward to next spring. How to live, how to hold on for the time being, was another matter. There was hardly a day went by without two or three people stopping at our place looking for work. Some were the familiar faces of lifelong friends and neighbors; others, strange faces, had the look of the road on them, miles of desperation carved deeply into their foreheads and their cheeks.

It pained my father to have to say no for he knew that for the men who came by gasoline was an expense that would not be recovered that day. Some of those who stopped spoke in low, plaintive voices that descended into outright begging. At first, for those people that my father knew, he kept a little money in his pocket. He would take them over by the fence, away from our inquisitive eyes, and force a dollar or two on them, a small loan for their gasoline and their trouble. When the men were certain that their pride would not suffer, they took the folded bills, stuffing them quickly in their pockets, shooting a quick glance at my brothers and me on the porch. We tried not to look, to pretend we had other things to think about. And we were thinking, thinking of how we would feel if we, too, were forced into taking charity. It was something that none of us ever gave voice to, knowing, somehow, that each of us thought about it.

At first, too, my mother did not interfere with my father's generosity to his friends and some of our relatives. It was her conviction that by sharing what we had we were twice as worthy to have it. Although my mother never quite understood money, she had a definite sense or an intuition of it. If my father were to have brought a sack of money equal to our worth, it would have been meaningless to my mother. She understood, though, that at times there was enough money and at other times there was not. In any event, she made do with what there was.

Toward the end of the month, she understood probably better than my father, who knew the exact dollar amount, that we were running out of money. We became afraid when, following another loan made by my father, she cautioned him, suggesting that he might want to hold on to some of those dollars. Just in case.

# Chapter 22

By mid-July, my school vacation was more than half over. There was little to do all day long except sit on the porch and daydream. Paulie and I had given up hunting because there was nothing to shoot at, not even buzzards.

For the first few weeks after school ended, I had Samantha Coleman. She would come by in her mother's car to pick me up and we would go for rides. Samantha left to spend the rest of the summer in Mobile, Alabama, with her aunt. She sent me a postcard every day with a scenic view of Mobile. When she ran out of scenic views to send, she used regular stationery. I wrote to Samantha, but not every day as I didn't have anything to say to her. The days in Schoolland were all the same. I thought about copying the same letter and changing a few things and sending it to her every day. I didn't think that was nice, though. With Samantha gone, I began to realize how bad things were. I had no choice but to notice.

My sister Celia's husband came for a visit, his first in months. After a brief reacquaintance with the kids, Celia standing by none too pleased with him, the two of them went for a ride. When they came back, the son-of-a-bitch didn't even bother getting out of the car to say goodbye to anybody. He left in kind of a hurry. Celia, for once, was not all in a gush to tell what happened. She spent most of the day to herself and at breakfast the next day she announced that she would give Frank another chance. There wasn't a whole hell of a lot of conviction in her voice, so we figured she was doing it for the children. Before any of us had much of a chance to say anything, Frank drove up to take Celia and the kids away. My father's face said it was bad business. My mother gave us all a look that warned us to stay out of it.

My grandfather was the only one working. He was still digging his well. Paulie and I volunteered all the time to help him with it. He wouldn't let us, saying he'd rather be out there alone. As we didn't have the enthusiasm to do anything, we didn't bother to argue with Grandpa. My father had kept up going off every morning as if to work. He did it out of habit and maybe because he wanted to keep things as normal as possible. My mother would fix a lunch for him. One or two of my brothers would go with him. Many times he came back in the early afternoon, his lunch sack untouched. He would hand the sack over to the twins who would take it to the mesquite grove for a picnic.

My father kept up the pretense as long as possible. He wasn't fooling anybody and so he gave it up. He began getting up earlier in the morning to go sit on the porch where he would smoke one Bull Durham cigarette after another. It seemed, too, that the words inside him became fewer. He hardly ever said anything and when he did, he did so sparingly in response to someone's question. After my mother's warning about the money, he began to go on long walks just so he wouldn't have to face the men who came by. He needn't have bothered because they stopped coming, too. In fact, no one seemed to be traveling much. It would be hours before a car would drive by on the road in front of the house. Paulie and I went to Candy's store one afternoon in Elpidio's truck only to find it closed. There were so few people coming by, and those that did bought so little that Miss Gretchen opened the store for just a couple of hours in the morning.

In Smiley, the stores and the gas stations were opened, but by midafternoon, everyone went home to sit in the shade of their yards and to take naps.

My mother wasn't used to having so many people in the house for the entire day. Even in the summers when we were out of school, we were usually put to work and so she enjoyed her quiet hours alone. With everyone in the house all day long, her whole life was disrupted. My mother started to take it out on us, scolding us for no good reason. She would be standing over the stove and as I came in for a drink of water, she would shoot me a look of anger, sharp and piercing. I would lamely say that I wanted some water, which I could damned well get for myself. Instead, my mother would fling a spoon into the pan and jerk a glass from the cupboard and fill it for me. Another time, when I surprised her in the kitchen, it was obvious that she had been crying. I asked her what was wrong and she told me to get what I came for and get out.

My brother Elpidio's condition had not changed at all since he was run off don Antonio Arreaga's place. He mostly kept to himself. Sometimes he went for the entire day without speaking to anyone. It was only in the evenings, at dusk, that he changed and became cheerful again. But that only lasted for a short little while, until he got into his truck and went off somewhere. There was no need to ask where he went. It would be very late when he returned.

I could tell that my mother and father were worried about him. I overhead my parents talking one morning about Elpidio having come in at daybreak. He had shut down the lights of his truck before he turned into our place, but my mother had heard him come in. To cover himself, he had not bothered to come into the house for something to eat as he did at other times. He had gone directly to the bunkhouse.

My mother and my sister Juana must have had a fight or something, as they had not been speaking to one another for several weeks. They tried not to make it so obvious, but it was obvious. Juana would spend long hours of the day in bed, reading her movie magazines and some books that she got from the Smiley library. When she wasn't in bed reading, she took to spending the rest of her time out at the old house with Marcos de la Fuente. She didn't even try to hide the fact that she was in love with Marcos. My mother still didn't like it one whit, but after so many months, and knowing that my sister Juana was as headstrong as anything, there wasn't much to be done about it. The upshot of it was that my mother didn't like it and my sister Juana knew it, and they each kept out of the way of the other.

With all our troubles, and the uncertainty of more hard times to come, the burden of Juana and Marcos was not trouble that my mother wanted to add to the family. To make matters worse, Paulie and I had gone to hunt rabbits along the dry creek by the old house. As we walked toward the barn, Paulie looked over at the house to see what new improvements Marcos had made.

Paulie whispered, "Goddamn, look at that!"

"What?" I said, turning to follow Paulie's eyes to the house. The bedroom window was open. Marcos de la Fuente lay in bed, naked, with a leg bent, fondling himself. Sitting on the bed beside Marcos was my sister Juana, also naked. She brushed her hair as Marcos raised his hand to touch her breast. My brother Paulie slapped my arm and began to walk inside the barn where they wouldn't see us. I followed, unable to take my eyes away from the window.

"We shouldn't be looking at them," said Paulie.

"So that's what they do when she spends all her time here," I said.

"What the hell did you think they were doing, asshole?" said Paulie. He was more upset than he let on.

"I'll bet you she never did that with Tony," I said.

"Probably not," said Paulie. He found a hay bale to sit on and began drawing circles in the dirt with a twig.

"Goddamned Marcos," I said.

"What do you think we should do about it?" asked Paulie.

"Shit, I don't know! What do you think?"

"If we tell the folks, they'll beat the shit out of us for snooping on them," said Paulie.

"Yeah, but Marcos de la Fuente is a dead man," I said, voicing the conventional wisdom on such matters.

"Naw, Daddy's not going to shoot him," said Paulie. "Now, Ma might.

She'll get mad enough to do it. I don't think she can shoot, though."

"We have to do something, don't we?" I asked.

"Nope. We don't have to do shit! We can just keep our mouths shut, that's what we can do," said my brother Paulie.

"How the hell are we going to do that? I mean, how are we going to face her from now on?"

"Same as always, idiot!"

"I don't know if I can do it," I said.

"You better," said Paulie, "or I'll kick the shit out of you!"

There didn't seem to be anymore to say about it. We went out the other side of the barn, swinging around the pigpens where we saw a badly constructed barbed wire corral inside of which were a dozen goats.

"What the hell is that?" I asked Paulie.

"Goats, idiot!" he said.

"I mean, where did they come from," I said, "we don't own any god-damned goats."

"Who do you think they belong to, shithead!" snapped Paulie.

I didn't say another word. It wasn't over by any means, but we had our hunting to get on with. We followed old cow trails along the creek, Paulie shooting to one side and I to the other. He spotted a cottontail and signaled for me to freeze. Paulie aimed, fired and missed. The report of the rifle through the branches of the mesquite spooked the rabbit into running across the trail over to my side. He stopped beside some cactus, where I shot and dropped him.

"Bastard!" said my brother Paulie under his breath.

I tied the rabbit to my belt and we continued onward, side by side. We didn't see any more rabbits and the one I shot was getting stiff. I told Paulie we ought to cut across what used to be the milo field and circle around to the house. He quickly agreed as he didn't want to go near the old house again for fear of disturbing Juana and Marcos.

"You think they'll get married?" I asked.

"I don't know, I guess," said Paulie. "I don't think Juana would go that far with him unless she was planning on getting married."

"Ma's not going to like that very much," I said.

"Anybody else, you'd probably be right. Not Juana, though. She's more like Ma than Ma is. Nobody pushes Juana around. She'll do what she wants."

"Let's make a bet on when they ask permission," I said.

"Let's not," said Paulie, disgusted by the idea.

I went straight to the mesquite grove to skin my rabbit. I yelled to my dog Jeff to come and eat up the rabbit innards. The dog raised his head when I called and then dropped it back between his paws. The son of a bitch wasn't going to move off the porch. I thought of being nice and dumping them in a bowl for him, but then he'd probably get blood and rabbit shit all over the porch and my mother would complain about it. I decided to leave them where they lay and let Jeff come and get them if he ever felt like it.

My bullet went through both shoulders of the rabbit, leaving dark, almost black splotches on the meat. I cut that part of it away and threw it in with the innards. That left a portion of the spine and its plump hindquarters.

I put the carcass on the sink for my mother to wash. She glanced over to the rabbit, saying, "What happened?"

"I ruined part it," I said.

"Why don't you learn to shoot!" she said, turning back to her stove.

My brother Paulie, sitting at the kitchen table, smiled. Jose sat opposite and when I caught his eye, he cautioned me with a shake of his head to keep my mouth shut. I came over to sit with them.

My brother Jose spent most of his time in the kitchen playing endless games of solitaire. He would arrange the cards, pull the first three, look from one side to the other at the row of exposed cards, and he would scoop all of them up and begin shuffling for another game. He and Paulie had both taken to smoking heavily and doing so in front of my mother and father. My mother was shocked by it at first. She was not shocked so much by the disrespect of indulging a vice in her presence as she was by the undeniable fact that Jose and Paulie were swiftly becoming men. She wanted to struggle to the last against losing her babies. My father settled it by snapping at her, "You want them to spend all day in the outhouse smoking? You want them to pretend they're not doing it?" His coarse comment brought her face to face with the inevitable.

Once they received permission, Jose and Paulie went through sacks and sacks of Bull Durham each week. My mother was not pleased at all that my father joined in with them. She complained about the smoke in her kitchen. After a while we figured that my mother needed to hear herself complain, that we weren't supposed to say anything in return. If we took too much notice of what she said, it made things worse. The one thing we all wanted was to lessen as much friction as possible.

Jose put aside his cards and asked Paulie and me if we wanted to get up a game of dominoes. Paulie said he didn't have any money. Jose agreed to let Paulie play on the cuff until better times. My mother turned and said she didn't want any gambling in the house.

"The way Jose plays and loses his money to me ain't gambling, Ma," said Paulie.

"I told you, no gambling," said my mother.

At that instant, my grandfather came in.

"Living is itself a gamble," he said, cheerfully.

"Don't you start, old man," said my mother.

"What're you doing home so early, Grandpa?" asked my brother Jose. "Aren't you digging your well any more?"

"Sure am, son. I'm just letting it drain. I hit some sulphur water and it stinks, I tell you."

"You smell like it," said Paulie.

"You should take some of the boys to help you," my mother said by way of apology for having snapped at Grandpa.

"I wouldn't want to disturb anybody," said Grandpa, just good naturedly enough to keep from being sarcastic.

"I can help you," said Jose.

"No, I'm doing fine by myself," he said. "I don't have too much more to go."

"Did you shore it up like I told you?" said Paulie.

"No, not at all, Paulie. It's holding up pretty well."

"I still say that thing is going to cave in and bury you, one of these days. All we'll have to do is fill it in the rest of the way and stick a gravemarker on it," said Paulie.

My father joined us after one of his long walks.

"The tank is filling up with water," my father said, after a long silence during which he kept stirring the coffee in his cup.

"The one over by the fence?" asked Jose.

"What other tank do we have?" snapped my father.

"You walked all the way out there and back?" asked my mother, but my father did not respond.

"I want somebody to take the cattle out there."

"That tank was dry as the desert," said Paulie.

"I know, I saw it," said my father. "I was by there day before yesterday and it was dry. Now, it's full of water."

"What the hell happened?" said Jose.

"There must be an underground spring pretty close to the surface near there," said Grandpa.

"By the way, what are we going to use for feed?" asked my brother Jose.

"How're we doing on hay?" my father asked Paulie.

"If we feed 'em every day, probably enough for a couple of weeks," said Paulie, drawing circles on the table with his finger.

"I guess I'll go out and try to find some to buy," said my father.

"You can put them on that piece where I'm digging my well. There's grass there and I expect there'll be some clear, sweet water coming up any day now," said my grandfather.

"Cows can't drink out of the well like that, Grandpa," I said.

"I didn't say it was going to be easy, son. We'll have to draw water for them every day, but there's some grass there," he said.

"You think it's worth the trouble?" asked my father.

"It is, if you want to save some of your animals," said my grandfather. "Otherwise, I'd be thinking about taking them to market."

"I might as well give them away for what I'd get for them," said my father, rolling another cigarette.

My sister Juana came in and began to look in the cabinets under the sink. "Didn't we have a water bucket in here somewhere?" she asked.

"What do you need it for?" said my mother.

"Marcos is pumping black water out of the well at the house," said Juana.

"Tell him to let it stand in a bucket for ten minutes or so, the dirt'll settle down at the bottom," said my mother.

"That can only mean that the well here will be pumping mud pretty soon, too," said my father.

"He tried that already, Ma," said Juana, desperately. "There's some kind of smell to it. Marcos thinks it's poison."

"It's sulphur," said Grandpa. "It's good for you, if you can get past the stink."

"I told him it wouldn't hurt anything, but he won't believe me," said Juana.

"Damned wetbacks," said Paulie.

My sister Juana let that one pass.

"We're going to be short on water ourselves here," said my father. "The stock tank is dry and every time the well at the old house starts pumping dirt up with the water, this well does, too."

"I suppose you'll be carrying water to him everyday, now. That's all we need," said my mother.

"He'll be needing water for his chickens, too, I expect," said my father.

"He's got goats, too, now," I said. "Paulie and I got a good look this afternoon."

Juana darted a glance my way and decided I couldn't be referring to what she was thinking. Still, if we were there in the afternoon, she was suspicious.

"I thought all he had was some chickens," said my brother Jose.

"Well, he's got some goats, so what?" said Juana.

"What's he want with goats, that's what I want to know," said Paulie.

"Not that it's any of your business, he slaughters them for barbacoa and he sells it to the other people from Mexico," said Juana, apologetically.

"First time I heard of him doing that," said my father.

"Those people from Mexico, are they the same ones as wetbacks?" said Paulie.

"Who gave him permission, is what I want to know," said my mother.

"I sort of told him no one would mind," said Juana, reluctantly. "He built a little pen in back of the pigsty for them. They don't bother anything."

"I think we should throw the son of a bitch out on his ass," said Jose, indignant that our good will had been trespassed.

Juana got on her knees, thrashed some pans around in the cabinet and found the bucket she looked for. Still down on her knees, she looked at my father.

"Daddy, Marcos wants to know if he can draw water for his animals for the time being," said Juana.

"It'll be two, three months, at least, before we get some rain, and probably all winter before things get back to normal, if ever," observed Grandpa.

"Why doesn't he come and ask for himself?" said my father.

"I thought it would be better if I asked," said Juana. "I didn't tell you. Half of the goats are mine."

"What?" yelled my mother.

"I bought half of the goats," said Juana.

"With what?" asked my mother.

"With my own money, Ma," she said.

"Your grandmother left you that money," said my mother, turning back to the pan on the stove.

"Not all of it. Some of it was my own. I earned it," said Juana.

"What else do you want to tell us?" said my father.

Paulie and I exchanged looks, remembering Marcos and Juana naked on the bed. Juana must have felt that her secrets with Marcos de la Fuente were written all over her. I don't think she suspected in the least that Paulie and I had seen them. I'm sure she was afraid that it wouldn't be too hard to put two and two together, though. It would never occur to her to lie. However, she knew there were only a few things she could tell us. The rest would have to wait for better times. The difficulty she had at the moment lay in selecting the proper things to say.

More disturbing for Juana was her inability to gauge my mother's and father's reaction. She sure as hell wasn't going into anything without first knowing how it would end. Going into business with Marcos de la Fuente, and it wasn't just business, was something that she ought to have discussed with them. My mother would certainly be suspicious of Marcos taking Juana's money. My father would insist on discussing it with Marcos.

Most of all, Juana was in love and she wanted the family's approval for Marcos de la Fuente. The only obstacle to that end was my mother. Marcos had breached some code for my mother from the very beginning and she had not forgiven him. Or, maybe it was the instant attraction between Marcos and my sister Juana that she had detected while the rest of us had been blind to it. In any case, except for my mother, none of us were particularly bothered by him, either way. But, then, it was my mother that Juana always wanted to please.

Marcos de la Fuente was far too different for us to take a liking to him right away. For one thing, he was more aggressive than most other *mojados* in trying to make money. He was shameless in the way he asked people for help, everything from getting someone to guarantee a loan for his truck to grabbing just anybody close by to help him unload his cargo on one of the many jobs he took on.

There were a few *mojados* in Schoolland, living with us for years, and though we existed tolerating and respecting one another, we knew and they knew that there was a tremendous difference between us. We were on our home ground, pledged to it in the timeless way of natives. The *mojados* had their homes in Mexico and for as long as they lived in Schoolland, Mexico remained home for them. They made no secret of it. Fortunately, I suppose, there wasn't enough of them to pose a threat to anyone.

My sister Juana couldn't deliberate forever on what she was going to say. Finally, in a quiet, almost submissive voice, she said, "I've been helping Marcos with the barbacoa on Fridays and Saturdays. We sell a lot."

"I didn't realize there were so many damned *mojados* in the county," said my brother Jose.

"They're not *mojados*," said Juana.

"What the hell are they?" asked Paulie, sarcastically.

"They are people, just like you. They come from Mexico, that's all," she said.

It was the wrong thing to say to Paulie. Before Paulie could say something, my father spoke. "So, you've made all your money back?" he said, hopeful.

"Well, no, not exactly," stammered Juana.

We waited for her to finish.

"Marcos says we can make more money if we buy more goats and raise them ourselves," she said. "He's been going to the livestock auction in San Antonio for more than a month and buying two goats at first. And when we went to deliver the barbacoa, there were more Mexicanos who wanted some and we didn't have any. And so, he brought three goats back and then four. And that's about all we can sell for now."

"Did you know any of this?" my father asked my mother.

"No," she said without turning to face anybody.

Juana continued. "I asked Marcos if it would be easier to raise the goats ourselves. He said he didn't have any place to raise them. I thought since we didn't have many cows anymore . . ."

My father exploded. "No! Goddamn it, no! I'm not going to turn my pasture over to raising goats! Not for you, not for anybody! Goddamn it!"

My grandfather started to laugh. The rest of us started to laugh, following Grandpa's example. My father's angry face looked at each one of us and slowly, he smiled, embarrassed at his outburst.

"I wish you had talked to me about all of this before going into it," said my father.

"Marcos says he only needs one or two acres. He'll put up the fence all by himself," said Juana, eagerly, urgently.

"You say he's built a pen for them?" said my father.

"Just for the time being," said Juana.

"He can keep them there for the time being, but that's all. You two are going to have to figure something else out on your own," said my father with his usual finality.

"I'll tell Marcos we can't raise goats here," said Juana quietly. She wasn't petulant or defiant, just resigned.

# Chapter 23

It was still daylight when don Antonio Arreaga drove up in the car he had owned for nearly twenty years. Tony was driving. Don Antonio's place had been sold by the bank after all and all he had remaining to him for a lifetime of hard work was his homestead. Even his animal pens were part of the parcel sold, but he kept them up because he could not bring himself to accept the fact that they no longer belonged to him.

The new owner had bought too late in the year to do anything with the land. Seeing that nothing was done with it, people began to talk about land speculators who, like vultures, were picking up every square inch of land they could get their hands on. It was also said that the land speculators did not intend to work the land but hold on to it until they could sell it back to the very people the bank had taken it from. They were buying at twenty and thirty dollars an acre and would as likely sell it back at a hundred. There were many farms and ranches in Schoolland that went unsold all that year, but the rumor of the land speculators was too good to pass up.

My father came out on the porch to greet don Antonio as he had done for so many years. He stopped just before descending to the first step.

"What's that old fool doing with a rifle in the front seat?" said my brother Paulie.

"They were probably out shooting rabbits, if there are any left," said my brother Jose. "That's all anybody is going to eat for the rest of this year."

Don Antonio Arreaga did not choose to wait for my father to get off the porch and invite him to visit. As soon as Tony braked the car to a stop, the old man was throwing the passenger door open and stepping down. He had the rifle in his hand.

"Don Antonio, it's been ages since you've come for a visit," said my father, smiling cordially, and offering his hand.

Don Antonio refused to shake hands with him. From the looks he gave to the rifle, held slackly in his hand, it appeared to me that he regretted having taken it from the front seat of the car. My father took the slight evenly, choosing to cross his arms over his chest.

Don Antonio took a few moments to work himself up to a proper rage. My father knew right away that it had something to do with Elpidio. Tony, meanwhile, remained inside the car, tapping his fingers on the steering wheel, wishing, I figured, that he were someplace else.

"You have got a problem with me, sir," said don Antonio, his pinched little face twitching, foam slobber building at the corners of his mouth.

"I won't know if I have a problem unless you tell it to me, Antonio," said my father, dropping the 'don,' as it didn't look like the old fool had come to be friendly.

"It's a problem alright, goddamn it!" don Antonio said in a rage. "Where's that boy of yours? I aim to kill him right here."

Don Antonio's rage, making him shake and tremble, also made him shrink in size. My father, who was not particularly tall, towered over him. It was all that the three of us on the porch could do to keep from laughing. My father remained serious in tone, but unaffected by don Antonio's words.

"Nobody's going to kill anybody," said my father. "You're upset about something. Suppose you come on up to the porch and tell me about it."

"I will do no such thing," said don Antonio. "Where is Elpidio?"

"He's not here. I wouldn't let him come out anyway," said my father. "You're gonna have to deal with me, for now. So, you might as well tell me what this is all about."

"It's my daughter, Concepcion!" yelled don Antonio.

From the tremor in his voice, he was angry and afraid at the same time.

"What about your daughter?" said my father, patiently.

"He has done her a serious injury."

"He loves her, Antonio. He wouldn't hurt her and you know it," said my father.

"Well, he has hurt me, then. He has hurt my family," said don Antonio in what seemed a mournful howl.

"That makes it a hell of a lot different, then, doesn't it," said my father, suspicioning but now knowing what it was all about. "Seems to me that in a situation like this, we ought to just marry them off and be done with it."

"No, sir," spat don Antonio, "not like this. Never! I will not have it! I intend to restore the honor of my family. Do you understand me?"

"Antonio, I can understand that you're upset, but let's not let this thing get out of hand. Let's fix whatever harm has been done."

"This harm cannot be undone. It is impossible for my family to live through this with any respect. By now, everyone's heard about it. If it's the last thing I do, I intend to salvage the honor of my family. At least, people will know I did the right thing by my family."

"We have to think of a way out of this," said my father.

"It's too damned late for that," said don Antonio. "Your boy should have put more thought to what he was doing before he did it. We were a decent family before this."

I felt like yelling something to him about his other daughter who was abandoned. At least Elpidio, I knew, would stand by Concepcion.

"There is nothing so serious that good men cannot come to some kind of an agreement," said my father.

"Not this time!" sneered don Antonio. "You tell him that I will shoot him on sight when I see him."

Don Antonio Arreaga tossed words before my father that were the beginning of a family feud. He got back in the car and the door slammed shut. My father kept looking at him through the windshield to see if he meant it. Tony slipped the gears into reverse, spinning the wheels, to back up enough so he could turn the car around. He didn't even slow the car down at the drainage dip by the side of the road.

"What the hell was all that about?" asked Paulie, acting as if he didn't know and asking more than anything what we should look forward to.

"Looks like you're going to have another nephew, that's what it's all about. As if we needed more trouble," said my father, wearily.

"I'll be goddamned," hooped Paulie.

My brother Jose had a worried look on his face. We had come down from the porch and were standing beside my father. The four of us stood side by side watching don Antonio's car disappear over the horizon.

"You think he means it, Pa?" asked Jose.

"Mean what?" I asked.

"Yeah, he means it," said my father. "He thinks he does, anyway. I'm not going to take any chances. There's no telling what a man will do when he feels as don Antonio does."

"You figure it's all the shit that's been happening to him, Pa?" said Paulie, quietly.

"Yeah, I guess so," said my father, continuing to look at the horizon.

"I think he drove them to it," said Jose, "trying to keep them apart like that. Dumb son of a bitch should know better."

"That's enough of that, Jose," my father warned. "Don Antonio still deserves our respect."

"What if he carries out his threat and does something to Elpidio?" asked Paulie.

"He's too chickenshit to do anything," I said.

"If we're not careful, that old fool will end up shooting Elpidio," chimed in my grandfather, coming up from the bunkhouse behind us.

"Were you listening in Grandpa?" my father asked.

My grandfather carried his Sir Walter Scott book.

"Couldn't help it," he said.

"So, you think don Antonio will try to make good on his threat."

"Not especially. Fact is, I don't think he really means any of it. He thinks he does, and that just about makes him more dangerous."

"Why is that, Grandpa?"

"That old fool has talked himself into something he never wanted to do and now that he has, he has no way out unless he does it. That's where the dangerous part comes in."

"Think we oughta just kill him, Grandpa?" said my brother Paulie, trying to make a joke.

"It won't come to that. Right now he thinks everybody in the world, Schoolland, is witness to his family's shame."

"If we can keep him at a distance for a few months, what with the drought and all, all of Schoolland will have starved to death. And then, it won't matter a goddamn to anyone. Will it?" said Paulie.

My father thought about that for a minute, and his initial smile gave way to a long, hearty laugh whose infectiousness overtook all of us, including my grandfather who looked at my brother Paulie in approval. Soon, we were all laughing like idiots as we got back on the porch.

My grandfather stopped laughing for a moment. "I've known that asshole for more than fifty years. Every few years, like clockwork, he gets himself into some shit where you just have to convince yourself that it ain't worth it to rid the world of him."

"You're probably right, Grandpa," said my father, smiling. "If we stay away from him for a while, he'll settle down."

"That's right," said my grandfather. "Let him be, I say, he's not going to hurt anybody. Let's don't provoke him and make him have to live up to his words. Fool like that doesn't know the value of words."

When the laughter subsided, my father became grim again. He began to roll himself a cigarette to hide his concern.

"What about an ambush?" asked Paulie. "Elpidio could be out riding one day and don Antonio comes out from behind the chaparral."

Paulie was still trying to carry on his joking. I slapped him on the shoulder. "That only happens in the movies, idiot!" I said.

"Where do you think the movies got the idea for it, stupid!" rejoined Paulie.

"All right. How is he going to know when Elpidio goes riding? Grandpa's the only one that's ridden his mare for months. How's he gonna know? Huh?"

"I don't believe don Antonio is the kind of person who would wait for somebody and shoot him down in the night," said my father, seriously considering what Paulie said.

My father went inside to tell my mother as much as he could about don

Antonio's visit. I was sure he would leave out the part where don Antonio felt like shooting Elpidio. It wasn't too long before he came back to smoke one of his cigarettes. My brother Jose rolled one for himself and tossed the sack to Paulie. Paulie didn't want one and he tossed the sack to Grandpa.

"What about the girl?" said Grandpa, reading my father's thoughts. No doubt Marcos the *mojado* and my sister Juana were included in his thinking.

"Poor girl," said my father.

"I wouldn't worry about it too much, said Grandpa. "They're both young. I say let nature take its course."

"Seems to me nature's already taken too much of its course with them," said my father, spitting over the side of the porch, his face serious and impassive.

We were anxious for Elpidio to come home so we could warn him, and more than that, we wanted to tell him what had happened. Wherever he had gone for the day, he did not come home after dark. He had been out to see a Czech farmer near Cheapside about mending some fences. My mother was worried about him. My mother could sense that there was more to it than my father told her.

The next morning, we discovered that Elpidio had returned home long after everyone had gone to bed. We figured it was his way of avoiding any explanation of things he did not want to talk about. However, even before he could reach his truck and be gone without joining the family at breakfast, my father saw him out in the yard pouring a quart of oil into the truck. He called him in. Elpidio was reluctant and annoyed. My father went to the outhouse to do his business and made Elpidio wait for him in the kitchen.

My sister Juana was in charge of waking us up. My mother thought there was something sinful in sleeping too much. The way things were going, there wasn't a goddamned thing for us to do and so there was no reason to get up. My mother's only response to our complaints was: idle people don't deserve to sleep.

When I came into the kitchen, I was surprised to see Elpidio sitting with a cup of coffee in front of him. My brother Jose was washing his face in the kitchen sink as Paulie was busy with the wash basin on the porch. I waited my turn.

"Are you here for a visit, or are you staying a while?" I said to Elpidio. He sipped his coffee without looking up.

My sister Juana pointed to the back door, meaning I should leave in the direction of her finger.

Paulie took his own time to wash himself and brush his teeth. Lately, he had taken to shaving a couple of times a week. It was useless to try to hurry him. Anyway, there wasn't anything to hurry for.

Marcos de la Fuentes' singsong voice startled me. "Good morning," he said.

Paulie held his chin firmly so he wouldn't cut himself with the straight edge razor and was unable to answer.

"Good morning," I said.

Marcos de la Fuentes placed a coffee can brimming with eggs on a corner of the porch. He didn't dare come any further. The son of a bitch smiled in a way that made me want to kick his teeth in. He saw my father coming up from the outhouse and waited to greet him. It was the proper thing to do, but it was something my father could have done without.

In the kitchen, Elpidio was trying to avoid looking at anybody. There were too many faces for him to avoid, despite his keeping his nose pretty close to the rim of his cup. My father didn't wait to be served and poured himself a cup of coffee. Elpidio said it was late and he had a long way to go.

"Did you get that job yesterday?" asked my father.

"No, the farmer's brother-in-law beat me to it. They sent me further up, near Yoakum. I was told to come back this morning. They might have something for me."

"Well, we have a few things to discuss," said my father gravely.

My grandfather came in, jovial and hearty. He slapped Paulie on the shoulder. "How is everybody this morning," he said.

"What the hell are you so happy about?" asked Paulie, sullenly.

"I was up early this morning. Read my book. It never fails to make me feel good, reading that book."

"Let's get to it," said Elpidio, impatiently.

"I'm ready for breakfast," said Grandpa.

My father deliberately took his time. Elpidio knew what was coming, and he knew as well that there was no way he could get out of the house until he had it out with my father. In the meantime, he tried to hide his face behind the steam rising from the cup. My sister Juana was the only other person in the house who happened to be madly in love at the moment and thus she felt more sympathy for him than did the rest of us. What was going on between Samantha Coleman and me was nothing compared to my sister Juana and my brother Elpidio.

The discussion didn't go as well as my father had planned. Elpidio, although he was hardly ever sullen or uncooperative, had little to offer in the way of details or comment when my father presented several possible solutions to him. My father spoke in a low voice, sometimes drawing out his words. It was his way of remaining reasonable when faced with something far beyond anything he had experienced before.

Elpidio's silence and his refusal to participate in more than a cursory manner, or to offer anything helpful to get himself out of his predicament, drove my father to the limits of his patience. My father realized that there was nothing to be done right away. He finally told Elpidio, in a gruff voice, to get on his way, and while he was at it, to spend a couple of minutes figuring out what he intended to do. Elpidio, of course, had been trying to figure out what to do for several months, now. It had occupied every moment of his waking day.

We were to find out later the reason for his coming home so late in the evenings, sometimes at dawn. He was spending his nights with Concepcion. With the help of her sisters and mother, all of whom were on her side with Elpidio, she had been going out of the house at night, after the old man went to bed. She would meet Elpidio near some abandoned chicken shacks by the side of the road. They had virtually been living in one of the shacks.

Concepcion's belly was already swollen and visible to God, man and anybody else who cared to notice. All of this served to infuriate her father even more.

Don Antonio had threatened to beat her on several occasions. He probably meant a spanking, as if Concepcion had been a naughty girl or something. Neither her mother nor her sisters would have permitted it. She would not tell Elpidio any of that, of course.

Tony, for his part, had his own problems with our family, namely my sister Juana. Marcos and she had been seen all over the place. It served to make Tony's loss all the more unbearable. Nevertheless, as much as he could, Tony kept himself at a distance away from the turmoil in his family. He didn't join in with his father on the trouble between Elpidio and his sister. He preferred to bear the burden of his troubles all by himself.

Tony had been giving in to it on the way out to our place with his father. He had wanted to see us humiliated. Once there, actually going through with it, and his father talking like a crazy man, he had repented and had seen how wrong it all was. What he had wanted after all was a glimpse of my sister.

Tony didn't believe for a minute that his father was capable of carrying out any of his threats. As a dutiful son, he listened and nodded at his father's fulminations. Other than that, he was not too concerned about them. If something were to happen, Tony wondered if he was up to avenging his family. Those thoughts weighed heavily within our family, too.

# Chapter 24

Near the end of July, in midweek, my father invited me to go to Gonzales with him. He had some business to take care of at the bank. He had intended to take my mother with him to do her weekly shopping a little early, but she balked at the last minute, saying it shouldn't take much too bring back a sack of potatoes, another of beans and a can of lard.

There was not much else to do; my father and brothers, who were not working anymore, had fixed and patched and repaired everything in sight with whatever materials we could salvage. To fix anymore would mean having to spend some money and my father did not want to do that.

In Gonzales, there did not seem to be as many vehicles parked in the town square or on the side streets. Normally, there would have been a few passersby, mostly townspeople, along the sidewalks, people who would nod to my father in greeting, occasionally stopping to exchange a few words. On this day, the sidewalks were virtually deserted, as if all the people had been plucked out of Gonzales and only the buildings remained. Gonzales had a feeling of desolation and solitude.

My father took me into the Courthouse Cafe where I ate a hamburger and drank a soda while my father drank a beer.

"You're not gonna eat, Daddy?" I asked.

"Not hungry," he said.

"I've never seen you drink beer before," I said.

"I guess, not," he said.

I was hungry and greedily gobbled the burger before my father finished his first beer. He drank a second beer while I finished my soda.

We walked to the northwestern corner of the town square to the bank. Inside the bank, it was cool and it smelled clean, almost sterile. My father strode past the empty teller windows to speak to a lady who told him to wait and take a seat. It didn't take but a few minutes before a man in a seersucker suit and black tie came to greet my father. He had his hand stuck out in front of him a long ways before he got to my father. I didn't trust him immediately.

As they went over the obvious, how bad the drought was, the man kept patting my father on the shoulders. The banker had reddish blond hair and he smiled a lot, exposing teeth that matched the color of his hair. The man turned to me and asked my father who I was, which should have been pretty goddamned obvious. Then he bent over to shake my hand where I sat. I liked him even less. My father told me to wait for him and he followed the man through a maze of desks into a private office. He closed the door behind them.

My father was in with the man for maybe twenty minutes or more. When he came out, his face was grave and he had his shoulders thrown back. That meant my father was angry.

"Come on, let's go," he said.

He didn't even turn to see if I followed. We crossed the street hurriedly and then my father slowed down and began to relax. We made a tour of all the shop windows, lingering only in front of the Hoskins Dry Goods, where my father kept his eye on a Stetson displayed in the window.

Every year, for as long as I could remember, my father had bought himself a new Stetson, passing on his old one to one of the children. This time, he looked in the window for a long time and tugged on my arm when he finished.

"I guess there won't be a new hat for us this year, squirt," he said, without any emotion in his voice. "What do you think about that?"

I kept my mouth shut.

We walked all the way around the square, coming to rest for a few moments opposite the jail and courthouse. In our perambulation we had not run into another soul, white or Mexican. My father asked if maybe we ought to run up to the grocery and load up on what my mother had sent us for. I didn't say much of anything because I could tell my father wasn't particularly asking me for an answer.

We leaned against the corner of the building, hoping to meet someone we knew. Across the square, we finally saw a woman tugging at two children. She seemed in a hurry to go somewhere.

My father spat on the sidewalk.

"White people are always moving so goddamned fast," he said.

"Grandpa's always saying shit like that," I said.

"When you get older, you'll hear what white people are saying about you right now," said my father.

After another ten minutes or so, my father tired of holding the building up with our backs and decided it was time to get our things and head back.

At the end of the business district, just before the residential section began, was the grocery store. We drove to it in the truck. Inside, the store smelled of sawdust and resin. The front door was open. As we walked in, we were struck by the swirling air of a large fan suspended from the ceiling. My father went to talk to the man behind the cash register, who kept nodding his head up and down as my father spoke to him. Neither of us had more imagination than to get what my mother ordered, but when it came to the sweets, I was pretty good at it. Once I piled my packages on the counter, the man stuffed them into a sack and my father paid. All the while, a clerk had been loading up the heavy stuff into the truck outside, ferrying it in a large-wheeled handtruck. As we left the store, he carried the last of it, a fifty-pound can of lard. My father stepped to one side of the doors to let the clerk pass. He was never a man to be rushed. My mother called it dawdling.

After the truck was loaded up, we simply stood in front of the hood. My father rolled himself a Bull Durham. The store had been empty, except for us. While we stood outside, a pair of gringas went in without giving us a look.

I was ready to go home because I didn't want to wait to get at the goodies I had thrown into the order. My father seemed to be in less of a hurry than I could stand. I waited for my father to finish smoking his Bull Durham. As a signal for him to hurry up, I went to the truck, pulled on the handle and jerked the door open.

It was very hot, the heat accumulating inside the cab of the truck. It began to seep out as I held the door open. The heat also sapped my energy, what with just standing around doing nothing. I felt sleepy and listless.

"Wait up," said my father, "I think I see somebody."

When I turned, I saw he was looking across the street toward a building housing the post office and some federal offices that had to do with agriculture, mostly. There were a half dozen cars in the parking lot and there were a lot of people, it seemed, going in and out.

"What's going on over there, Daddy?" I asked.

"Government food," said my father.

"What?" I said.

"The government buys up corn, wheat and the like. Crops nobody can sell. Milk and dairy things, too. That way we'll keep a good price when we sell," said my father.

"They buy it up and then give it to poor people," I concluded.

"That's right. Except, it may not be just poor people this year, boy. We may come to it ourselves," he said, glumly.

"Are we going to be poor, Daddy?" I asked, curious, not knowing if he was kidding me as he did sometimes.

"We are poor, squirt. We have always been poor people," he said.

"How come? We have our land and the government is not giving us food, not yet anyway," I argued.

"Not yet, maybe, but that doesn't mean we are not poor. Remember that. Come on, walk with me," he said.

We walked across the street, stopping beside a gray Dodge of the kind built during the war, a large lumbering car whose ass-end resembled a tailless armadillo. A woman of about my father's age sat in the passenger side of the car. The back seat was full of kids. My father nodded to the woman, but did not speak to her.

We stood by on the concrete while my father rolled himself another Bull Durham. Not long after, the man my father waited for came out. He had a pronounced limp which tended to distort his body shape each time he took a step forward. He was aided by a gnarled cane which, though worn, was brightly polished.

"Simon, it has been a very long time since we've seen you," said my father.

The man to whom my father spoke ignored him and limped his way in between the Dodge and another car. My father walked quickly around, placing his hand on the roof of the car.

"Simon, didn't you hear me? Don't you remember me?" asked my father, leaning his face to one side so that the man, who wouldn't raise his head, could get a better look.

"I remember you," said Simon.

The man was at a loss to conceal the packages he carried under one arm.

"Why don't you say hello, then," said my father, trying to be congenial about the matter. "You don't have to be glad to see me, or anything, but we're family, Simon. That counts for a hell of a lot, you know."

"You're right, you're right," said Simon, still refusing to look my father in the eye. He kept his head bent, his voice was low and apologetic.

There was a long silence between them. Finally, Simon spoke again.

"It's that I don't like for anyone to see my family like this," he said. "It ain't right for a man to have to beg for food."

"We grew up almost like brothers, Simon, what kind of trouble can you be in that I can't help?" said my father, sympathetic and yet, scolding him at the same time.

Simon became angry. "Come around here and see this," he said. Simon walked around to the passenger side of the car and opened the rear door. He took the sack he carried under his arm and tossed it on the floorboard where lay other packages of cheese and corn meal.

"Get out of the damned way," he yelled at the children who took up every inch of the back seat, piled on top of each other.

"That's what we've been living on ever since we got back from up north. We ain't had no meat, or even beans and tortillas, in the last month," said Simon, angrily.

"You could have come to see me, Simon. Why haven't you come out to see us? You could have done that, couldn't you? We might be able to put a few dollars together for you, you know," said my father, softly, trying to keep Simon's dignity intact.

"I don't want your charity. It's bad enough having to take it from the goddamned government, from those people inside that building there. You'll never know what it's like until you go in there," said Simon.

"I may have to, yet, Simon," said my father. "But, that is not enough reason not to let me help you. While the family is able to, you know we'll do everything we can."

Simon broke down and began to cry, which served to spur the children into crying themselves. His wife, a gaunt, taciturn, woman, kept looking straight ahead through the windshield into the entrance of the federal building. She tried hard to ignore her husband and children, feeling a special kind of humiliation. As the crying eased somewhat, she turned her sharp, penetrating gaze directly at me and it made me nervous. I had never seen a face so full of despair.

My father touched Simon's shoulder, which made him flinch upon contact. "Come with me to the store, Simon. We'll get some things for you, whatever you need. You're family, Simon. That's why I'm offering. If you're too proud, do it for the children," said my father, keeping his voice steady.

"No, I can't," said Simon. "I just couldn't."

Simon's wife spoke for the first time. "You can starve, if you want to, Simon, but I won't let my kids starve!" She leaned across the seat to look my father in the face. "I'll go with you, mister, even if this man won't." There was a suppressed rage in her voice.

My father was instinctively affronted by the woman's forwardness. I guess that had he thought about it, he would have understood her desperation. However, the suddenness of it and the sharpness of her voice, made my father uneasy. But my father was not about to go anywhere without Simon and certainly not without Simon's permission.

I noticed that Simon, too, was taken aback by the violent hiss in his wife's voice. Instead of becoming angry with her, he seemed to accept the fact that the order of his family authority was breaking down. When a man can't provide for his family, he relinquishes certain aspects of his manhood. Simon seemed to collapse against the side of the car in complete submission to his circumstances. He did not seem to have the least bit of fight left in him. He shifted more of his weight to the cane at his side. The children still whimpered in spurts in the stifling heat inside the car.

"Come on," said my father. Simon could no longer struggle in the least and my father took him by the arm, leading him away from the car.

Simon's voice was husky as he told his wife to stay with the kids and the three of us walked across the street back to the store. Once inside the store, my father handed him a basket and told him to fill it with whatever he wanted. Simon's face was long and mournful and at every step he seemed to hesitate, alternating between wanting to cry and not knowing what to do.

The two gringas who had come in before were having their groceries tallied and they looked in our direction with disdain. I wanted to ask my father why they looked at us that way, but that would be the least of his concerns at the moment.

Simon took some boxes of *fideo,* a couple of bags of beans, some potatoes and a couple of small cans of shortening. As we walked along the aisle, I picked up two packages of cookies, questioned my father with a look, and when he nodded, I threw them in Simon's basket. Simon wanted to protest but my father was looking the other way. I smiled at Simon. Simon froze in his tracks, unwilling to move anymore. My smile made him ashamed of himself. My father took Simon to the meat counter and had the butcher wrap up some beefsteaks, sausages and salt pork. Meanwhile, I went back to the produce section and brought him apples and oranges.

Simon remained far to one side as my father paid for the groceries, trying to dissociate himself from the charity he was forced to accept. My father had made it plain that it wasn't charity at all, but then a proud man is likely to believe the worst. We had an account at the store, but because the drought had eaten up everybody's money, the grocer was not giving anything out on credit anymore. This irked my father a little, but he understood the man and his business. The grocer was perplexed that we had come back for more things, but he kept his peace and took the money my father handed to him.

We helped Simon to the car with the bags of groceries and before saying goodbye to Simon, my father pressed a ten dollar bill into his hand. By this time, Simon was completely submissive and made no move to resist this last gesture from my father.

Simon's wife gave us a thin smile of thanks, but her face was so bitter, it was difficult to tell at first. Simon, before sliding in behind the wheel, tried to mumble some thanks and assurances that he would make sure my father was repaid. My father told him not to worry about it ever.

My father walked back to our truck, taking exceptionally long strides. It was all I could do to keep up with him. He kept his silence until we were well out of Gonzales and had crossed the Guadalupe River bridge. After a long while, my father began to speak. "Our people are not used to handouts," said my father. For a moment, I was not sure he was talking to me, as he just suddenly began to speak and it did not seem directed at me in particular.

"That goddamned Simon's had bad luck all of his life. He should be used to it by now, but I guess it must be something you never get used to," said my father, without sounding malicious in the least.

"We're not in too good a shape ourselves, are we, Pa?" I asked, suddenly realizing what the manner of my father's speech meant. "Is that why you're so mad?"

"No, son, we're not in too good a shape ourselves, you're right about that," he said, sadly, expelling a long breath of air. "I'm pretty sure we can make it through the year, if no further disaster falls on us. We might lose some acreage and a lot of our pride with them, maybe, but we won't go hungry. You can thank God for that."

We passed the Apache Drive-In to the left as we rounded the curve and headed for home. I mentioned that it had been a long time since we had been to the movies at the drive-in and then I realized it wasn't the best thing to say at the moment.

# Chapter 25

We drove all the way out from Gonzales without saying a further word between us. My father kept his eyes intently on the road ahead, his hands firmly gripping the steering wheel. As we rounded the curb by the cemetary in Wrightsboro, I thought of our family buried there.

"I think I have a way out of Elpidio's problem," said my father as we pulled into our driveway.

I wanted to ask him what it was, but I knew that he wasn't really talking to me at all.

Little Albert and little Julian were tracking one of the hens with a stick gun in the mesquite clump when they spotted the truck. They were waiting for us, jumping up and down, as my father killed the ignition. The twins wanted to be the first to look through the sacks we brought. They climbed in the back and rummaged in the box of groceries until they came up with the sweets. They knew better than to break into the bags, but each of them took a bag to carry inside to present to my mother, hoping she would give them permission to open it.

My father lifted the can of lard and waited for my brothers Jose and Paulie to come outside to help. Jose took the can of lard from my father. Paulie struggled to lift the sack of potatoes over the side of the truck. I told him to drag it to the tailgate before trying to throw the sack on his shoulders. It only served to make him more determined to lift it straight up and toss it over his shoulder. He finally managed to do it, but at considerable pain, after which he began a wobbly, uncertain walk up the porch stairs and through the front room into the kitchen. I carried a small box of canned things.

My mother reviewed what we brought, checking off the items against a list that she had memorized. Afterward, she began to complain and enumerate all the things she needed which we had not even thought to bring. My father apologized because I had not reminded him. Actually, it was a sort of ritual between them. My mother complained because she had wanted to go to Gonzales, just to get out of the house for a few hours. But the pressures of the many things to do had forced her to sacrifice herself once more.

Once my father and I had gone to town, she brooded about it and had not accomplished nearly as much as she had intended. This is why she got pissed every time.

Grandpa came in about the time when all the goods had been stored away. He was in a foul mood, having just gotten up from a lengthy afternoon nap, a nap long enough to disorient him and make him cranky. Paulie began to grin from ear to ear as he thought of the perfect thing to set off Grandpa. My father noticed Paulie right away and gave him a warning look. As usual with Paulie, getting caught just as he prepared to do something was as good as doing it and getting by with it, as in neither case was he punished. Paulie settled back in his chair to enjoy himself.

"Elpidio?" said my father, forming the name into a question.

"He went with Heriberto. He was supposed to help with something or other," said my mother.

"Jose, you and the squirt, here, I want you to do something for me," said my father. The way he spoke signalled that he had made up his mind on something and he was now ready to go through with it.

"Sure, pa, what is it?" asked my brother Jose.

"Come on outside I'll explain it to you," he said, placing his arm on Jose's shoulder.

I got up to go with them.

"You stay, for now, squirt. This part doesn't concern you," said my father.

My mother's ears perked up at that. It was not my father's habit to be secretive; and when he was, the only one in on it was my mother. If he was going to leave her out of this, she was not pleased about it.

"What is he up to?" my mother asked me.

"I don't know, he didn't tell me anything," I said, sullenly.

She gave me a black look that would not take no for an answer.

"All I know is he said he had figured a way out of Elpidio's problem. That's all I know . . . honest," I squealed.

My father and my brother Jose went out the front door and around the house to the mesquite clump and stood beside the water trough. Jose leaned against the trough, his arms folded across his chest. My father stood facing the road. They talked for a few minutes and my father began to walk to the horseshed where he saw a lot of things strewn about and began to gather them up as he talked. My brother Jose did little more than listen, nodding his head in agreement each time my father looked directly at him. Grandpa had left a bridle hanging on a hook outside. My father just shook his head and took it into the tack shed.

I figured the best thing for me to do was put some distance between me and my mother's worry and anger. I went outside to the back porch. My dog Jeff groaned or growled, it was difficult to tell which, when I petted him on the head. The damned dog didn't like it too much, but I loitered on the porch expecting that my father would call me.

"It's very important," said my father for my benefit, "that you repeat my message exactly as I told it you. Now you think you can do that?"

"Sure, Pa," said my brother Jose. "You know I always do like you tell me."

"I know, son, but I haven't ever asked you to do something this important. I guess, what I mean is, I don't really know if it will work or not. That's what makes me so goddamned nervous, you understand?" my father asked, arching his eyebrows.

My brother Jose, of course, did not understand at all. I did, or so I thought.

"I'm going to say it again. You pay close attention, squirt, your brother's going to need whatever help you can give him, understand?"

Without bothering for me to answer, he continued.

"You go to don Antonio's. You stay in the truck. Don't get down, even if you're asked. Tell don Antonio that I want to meet with him. Tell him that I have a solution to our problem. If he wants to know more, tell him I've instructed you to ask for a meeting and nothing else. You don't know anything."

"Is that why you're not going to tell us the rest, Pa?" I asked. "I mean, what you're going to do to help Elpidio."

"Not now, squirt," said my father, cutting me short. He spoke a little more harshly than I thought necessary.

"Tell don Antonio that I will meet with him tomorrow morning behind Candy's store. Tell him I said it has to be tomorrow, because it is Sunday and there won't be anybody out. Nobody will see us. Ten o'clock, about half a mile up the road behind the store. We can settle everything once and for all, and we'll be able to live a lot easier."

"You want we should go now, Pa?" asked my brother Jose.

"Yes, go right now. Don Antonio will probably insult you and me and say all kinds of things. But, you just don't say nothing back. Pay no attention to it at all. Understand?"

"Yes, sir," said Jose.

The trip and delivery of the message to don Antonio went without major incident. My brother Jose was able to get his message out and don Antonio didn't have any questions at all to ask. Tony Arreaga, too, was friendly, laughing with us for the first time in many months. Don Antonio's rage, we noticed, seemed to be bent back a lot. There was just a little of the banty rooster left in him. I guess he had been carried away by the moment when he saw his daughter pregnant. Being that nothing much had happened, he began to think about what it means to have an open challenge like that. No one knew what my father would do about it, either. Don Antonio seemed more than a little grateful to know the feud had not been fired up exactly and the prospect of a solution was very appealing to him.

When we got back to the house, my father wanted to know how don Antonio had taken to the offer and we reported that he had been extremely courteous, almost relieved at the possibility of ending the trouble once and for all. I don't think my father was about to rely on our assessment of don Antonio's temper. If we were right, then things might go fairly well.

On Sunday morning, my mother, my sister Juana, little Albert and little Julian went to church, with Juana driving the truck. I had already received my spankings for refusing to go to church. My mother had rendered me to the pile of incorrigibles and no longer bothered to get me to go. Little Albert and little Julian were not yet old enough to say no to my mother and the both of them looked at me with hatred in their eyes.

My father knew that don Antonio was extremely religious and always went to the ten o'clock Mass in Nixon. My father allowed that don Antonio would need to visit people after church and then he would have to drive home to leave off the family. He figured don Antonio would as likely be an hour or so late.

Just before eleven o'clock, my father and I were on the porch. Grandpa had a straight back chair in front of the bunkhouse and was reading his Sir Walter Scott. Paulie and Jose were playing cards at the kitchen table. Elpidio and my father had discussed something the night before, but neither of them would say anything about it.

On this morning, Elpidio seemed to be a bit more agitated than usual. It seemed to me that he simply did not want to be idle for one second at the same time that he wanted to stay out of everybody's way.

My brother Jose had approached my father earlier in the morning, after the family had gone off to church, to ask if he was going to the meeting with don Antonio. My father told him he was taking me and that was all. He offered no further explanation. More than going along, my brother Jose wanted to know what the solution to Elpidio's problem was. And that's the part that my father was not ready to tell.


Candy, in observance of the Sabbath, had never opened his store on Sundays. My father parked the truck to one side of the white clapboard building, inside a grove of lilac trees. A little beyond, we could see the concrete supports for a windmill.

"What if somebody sees us?" I asked my father.

"You would have to be looking for us to see the truck from the road," he said in response.

We got out of the truck and stood by a rusted shed where we had a clear view of the ochre gravel road. I hunkered down on my heels while my father leaned against the tailgate of the truck. My father had smoked two Bull Durhams before we saw the cloud of red dust off in the distance coming from the north. Instead of continuing toward us, it stopped about a half mile away.

"That's them," said my father. "Let's go."

My heart raced with excitement. To me, it was like a gunfighter showdown in the movies. My father walked along the red sand scalloped by the speeding rubber tires. I walked on the hump of sand between the ruts. I wanted to ask all sorts of questions, say all kinds of things, to mask the thumping in my chest. I figured my father had enough on his mind without having to put up with me.

Don Antonio had driven out by himself in an old truck. He had not parked the truck so much as he had simply stopped and turned off the ignition, not bothering to move to the side of the road. He had remained sitting inside the truck in the sweltering heat.

My father and I walked to within ten yards or so of the truck. My father stopped to look at don Antonio inside the truck. The glare of the reflected sun made an indistinct shadow of don Antonio. My father turned and began to walk to one side of the road, his boots sinking into the soft sand of the road shoulder. He crossed the barbed wire fence and began pacing up the sharp incline of the field. Whatever crop had been planted on it had already been burned and shriveled by the drought and plowed under. The dark, ochre earth beside the fence changed abruptly in color to deep black soil, the top of it having an ashen, ghostly hue to it. Our footsteps made deep black indentations on the ashen hue.

Don Antonio surely had been watching us all this time, but he made no movement to step down from the truck. When we got to the top of the rise in the land, my father hunkered and began to sift dirt between his fingers. I started to pick up clods of dirt and tossed them in all directions.

"Don't throw them in don Antonio's direction, he'll think you're being disrespectful," said my father.

"Yes, sir," I said, and began tossing them at the far horizon.

We waited for a full ten minutes, with the sun becoming hotter and hotter. Several times my father took off his hat and wiped the sweatband with his handkerchief.

"What the hell is he waiting for, Daddy?" I asked, irritated.

"He's doctoring up his pride, son," said my father.

"By making us wait?" I asked.

"That's it, exactly," my father said.

"He must be a bigger fool than we thought," I said, grown-up like.

My father smiled.

"Don't say anything when he comes, all right?"

"Yes, sir," I said. I walked a few paces away to find more clods to throw.

Don Antonio finally stepped down from his truck. He looked from one side to the other for a place to cross the fence and seeing that one place was as good as any other, he moved forward. He tried to maintain an air of dignity as he bent over, pressing down on the barbed wire to cross through. He snagged his black suit on a barb as he slid through the top and second strands. He had not changed from the black suit he wore to church every Sunday. The high-top shoes were brightly polished but, as he approached my father and me, they acquired a thin film of grayish dust.

Don Antonio came up to within a few feet of us and stopped, looking at my father directly in the eye. "What's your solution?" he said, avoiding all the pleasantries and any sense of civility.

"It's a simple one," said my father. "We agree that our children will leave Schoolland. We tell them to run away together. Elope."

"I don't see that that's much of a solution," said don Antonio, his eyes downcast.

"I don't have a perfect solution, Antonio. If I could, I would undo everything, but the fact is that I can't and you can't. That means we have to be satisfied with what we can do, that's all."

"My daughter would not elope," said don Antonio, unhappily, not realizing that the days of strict obedience were over.

"Happens all the time," said my father, trying to be gentle with the old man. "We'll say they wouldn't wait for a proper wedding and they ran away."

"No one will believe that my daughter would do that," said don Antonio, persistent. "She was not raised that way!"

My father was exasperated. He was about to say something snide, but he thought better of it. Instead, he thought for a long time, trying to find the right words to convince don Antonio to accept his plan.

"Look, Antonio, we will both be disgraced much worse if you don't listen to me," said my father.

"You have it all planned out, don't you?" said don Antonio. "You're just looking out for your own. Well, what about mine, I have to look out for my own, too."

He was clearly defeated and simply argued the point out of a vanquished sense of pride.

"We have been friends all of our lives, don Antonio," said my father. "A marriage between your children and mine is something we both have been expecting for a long time. I would have preferred that they waited to do it properly, in the ways of my father and yours. Times are not as they once were, Antonio. It's something we have to live with. This is the best I can think of. If you have something better, I'm willing to listen and go along with it."

"You called me here because you think I don't know what to do," said don Antonio, a look of pain and anxiety crossing his face. He walked off to one side, concentrating his gaze on the tops of his shoes.

"I am responsible for Elpidio. I will give him whatever money he needs to go to San Antonio, or wherever else they want to go. They must stay away at least for a year. As far as anybody will know, they eloped. It is not so unusual for young people to do that these days. You and I in public can be angry with them for doing it, but we will forgive them when they return after the year is up. Is that understood?" My father's voice became hard then.

The harshness of it stunned don Antonio and he meekly nodded his head in agreement. Don Antonio had finally relented. He had spent all the resistance he had. "When do you want this to happen?" he asked, meekly.

"The sooner the better," said my father. "Tomorrow night. I can get some money from the bank tomorrow, give it to Elpidio and after that, it's up to him how he sneaks away with Concepcion. I've already explained to Elpidio and he understands what he has to do. I suggest you do the same with Concepcion."

"How will they arrange to meet?" the old man asked.

"It's none of my business how they do it. I just want it done," said my father, unconcerned.

"You say they should be gone for a full year," said don Antonio.

"At least. There's too many people who suspect too much as it is. We could have handled it better, I suppose, some time ago. But, that's passed now. This is all we have."

"It'll be as you say," said don Antonio. "And, I'll be goddamned for agreeing to it."

I had expected my father to stay longer and try to console don Antonio, but he didn't. Once don Antonio agreed to the plan, my father turned swiftly and in long strides reached the fence. I followed behind at a trot, trying to keep up with him.

All the way home, my father didn't say another word.

My mother cried most of the day as she prepared Elpidio's things. She wanted him to take along some things she had saved from when he wore them as a baby. My sister Juana scolded her all day long, trying to convince her that a year wasn't all that long. My mother wouldn't hear of it. She made Juana cook fried chicken, biscuits and two cakes for Elpidio to take with him. In addition to Elpidio's clothes, my mother packed sheets, pillows and pillowcases, blankets and a goodly assortment of dishes and kitchen utensils.

Elpidio was gone for most of the day, returning shortly after we had finished supper. He came to each of us to shake our hands in goodbye. He embraced my grandfather, my father, my mother and my sister Juana. My father had already given him the money from the bank. My grandfather handed him some folded bills that looked like twenties. My sister Juana handed him one of the cakes because she knew he wasn't going to take the other stuff with him. Lastly, in a gesture that brought tears to our eyes, the twins each handed him a dollar.

Elpidio looked around him and saw all the stuff my mother had prepared for him. He picked up a suitcase and another box filled with clothes and took them out to his truck. My mother told Paulie and me to help him, which we began to do. Elpidio stopped us on the porch and said he wasn't taking any more than he had loaded up already. My father patted Elpidio on the shoulders and my mother hugged him one last time.

Waving to everyone, Elpidio got into his truck and drove off.

# Chapter 26

Everything seems to have gone to shit during the dog days of August. The dry persistent heat became unbearable. We didn't think it could get much hotter, but it did. We had given up all attempts to keep a normal life going; there was no use in pretending. All goddamned day long we sat somewhere, sweating, not having the strength to even move.

I took to going out into the mesquite grove and climbing up on the branches of an old mesquite. I would stretch out on the thick branch and lie there for hours.

"What the hell are you doing?" my brother Jose groused one afternoon.

"I'm a fucking python," I told him.

The boar and our brood sows died. We fed them and we watered them and we kept the sty from drying up. In fact, we did everything we could for the sons of bitches, but they died anyway. My father ordered my brothers Jose and Paulie and me to dump the carcasses farther down the dry creekbed. We heard him clearly enough, only we continued sitting where we were, not bothering to answer him. When he repeated his orders, my father was genuinely angry.

Jose and Paulie almost got into a fight in front of the house because Paulie wanted to drive Jose's truck and Jose decided that Paulie wouldn't. I don't think it mattered a whole hell of a lot to my brother Jose. It was just that Paulie said he was driving and no son of a bitch was going to stop him. That's what did it. Jose grabbed Paulie by the shoulders and shoved him aside. Jose saw the punch coming and stepped out of the way, hooking his arm over Paulie's, spinning him so he could hook his other arm in a Full Nelson.

"That's right," said my father, who had been watching from the porch. "Go on, kill each other!"

At that, my brothers settled down. "Go on, get in the truck," said Jose. Paulie climbed in the back and I got into the front seat with Jose.

It was hard to tell when all three pigs had died. By the time we got to them they were already bloated and there was a swarm of horseflies buzzing around them. The three of us stood with our arms resting on the fence, staring at the dead pigs.

"How the hell are we going to load them in the truck?" I asked.

"We ain't," said Jose, spitting over his shoulder.

"You don't mean you're going to drag them away," said Paulie.

"Why not?" said Jose.

"Those fuckers are already pretty ripe," said Paulie. "You try and pull them and the heads are gonna come off."

"They just died last night, Paulie," I said.

"Why don't we go borrow somebody's caterpillar? We can pick them up with the scoop and just drive them down the road," said Paulie, proud of himself.

"Who do we know that's got a caterpillar," said my brother Jose, which was as close as he would get to saying Paulie had a good idea.

"Old man Badel's got one. He uses it to haul chickenshit," said Paulie.

There was no point in going any further with it. Otto Badel would never loan it to us. In fact, we'd be lucky not to get shot if we went on his place. During the war, some men had come on Otto Badel's place in the middle of the night. They had intended to hang him on account of he was German. Earlier in the day, the citizens of Schoolland had buried the first casualty of the war with Germany. By eveningfall, some of the men had drunk enough to bolster their courage and had chosen Otto Badel for their neighborly revenge. They dragged Otto Badel out of his house, hogtied him and took him out a couple of miles to a suitable tree. There, the men came to their senses and left Otto Badel with his hands tied behind his back and a rope around his neck.

Otto Badel, who had never been friendly with anybody in his whole life, was never quite the same after that. Over the years, he'd shot at several people who came onto his place. I guess he figured someone was bound to come and finish the job started on him.

My brother Jose backed up the truck while I opened the gate to the pigpen. Paulie ran across the fields back to the house to get some rope. While we waited for him to come back, the stench from the dead pigs began to rise up.

"Grandpa says human corpses smell worse than anything," I said.

Jose didn't respond. Through the trees, I saw Paulie riding up on his horse. He rode his black horse right up to the pigpens. When the horse got a whiff of the stench, he reared up on his hind legs. I moved out of the way.

"Take him back to the barn!" Jose yelled.

"Funny how animals understand about death," I said.

"Nobody understands death, squirt," said my brother Jose. "The best we can do is stay away from it."

"I don't see how we're going to get away from death right here," said Paulie. "Come on, let's get this shit over with. It's stinks here!"

Paulie and I went to tie the rope around the boar's head. Jose tied the other end of the rope to the trailer hitch on the truck.

"I don't have much clearance to pull this son of a bitch out of the pen," said Jose. "If I don't drag him past the gate here, grab his feet and pull on him off to the side there. I don't want to get snagged up on the post there."

"I ain't going to touch the son of a bitch," said Paulie.

Jose eased the truck forward until the slack went out of the rope. Paulie yelled for him to stop while he checked once more to see that the rope wouldn't slip. He tapped the taut rope with his toe. When Paulie was satisfied, he whistled for Jose to begin. The pig's body moved out of the pen slowly until just its hind quarters were inside. Paulie yelled to Jose that it would clear and Jose backed up the truck a little and then turned it up the road that wound around behind the barn. I followed on foot. Paulie went to the barn where he tied his horse. Once Jose got the animal past the barbed wire fence, he stopped for me to get in the truck. I told him Paulie was going to follow us on the horse. We didn't have any trouble dragging the pig's body along the tractor road at the edge of the milo field. The dry creek was nothing more than a scar on the land, overrun by chaparral and spotted here and there with a mesquite tree.

We found a good opening in the chaparral. Jose told Paulie to take the horse into the creek bed. We untied the rope from the hitch and handed to it Paulie. The horse was skittish, but Paulie managed to keep it under control. He wound the end of the rope around the saddlehorn and began to gently kick the horse forward. The dead pig was too heavy for the horse to pull. Jose told me to pull on the rope while he lifted the pig by the feet. The dead weight began to move until it slid over the foot-high bank.

We did the same thing for the two sows without too much incident. After the last one, Paulie took a shortcut back to the house. Jose and I went to close up the gate. As we drove by the old house, we saw Marcos de la Fuente standing outside on the porch he had reconstructed. Jose waved to him. Instead of waving back to us, Marcos de la Fuente turned and went inside the house.

"I wonder what the hell is wrong with him," said Jose, scratching his head.

At the house, we found out what was bothering Marcos de la Fuente. We went into the kitchen and found my sister Juana and my mother with their eyes red from crying. My father's face was stern and severe. The twins sat at the table solemn and quiet for a change. Through the kitchen door, I saw Paulie running the black, pretending he was racing him.

"What's happened?" asked Jose.

My mother began to cry in loud, heaving sobs. My sister Juana started to cry again. The twins fidgeted and little Albert began to cry, too; and this made little Julian begin to cry as well.

"Your sister wants to get married," said my father.

"So, why is everybody crying?" said Jose, disgusted.

"Shut up, Jose! You don't know anything," hissed my sister Juana.

"I just thought we should be happy when somebody wants to get married," he replied.

"This is not the time for anyone to be getting married," said my father.

"She won't listen," sobbed my mother. "She's going to do it anyway."

"Ma, I don't understand why you don't want to me to do it," said my sister Juana.

"Listen to your father," my mother said.

Marcos de la Fuente had bought himself an old truck which clattered as if it were falling apart. We heard it pull up outside.

"He's here," I said.

"I told him to come, so we could share the good news like a family," sobbed my sister Juana.

"Go tell Marcos to come in," my father instructed me.

Marcos de la Fuente came into the kitchen, smiling, expecting that everything would be as he and Juana had planned. His face changed immediately when he saw her. He stood in the kitchen doorway, working his fingers around the edges of his hat brim, twirling it slowly. He had come in on shit he hadn't counted on.

"Marcos," began my father, "I was telling Juana that this is a very bad time for the two of you to get married."

"Yes, sir," said Marcos de la Fuente. "We know it's not a very good time to do this."

"I want to do what's right for my daughter. And, I don't have the money to do it right now. I've asked Juana to wait until next year when things'll get better for everybody. Then we can have a proper wedding and I won't be ashamed to invite all of my friends and neighbors."

"I never thought that it would cost you anything," said Marcos de la Fuente. "It's just Juana and I that are getting married."

"Well, around here, it's more than that," said my father.

Grandpa came in from the bunkhouse to join us. The skin on his face had loosened up; the creases had become thick and lumpy. He had lost some weight and his movements were a lot slower. He was limping as he came to sit at the table. Little Julian got up to let him have a chair.

"I'll pay for the goddamned wedding, if that's what's bothering everybody," he said, growling.

No one said anything. My grandfather looked up at my mother. "Well, now that that's settled, how about let's eat," he said.

"No, Grandpa, this is for me to do," said my father.

"Are you going to run away if you don't get a wedding?" my grandfather asked my sister.

In spite of the fact that our brother Elpidio had gone off on an arranged elopement, I don't think my sister Juana had quite thought of running away. Not yet, anyway. Marcos de la Fuente had thought of it. It became evident when he stepped forward, his hat held high against his chest.

"We want to have an honorable wedding, out of respect for the family," he said. That shifty son of a bitch! He was scared that he would have to run off with her. But, he couldn't. He had too much going for him to steal my sister and go someplace else to start over again.

"I think they'll run away if we don't do something," said Grandpa. "First, Elpidio's gone away, and now Juana."

"No," screamed my mother. "Juana is not running away! I will not let her run away. No more!"

Marcos was visibly nervous, probably thinking of how he was going to talk Juana into waiting. Having made up her mind, it was not likely that my sister would wait.

My father remained silent, tapping his fingers on the table. After what seemed a long time, he made his decision.

"I've got a note coming up at the bank in Gonzales," he said. "We're going to have to sell the cattle to make good on it."

"What's this?" asked my mother.

"The bank wants their money, crop or no crop," he said.

"But, I thought, when you went to the bank two weeks ago . . ."

"I didn't know how to tell all of you," said my father.

"There's four or five banks between Nixon, Smiley and Gonzales," said my grandfather. "It don't make a whole hell of a lot of sense if they end up owning everything. What the hell do bankers know about animals and raising crops?"

"They're not closing in on everybody. Just the ones they feel aren't going to be able to make it back," my father said.

"Sons of bitches are probably selling out the little guys so's the rich sons of bitches don't go broke," said Paulie.

My mother didn't even blink an eye at the profanity.

"White people take care of themselves," said my grandfather.

"So, they figure we're not going to get on our feet again?" I asked. Even as I spoke, I knew it was the wrong thing to ask. My father didn't see any need to answer that.

"Daddy, I didn't know," said my sister Juana, tearfully. "I really had no idea."

"No, it's my fault," said my father. "I should've told everybody when I first learned of it."

"Why didn't you?" asked Paulie.

"Paulie, behave," said my brother Jose.

"He's got a right to ask that question," said my father. "I guess I figured I would wait for a couple of weeks and go to the bank again. See if I could get them to change their minds."

"I don't see how," said my grandfather.

"Juana," began my father, relieved, "we'll have more than enough money to pay off the bank and have your wedding."

"I wish I'd known, Daddy," said my sister Juana.

"You're not kids anymore. Your mother and I have to face that. You won't have much of a life if you have to wait on your mother and me."

My sister Juana left the kitchen to go to her room. Marcos de la Fuente was uncomfortable, feeling that he was responsible for our troubles.

"Well, I guess that settles it, then," said my father. He got up from the table and went out the back door of the kitchen to scold Paulie for running the horse for no good reason on such a hot day.

No one was happy with the decision. We ate our supper in a gloomy atmosphere. Jose, Grandpa and I played a cheerless game of dominoes after the dishes were cleared away. Juana stayed in her room and didn't come out the rest of the night. Marcos said he had some business in Nixon and left. He wasn't part of the family, yet, and none of us particularly wanted him in the house.

My father and Paulie stayed out with the horses for several hours. They had ignored my mother's calls to come in and eat. When they did, my mother had already gone to lie down and they had to serve themselves. We finished a couple of games of dominoes, but none of us had our hearts in it. My grandfather kept score and that usually brought forth plenty of accusations of cheating. On this night, we didn't much care who won.

I looked into my grandfather's eyes and saw how deeply set they were in their sockets. Their lustre appeared gone. I saw once again the image of my grandmother in her casket. For the first time in my life, I felt a great emptiness in the kitchen that evening.

School began in September and the effects of the drought were visible on all the school kids. For me, it was good to be back. I forced myself to concentrate on my studies and that was a useful distraction.

Samantha Coleman's cousin had come to stay for the term. Her parents were divorcing and she had come to live in Smiley until it was over. She and Samantha were inseparable. Whenever I joined them, I was clearly the outsider. They talked of things that did not include me at all. It got so I was embarrassed to be with them. It was only when Samantha and I were alone that things went back to how they had been in the spring. That was an even better distraction.

About the middle of September, my sister Celia came for a visit. She had changed to where it was nearly impossible to recognize her as the same person. For one thing, she was in a hurry to leave as soon as she arrived. It was like she couldn't bear to stand still for a moment. She kept fidgeting, sitting at the table for a minute and then getting up to pour herself some coffee from the stove, and sitting down again. Several times she stood up to open the refrigerator, looked inside and sat back down. All the while, she talked non-stop. She had lots of important news to tell us.

She told us first of all that she could not stay the night, or several days, as she usually did. She held back on her important news. We more or less knew what it was, but we waited for her to tell us anyway. She began with the news about Elpidio and Concepcion. They had rented a nice little house, their baby was due in early September and Concepcion was real big and healthy. Elpidio still had his job and they were getting to like San Antonio real fine. My mother became apprehensive that Elpidio would get to liking it too much in San Antonio and remain there permanently.

Jose said that with Juana's wedding coming up, maybe it was time to let Elpidio come back. My father said it was not possible. They had only been gone less than two months and with the baby on the way and Antonio Arreaga still upset with Concepcion. . . . The deal with don Antonio called for Elpidio to stay away for at least a year. When my father said that, my mother began to cry softly.

My sister Celia seized the opportunity and blurted out that she and Frank were getting divorced.

I was surprised that my mother and father took the news calmly. In fact, my mother stopped crying. Paulie said it was a good thing that she was getting rid of the son of a bitch husband. Celia told us how Frank had moved out of the house for good. She said she had tried to keep the family together for the sake of the children. The children were more afraid of Frank than ever. She was through forgiving him, also for the sake of the children.

Celia had been working for several months in an office, where she was learning to type and to be a secretary. The owner of the business, she said, was a widower who was interested in her. Celia laughed, nervously, saying the man was older and fat and not very handsome. Frank was young, slender and handsome, she said, and she'd had quite enough of that. She wanted to get the divorce so she could start seeing her boss.

My father told Celia to be careful, as Frank was crazy and there was no telling what he might do once he found out she was seeing another man. Celia said she could take care of herself. She had already gone to court to force Frank to pay something for the children. The judge had ordered him to pay ten dollars a week for each of the children. She didn't know whether Frank was ashamed of himself or whether he was angry about being in court, but when the judge announced what he was ordering Frank to pay, Frank had stood up and told the judge that he would give twice the amount. The judge couldn't be sure whether Frank was making fun of him, but anyway he ordered Frank to pay twenty dollars a week for each child.

My sister Celia said that Frank was supposed to go to the courthouse to leave the money for her, but he had come to the house instead to leave her the sixty dollars for the first week. And that was the last she had seen him. She had gone to the courthouse to see if they could find him and get the money from him. The courthouse people told her that very few fathers ever paid for their children. They told her to get a job and take care of herself and the children. Celia was not angry or bitter about it. She told us it was the best advice she had gotten from anybody in San Antonio. Once she found a job and starting bringing home her own paychecks, she felt a whole lot better about things. She had even saved up enough money to pay a lawyer for the divorce.

It had not been very difficult to find Frank, as he kept going to the same place all the time. Her boss gave Celia an afternoon to go with her lawyer to find Frank and give him the papers to appear in court. Frank didn't get angry or anything. Maybe he was a little embarrassed to be served with the papers in front of his friends. They were supposed to be in court to end the marriage in three months and that's the important news she had for us.

As soon as she finished, my sister Celia gathered her children together, herded them into the car and was gone as quickly as she had come.

My mother was upset about the divorce business. No one she had ever known had gotten one. Celia did not appear to be grieving at all and that made it a bit more bearable.

"I don't know what this family is coming to," said my mother, expelling a long exhausted sigh.

"Celia is becoming a full-grown woman," said my father.

"She's had three children! She was a woman long ago!" snapped my mother.

"She's always been a child," said my father, "until now." He smiled, proud of his daughter.

# Chapter 27

What with school, Samantha Coleman, Celia's divorce, the waiting for news of Elpidio's baby and Juana's wedding less than a month a way, I didn't have much time to think about Grandpa's well. My father had sold what cows we had, and with them went two of the horses. Concepcion had written us a letter saying Elpidio wanted his mare sold and for my daddy to go on and keep the money he got for her. My father sent him his money anyway.

The well at the old place had gone completely dry and Marcos de la Fuente got his drinking water from the well at the main house. He got water for his animals elsewhere; he never told us where. The only water we had was in the main well in the mesquite grove. The water trough, meanwhile, became black and smelly as the pump starting spewing up silt. As the silt collected at the bottom of it, we shut off the feed to it. We found an old washtub and used that to water the horses we had remaining. In the kitchen, my mother and my sister Juana poured buckets of water and let them stand on the sink while the black, grainy dirt settled on the bottom. When it got too smelly, they boiled it for us. Even so, the water still retained a brackish taste and we took to drinking only as much of it as we needed to stay alive. My mother took to ordering a lot of sodas from the store.

We were forced to take fewer baths. When one of us couldn't stand it anymore and demanded a bath, it became a family affair, as we had to share the bathwater. Little Albert and little Julian complained because they were usually the last in line and by then the water got pretty ripe. And then we complained because it was my mother and Juana who had first dibs on the bathwater. We each were allowed half a bucketful to rinse off. Most of the time, we had to settle for sponging ourselves clean.

Since no one had taken seriously Grandpa's determination to dig a well, we quit kidding him about it and didn't notice too much that he continued to go out there every day. There wasn't any need for the goddamned well anymore. But, no one had the heart to tell him so. Besides, there was something funny going on with my grandfather. He would come home from digging the well and after washing up would go immediately to bed. He would spend hour after hour in his bunk, reading the Sir Walter Scott novel by the light coming in through the screendoor. After dark, he would pull on the lightstring and keep reading.

"Don't you ever get tired of reading the same book, Grandpa?" I had asked him once.

"It's the only book I got," he said.

"Why don't you read one of mine," I said.

"I don't read English," he said.

"That book there is written by an Englishman," I said.

"Maybe, but he does all right in Spanish," he said.

Many times my mother would send us to wake him up for supper, but he either refused or ignored us. She would leave a plate on the stove for him and he would eat it for breakfast in the morning. All of us, my mother and father included, were waking up later in the day. Not my grandfather. He'd eat, boil his coffee, and be on his way to the well long before anybody else was up. He had tired of going out there on horseback and took to driving the long way around in the truck that he hardly ever used.

Late in the summer, Grandpa had given up his solitude and for the sake of my mother had agreed to take Paulie and me with him to the well every day. He did it as a favor because my mother was growing more resentful every day at having so many damned people in the house all damned day.

Paulie and I went with him every day for a couple of weeks. He told us to go hunting or something and to keep out of his goddamned way. He had gotten rid of the tripod he and Paulie had put over the hole. Instead, he had a long-ass ladder that stuck out of the hole about four or five feet. He used three buckets to empty out the dirt. He would go into the hole, dig for a while and then climb up out of the hole. The buckets were attached to three ropes that had a noose at one end. The noose he draped over the ladder. These he would pull up and empty.

Paulie and I noticed that Grandpa disappeared for a long damned time down in the hole. It took him maybe half an hour to get back up again. It was a considerable strain for him to pull up the buckets of dirt. We approached him and made an attempt to take the ropes from him to help, but he brushed us away, saying he could do it by his own damned self. Paulie and I asked him if we could go down and get a look. Grandpa said there wasn't anything to look at. It was pitch black. Then he softened up a bit and told us he had a flashlight tied to the ladder on a string. If we wanted to see it bad enough, we could use that.

I was very scared as we descended the ladder, Paulie going first. The goddamned ladder wobbled and I was sure I would fall. As soon as Paulie got to the bottom, he found the flashlight and I felt safer as I found firm footing on the muddy dirt.

He was already about twenty feet down and there was no sign of decent water yet. A couple of days later, when we were with him, watching more than helping, there was a false finish when he struck a layer of water and the hole filled up to his ankles.

When he started sending up the buckets full of brown water and then thin mud, Paulie and I breathed a sigh of relief as we were convinced that it was over. We were hoping he would come up, happy as shit that he had brought in the well. But he kept on digging and before the day's work was up, he had drained all the water and was back to sending up buckets of black mud which had the consistency of tar.

After school started, Paulie continued going out with him. It kept Paulie occupied and it seemed as if he really was interested in finishing the well. There were days when my grandfather didn't feel well enough to go out, but Paulie would take Grandpa's truck and go out by himself. Nobody mentioned it for fear that Paulie would change his mind and return to being a pain in the ass.

My brother Jose had talked about going out to Ohio to find work, but my mother talked him out of it.

My sister Juana was nervous as hell about getting married. She and Marcos de la Fuente had a pretty serious fight over something and she had come back to the house in tears, vowing never to marry the wetback son of a bitch. They ended up not speaking to each other for a whole day.

About a week before the wedding, my father and my brother Jose got jobs working cattle in Leesville. It was sunup to sundown jobs and they had to stay on the ranch where they worked. They managed a brief visit of a couple of hours on the Sunday before the wedding. The following Friday, they had finished and came home.

The wedding itself went off just fine. The only sad part was the absence of my brother Elpidio. He wouldn't disobey my father about being gone for a year and besides, he and Concepcion had a little girl, just a few days old.

My brother Heriberto was already shitfaced by the time he got to the church. Several times during the ceremony, he got up to go take a leak and chug down some more whiskey. After the marriage ceremony, I was standing next to my brother Heriberto, watching my mother and father, Juana and my brother-in-law Marcos de la Fuente shake hands with the well-wishers. My brother-in-law Marcos wore a powder blue tuxedo and a powder blue ruffled shirt with black trim.

"Look at that wetback asshole!" said my brother Heriberto, weaving to and fro in his drunkenness.

"What about him?" I asked, annoyed. "It's his wedding day. He's family now, Beto, leave him alone."

"Look at how he's dressed! No white man would dress like that!"

"Well, he's not white, and you ain't either," I said.

"You wouldn't catch me wearing something like that on my wedding day!" He staggered some more.

"You didn't even wipe the pigshit off your boots when you got married," I said, and started to walk away from him.

"You're getting a smart mouth on you, you know that?" Heriberto said after me.

Grandpa's heart attack came after we had completed a pleasant Saturday working at the well. Paulie had behaved himself. We had advanced a couple of more feet on the well, although by now, not even Grandpa pretended any more that the well would ever be serviceable. It was just something to do to keep busy.

On the way home, Paulie drove Grandpa's truck roughly. He wouldn't slow down for the bumps and he ignored me when I asked him to take it easy. At one of the bumps, when the truck was sent flying into the air, I noticed that Grandpa winced in pain as the truck landed first on its front wheels and just as suddenly on the back wheels. The force of the last landing jerked us backwards and I struck the metal of the truckcab with the back of my head. Once the truck settled a little, Grandpa grabbed his shirt in the center of his chest. He groaned and twisted to one side as if he had cramps or something.

"Are you all right, Grandpa?" I asked him.

It took him a little while to answer. His voice was thick and groggy when he did. "I'll be alright if this goddamned idiot doesn't kill us all before we get home," said Grandpa.

In front of Candy's Store, Paulie took a sharp turn to the right. The rear wheels skidded on the loose gravel, raising a cloud of dust.

"Why don't you watch for cars, Paulie?" said Grandpa.

"They ain't any," said Paulie. "The bank took them all back!"

The farm to market road was fairly smooth and Paulie took advantage to race the truck as fast as he could before the sharp right angle turn that led to Smiley. It was about a mile run.

Paulie had the truck up to eighty when I saw the turn coming up. He was approaching it too fast. I grabbed Paulie's arm.

"Don't fuck it up," I said.

"Ha!" retorted Paulie.

Paulie let go of the accelerator and began to tap the brakes rhythmically, the truck lurching forward each time he did so. The muffler pipe roared busily behind us. When we went into the turn itself, the truck lurched to the left, seeming to spin through the curve on its two left wheels. Paulie's face was blank. His hands gripped the steering wheel tightly. His lips were pressed together. In what seemed an eternity, we came out of the turn with the truck swinging from side to side as the weight shifted and Paulie was laughing his asshole head off.

We were already past Pruitt's mailbox before I leaned over to see how Grandpa was doing. He was limp, keeled over to one side, his forehead leaning against the side window.

"Grandpa, are you all right?" I asked, nudging his side.

Other than moving with the rhythm that the truck took from the road, Grandpa was very still.

I grabbed Grandpa's shoulder and shook him. He seemed asleep, his eyes closed, his lips slightly parted.

"What the hell's wrong with him?" asked Paulie. "He wouldn't go to sleep on us, would he?"

We were almost at the creek that ran beside the old house.

"He's dead!" I said.

"Fuck you!" said Paulie.

"Grandpa! Wake up!" I said, shaking him harshly.

Grandpa did not move. We were adjacent to the old house now. My new brother-in-law Marcos, shirtless, was outside clearing some weeds from the front of the house. He waved as we went by.

"What's the matter with him?" said Paulie, scared.

"I told you! He's dead!" I squealed.

Paulie had downshifted as we neared our house. The muffler of the truck fluttered a noisy report. Paulie leaned over to get a good look at Grandpa's inert body. So doing, he slammed down the clutch and threw the truck into third gear. The engine groaned and we shot forward.

My father and my brother Jose were on the porch as we roared past the house. Paulie pressed hard against the horn in the center of the steering wheel. There was nothing I could do to warn them or to let them know what Paulie had in mind. I hoped they could see Grandpa's body slumped against the window.

"What're you doing?" I said.

"Taking him to the hospital, idiot! What the hell do you think I'm doing?"

"You think they can help him?" I asked.

"Won't know until we get there," said my brother Paulie.

We were on the other side of Wrightsboro, on the paved road, when Paulie asked me to feel and see if Grandpa was getting cold.

"What the hell kind of thing is that?" I asked.

"If he's dead, he'll be getting cold, idiot!" yelled Paulie over the roar of the truck's engine.

I didn't want to touch Grandpa if he was dead. But if he was still warm, there was a chance he might live. I reached out my hand to touch his thigh, just above the knee.

"Not there, shithead! On his cheek. Touch him on the cheek!" screeched Paulie.

I did as he said. I couldn't tell the difference. It had never occurred to me to notice the difference between cold and warm bodies.

"Well, what do you think?" said Paulie as we came upon a straightaway and he pressed down on the gas pedal.

"I don't think nothing," I told him.

"Goddamn you!" said my brother Paulie.

He pressed down on the gas pedal some more. Neither one of us said shit as we pushed forward, over the twin bridges crossing the Guadalupe and on into the center of town.

Paulie knew the way to the hospital. He stopped short of the courthouse and went left and then right at the next block, past Marrou Bros. Chevrolet. From there, he went right by the stop signs until we got to the hospital.

Paulie parked on the curb in front of the hospital and ran inside. I had been in the middle between him and Grandpa. I didn't feel right sliding out the driver's side, but there was little I could do where I sat. I got out and stood on the curb with my hands in my pocket. Two men came running out from inside the hospital building. They were dressed in white. Paulie, looking as if he was in charge, followed them out. One of the men shoved me aside and ran around to the passenger side of the truck. Carefully, he opened the door, slipping his hands in to take hold of my grandfather. When he had the door fully opened, he pushed Grandpa back to a sitting position. The other man stood by useless. At a nod from the first man, he went inside and returned in seconds hauling a stretcher. Together they placed my grandfather on it, after which they wheeled him inside.

Paulie and I went inside the hospital into a small reception area that smelled of disinfectant. A white lady, in a starched uniform with a face to match, gave us a dirty look. She told us to take a seat.

We had been sitting there, the white lady shooting us dirty glances from time to time, when my mother and father came in. They arrived about ten minutes behind us. They came directly to us wanting to know what had happened.

"Grandpa died," I blurted out.

"No, he didn't," said Paulie. "They got him in there somewhere. We don't know how he is."

"May I help you?" said the white lady.

"We want to know about my father-in-law," said my father.

"The doctor is with him right now," said the white lady. "Please, take a seat."

My mother was on the verge of tears. My father took her by the shoulders and led her to a chair. My brother Jose, my sister Juana, the twins little Albert and little Julian had come separately in Jose's truck. Marcos de la Fuente was with them, keeping his distance.

We waited for about three hours. The doctors and nurses walked by, looked at us, and kept going.

"We have to let Heriberto and Celia know about this," said my mother.

"Elpidio, too, don't forget," said my father.

"There's too damned many of us," said Paulie.

We had more or less figured out for ourselves that there was nothing to do but wait. Juana and Marcos de la Fuente went outside for a walk.

My father gave me a handful of coins and sent me with the twins to buy them some sodas. The Greyhound bus station was a block away on the corner.

When the twins and I got back, we were told that Grandpa was doing fine. The doctor said my grandfather was lucky to have been brought in so quickly. Another half an hour and they couldn't have done anything for him. He would have gone. My father tousled Paulie's hair.

The doctor told us it wouldn't be until the evening visiting hours the next day before they could allow anyone to see my grandfather. My mother insisted on staying at the hospital. My father stayed with her. My mother told the rest of us to get on home.

Paulie wanted to stay with them, but my father told him to go on home.

It was a sad trip back to the house. I mean, we knew he was alive and doing fine, so the doctors said, but so long as he was in the hospital we worried about him just the same.

My sister Juana finished the supper that my mother had been making before Paulie had driven by tooting the horn. She kept the light on in the kitchen only as long as it took for us to eat. Marcos wouldn't eat with us. He stayed on the porch smoking cigarettes.

"How come Marcos won't eat with us?" asked little Albert.

"He'll have to get used to us, that's all," said my sister Juana.

After supper, she put the twins to bed, turned off all the lights and she and Marcos walked home. The only light in the house that evening was a votive candle in the front room. We sat in the front room for most of the evening. We worried about Grandpa and no one said much of anything.

My brother Heriberto came to visit just as we were getting ready for bed. It didn't take hardly any time to fill him in on what had happened. He was going to go to Gonzales right away, but Jose told him it was no use.

They kept my grandfather in the hospital for ten days. When the let him go, he was strapped to a wheelchair. The stroke had partially paralyzed him down the left side of his body and he couldn't talk. Other than that and some weight he had lost, he seemed like the Grandpa of old. The only difference I could tell was his shave. They had shaved his parchment-colored cheeks so closely that they appeared to be almost pink.

The doctors sent him home with strict orders on what he was to eat and what he could do. The food he was allowed to eat wasn't fit for humans. It was mostly mushy shit that smelled bad. The worst part of it for Grandpa was not being able to get around. He was allowed to be in the wheelchair for a couple of hours a day. The rest of the time, he was confined to bed.

My mother decided to keep Grandpa in the big bedroom. That meant my brother Paulie took Grandpa's bunk outside with my brother Jose, who had inherited Elpidio's bunk. It was a pain in the ass to sleep with the twins, so I took to sleeping on the floor, at the foot of Grandpa's bed.

Grandpa's medicines, and there were a lot of them, were on a little table beside the bed. My sister Juana was in charge of making sure he got his medicine on time.

I was putting my books and tablets together after school one afternoon when I heard my grandfather grunt behind me. I turned and asked if I could bring him something. He lifted his right arm and with one crooked finger he pointed to my school stuff. It took a little doing, but he got me to understand that he wanted my writing tablet. I took it to him and he wrote, in large scrawling letters, "libro."

I couldn't read a lick of Spanish, but after I recited the letters a couple of times, speeding up as I did so, I managed to say "book" in Spanish. My grandfather blinked his eyes and managed a weak nod of his head. I knew I was on the right track. I lifted up all of my own books for him to inspect and he shook his head, no, each time. In a flash of inspiration, I ran to the bunkhouse and found his Sir Walter Scott novel. When I came back and held it up for him, he nodded his head, yes.

"Do you want me to hold it up for you to read, Grandpa?" I asked.

He indicated the tablet again. This time, he wrote, "no," and I had no trouble understanding it.

"Well, what, then? Do you want me to read to you, is that it?" He nodded his head, yes.

"Grandpa, I can't read this shit. It's all I can do to read in English."

My grandfather wrote on the tablet, "I tich u." It took most of his strength to get that much on paper and it took me quite a while to figure out what it said.

"How're you gonna do that?"

On the tablet, he scrawled out the vowels. He pointed to "a." I said "a" as in "hay," and my grandfather shook his head from side to side several times. I looked at him and he opened wide his mouth as if saying "ah," and I got it.

The first thing I had to do was figure out that he was trying to teach me right then and there. It took most of an hour, with me coming with every sound I could make out of each vowel until he would shake his head, yes.

I went out to play when he fell asleep and promptly forgot all the sounds I had learned to make. Later in the evening, he tried me again and we had to repeat the entire process from the afternoon; however, I hit upon the right sounds a lot sooner.

The next day he decided I was ready to begin reading the book to him. I held it in front of his eyes while he read and memorized the first line on the page. For the next couple of hours, I repeated each word, watching him for a sign that it was correct, until I got through the entire line. I kept repeating the line in Spanish, just like it was my normal way of talking.

The next day I lost the place in the book and we had to start all over again with another line. I had trouble making the connection that the Spanish we spoke all the time was written, too, just like the English in our textbooks. It had never occurred to me that Spanish was also a written language.

Little by little as the days wore on, I got better at it and within a month, I was able to read an entire page to Grandpa at one sitting. I would sit by close to the bed reading to him. He would place his hand on my arm. Each time I made a mistake, he would pinch me. Pinched me hard, he did.

There was still no let up in the heat and the dryness of Schoolland and it was already well into October when the days should have begun to cool. We had grown so accustomed to the hot weather and the drought that we hardly notice the heat wave. My mother had bought a fan for Grandpa, but he didn't like it and we didn't use it much.

My brother Paulie, without being told and without telling anyone, had been going out to Grandpa's well. He had taken over the digging of it all by himself.

I knew what he was doing and I asked if he wanted me to go out with him on Saturdays. He said he would rather finish it by himself. I persisted, and he reminded me, sarcastically, that when he said no, he meant no.

# Chapter 28

The rains came a few hours before dawn. They began as a fine mist swept from the south carried along by a soft quiet breeze. When the family awoke, the world outside was a deep metallic blue that glistened a wet gray. My grandfather was the first to see it. He had not slept more than an hour or two at a stretch since his stroke. He still had not recovered his speech and could not alert us to it.

My mother noticed the chill in the air first thing. She went outside on the back porch to have her face bathed immediately by the rain. My father shivered as he came into the kitchen. The back door was open wide. He went to join my mother. They stood closely together. Their tears were indistinguishable from the rain.

The twins and I got dressed and had our breakfast while my mother fixed our lunches. We told her we wanted to stay and watch the rain.

My father had gone to the front porch. I joined him briefly. He had changed to a flannel shirt and again was soaking wet. At that hour, it ought to have been daylight full. As the sun rose higher, the metallic blue of dawn had been changed by the rain to a rich cottony white. There were pockets where the rain was thick and they seemed as sheets fluttering gently on the line. We could see the hazy outlines of the beginning of Huntley Poindexter's pasture.

Little Albert and little Julian came out, wearing their yellow rain slickers. I had an opaque raincoat draped over my arm. The twins brought my lunch to me. I took the sack and waited for the bus.

My brothers Jose and Paulie finished their breakfast and came to the porch to smoke their first cigarettes of the day.

"I guess there ain't no school today," said my brother Jose.

"It's after eight already," said my brother Paulie.

The bus never came that day. My mother made the twins stay in the front room. She didn't have to tell them to be quiet.

I went into the big bedroom to see about Grandpa. I turned on the overhead light and Grandpa grunted. I asked if he wanted the light out and he nodded yes.

"You want to enjoy the rain, Grandpa?" I asked.

Grandpa nodded, yes.

In the two months since his stroke, he had gotten to where he could grunt. The doctors told us he would probably be talking in another six months.

My mother made another pot of coffee. It would be a day when she would have to endure the entire family in her kitchen.

Paulie and Jose were at another of their interminable hands of gin rummy. Paulie had streaks of luck where he won three or four times in a row. Jose was more methodical, memorizing each card, and with the persistent plodding that we often saw in my father, he won more games than he lost.

My mother was at her happiest when she was cooking. By midmorning every day except Sundays, she had the beans on the boil. On the day the rains started, she was trying to figure out what to make for lunch. There wasn't much in the refrigerator and she didn't want to send anyone to town. Then my brother Heriberto came over to eat. He confessed that Alva had thrown him out of the house and he asked if he could stay for a few days. No one answered him directly, but he knew he could stay. So, he ate lunch and went on home to settle things with Alva. Juana and Marcos de la Fuente dropped by for lunch. Juana started to help my mother.

Suddenly, the sky brightened up into a blinding white light that lasted a second or more. And just as suddenly, the crack of thunder exploded with such force that it felt like it went off right in the goddamned kitchen.

As the sound of the thunder sputtered off into the distance, the electric power went out. The twins came into the kitchen hugging one another and crying. My mother sent me to sit with Grandpa. There was a smile on Grandpa's face as though he had seen something and was keeping the secret of it.

"The lights went out, Grandpa," I said.

Grandpa kept smiling in the darkness of the bedroom.

The wind struck next. The first wave of it, a loud vicious gust that uprooted a mesquite tree, struck with such force that the house shook to its foundation. My grandfather made a sign of the cross. After a few more minutes, the electric power came back on. There was more lightning and more thunder and the rains began in earnest.

The rains continued for three straight days. They were hard, powerful rains which let up for a couple of hours and were followed by a wet mist or drizzle before beginning again in full force. By the second day, the uppermost layers of ground were saturated. It wasn't enough to replenish all the moisture that had evaporated in eight months. The rains were falling faster than the ground could absorb them. Espinoza creek, a mile up from our house, flooded a foot or two over the road.

The school bus had not come by morning and so we figured there was no school.

On the third day of the rains, my father told us that he had another bank note due in the middle of December. There was no money to pay it and little likelihood that all of us together could earn it in so short a time.

"They're taking the land, then," said my brother Paulie.

"That's right," said my father.

"How much of it?" asked my brother Jose.

"Not all of it," he replied. "About half. If it sells quickly enough, we'll likely get some money out it. If not, I hope it'll be on the market long enough for us to put some money together and buy it."

Marcos de la Fuente understood and accepted that it was going to take him a long time, maybe years, before we would consider him a family member. What he said next sure didn't help things.

"I want to buy my place from you," said Marcos to my father.

"Your place?" said my brother Jose.

"You know, where Juana and I live. I'll take the barn and the corral, and that little piece of mesquite where the pigpens are."

My father's jaw muscles worked furiously. If he could, he would've bitten the wetback's head off. "That place belonged to my father. I wouldn't sell it to you or anyone else. This house and that is all we have left that is not pledged to any loans."

"Daddy, Marcos and I need a place to live," said my sister Juana.

"You have a place. You can stay there for as long as you like."

"That's not what I mean, Daddy."

"It's just not fair that Juana and I don't have our own place to live in," said my brother-in-law Marcos de la Fuente.

"You think it's fair that we're going to lose everything ourselves?" asked my brother Paulie.

"We're not going to lose everything," said my mother emphatically.

"I just thought I would help out," said Marcos.

"We don't need that kind of damned help," said my brother Paulie. Paulie got up and went outside to stand in the chilly night.

On the fourth day, the rains stopped once and for all. The sun came out pale yellow but strong. In a matter of hours, the floodwaters receded and the ground stayed damp but it wasn't muddy.

Paulie went out to the well and came back to tell us there was five feet of water collected at the bottom of it. My grandfather overheard Paulie telling me about it. He was in his wheelchair, in which he spent more time, now that he was getting better. In a groggy, faltering voice, the first words he had spoken, fully articulated since his stroke, were, "see, well." "We can ask the doctor the next time he comes to see you," I said to my grandfather.

Grandpa took the tablet that was always upon his lap and wrote, "ride, truck."

"Grandpa," I said, "it's too rough a trip for you." He shook his head vigorously, no.

"Let's see what Ma says," said Paulie.

My mother reacted with typical horror. Luckily, the doctor came to see Grandpa for his weekly check-up.

"How far is it?" asked the doctor.

"It's about three miles on horseback," said Paulie.

"I take it he insists on going out there on his horse," said the doctor.

"Five miles," I said. "We can drive there."

"Well, I don't see where there's any harm in it," said the doctor. "Make sure you keep him warm and somebody rides with him in the back of the truck. I don't want him out of the wheelchair."

It took four of us to lift my grandfather, wheelchair and all, up onto the truck bed. My mother had bundled him up into a shapeless mass with two pairs of trousers, two shirts, a blanket folded and strapped around his legs and another blanket over his chest. She put a woolen cap on his head and then tried to fit his hat over it. It didn't work. My father intervened at that point and Grandpa was ready without the cap. In our unsteady lifting, his hat went askew and I fixed it for him.

The drive out to the well was slow and steady. My brother Jose drove the truck, with my father beside him in the cab. Paulie and I rode in the back with Grandpa.

At the well, Jose backed up the truck as close as he could to the well. The hole itself was a round gaping pit in the ground. The ladder came up within a foot of the rim. My brother Paulie took a long bamboo pole he had cut and descended the ladder. My father and Jose stood on the rim of the well watching him go down. A few minutes later he came back up. He had notched the bamboo pole at the water level. There was two feet of water at the bottom.

"I ought to begin hauling up that water," said Paulie.

"Did you ever think that you've struck permanent water?" asked my father.

"Shit, no! That's just seepage from the rains, Daddy," said Paulie, serious and less obnoxious than usual. Paulie took one of the buckets and dropped into the hole. He pulled it back up full of water.

"See? That ain't well water. Not yet," he said.

I took the pole from Paulie and showed my grandfather the water level, explaining it to him slowly.

He had heard and understood every word and he looked at me angrily. I felt like an idiot.

"We don't need the well," said my brother Jose. "Not now."

My father didn't answer. Instead, he looked up to my grandfather.

"Seen enough?" he asked.

Grandpa nodded, yes.

On the way back, we stopped at Candy's for sodas. Grandpa drank a little of my Dr Pepper.

Since I had learned to make out the words in Grandpa's Sir Walter Scott book, I had gotten to the point where I did a fair job of reading it. It had become our habit that after school every day, as soon as I put my things away, I would read to Grandpa. Not very much, just a page or two. I told Grandpa once that the parts I was reading sounded interesting to me and what I wanted to do was begin the book from the beginning. It wouldn't be the beginning of the novel itself because about a dozen pages were missing.

Grandpa had shaken his head, no. I had asked him, how come, but with a pained expression on his face, he had waved for me to go on reading as I had been.

Every day, I would open the book up to a different page and I would read until long after Grandpa was asleep. I had to do it that way because Grandpa had the habit of listening with his eyes closed. On several occasions I had stopped reading and he would startle me by grunting and waving to me to come back. I had gotten to the point where I would read until there was a break in the story. This allowed me to get a sense of what was going on in the story. I found it to be a good idea because Grandpa would be sound asleep whenever I stopped.

At the beginning of November, things were looking up. My brother Heriberto had decided to stop being an asshole and had taken a permanent job in the packing house in Smiley. It was a dirty job, hauling barrels of chicken guts. My sister-in-law Alva didn't mind that he stank up the house when he came home. She made him take a bath every day and she washed his clothes every day, too. She didn't mind it at all now that he paid more attention to the kids and was drinking less.

My sister Celia's divorce came through. Her oldest was in school and she was proud of that. The last time she had come for a visit, her boss had come with her. I guess that meant they were serious about each other. The guy seemed like a nice enough fellow, except that he had a gold tooth in his mouth and that made him look a little stupid to me. Celia liked him and so it didn't matter what I thought.

My mother and father finally went to see Elpidio and Concepcion and the baby. My sister Juana had taken them. Marcos de la Fuente didn't like it that he wasn't invited to go along on the trip. The way Juana spent so much time at our house after the trip probably meant that they weren't speaking to each other. Again. Marcos and Juana found a little house with a large lot in Nixon and they bought it. They then came to tell Daddy that they were going to knock down my grandmother's house and go into the pig raising business. My father had not bothered to answer them and had walked out of the house. It was up to my mother to explain things to them.

People began to hire workers again and my father, Jose and Paulie had steady jobs, at least, through the winter. The bankers softened up and renewed his loans, even extending him some credit to plant the next year.

Samantha Coleman had gotten mad at me and wouldn't talk to me anymore. As soon as it happened, I began to notice all kinds of girls. Some of them even smiled at me when they caught me watching them.

My grandfather had become much stronger and could sit up on the bed for hours. Lately he could swing his legs off the bed and get into the wheelchair all by himself. The best part was his speech. He could speak short sentences in a hoarse and stammering voice. It wasn't perfect yet, but it was much better. His sleeping was more regular and he had put on some weight. The doctor had cut his visits to once a month and had stopped many of the medicines Grandpa had been taking.

I had gotten to enjoy reading the Sir Walter Scott book so much that I felt bad when I came home after school to find Grandpa sitting up and reading for himself. I think Grandpa understood that the reading I did was as much for me as it was for him and he would offer the book to me whenever I came in.

No one in the family was particularly impressed or pleased that I could now do a passable reading in Spanish. In fact, my mother had warned me to stop my nonsense. If I was ever going to amount to something, I had better concentrate on English and that's all there was to it.

I was reading a passage, a lengthy battle between King Richard and the Moslems, when my mother came in. Grandpa was listening quietly with his eyes closed.

"Is he asleep?" asked my mother.

"I don't think so," I replied. "Are you asleep, Grandpa?"

My grandfather smiled and winked at me.

"He's awake," I said. "Is anything the matter?"

"No," said my mother. "I just thought . . ."

As I went back to my reading, I heard Grandpa's truck, driven by Paulie, come roaring up the driveway. He slammed the door shut and bounded up the porch stairs. He came running into the bedroom. I was still reading to Grandpa. Paulie was about to say something when I held up my hand to silence. I put my forefinger to my lips. From the look of him, my grandfather was asleep. I wanted to get to the end of the battle and so I kept on reading.

I could hear Paulie talking to my mother in the kitchen. "There's water in the well! Clear, clean, water! I was wrong," said Paulie. He had not been out to work on the well for weeks and had probably stopped by to take a look after work.

I smiled as I went back to my reading. Grandpa was in for a pleasant surprise when he woke up.

My mother came back into the bedroom. Something was bothering her, all right. She had never interrupted our readings like this. She walked between the bed and the chair on which I sat. She bent over Grandpa and placed her hand on his forehead. My mother took my grandfather's right hand in both of hers and she dropped to her knees on the floor. She began to softly kiss my grandfather's hand. Slowly, I closed the book and came to stand over my kneeling mother.

"What's wrong, Ma?" I asked.

It took my mother a long time to answer me.

There were tears in her eyes as she looked up at me and made the sign of the cross.

ACZ - 2759

2/20/9

PS
3563
A73344
S36
1988